DRAGON'S EGG

ROBERT L. FORWARD

A Del Rey Book

BALLANTINE BOOKS • NEW YORK

Thanks to:
  Frank Drake—he invented them.
  Mary Lois—she named them.
  Larry Niven—he gave them
    something to do.

—and David K. Lynch, Mark Zimmermann, Carlton Caves, Hans Moravec, David Swenson, Freeman Dyson, and Dan Alderson, who helped me in several technical areas. My special thanks to Lester del Rey, who took what was practically a pedantic scientific paper and helped me to turn it into something interesting to read, and to George Smith and the Hughes Aircraft Company for giving me the intellectual environment that made it feasible.

Prologue

TIME: 500,000 B.C.

Buu lay in his leafy arbor nest and looked up at the stars in the dark sky. The hairy young humanoid should have been asleep, but his curiosity kept him awake. A half-million years in the future that twinkling of curiosity would have led his mind out into the universe to explore the mathematical mysteries of relativity. Now . . .

Buu continued to stare at the bright stars above him. One speck suddenly flared brighter. Frightened—but fascinated—Buu watched the growing point of intense light until it went behind a dense tree branch. He would be able to see it again if he went to the nearby clearing. He clambered down from his nest—into the striped coils of Kaa.

Kaa did not enjoy his kill for long. Things were difficult for him in a world with two suns. The new sun was tiny and white, while the old one was big and yellow. The new sun circled constantly overhead. It never set, and he could no longer catch things at night. Kaa died—along with other hunters who could not change their habits fast enough.

For a year the new light shone from above, searing the sky. Then it slowly grew dimmer and dimmer, and within a few years night returned to the northern hemisphere of Earth.

Fifty light-years away from the Solar System there was once a binary star system. One star was in its normal yellow-white phase, but the other had bloated up until it turned into a red giant, swallowing the planets around it. The nuclear fuel for the red giant ran out just fifty years before Buu's curiosity got the better of him. With its fusion-bomb center turned off, the energy the star needed to hold itself up against its self-gravitation was no longer available, and the star collapsed. At the center, the infalling matter became denser under the terrific gravitational pressure until it turned almost completely into neutrons. The neutrons pressed closer and closer until they were packed radius to radius.

Under these cramped conditions, the strong nuclear repulsion forces were finally able to resist the gravitational pressure. The inward rush of matter was quickly reversed, and the outward motion turned into an incandescent shock wave that traveled upward through the outer shell of the red giant. At the surface, the shock wave blew off the outer layers of the star in a supernova explosion that released more energy in one hour than the star had released in the previous million years.

Beneath the expanding cloud of blazing plasma, the core of the red giant had changed. What had once been a large, red, slowly rotating balloon 200 times bigger than the Sun was now a tiny, white-hot twenty-kilometer ball of ultra-dense neutrons, spinning at over 1000 revolutions a second.

The original magnetic field of the star had stayed trapped in the highly conductive collapsing cloud of star stuff. Like the sunspot pattern on the original star, the magnetic field was not aligned with the spin axis of the neutron star, but was sticking out at an odd angle. One magnetic pole was very concentrated and a little above the equator. The other (really a group of poles) was on the opposite side of the star. Part of its complex pattern was below the equator, but most of it was in the northern hemisphere.

The almost solid trillion-gauss magnetic fields reaching out from the two magnetic poles of the rapidly spinning star tore into the glowing debris remaining from the supernova explosion. Driven by the rapid rotation of the ultra-dense sphere, the magnetic fields threw the massive clouds of ions away from the star in scintillating gouts. Like a Fourth-of-July pinwheel on the loose, the neutron star accelerated off to the south, directly toward its nearby neighbor Sol, the magnetic propeller leaving a glowing wake streaming out behind. After a short while, the plasma density became thinner and the rocket action stopped, but by then the star had achieved a respectable proper motion of thirty kilometers per second or one light-year every 10,000 years, a tiny wanderer jaywalking across the star lanes of the Galaxy.

TIME: 495,000 B.C.

As the neutron star spun its way through space, the debris it attracted by its gravitational field fell inward. When the interstellar material approached to within a few thousand kilometers of the twenty-kilometer-diameter ball, it was heated and stripped of its electrons by the intense gravity and the whirling magnetic fields. The ionized plasma then fell in elongated blobs toward the star, its velocity reaching 39 percent of the speed of light as it struck the crust in the east and west magnetic polar regions. The bombarded crust responded with flares of charged particles that shot back out into space, gaining speed and radiating pulses of radio energy as the spinning magnetic field lines whipped them outward.

Inflated by the pulsating radiation and streams of hot plasma from the spinning star, the cloud of gas from the original supernova explosion continued to expand at a speed of one percent that of light. After 5000 years, the front of the shock wave passed through the Solar System. For a thousand years the shielding magnetic fields of the Sun and Earth were buffeted by the invisible hurricane-force interstellar winds. The wiggling magnetic field lines lost their ability to keep the dangerous high-energy cosmic ray particles away from the fragile Earth. The ozone layer in the upper atmosphere collapsed, and the life forms on Earth were subjected to a harrowing barrage of mutating radiation.

When the millennia-long storm finally waned, a new species of nearly hairless humanoids had emerged on Earth. The original band was small, but the individuals were smart. They used their intelligence to control things around them, instead of letting nature and the strong-muscled have their way. It wasn't too long before their ancestors were the only humanoids left on the planet.

TIME: 3000 B.C.

Traveling at its leisurely pace of one light-year every 10,000 years, the neutron star began to approach the Solar System. The intelligent beings who had been born in its baptism of invisible fire a half-million years ago had progressed to the point at which they began seriously to study the heavens. The neutron star glowed with a white-hot heat, but it was too tiny to be seen by mere human eyes.

Although many times hotter than the Sun, the neutron star was not a hot ball of gas. Instead, the 67-billion-gee gravity field of the star had compressed its blazing matter into a solid ball with a thick crust of close-packed, neutron-rich nuclei arranged in a crystalline lattice over a dense core of liquid neutrons. As time passed, the star cooled and shrank. The dense crust fractured and mountains and faults were pushed up. Most crustal features were only a few millimeters high, but the larger mountain ranges rose up almost ten centimeters, poking their tops above the iron-vapor atmosphere. The mountains were the highest at the east and west magnetic poles, for most of the meteoric material that fell on the star was directed there by the magnetic field lines.

The temperature of the star had fallen since its birth. The neutron-rich nuclei on the glowing crystalline crust could now form increasingly more complex nuclear compounds. Since the compounds utilized the strong nuclear interaction forces instead of the weak electronic molecular forces that were used on Earth, they worked at nuclear speeds instead of molecular speeds. Millions of nuclear chemical combinations were tried each microsecond instead of a few per microsecond, as on Earth. Finally, in one fateful trillionth of a second, a nuclear compound was formed that had two very important properties: it was stable, and it could make a copy of itself.

Life had come to the crust of the neutron star.

TIME: 1000 B.C.

Still unseen by human eyes, the white-hot neutron star continued to approach the Solar System. As the surface of the star began to cool through that small temperature range that was most conducive to nucleonic life, the original replicating nuclear molecule diversified and became more complex. Competition for the simpler nonliving molecules that served as food became more intense. Soon the primordial manna that had covered the crust was gone, and in its place were clumps of hungry cells. Some clumps of cells found that their topsides, which faced outward toward the cold, dark sky, were constantly at a lower temperature than their undersides, which were in contact with the glowing crust. They raised a canopy of skin up away from the crust and soon were running an efficient food-synthesis cycle using the heat engine that they had arranged between a stiff taproot penetrating deep into the hot crust and the cool canopy above.

The canopy was a marvel of engineering. It used stiff crystals embedded with superstrong fibers to form a twelve-pointed cantilever beam structure that raised the thin upper skin against the 67-billion-gee gravity field of the star. Of course, a plant's beam-structure couldn't lift its topside very far. A plant might be as much as five millimeters across, but it could only raise a canopy up a millimeter.

The plants paid a price for their canopies and supporting frame. They were rigid and had to stay where they had rooted. For many, many turns of the star, nothing moved except for an occasional spray of pollen from the tip of a cantilever beam on one plant, followed by the contraction of a flap at the tip of a nearby plant. Then, many turns later, that action would be followed by the dropping of a ripe seed pod, which rolled away in the continual winds.

One turn, a rolling seed pod broke against a chunk of crust. Its seeds scattered and several of them started to grow. One was more vigorous than the others, and soon its canopy began to rise above those of its slower siblings. Suffocated in the heat radiated from the star below and the underside of the taller plant above, most of the smaller seedlings died.

One, however, underwent a strange transformation as its body functions started to fail. It had a mutant enzyme whose normal function was the fabrication and repair of the crystalline structure that held up the canopy. But under the influence of the distorted nucleonic chemistry of an organism near death, the enzyme went wild and dissolved the crystalline structure it was designed to protect. The plant turned into a sac full of juice and fibers, and flowed down the slight slope upon which it had been rooted to a new resting place. The twelve pollen sprayers, slightly photosensitive in order to provide the optimum orientation for the canopy of the plant, worked their way around to the top. Now that the organism was out from under the blocking canopy of the larger plant, the errant enzyme controlled itself again. The plant sent down roots, rebuilt its canopy, and proceeded to give and receive many sprays of pollen. The mobile plant had many seedlings, all of which had the ability to dissolve their rigid structure and move if the conditions weren't right for optimum growth.

Soon the first animals roamed the surface of the neutron star, stealing seed pods from their immobile cousins and learning that there were many good things to eat on the star—especially each other.

Like the plants they came from, the neutron star animals were only five millimeters across, but, lacking stiff internal structures, they were flattened by the gravitation. The twelve photosensitive pollen sprayers and flaps became eyes, but they still retained their original reproduction function. The animals could grow "bones" whenever they wished. Most of the time these were degenerate forms of the cantilever beams that were used to hold their eyes up on stalks so they could see further; but, with a little concentration, a bone could be formed anywhere inside the skin sac. However, speed of bone forming was paid for in quality: the bones were made solely of crystallized internal juices; they did not contain the embedded fibers that made the plant structure so strong. That procedure took too much time.

Unlike the plants, the animals had to contend with the star's magnetic field. The plants didn't move, so they didn't mind that they were stretched into a long ellipse aligned along the magnetic field lines. The bodies of the animals were also stretched into long ellipses, but since their eyes were stretched by the same amount, they were not aware of the distortion. However, the animals found that it was much harder to move across the magnetic field lines than along them. Most gave up trying. To them the world was nearly one-dimensional. The only easy directions in which to travel were "east" and "west"—toward the magnetic poles.

After a long time, plants and animals existed all over the surface of the neutron star. Some of the smarter animals would look up at the dark sky and wonder at the points of light they saw moving slowly across the blackness as the neutron star turned. The animals in the southern hemisphere of the star were especially bewildered by the very bright spot of light that stayed fixed over the south pole. It was Earth's Sun. The light was so bright and close that it didn't twinkle like the other specks of light. But except for using the star as a convenient navigation beacon to supplement their magnetic directional sense, none of the animals bothered to think more about the strange light. There was always plenty of food from the constantly growing plants and the smaller animals. An animal doesn't need to develop curiosity and intelligence if it has no problems that need solving.

TIME: 2000 A.D.

The blinking, radiating, spinning neutron star was now one-tenth of a light year from the Sun. After a half-million years the star had cooled, and its spin speed had slowed to only five revolutions per second. It still sent out pulses of radio waves, but these were but a weak remembrance of its brilliant earlier days.

In a few hundred more years the neutron star would pass by the Solar System at a distance of 250 astronomical units. Its gravity would perturb the outer planets, especially Pluto, way out at 40 AU from the Sun. But Earth, snuggled up to Sol in its orbit of one AU radius, would scarcely notice the passage. The star would then leave the Solar System—never to return.

By now the life forms on Earth had invented the telescope, but even this was inadequate to see the tiny pinpoint of light in the vast heavens unless one knew exactly where to look.

Would it pass unseen?

Pulsar

Jacqueline Carnot strode over to a long table in the data processing lab in the CCCP-NASA-ESA Deep Space Research Center at CalTech. A frown clouded her pretty face. The cut of her shoulder-length brown hair and her careful choice of tailored clothing stamped her at once as "European."

Her skirt, blouse and clogs were her only items of clothing. It was not that she did not own stockings—and purses—and makeup —and rings—and perfume—and other "women's things"; it was just that she was in too much of a hurry in the morning to bother with them, for she had work to do. The French government had not given her a state fellowship to study at the International Space Institute so she could spend all morning getting dressed.

The slender woman swiftly cleared the table of its accumulated scraps of paper and tossed down a long data record at one end. The cylinder of paper rolled obediently across the table, then obstinately off the end and five meters across the floor before it finally stopped. Jacqueline left the roll on the floor and started to analyze the data. This menial task would normally have been handled by a computer. Unfortunately, computers now insisted on a charge number for everything, and when Jacqueline had logged on this morning she had found that the meager balance that she had been saving out of Professor Sawlinski's allocation for her thesis had been swallowed up by another retroactive intercurrency account readjustment. She knew that Sawlinski had plenty of rubles in his research budget; but, without his budget authorization and his personal approval to the computer (by the crypto-password that she knew, but dared not use), she was reduced to waiting and hand-processing until he returned.

Actually, it was fun working with the numbers in this personal way. With the computer doing the analysis, the numbers would be crammed into digital bins whether they were real data or noise, and right now there was a lot of scruffy noise on the graph.

The data Jacqueline was analyzing came from the low frequency radio detectors on the old CCCP-ESA Out-of-the-Ecliptic probe that was the first major cooperative effort between the Soviets and Europeans. Back in the early days of the race to the Moon, the Europeans had supplied the first Soviet lunar rover with laser retroreflectors. Then, after a disastrous experience with the Americans in which one of America's four precious Shuttle spacecraft and Europe's only SpaceLab had exploded on the launch pad, the Europeans had turned back to the East for cooperation. The Europeans built the instrumentation for an Out-of-the-Ecliptic spacecraft that was launched by one of the giant Russian launch vehicles. The craft first traveled five astronomical units out to Jupiter. But once there, instead of taking pictures and going on to other planets as previous spacecraft had done, it went under Jupiter's south pole—to shoot straight up out of the plane formed by the orbits of the planets.

As the spacecraft climbed up out of the ecliptic plane, its sensors began to see a new picture of the Sun. The magnetic fields that blossomed out from the sunspots at the middle latitudes of the Sun were now attenuated, while new effects began to dominate the scene.

The data from the CCCP-ESA Out-of-the-Ecliptic probe had been thoroughly analyzed by many well-funded scientific groups early in the mission. The information gathered had shown that the Sun had a case of indigestion. It had eaten too many black holes.

The scientists found an extremely periodic fluctuation in the strength of the Sun's polar magnetic field. The magnetosphere of the Sun had many variations, of course. Each sunspot was a major source of variability. However, sunspots were irregular in time and were so strong in the middle latitudes that they dominated everything. It was not until the OE probe was above the Sun, sampling data for long periods of time, that the finely detailed, highly periodic variations in the radio flux were found and interpreted as periodic variations in the Sun's magnetosphere. It was finally concluded that the Sun had four dense masses, probably miniature primordial black holes, orbiting around each other deep inside the Sun. These disturbed the Sun's normal fusion equilibrium by gnawing away at its bowels. The effect of the black holes on the Sun would become serious in a few million years, but all they did now was bring on an occasional ice age.

Although the human race realized that the Sun was not a reliable source of energy for the long term, there was little they could do about it. After a short flurry of national and international concern over the "death of the Sun," the human race settled down to solving the insoluble problem in the best way that they knew —they ignored it and hoped it would go away.

It was now two decades later. Miraculously, one of the two communication transmitters on the satellite and three of the experiments were still running. One of them was the low frequency radio experiment. Its output was sprawled across a table and down a computation-lab floor, slowly being marked up by the swift, slender fingers of a determined graduate student.

"Damn! Here comes the scruff again," Jacqueline muttered to herself as she slid the long sheet across the table and noticed that the slowly varying trace with the complex sinusoidal pattern began to blur. Her job for her thesis was to find another periodic variation in that complex pattern that would indicate that there were five (or more) black holes. Failing that, she needed to prove that there were only four. (At least she had been able to get her peripatetic advisor to agree that a well-documented negative result would be an adequate thesis.)

However, she was worried. The scruff was blurring the data, ruining a good portion of it. It wouldn't have made much difference if the good part had shown some new pattern and she could have ferreted out a new black hole to add to the Sun's problems. However, it was now pretty obvious that she would have to be content with a negative thesis, and this noise was going to make it difficult to convince the examining committee that there were only four black holes in the Sun. She stared at the noisy portion as her arms rapidly slid the long sheet of paper across the table.

"I shouldn't complain about this antique spacecraft," she said. "But why did it have to start stuttering now?"

She moved along the trace. The scruff got worse, then slowly faded away. When she got to the clear section, she started to measure the amplitude averages again. In a way it was good that the computer was not blindly working on this data. She had enough sense to ignore the noisy parts, and thus end up with a very clean spectrum. But if the computer had been handling the data, it would have folded the scruff in with the good data and the resulting spectrum would have had a lot of spurious spikes that would have given the examination committee plenty of ammunition. Jacqueline finished her data analysis late in the evening. She looked at the neat figures in the notebook.

"That is the hard way to analyze data," she said to herself. "Tomorrow it gets worse, when I have to read it all into the computer. I hope old Saw-face has loosened the purse strings by then." Jacqueline glanced wearily at the long tumbled ribbon of paper on the floor and, swirling it around, finally found a loose end and started to roll it up.

"Up and down with a double hump, triple hump, bump—repeat twice more, then scruffffff, then up and down with a double hump, triple hump, bump—repeat twice more, then scruffffff . . ." Jacqueline stopped her semiautomatic mouthing of the pattern on the roll. She quickly gathered up the whole pile of paper and carefully carried it to one end of the long room and stretched it out on the floor. She then went to one end and strode rapidly along it, looking for the noisy portions. "The scruff is periodic!" she exclaimed.

The noise seemed to have a period of about a day, and, as she went from one end of the roll to the other, it slowly drifted with respect to the more regular periodic bumps that were the meat of her thesis. She had previously thought that the noisy portions were due to random malfunctions of the spacecraft, but now the periodic nature of the scruff made her look elsewhere for the cause.

"It could be that the spacecraft develops an arc in the transmitter for a few hours every day, but that doesn't sound very likely," she said. She finished rolling up the paper and, carrying the roll with her, went into the communications lab. The first thing she looked up was the spacecraft log. Fortunately, that information was in the general library file and the computer would let her look at that without charging her. She flashed the log backwards, page by page. Most of the entries had her name entered:

J. CARNOT: ESA: ACCOUNT SAW-2-J: LFR DATA DUMP

"I seem to be the only one using this satellite," she said.

Finally she came to an engineering note. Once every few days or so, during slack periods, the spacecraft engineers at the CCCP-NASA-ESA Deep Space Network communications center would take the spacecraft through its engineering check list.

POWER 22% NOMINAL
X-BAND DOWN-LINK 80% NOMINAL
K-BAND DOWN-LINK DEAD
ATTITUDE CONTROL DEAD
SPIN RATE 77 MICRORAD/SEC
FUNCTIONING EXPERIMENTS
    LOW FREQUENCY RADIO
    SOLAR IR MONITOR
    X-RAY TELESCOPE (STANDBY)

"Only two experiments on," she said. "The engineers must have turned off the X-ray telescope since the last time I checked." She looked at the number for the spin rate, flipped the computer terminal into compute mode, and made a quick calculation.

"Seventy-seven microradians per second comes out to be a little more than one revolution per day—about the same period as the scruff. The scruff must be caused by the effect of the solar heating on the transmitting antenna or some other solar effect."

She logged off the terminal, took the roll of paper, and headed back through the pre-dawn hours to her room. The roll would join the many other rolls that lay stacked in a pile on her bookshelf, while she joined the rest of Pasadena in sleep.

TIME: FRIDAY 24 APRIL 2020

In her sleep, Jacqueline was flying. No, not flying, but drifting through empty space. She looked down and finally realized where she was. Below her was the bright globe of the Sun. Spread out before her was the whole Solar System as seen from above. Her astronomically trained mind had placed the dream planets in their proper positions and she could almost imagine faint lines tracing out the nearly circular orbits that gave the Solar System the appearance of a bull's-eye target from this perspective. She found the tiny double-planet system that was the Earth-Moon pair and was straining to try and make out detail on the Earth when the slow, inexorable rotation of her body dragged her eyes away from the scene. Unable to turn her head around any further, she was forced to gaze upwards away from the Sun, her arms and legs outstretched in the form of an X. "Just like the low frequency radio antennas sticking out of the OE probe," she thought.

Soon the rotation brought her body around again and she admired the view. She finally concentrated on looking at the north pole of the Sun. She had no trouble looking at the Sun despite its brightness, and she searched for any variations on the nearly featureless surface. As she stared, she saw nothing with her eyes, but she finally began to notice weak pulsations in her arms and legs. A double pulse, triple pulse, pulse . . .

"I'm picking up the complex radio signal of the orbiting black holes!" she thought, as her body continued to revolve. Soon she could no longer see the Sun, but she could still feel the pulsations in her arms and legs. Then, while staring out at right angles from the Sun, she felt a rapid tingling sensation building up in her right arm. It became stronger and stronger, nearly blotting out the slower, rhythmic pulsations. "The scruff!" she exclaimed, and then began to laugh at herself . . .

"Nothing like getting yourself so wrapped up in your thesis work that you dream you have become the spacecraft yourself," said Jacqueline as she sat up in her room. She looked at the bustling noonday traffic out her window and rubbed the prickles out of her right arm, restoring the circulation it had lost while trapped under her exhausted body.

She was halfway through her belated breakfast when the dream surfaced again in her mind. Although she knew the spacecraft's operational characteristics almost as well as she knew the operating characteristics of her own body, it did seem strange to her that in the dream the scruff came when she was looking away from the Sun, not toward it.

She thought about it for a while, then went to her bookshelf and got down the roll she had been working on the previous night and an older one from several months ago. She unrolled a section from each of them on the floor, one above the other, and slid the old one back and forth until the slowly varying complex pattern caused by the orbital motion of the black holes was matched up on the two rolls. She then looked along both sheets and came to the noisy portions. They were different. First of all, the scruff a few months ago was significantly weaker (although that could be explained by a degrading piece of equipment or insulation), but there also seemed to be a definite shift in the position of the peak of the scruff activity with respect to the position of the Sun. She got out an even older roll, and checked it. The scruff was very weak now. In fact, she remembered that the computer had had no trouble obtaining a nice, clean spectrum from this data since the spectral energy in the noise had been so small. Again, however, there seemed to be a delay in the position of the peak intensity of the scruff.

"Well, this is one time when the number-crunching objectivity of the computer is orders of magnitude better than the highly subjective human hand and eye. It is back to the computer for you, Jacqueline," she said to herself. "But first you have to get some more computer time from old Saw-face."

Jacqueline walked across the CalTech campus to the Space Physics building. The huge edifice, built in the days when space budgets were a significant fraction of a nation's budget, was now the Space Physics building in name only. Only the basement computer room and the first floor offices contained space research activities. The remaining floors of the building had been taken over by graduate students of the Social Sciences department. If the CalTech-Jet Propulsion Laboratories combine had not been able to talk NASA, the Europeans, and the Russians into combining their dwindling national space budgets into supporting one international space research center with a single Deep Space Network, then there would be no deep space research at all.

After the Americans had given up sponsoring deep space probes and the European Space Agency had broken into squabbling factions after the loss of SpaceLab, the Russian planners, without visible competition, had lowered their priority for deep space research to almost zero and concentrated their funding on manned and unmanned Earth orbital ventures. The cold war was still on, but it had degenerated into an almost automatic name-calling at the United Nations. The Russian standard of living rose, and as it did, the party planners found that they had to give more and more attention to a no-longer docile population and could not justify a separate deep space program.

Jacqueline walked down the almost deserted corridors of the Space Physics building to Professor Vladimir Sawlinski's office. Jacqueline hesitated, then knocked.

"*Da?*" said a gruff voice.

Jacqueline opened the door and walked in. A thin, middle-aged gentleman swiveled away from a computer screen filled with text in Cyrillic characters and turned to look at her. Jacqueline's Russian was good enough that she could tell that he was reading a science news article about the supposed discovery of a magnetic monopole in some iron ore in Nigeria.

Sawlinski's clothing was unusual for a Russian. It was a tailored suit in the latest European style. Its very presence on his spare frame advertised that the wearer was a multi-cultured world traveler who was given significant freedom and even more significant financial reimbursement by a worldly wise Russian government that expected great things from him. The man's balding head bent forward as he peered over his reading glasses at the young woman.

"Jacqueline!" Sawlinski said, his face beaming with pleasure. "Do come in, young lady. How is your thesis work coming? Have you found another collapsed substellar object?"

Jacqueline grinned inwardly at the Russian's refusal to call them miniature black holes. Unfortunately, the Americans and Englishmen who had first popularized the concept of black holes were not aware that the phrase "black hole" had a context in the Russian language that was not used in polite company.

"I have used up my account and the computer will not talk to me anymore," she said. "I thought I had plenty of computer time left, at least for another month of work, but a retroactive inter-currency adjustment canceled it out."

Professor Sawlinski flinched. He had been afraid of something like that. His budget from the Soviet Academy was quite limited, but worst of all, it was in rubles. Now that the Chinese and Russians were heating up the border war in Mongolia again, the Russian ruble had been falling fast in the international money markets. He had been glad to have Jacqueline working for him, for she came free. As one of its few full-time graduate fellows, ESA paid all her expenses. When he had come to America to work in the International Space Institute, he had despaired of being able to afford any graduate student help, so getting Jacqueline had been a lucky break. She was smart (and pretty besides).

"All right," he sighed. "I will transfer more money from my main account. But my account will also be depleted by the same adjustment. I am afraid that this means that I won't be able to go to the Verona conferences this summer." He turned to the computer terminal at his desk and carried out a short dialog with the financial account program.

He turned after a minute and said, "The computer will now talk to you again. However, please be prudent in what you ask it to do, for the rubles are getting scarce."

"Thank you, Professor Sawlinski," Jacqueline replied. "However, I still have much work to do to finish my thesis. As of now, I cannot find any other periodic signals in the data. Also, the records from the probe are getting worse. The noise on the traces is growing in amplitude, and I have to throw out a good portion of the data. The noise itself is interesting though. I went back through some old traces and I find it is not only increasing in amplitude but the peak seems to shift in time with respect to the radio signals from the Sun."

"*Da*, the 'scruff,' as you call it," he said. "It is not going away, but getting worse? Well, we should not expect much from a spacecraft that is so old."

"But the shift with time is strong evidence that the scruff is not generated by the Sun," Jacqueline protested. "I think we ought to look into it."

"I can think of many mechanisms whereby the failing electronics on the spacecraft could produce this static," he replied with a smile. "We want you to get your thesis done without spending too many of my precious rubles, so I think we ought to concentrate on the analysis of the radio data that is not bothered by the noise."

"But it would not take long for me to have the computer go back through the data and get a good estimate of the drift," she said. Then remembering the tingling in her right arm, she suddenly became sure of something else, although it was against all logic that her position in bed in Pasadena had anything to do with an inanimate spacecraft cruising through space two hundred astronomical units away. Yet many a scientific idea had first surfaced in a dream of the researcher. Perhaps her subconscious was trying to tell her something.

"I am almost positive that the scruff is being picked up by just one of the four antenna wires," she said eagerly. "If I could get the engineers to switch the data collection mode to read each antenna separately . . ."

"*Nyet!*" boomed Professor Sawlinksi. "Paying the Deep Space Network to point their antennas to a given spacecraft to collect a one hour prearranged data dump is expensive enough. Do you realize how much it costs to send a command to a spacecraft?"

She started to speak, but Sawlinski cut her off as he dropped his recently acquired "American Professor" image and reverted to his autocratic old school Russian stance. "*Nyet! Nyet! Nyet!*" he said as he turned his back on her and switched on his computer console. "*Do svidaniya,* Mademoiselle Carnot."

Jacqueline started to speak, but realized that the interview was over. She seethed inwardly, but finally decided to leave and take her frustrations out on the computer. At least he had transferred the money to her account before he had turned her off. Quietly closing the door behind her, she made her way downstairs to the computer console room.

"I wonder how much a command change really does cost?" she thought as she made her way down the steps. "I will go out to Jet Propulsion Laboratories, talk to the Deep Space Network engineers and find out if it is as expensive as he thinks it is."

With the computer glad to see her again, now that she had money in her account, she read in the figures that she had laboriously extracted the previous evening. She then ran an analysis of the collected data. The peaks in the power spectral density curve were still in four families. The four lowest peaks were the fundamental orbital frequencies of the four black holes, while the higher harmonics were evidence of the slight ellipticity of the orbits. The basic pattern had not changed for decades. Although the black holes were orbiting in the interior of the Sun where the densities were hundreds and thousands of times greater than water, as far as the ultra-dense black holes were concerned, they were orbiting in a near vacuum.

She searched carefully between the four lowest spikes, but could find no evidence of another peak. She had the computer repeat her search, and it came up with three two-sigma candidates, but they looked like noise to her and a quick check with a random half-data set proved her right. She was through for the time being, for a data dump was not scheduled for another week. But while she was on the computer, she decided to have another look at the noise problem.

She first wrote a program to extract the noisy portions from the data sets, then to find the maximum of the amplitude of the scruff (which was a hard concept for the computer to grasp), then to plot the phase of the scruff maximum with respect to the position of the Sun. In the process, she learned that the spin rate of the satellite had increased slightly in the past years, somehow gaining angular momentum from the solar wind and light pressure.

Further examination of the drift of the phase and some calculations of the orientation of the spacecraft with respect to the Sun found that the peak in the scruff stayed constant with respect to the distant stars.

"That means that whatever the source of the noise, it is outside the Solar Sytem!" Jacqueline exclaimed.

Then she realized that she had never asked herself what the "scruff" really looked like. On the hardcopy printout of the reconstituted analog signal from the spacecraft, the scruff just looked like random fuzz. She cleared the screen and called up the latest data dump. The curve of the low frequency radio readout wound its familiar way across the screen. She stopped it as she came to the maximum of the scruff. The scruff was so strong in this section that it often saturated the screen.

She called on a section of the data analysis program that she had seldom used before, and a small section of the data was expanded on the screen. The hours-long humps that were the subject of her thesis were now stretched out so much that only a portion of one of them could fit into the screen. The scruff now dominated the screen and looked as noisy and nasty as ever. She called for another expansion, and the computer activated an override warning circuit.

WARNING!
PLOT SCALE INCOMPATIBLE WITH DATA DIGITALIZATION
    RATE.
PLEASE CONFIRM COMMAND.

Jacqueline hesitated slightly, then hit the confirm key. Immediately a set of almost random dots filled the screen. The short-term variation from point to point was strong, but the general amplitude level seemed to rise and fall slowly, with a period of many minutes.

Again, she called on the computer to carry out an operation on the data that she had never used before. She had been interested solely in the variations of the data with periods of weeks to days. Now she asked it to carry out a harmonic analysis with periods of seconds. Again the computer complained.

WARNING!
SPECTRAL ANALYSIS SCALE INCOMPATIBLE WITH
    DATA DIGITALIZATION RATE.
PLEASE CONFIRM COMMAND.

There was no hesitation this time: Jacqueline had hit the confirm key long before the computer had printed its objections. The spectral analysis plot flashed on the screen. There was a large spike around one Hertz that represented the one per second data digitalization rate, but at 0.005 Hertz there was a strong spike, indicating a periodic fluctuation with a 200-second period. However, the 200-second variation could have been caused by a beating between the one Hertz data sampling rate of the spacecraft and some high frequency oscillation that was close to some harmonic of the sampling rate. Jacqueline felt from the behavior of the data that a high frequency variation was causing the scruff, but it would be hard to prove it with the spacecraft sampling rate set at one sample per second.

Jacqueline, her enthusiasm finally exhausted by confusion and sleepiness, dropped the hardcopy printouts of the data into Professor Sawlinski's mailbox and went off to bed. She again had a dream about flying above the Solar System, only this time she was whirling around rapidly. She awoke feeling dizzy, then went back to sleep to dream ordinary, quickly forgotten dreams.

After awakening the next day, Jacqueline went by Professor Sawlinski's office. His door was open, and her data sheets were spread out on his desk. He was talking with Professor Cologne, the astrophysicist.

"This high frequency scruff is definitely not random noise, for there is evidence of a strong periodicity of 199 milliseconds, or a little over five cycles per second. The beating between the 199-millisecond pulsations and the one-Hertz data sampling rate gives it the 200-second beat pattern. However, it is not a 200-second fluctuation because the engineering interruptions in the science data are not exactly an even number of seconds long, and the 200-second beat starts with a new phase after each engineering readout. If you take enough data, and do an analysis of it, you find the 199-millisecond periodicity."

As he spoke, Professor Sawlinski held up Jacqueline's printout. Professor Cologne studied it briefly, then returned it with the comment, "It has all the earmarks of a pulsar, but there just isn't any known pulsar of that frequency. I would suspect the spacecraft somehow has found a way to become a low frequency radio oscillator."

Professor Sawlinski saw her standing in the door. "Ah, Jacqueline, come in. I was just showing Professor Cologne our latest data. I have decided that we ought to arrange to have the data digitalization rate increased to at least ten times per second, so we can obtain a better idea of the time varying nature of these pulsations."

"But the cost . . ." Jacqueline interjected.

"Yes, it will cost some money, but by the time the computer billing gets to us, we will be well into the new planning year," he replied. "Could you visit the JPL people and arrange for the change?"

"*Nom de Dieu!*" muttered Jacqueline under her breath. "First, not enough money, and now plenty of money."

Aloud, she replied, "Yes, Professor Sawlinski. Do you also want to try reading out the antennas sequentially?"

"*Nyet!*" he replied brusquely. "How many times must I remind you, only change one parameter at a time in an experiment!"

"Yes, Professor," she said, and practically bowed her way out of the office.

Once in the hall, she found herself automatically heading down the stairs to the computer room. She stopped and started to turn back to go to JPL, but then she decided to spend a little more time learning how the spacecraft command system operated. She felt that perhaps she could not only satisfy Professor Sawlinski, but also her own curiosity.

After a few hours spent browsing through the engineering handbooks, she smiled and headed up the stairs, where she caught the CalTech jitney bus to JPL. Sawlinski's name moved her swiftly through the administrative maze and she shortly was assigned to Donald Niven, one of the JPL project managers.

When she walked into the office she had been directed to, she saw a chunky young man with neatly trimmed dark hair and the slacks, sports coat, and tie that seemed to be the professional uniform of the engineers at JPL. She guessed that he was in his late twenties. She had thought that a project manager would be someone older, but as their conversation proceeded, she could tell from his cool, calm, methodical questions that, despite his age, he had acquired years of experience in the Deep Space Network organization. Their discussion was half technical, half financial.

"So the length or complexity of the command has almost no bearing on the cost?" she asked.

"That's right," Donald said. "So that groups like yours could plan their expenditures, we worked out a standard rate for each command cycle."

"Suppose a command has a series of steps in it?" she asked.

"As long as the steps are something for the spacecraft computer to go through and do not involve us, then the charge is the same for one or ten steps," he replied. "What do you have in mind?"

Jacqueline got out her program sheets. Donald swung his computer console around so they could both look at it. He typed in the code for the OE spacecraft operations manual.

"The first thing I want to do is to increase the low frequency radio data digitalization rate to its maximum," she said. "Then, after a week of high rate data collection, I want to have the data taken alternately with the four antennas, each one taking data for one minute at a time. After that, I want to have the X-ray telescope reactivated. It has a one-degree field of view, and I want it to scan between these two angles at a rate of one degree per day." Jacqueline handed over the sheet of paper and he took it.

"I see these are in spacecraft coordinates," he said, his opinion of the young woman increasing with every second. "Thanks for taking the trouble to convert them for me."

"It was no trouble," she replied calmly. "I have been living with that spacecraft so long that I practically think like it."

Together they worked out the command procedure, and Donald transferred it to the programming section. The computer would actually do the programming, but the programmers had to take the computer result through several tests to make sure that some bugs had not crept into the computer simulation in the decades since the spacecraft had been launched.

"I'll give you a call when the command is ready," Donald said. "It'll be a few days before the formal procedure is finished. Fortunately, I don't think we will have any trouble getting permission from the sponsoring agency. Although the experiment package was built by ESA, the spacecraft itself was built by the Russians, so the authority for command changes rests with the Soviet Academy of Science, and Professor Sawlinski's name should be good enough for them. Do you have a telephone number where I can reach you?"

TIME: FRIDAY 1 MAY 2020

As the days passed, Jacqueline and Donald spent many hours poring over the command time line. It was a long sequence, with even longer delays in it.

"Why can't we leave the low frequency radio on high digitalization rate while the X-ray telescope is scanning?" Jacqueline asked. "That way, if the X-ray telescope picks up something unusual, we can check the low frequency radio to see if the scruff is active."

Donald paged the screen to the section describing the operational characteristics of the low frequency radio digitalization block. "The X-ray telescope uses a lot of power, especially when it is in the scanning mode," he said. "I'm afraid that, because of the age of the radioisotope power generators, the voltage on the power bus will drop so much that the low frequency radio digitalization will blank out if we ask it to keep operating at its highest rate."

"How fast can it operate?" Jacqueline asked.

"Well," Donald said as he looked through the table, "it was minimum-voltage designed for an upper rate of eight times a second, and we have it pushed all the way to sixteen times per second. With the low voltage on the bus, we ought to come back to either eight or four times per second."

"Leave it sixteen times a second," said Jacqueline firmly. "No data is preferable to poor data."

Donald looked at her with a slightly bewildered expression as if he were seeing past her pretty face for the first time. He started to protest, but decided against it and made the short change in the command sequence as she wanted it.

Slowly the command was assembled. Jacqueline and Donald worked on it periodically during the day when Donald was charging to Sawlinski's account. They also talked about it over lunch and in the evenings, when Sawlinski's budget received an extra dividend of Donald's time.

TIME: SATURDAY 2 MAY 2020

Donald lay back on the grass of the recently mowed lawn of the Griffith Park Observatory. It was Saturday and a pleasant evening lay before him. First, a visit to the early show at the planetarium where he would see the highly touted Holorama show. Then an evening under the stars at the Greek Theater down the hill to listen to the Star Crushers, the latest sensation in popular music. And, to go with it all, a fascinating and beautiful, but perplexing, girl.

The Sun had set and Donald's mind wandered up into the lightly star-sprinkled sky as it had been doing ever since he was a little child and he and his father would go out into the back yard in the evening to look at the stars. Occasionally they would both be rewarded by the quick slash of a meteor or the slow progression of a satellite. Donald knew that since those days, his life had been fixed. He wanted to go to the stars!

Unfortunately, mankind's reach for the stars had faltered as Donald came of age, but his persistence had garnered him one of the few jobs left in the field. Although it now looked as if he would never get off the Earth himself, he was out there in proxy in the spacecraft that he tended.

Jacqueline took another sip of wine and watched Donald's eyes as they peered into the darkening skies. They were as vacant as the deep space they were contemplating.

"Next time he will make the picnic supper and I will bring the wine," she said to herself as she thoughtfully slid the sip of wine back over her tongue. "These California vintages are good, but he has a lot to learn if he thinks this is better than a good French wine."

Jacqueline knew Donald well enough to realize where his mind was. "Which one are you looking at?" she asked, knowing that he knew the position in the sky of every one of the six deep-space spacecraft that he was responsible for monitoring.

"Not one of mine," he replied, "but the first one to leave the Solar System—the Pioneer X. It went out between Taurus and Orion. It must be at 10,000 AU by now. I was imagining that I was out there, no longer able to communicate with Earth, pushing on alone, buffeted by micrometeors and the interstellar wind, getting more and more tired but pressing onward and outward . . ."

Jacqueline's tinkling laugh brought him back to Earth. He rolled over and glowered somewhat shamefacedly at her.

"Don't be mad," she said. "You and I must be more alike than we realize, for I too sometimes dream that I am a spacecraft."

She told him of her strange dream, and then they both talked about the well-known phenomenon of graduate students living, eating, and even dreaming their thesis problems.

"Your subconscious was probably trying to tell you something," he said.

"I know," she replied, "and I take that dream almost as seriously as I do the results of my calculations, or at least I will until we get something out of the spacecraft that contradicts it. But I was thinking, perhaps if we delayed the start of the X-ray telescope scan, and first stepped through the various digitalization rates on the low frequency radio, we might pick up some additional information on the exact spectrum of the scruff."

As Jacqueline shifted from being a companion for the evening to a colleague at work, Donald realized that the drifting mood of the picnic had disappeared, and they could talk shop standing in line just as easily.

"Maybe," he said, as he started to pack the basket. "Let's put this in the car and then get in the line for the show. We can talk about it more there."

TIME: TUESDAY 5 MAY 2020

The Deep Space Network spent five minutes (and many rubles) to launch the command into space. The five light-minute long string of radio pulses traveled for over a day before it reached the OE probe 200 AU away in its high arc over the Sun. The command was stored, and the spacecraft computer rapidly computed the check sum. It found no obvious errors, but the string of bits was treated like a potentially dangerous cancer virus. It was not allowed to get into the command mechanism just yet, for if there were something wrong in that string of bits, it could kill the spacecraft just as surely as a meteor strike. A copy of the bit stream stored in the holding memory was sent back to Earth. There the copy of the copy was checked with the original. Finally, another copy of the original command string, followed by a separate execute command, was sent out to reassure the OE probe that it could now change its operational state.

Jacqueline was waiting when the next data dump came into the computer. It was nearly midnight—a typical working hour for a graduate student—only now she was not as lonely as she had been in previous months when she had sat at this console in the early morning hours.

"Looks like a good dump," said Donald as he watched the Deep Space Network report build up on his screen.

Jacqueline turned to smile at him, but was interrupted by another, less kindly voice.

"Clean up the low frequency radio data and do a quick plot on the screen," Professor Sawlinski commanded.

Jacqueline's practiced fingers flew over the keyboard, and soon the computer was rearranging the data from spacecraft format to plotting format. There was a lot of data now that the digitalization rate had been increased, and it took some time.

"Here it comes," said Donald, as he watched the plot start to build up on Jacqueline's screen. The complex, humped pattern of the low frequency radio variations snaked their way across the display, crowding all their variations into a few inches of screen. Jacqueline peered closely at the display and slowly the greenish white line changed texture, as if it were going out of focus.

"The scruff is starting," she said.

They all looked as the slow variations became almost submerged in a flurry of noise.

Jacqueline noted the time of onset of the scruff and stopped the slowly moving plot with a few strokes of the *delete* key. A few more commands, and soon a new plot came on the screen. This time the sinusoidal variations were well spaced, and the scruff was now a distinct pulsation.

"It is definitely periodic!" Sawlinski said. "Expand it further!"

In the next plot, the slow variations that were the basis of Jacqueline's thesis had been reduced to a gradually increasing trend line. And on that line there marched a series of noisy spikes, as equally separated as soldiers in a parade, but varying greatly in their size.

"It certainly looks just like a pulsar," exclaimed Sawlinski. "What is the period?"

"I'll run a spectral analysis of this section," Jacqueline said.

Soon the spectral analysis was on the screen. There was a lot of noise and some sideband spikes, but there was no doubt that the data centered predominantly at a frequency of 5.02 Hertz or a period of 199 milliseconds.

"Something that regular can only be manmade—or a pulsar," said Sawlinski. "I want you to find the other sections of scruff and see if the periods are the same. If they are, see if one section of scruff keeps in step with the beat set up by the preceding sections. I will check the library to get the latest data on pulsars." He went across the room and activated another console.

Jacqueline peered at the screen and said, "If you are going to look up pulsar periods, I would say that the period is 199.2 milliseconds, although the last number could be off by a few digits."

By the time Sawlinski had put the console into library mode and had obtained a list of the known pulsars with periods of less than one second, Jacqueline had determined that the pulses indeed kept very exact time. Although they faded away and reappeared a day later as the spacecraft slowly rotated, the new line of marching pulses was still in step with the first batch. She followed the pulses through the whole set of data. They kept accurate time during the whole week.

"The period is now 0.1992687 seconds and seems to be good to at least six places," Jacqueline said as Sawlinski glanced at her.

He looked through the tables of pulsar periods on his screen. "There are no known pulsars with that period," he said. "Yet it must be a pulsar. If we only knew exactly where to look, maybe the radio telescopes here on Earth could find it."

Jacqueline finally decided to tell him of her decision to add an additional command to the original one. "Professor Sawlinski," she said, "while Donald and I were working out the details of the command to the spacecraft to have it speed up its data digitalization rate, we realized that the length of the command made no difference to the cost of sending the command. We also figured that, after a week of high rate data, we would have obtained most of the information on the nature of the high frequency scruff, and we could then have the spacecraft do something else."

"What did you do!" Sawlinski barked at her.

Jacqueline faced him and patiently explained. "After a week of data collection at high rate, we programmed the spacecraft to continue at a high data rate, but to switch cyclically between the four antenna arms. I hoped that the scruff would show up more on one arm than another, and we could at least tell from what quadrant of the sky the signal was coming from."

Sawlinski's face glowered while he thought over what she had told him. Finally he relaxed and said, "*Horosho!*" He then turned to Donald and asked for the time of the next data dump.

"One week from now, minus about a half-hour."

"*Horosho.* I will see you both then," he said. "Meanwhile, Jacqueline, you had better get this information ready for publication in *Astrophysical Letters*. We will want the period, the apparent strength, and anything else you can extract out of the data. We will hold off sending it in for review until we have had a chance to see next week's data. *Dobri vecher.*" He turned on his heel and left them.

TIME: TUESDAY 12 MAY 2020

The following week, the console room was crowded. Professor Sawlinski had brought a few radio astronomers with him, and several of the faculty and graduate students, having heard rumors in the halls, had also gathered to get in on the excitement. Donald had brought along a spacecraft antenna design engineer; together they had dredged up the exact configuration of the low frequency radio antennas on the spacecraft and calculated the exact radiation pattern of each arm. The antenna patterns were very complex because the response of an individual arm depended strongly on the detailed shape of the spacecraft on the side where that particular arm was attached.

Jacqueline was also ready with a complex data reduction program that would produce five plots on the screen, one showing the signal detected in each arm, and one showing the combined response of all the arms.

Donald turned from his console, where he had been monitoring the engineering data from the Deep Space Network.

"The dump is finished. You should find the data in the computer files now," he said.

Jacqueline's hands flew over the keyboard and soon five greenish white lines were snaking their way across the screen.

"Here comes the scruff," she said. Then leaning forward she looked at the four top traces and exclaimed, "The pulses are showing up in only one of the antenna arms!"

It soon was obvious that, as the spacecraft tumbled slowly through space with its four long antenna arms sweeping across different portions of the sky, one of the antennas was doing a much better job of picking up the high frequency pulses than were the others. They would now be able to do a better job of pinpointing the source in the sky.

The spacecraft antenna design engineer shook his head in puzzlement. "It doesn't make sense that one of those antennas would be that much more sensitive than the others. After all, they are only long hunks of wire, and their antenna patterns should not look all that different. Which one is it?"

"Antenna number two," Jacqueline said.

The engineer turned to his console and soon a directivity pattern, fleshed out in pseudo-three-dimensional shape by the computer, flashed on the screen.

"I don't see any significant directivity here," he said.

Donald had been watching, and had noticed a frequency number at the bottom of the screen.

"The pulses could be high frequency bursts that are higher than the nominal design frequency for the low frequency radio antennas," he said. "Can you calculate the antenna pattern for a higher frequency?"

"I already have that calculated and stored," said the engineer. He typed in a command and soon the pattern was replaced by another one. Sticking up out of the center of the pattern was a high-gain spike.

The engineer looked at it for a second and then announced, "That spike is called an 'end fire' lobe and is a complex interaction of the antenna with the panel and instruments on that side of the spacecraft. We often see such spikes showing up at the high frequency end of the design range." He turned to Jacqueline and said, "That makes it easy; your pulses are coming from the direction the antenna is pointing."

The radio astronomers began to get interested. They now knew in which direction relative to the spacecraft the pulsating signals came from. However, it took a few hours of work with the Deep Space Network and the spacecraft engineers before they knew exactly how the spacecraft was oriented with respect to the stars when the pulses were at their maximum.

Within two days, several radio dishes were pointing their narrow beams out into space, searching for the new pulsar. Even though they knew the exact period and even to a fraction of a second when they should see a pulse, none was found. The mystery grew deeper.

TIME: TUESDAY 19 MAY 2020

"Little green men begin to sound more and more plausible," Donald said as he lay on the grass next to Jacqueline. He had taken her to a show and had been pleased that she had taken the trouble to put on her "women's things." Behind her prettied-up face, the intelligence that was Jacqueline peered out and frowned disapprovingly.

"Don't be silly," she said. "There has to be a perfectly simple explanation, but we just have not thought of it yet. Perhaps the X-ray telescope will tell us something. Fortunately, it scanned over the probable position in the sky in the second day of this week's data collection, so we won't have to wait too long."

"Does Sawlinski know about that part of the command?" Donald asked.

"No," Jacqueline said, "I didn't get a chance to tell him. In fact, he has been so busy giving seminars and visiting radio astronomy antenna sites that I haven't seen him for a week."

Donald looked at his watch and said, "Well, it is almost time for the next data dump. Let's go in and monitor it on the consoles." They rose and walked through the darkness to the Space Sciences building.

This time the console room held only two people. Donald sat behind Jacqueline and leaned on the back of her chair, smelling her perfume and watching her slender fingers play over the keyboard.

"The X-ray data is in a different format from the radio data since it is just a count of the number of X-ray photons detected," she said. "First, I will get the directional plot and see if there is any significant increase in counts in the same direction as the low frequency radio experiment detects radio pulses."

Soon a histogram of pulses versus the direction in the sky flashed on the screen.

"Look at that spike!" Donald said. "Is that the right direction?"

"*Mais oui!*" Jacqueline's fingers stumbled in the excitement, and she had to erase a distorted plot before she slowed down and finally got the computer to show the number of counts versus time when the telescope was pointing in the right direction.

"There they are, just like little soldiers, five times a second!" said Donald.

"5.0183495 times per second," Jacqueline retorted. "That number is engraved in my memory. What I really hope to get out of this X-ray data is some evidence of delay between the X-ray pulses and the radio pulses. The X-ray pulses will travel at the speed of light, but the radio pulses will be delayed slightly by the interstellar plasma and will arrive later. The more they are delayed, the more plasma they had to travel through. The combination of X-ray data and radio data will give us a rough idea of the distance to the pulsating source."

As she talked, she was working the keyboard, and soon, underneath the marching row of X-ray spikes, there was a similar row of spikes from the radio antenna.

"It is a good thing you decided to digitalize the radio data sixteen times a second so we could see the individual pulses," Donald said. "If we had tried four times a second as I recommended, we would have missed most of them."

"There is no delay!" Jacqueline cried, bewildered.

"Hmmm," said Donald, "maybe the delay is almost exactly 200 milliseconds and they are just shifted."

"No," Jacqueline said, pointing to the screen. "Look—there is a very weak X-ray pulse followed by three strong ones and then two weak ones. You can see the exact pattern in the radio pulses, right below them. The delay is almost zero. That must mean that whatever the source of the pulses, it is very close to the detectors."

" . . . and the closest thing to the detectors is the spacecraft itself," Donald said. "I am afraid that somehow the spacecraft is putting spikes into both the low frequency radio antenna and the X-ray telescope."

Jacqueline frowned, then quickly produced two more plots with much larger scales. The pulses were now so close together that they were back to being scruff again. But the scruffy region on the X-ray plot was much shorter than on the radio plot.

"No, it is not the spacecraft," she said. "Look here, the pulses come and go with time much faster for the X-ray telescope than for the radio antenna. The X-ray telescope has a field of view that is limited to one degree, while the high sensitivity spike in the radio antenna has a beam width of almost three degrees, and these plots are consistent with the width of those patterns."

"Well, if it isn't the spacecraft," said Donald, "then what is it?"

"Give me a few minutes," she said, and went back to typing on the keyboard.

Donald got up, walked down the hall to the coffee machine and bought them both a cup of coffee. It looked like a long evening ahead. When he returned, she had the X-ray and radio-pulse trains up on the screen again, but now they were blown up so far that only three pulses appeared on the screen.

"There is a very slight time delay," she said as he walked in. "I wish I could remember the number density for the interstellar plasma near the Sun. I worked out the values for the latest solar wind cycle last month; I will have to go upstairs and look it up."

She made a hard-copy printout of the graph on the screen, then ran quickly upstairs. Donald followed slowly behind, carrying the two cups of coffee. By the time he made it up the stairs, she had found the number for the interstellar plasma density. She was punching away on her hand calculator when he walked into her office.

"2300 AU!" she exclaimed. "That pulsar is only one-thirtieth of a light year away!"

"A star that close?" Donald asked. "Surely we would have seen it moving across the sky long ago."

"No," she said, "a pulsar is a spinning neutron star, and a neutron star is only about twenty kilometers in diameter. Even if the temperature were high, the size of the light-emitting area is so small that we wouldn't be able to see it unless we looked in just the right place with a very large telescope. But you are right, it is strange that it has not been picked up in one of the sky surveys."

"If the pulsar is that close, then why didn't the radio astronomers find the pulses too?" he asked.

"Neutron stars give off their radiation in beams that shoot out from the magnetic poles, and you have to be in the direction of the beam to see the pulses," she replied. "That is why the spacecraft sees the pulses and we can't. The spacecraft is up out of the ecliptic by 200 AU and has moved up into the path of the beams." She walked over to the whiteboard in the office, picked up a colored marker, and started to pace and scribble.

Donald kept silent as slender feet clicked back and forth across the floor in their dress shoes. He waited patiently while long fingers scrawled diagrams and calculations on the board. He watched in admiration as the pretty face puzzled out the complexity of the mathematical transformation from one set of astrophysical coordinates to another. Five minutes later, he was still admiring Jacqueline from behind when she finally turned and spoke.

"It is up in the northern sky," she said. "But it is not where we thought it was. Because the neutron star is so close, there is a difference of over five degrees in the angle from the spacecraft to the star and from the Earth to the star. No wonder the radio astronomers could not find it. We told them the wrong direction."

She went over to a star chart on her wall and carefully made a tiny cross. She turned and, with a wry grin on her face, remarked, "And the reason it was never picked up in a sky survey is that it is right next to Giansar, the fourth magnitude star right at the end of Draco, the Dragon constellation. It would take a good telescope to see the neutron star image in that bright glare."

She drank down the rest of her coffee.

"Let's go wake up old Saw-face," she said. "We've got a paper to publish."

TIME: FRIDAY 22 MAY 2020

In two days the paper was prepared and accepted into the *Astrophysical Letters* computer. The next day it was on the astrophysical information net, along with a note from the radio astronomers that very weak 199-millisecond pulsations had been detected from a region in the northern skies right at the end of the constellation of Draco. Shortly thereafter, the new ten-meter telescope in China found a faint speck in the sky, and pictures of "The Egg of the Dragon—Sol's Nearest Neighbor" appeared in *Sinica Astrophysica*. The popular press copied the picture—along with the picturesque Chinese name, and soon people were peering up at the night sky, vainly trying to catch a glimpse of "Dragon's Egg," resting just off the end of the constellation Draco, as if the star were a recently laid egg.

TIME: SATURDAY 13 JUNE 2020

It was Saturday evening. Donald and Jacqueline sat on the grass of the Griffith Observatory and talked. They were much more relaxed than they had been for months. Jacqueline's thesis was completed, and her formal oral defense the day before had been a mere formality, what with the world-wide scientific acclaim and video-news publicity being made over the discovery.

"I still don't understand why Sawlinski is doing the video-news interviews," Donald said with a frown. "You were the one who discovered the neutron star first, not he."

"That is not the way science works," Jacqueline explained. "A Professor starts a research project hoping to discover something new. The student sometimes makes the discovery, but without the Professor's research project, the discovery would not have been made. Since the Professor gets the blame if the project is a failure, he should get the benefit from any successes. Besides, it doesn't upset me—after all, my career is off to a great start!"

Donald only felt a greater admiration for the woman of whom he had become so fond. He kept silent and continued to look upward at the stars.

After a long time, Jacqueline spoke. "I wonder if we could ever go visit Dragon's Egg. At the speed it is traveling, it will be gone from the Solar System in a few hundred years. I wish I could go myself, but I guess maybe it will be my grandchild or great-grandchild."

"We may be going sooner than you think," Donald said. "The latest news on the Nigerian magnetic monopole discovery is that they have used the first monopole in a large magnetic accelerator to generate other monopoles, and some of those have already been used as a catalyst for a deuterium fusion reaction. The JPL engineers are excited about the fusion results. They are already starting to design fusion-rocket concepts for interstellar spacecraft. I don't think a ship will be ready soon enough so that you and I could go for a visit, but I wouldn't be surprised if, in twenty or thirty years, one of our children will be looking down at Dragon's Egg from a close orbit."

And inevitably, the years passed . . .

TIME: SUNDAY 15 AUGUST 2032

Quick-Mover was getting tired. He only hoped the Swift was tiring faster. The Swift was much quicker than he, but its brain was slow, and it never seemed to learn from its repeated failures to catch him. This particular beast had been harassing his clan

for the last three turns of the sky, and the clan had been forced
to retreat to a cluster of boulders that blocked the Swift's rush.
There was nothing they could do until the huge beast tired and
went away, or else caught one of them out in the open—like
Quick-Mover—who was now beginning to regret his attempt to
get a food-pod from a nearby plant.

He watched carefully with six of his eyes as the Swift laboriously moved in the hard direction until it figured it was
directly east or west of its intended prey. Once there, it would
start accelerating, swiftly slithering toward him as its long narrow body twisted across the crust. As it neared, the great, glowing maw would open, and out from under each of the five eyes
ringing the gaping mouth would spring a long, sharp fang of
crystal.

Quick-Mover knew how sharp those fangs were, since he had
one stored in a tool pouch in his body. He had retrieved the fang
from the mangled carcass of a Swift that had been the loser in a
mating duel and had used it to cut up the drying carrion that he
and his clan had enjoyed as a supplement to their food-pod diet.

The Swift launched its rush. Quick-Mover waited until the
Swift had committed itself to its attack; then, thinning his flexible, opalescent body down, he pushed into the hard direction
with all the speed that his muscles could command. The Swift
was now moving so rapidly that it could not change its course,
but it was close. One of Quick-Mover's trailing eyes winced
when a fang nicked its thick support stub.

As the Swift slowed its rush and turned to attack again, Quick-
Mover became desperate. Soon one of those sharp fangs was
going to slash a large hole in him, and the next time the Swift
made its rush, it would catch him.

Then suddenly, Quick-Mover had a thought. He had a fang
too! He watched the Swift shift position off at a distance and
begin its rush. He quickly shaped a section of skin into a short
tendril and, reaching into the tool pouch orifice, pulled out the
fang. He enlarged the tendril into a strong manipulator, backed
up with a thick crystal bone core, and pushed the rest of his
body into the hard direction again. This time, he left a portion of
his body out in the path of the Swift. It was the thick manipulator holding the fang. Quick-Mover felt a jar, then his eyes
glowed as he saw the Swift stumble to a halt, fangs snapping at

its flank, where the glowing vital juices poured out onto the crust.

Quick-Mover looked in awe at the fang held in his manipulator. Both were covered with dripping gobs of glowing juice. He sucked them clean, enjoying the unaccustomed taste of fresh juice and meat. He moved over to the still-thrashing Swift. Carefully keeping well off in the hard direction, he watched the Swift as it grew weaker. Finally, feeling bolder, he moved the manipulator with its fang over the center of the long thin body and struck downward. The sharp point sank deep into the body. The Swift, struck in its brain-knot, shivered and flowed into a fleshy pile.

Quick-Mover raised the fang and struck once more.

It felt good.

He was mightier than a Swift! Never again would one of these beasts terrorize his people!

The fang struck again and again and again . . .

TIME: FRIDAY 5 NOVEMBER 2049

Pierre Carnot Niven floated in front of the console on the science deck of the interstellar ark, St. George. The thin young man pulled thoughtfully at the corner of his carefully trimmed dark brown beard as he monitored the activities out in the asteroid belt surrounding the still-distant star, Dragon's Egg.

"It's still 'Mother's Star' to me," Pierre thought as he recalled his childhood years, lying in his father's arms out on the lawn to watch the first interstellar probes go out to explore the neutron star his mother had found.

There had been some whispers of "favoritism" when he had been picked to be Chief Scientist of the Dragon's Egg exploration crew, but those who whispered had not been as driven as he. He had felt his mother had received too little scientific recognition for her discovery, and his whole life had been spent rectifying that supposed wrong. He had not only made himself the world's expert on neutron-star physics, but had also taught himself to be a popular science writer so that everyone—not just a few scientists—would know of the accomplishments of the son of Jacqueline Carnot. Pierre had been successful, for his ability to communicate science concepts at every level had led to his being chosen leader and spokesman for the expedition. Now the talking and selling and explaining were through, and the scientist in Pierre took over.

The expedition was still six months away from Dragon's Egg, but it was time to start the activities of the automated probes that had been sent ahead by St. George. There would be a lot of work to do in preparation for their close-up view of the star. Now that they had found and identified the asteroidal bodies around the neutron star that they would need, the work could be done as easily by robot brains as human ones.

The largest of the probes was really an automated factory, but its single output was very unusual—monopoles. It had some monopoles on board already, both positive and negative types. These were not for output, but the seed material needed to run the monopole factory. The factory probe headed for the first of the large nickel-iron planetoids that the strong magnetic fields of the neutron star had slowed and captured during its travels. It started preparing the site while the other probes proceeded with the job of building the power supply necessary to operate the monopole factory, for the power that would be needed was so great that there was no way the factory probe could have carried the fuel. In fact, the power levels needed would exceed the total power-plant capability of the human race on Earth, Colonies, Luna, Mars, asteroids, and scientific outposts combined.

Although the electrical power required was beyond the capability of those in the Solar System, this was only because they didn't have the right energy source. The Sun had been—and still was—very generous with its outpouring of energy; but so far the best available ways to convert that radiant energy into electricity, either with solar cells or by burning some fossilized sun energy and using it to rotate a magnetic field past some wires in a generator, were still limited.

Here at Dragon's Egg, there was no need for solar cells or heat engines, for the rapidly spinning, highly magnetized neutron star was at one time the energy source and the rotor of a dynamo. All that was needed were some wires to convert the energy of that rotating magnetic field into electrical current.

The job of the smaller probes was to lay cable. They started at the factory and laid a long thin cable in a big loop that passed completely around the star, but out at a safe distance, where it would be stable for the few months that the power would be needed. Since a billion kilometers of cable was needed to reach from the positions of the asteroidal material down around the star and back out again, it had to be very unusual cable—and it was. The cables being laid were bundles of superconducting polymer threads. Although it was hot near the neutron star, there was no need of refrigeration to maintain the superconductivity, for the polymers stayed superconducting almost to their melting point—900 degrees.

The cables became longer and longer and started to react to the magnetic field lines of the star, which were whipping by them ten times a second—five sweeps of a positive magnetic field emanating from the east pole of the neutron star, interspersed with five sweeps of the negative magnetic field from the west pole. Each time the field went by, the current would surge through the cable and build up as excess charge on the probes. Before they were through, the probes were pulsating with displays of blue and pink corona discharge—positive, then negative. The last connection of the cable to complete the circuit was tricky, since it had to be made at a time when the current pulsating back and forth through the wire was passing through zero. But for semi-intelligent probes with fractional-relativistic fusion-rocket drives, one-hundredth of a second is plenty of time.

With the power source hooked up to the factory, production started. Strong alternating magnetic fields whipped the seed monopoles back and forth at high energies through a chunk of dense matter. The collisions of the monopoles with the dense nuclei took place at such high energies that elementary particle pairs were formed in profusion, including magnetic monopole pairs. These were skimmed out of the debris emanating from the target and piped outside the factory by tailored electric and magnetic fields, where they were injected into the nearby asteroid. The monopoles entered the asteroid and in their passage through the atoms interacted with the nuclei, displacing the outer electrons. A monopole didn't orbit the nucleus like an electron. Instead, it whirled in a ring, making an electric field that held the charged nucleus, while the nucleus whirled in a linked ring to make a magnetic field that held onto the magnetically charged monopole.

With the loss of the outer electrons that determined their size, the atoms became smaller, and the rock they made up became denser. As more and more monopoles were poured into the center of the asteroid, the material there changed from normal matter, which is bloated with light electrons, into dense *monopolium*. The original atomic nuclei were still there; but, now with monopoles in linked orbits around them, the density increased to nearly that of a neutron star. As the total amount of converted matter in the asteroid increased, the gravitational field from the condensed matter became higher and soon began to assist in the process, crushing the electron orbits about the atoms into nuclear dimensions after they had only been partially converted into *monopolium*. After the month-long process was complete, the 250-kilometer-diameter asteroid had been converted into a 100-meter-diameter sphere with a core of *monopolium*, a mantle of degenerate matter of white dwarf density, and a glowing crust of partially collapsed normal matter.

After the first asteroid had been transformed, the factory turned to the next, which had been pushed into place by a herder probe that had started its task many months ago. The process was repeated again and again until finally there was a collection of eight dense asteroids circling the neutron star: two large ones and six smaller ones, dancing slowly around each other as they moved along in orbit. They were kept in a stable configuration with thrusts from the probes, which used the magnetic fields from a collection of monopoles in their noses to exert a push or pull from a distance on the hot, magnetically charged, ultra-dense masses.

The probes, herding their creations along, now waited patiently for St. George to arrive. As the humans approached the neutron star, the herder probes became more active. They pushed, pulled, and nudged the two larger asteroids until they approached one another. As the ultra-strong gravitational fields of the two asteroids interacted, they whirled about one another at blinding speed and then took off in opposite directions on highly elliptical orbits that would meet again many months later at a point much closer to the nearby neutron star.

Volcano

TIME: 14:44:01 GMT SUNDAY 22 MAY 2050

Broken-Petal flowed his elongated body down through the ragged rows of petal plants, anxiously feeling the swellings of the ripening pods on the underside of each plant with his tendrils. He subconsciously counted the pods as he went along, but not in terms of numbers, since his total mathematical knowledge consisted of: one, two, three—many.

Although Broken-Petal could not count, he was very good at equating large numbers. He knew that, sometimes, what seemed to be many pods was still not enough to feed the clan—for there were many in the clan and all were always hungry. As he moved and felt, the many pods in his mind grew and, as the number grew, his anxiety for the many in the clan became less and less. He found his undertread adding a youthful t'trum pattern to his smooth flowing motion as he came to the end of the last row. He let his opalescent body resume its normal flat, ellipsoidal shape and looked at the crop with pride. The petal plants were tall. He would have liked to have seen them all, but he was content to rest at one end and look with only three or four of his dozen dark red eyes down between the rows that he had struggled so hard to get the clan to dig.

Broken-Petal remembered the time, many turns of the stars ago, when he came across proud old Dragon-Flower with a stub of a broken dragon crystal in her manipulator.

"What are you doing, Aged One?" Broken-Petal asked.

"I'm tired of having to wander in the wilderness to find a petal plant that has not already been stripped of all of its pods," she said. "I'm going to have my own plants, right here outside my wall." She left the dragon crystal sticking in the crust, and flowed back to let him see what she had been doing. As she did so, the strong crystalline bones in her manipulator dissolved, and the muscle and skin that had covered the thick, articulated appendage shrank back into her body until her surface was smooth again.

"Why are you digging those holes, Aged One? How will that get you your own petal plants?"

She replied, "I may be old, but I still see well and remember well. The last time the young ones came back from a hunt, they had traveled so far away they had found some petal plants that had never been picked. They brought home as many pods as they could carry. There were many delicious ripe ones and some that looked all right, but, when opened, were runny and the seeds inside were hard. Naturally, being an Aged One, I got the overripe pods. I ate all that I could—the taste is not bad once you get used to it—but the seeds inside were too hard to crack, so I rolled them outside."

"I remember that hunt," Broken-Petal said. "We never did find a sign of a Flow Slow or even a Slink, but that patch of untouched petal plants made up for it all."

Dragon-Flower continued, "One turn I noticed that one of the seeds had rolled into a crack in my wall. It had a little petal growing from it. I watched it turn after turn as it became larger and larger. It grew into a petal plant! I was happy, I would have my own petal plant right near my door. I would dream of picking the pods whenever I wanted, without having to go far distances. Maybe I could even wait and have a ripe pod to eat all by myself, as I did in the old times when I was a young warrior and went on hunting expeditions."

Her t'trums became sadder as she went on, "But the stones in the wall kept the petal plant tilted to one side—and it fell over and died."

She added, "I watched the other seeds, but none of them grew into petal plants. They just sat there under the sky and did nothing. Then many turns ago, having nothing better to do, I cleaned out my stockade and pushed a pile of dirt, old pod skins and Flow Slow nodes out the door. The pile covered one of the seeds. Later I noticed it too had started to grow into a petal plant!

"That's it over there," she said, rippling her eye-stubs.

Broken-Petal's eyes followed the ripples and saw a small plant growing up from the corner of a decomposing heap of trash. The plant was still small enough that he could look down on its concave topside, cooled to a dark red by the black sky above, while the lumpy underside of the many-pointed leaf structure reflected the healthy yellow glow of the crust.

"It should be big soon," Dragon-Flower said. "I can already see some pod swellings on the underside."

Several thoughts ran through Broken-Petal's mind as he looked at the plant, with its promise of food. But there was one thought that made him feel in a funny way that he had never felt before. He felt the spark of inspiration.

"Aged One! I have thought of a new thing! Let us take all the hard seeds we can find and put them under piles of trash that we take out of our stockades. The seeds will grow into petal plants and we will have all the pods that we want!"

Dragon-Flower paused a moment, reformed her manipulator, and grasped her broken shard of dragon crystal. "You are wrong, Broken-Petal. The seeds do not need trash. My first petal plant was not under trash, it was in a hole in my wall," she said. "It is obvious that the petal plants just want to see the sky. As long as the seeds stay out on the crust where they can see the sky they are happy and do not grow. But if you take away the sky, they get unhappy and break out of their hard coats and grow until they can see the sky. That is what I am doing with this broken crystal. I use the sharp point to make a little hole in the crust. I put the seed in the hole and cover it up so that it cannot see the sky. The seed will get unhappy and start to push up until it can see the sky once more, only by then it will be a petal plant, instead of a seed."

Broken-Petal knew better than to get into an argument with an Aged One, even if he was Leader of the Clan. He watched as Dragon-Flower continued with the arduous task of poking the sharp end of the broken crystal into the hard crust. She soon tired and quit, but not before there were many holes around the perimeter of her stockade, and in each hole was an unhappy seed, covered over with powdered crust.

Dragon-Flower's experiment was both a success and a failure. Most of the seeds grew into plants, and soon Dragon-Flower was on friendly terms with many, as she had more pods than she could eat. Broken-Petal had to put his weight on a few of the more rash youngsters and give them a good drubbing before they stopped their raids on her plants.

"You lazy flats!" he would holler on their hides. "Go out and find your own pods! And make sure you bring back the best one for Dragon-Flower to replace the one you took!"

He couldn't let them get lazy and weak; he would need their strength on the next raid or hunt.

Then, things got worse. The plants grew and grew until they blocked the sky over most of Dragon-Flower's stockade. Although no one really minded reaching a manipulator under a plant to take a ripe pod to eat, it was really nerve-wracking to have those heavy-looking petals hanging over one. Dragon-Flower had to tear down her walls and build a new stockade away from the plants. It was good she did, for as the plants aged, their support crystals grew weak; then one or more of the petals would break off under the extreme gravity; and would instantly reappear on the crust, its crushed mass sending out a shock of vibration that went rippling through the clan compound, making everyone nervous.

Broken-Petal knew a good thing when he saw it, and the most important trophy from the next hunt was not the torn-up carcass of a Swift, but many overripe pods, bursting with hard little seeds. Then his problems began, for the cheela in his clan were hunters.

Hunting was not hard work. It consisted of a leisurely stroll in the country with a bunch of friends, followed by a short period of exhilarating terror and a chance to demonstrate how brave and strong one was, climaxed by an orgy of eating and lovemaking that compensated for the long trek home carrying hunks of flesh.

Farming, however, even poke-and-cover farming, was hard work, especially in the tough crust of Egg, and there was no heroism or fun involved to make up for it. And worst of all, after all that hard work, it took many, many turns before there was any food to show for the effort. Broken-Petal had to tread on the edges of quite a few before he finally saw all the hard little seeds safely tucked into holes in the crust, unhappy at the loss of the sky.

Broken-Petal moved to the next row and the next, feeling proud. This had been their third crop of petal plants. The first crop had gone well, but there had not been enough plants for the whole clan, and they still had to forage to feed everyone. Broken-Petal had made sure that there were enough holes the next time, and his care was made easier by the cooperation of the digging crew, who now appreciated the long-term consequences of their labor.

As Broken-Petal moved between the rows, he saw a white patch in the crust. As he passed over that section of the crust, it seemed strangely hot. He moved back and forth, feeling the crust with his underside. He was bewildered. This had never happened before. As he went between the plants to check in the next row, the crust trembled underneath him. The automatic sonar sensors that he used to track his prey sprang into action and his bewilderment changed into shock. The source of the trembling was directly below him! He was scared.

"Is it a *dragon?*"

"No. No. There is no such thing as a dragon," he reassured himself. The old hunters used to tell tales of a tall, fire-shooting monster that came up out of the crust and stopped a cheela in his tracks by searing his outer edges with its violet-colored fire. The dragon would then fall on him from its tremendous height, smashing him like an egg sac and then absorbing him for dinner. No one had ever seen a dragon, but the large, very strong crystal bones that were found scattered in profusion over and underneath the crust certainly gave a taint of credibility to the tales, for no one knew where the dragon crystals came from.

Broken-Petal moved away from the area as the crust got hotter and hotter and the trembling from underneath continued. He was halfway back to the clan stockades when some of his rear eyes saw a spurt of bluish-white gas shoot from a crack in the crust, searing a petal of the plant overhead.

A group from the stockades met him as he approached. "It feels like a crustquake," one said, "but it keeps on repeating in the same place."

"It is not far," said Many-Pods, one of the clan's best trackers.

"You are right, Many-Pods," Broken-Petal said. "Whatever it is, it is right in the middle of our field."

The clan flowed carefully to the edge of the field and took

turns looking down the affected row as the hot smoke and gas continued to pour from the crack. More plants were burned now.

Broken-Petal had been thinking, and when the clan had finished looking and formed to the east and west of him, he knew what he had to do.

"The smoke and hot gas are going to kill our plants," he said. "Pretty-Egg, get back to the stockades and get everyone here fast. Even the littlest hatchling can carry a few pods. The rest of you, start picking as fast as you can. Start by going as near the smoke as your treads can take, then pick everything off those plants. Even the unripe pods will taste good after the ripe ones are gone." Broken-Petal led the way down the row as his instructions radiated away through the crust.

"Just when things were getting better," he thought. "The gods shall tread the edges of the proud," the old storytellers had always said. Well, he had let himself get complacent, and the Old Ones were right.

He moved as close as he dared to the vent. The smoke was reaching high up into the atmosphere now. The heat radiating down on his dark red topside from the billowing bluish-white column was uncomfortable. Although the crust was hot, he could still get to within three plants of the vent. He paused for a moment, formed three manipulators, and started picking pods, ripping most of them away from the flesh of the plant, although some of them were near-ripe and came away easily. He stored the pods in a carrying pouch he formed in the upper part of his body. He moved back and forth, picking pods as he went, approaching the crevasse at a distance that was mediated by the desire for food overcoming the unwillingness of his tread to move to hotter crust.

The first section of plants nearest the crevasse went quickly. Broken-Petal organized things so that the pods were dropped by the pickers at the edge of the planting, to be taken back to the stockade by the younger ones and stored away by the Old Ones. Although they moved as fast as they could, they lost many pods from the plants that were too close to the crevasse. The tedious work continued, with the laborers constantly harassed by shocks and crust dust falling on their topsides.

Soon, all were back from the field, their eating pouches sucking quietly on pods as they rested at the outskirts of the clan compound. Some of their eyes scanned the small, blue-hot hill that now grew in the middle of the devastated petal plant field, while other eyes followed the pillar of smoke that went far up into the sky until it seemed to touch the stars. The smoke went from an intensely glaring blue-white column at the base, to deep, deep red clouds far up in the cool black sky, the bottoms of the billowing red clouds tinged with a yellow glow from the crust below.

The times grew difficult. The food they had harvested lasted a long time, but the diet of immature pods was a great deal less tasty and nourishing than the steady turn after turn of feasting that they had enjoyed after they had learned about farming.

Broken-Petal tried to salvage things. There were no overripe seed pods from the recent crop, so he sent out a team to forage in the far regions for more, while he had the rest gouge holes in the crust away from the towering column of smoke. After much labor, the holes were ready, but the hunting party returned empty-handed.

Broken-Petal knew better than to berate them. In times like these, a successful hunting party had its pick of love partners, while these would only have each other for many, many turns.

"What was the problem?" he asked.

See-High spoke for them. "We saw many hunting parties that were doing what we were doing, out gathering every pod and hunting every animal they could find, even the almost worthless Tiny Shell."

He went on. "We went as far as we could before our own food ran out. It was the same everywhere. Everyone was so busy hunting that there was no fighting. We thought about attacking one of the other groups, but it was obvious from their thinness that they were carrying very little in their pouches in the way of catch, and were as bad off as we were. We even attempted to talk with some of them using long-talk. Although they don't speak just the way we do, it was obvious from what we could make out that all the clans are afraid of the tower of smoke and the constant trembling of the crust."

Flow-Hunter, the clan's bravest hunter, who had been allowed to change her egg-name after her third kill of a Flow Slow, interrupted with a laugh. "Some of them think that the tower of smoke is from the fire of a dragon, and the trembling is the dragon moving over the crust to get them! All of them are talking about leaving, saying the place has become taboo."

Then Broken-Petal had a flash of inspiration born out of the natural instincts that had made him Leader of the Clan. "If every clan is out hunting and stripping the crust bare of food," he said, "we will go where they don't go."

He spoke to the hunting party. "Go eat and load up with food. With the next turn you are going out hunting again, only this time you are to go southward—in the hard direction."

There was a shuffle of discontent from the group. They had been expecting to be sent out again in an attempt to redeem themselves, but to be sent in one of the hard directions sounded like punishment. No one ever went in the hard direction unless he had to—not even the powerful Flow Slow. See-High started to object, but Broken-Petal tapped him to silence with a sharp ripple from his tread. His tread started again, softer this time, and the encouraging words rippled through the crust to vibrate against the treads of the hunting party.

"I'm not angry with you, and I know that to travel in the hard direction means that you will move so slowly that you will still be within sight after three turns," he said. "Think—every clan we know is east or west of us, and we all go back and forth over the same territory, stripping it bare. If you go in the hard direction far enough, you may find land where there are fewer clans and more food. Now, eat and go!"

Long before the turn was complete, the hunting party was ready to leave. Broken-Petal gave them last instructions. "Go neither east nor west until you can see mature petal plants; then you can go off to examine them to see if there are any seed pods. If not—continue south until you do. But don't go beyond your food supplies. I want you back." His tread rippled with wry humor. "After all, there are two directions that are hard going, and if you don't find anything in one direction, you could always try the other one."

With a rumble of bitter humor, the hunting party pushed off toward the south. After a half a turn, they were out of reach of short-talk, but still were visible as figures halfway to the horizon. After three turns they disappeared over the horizon and the rest turned to their chores—and waiting.

See-High pushed slowly into the springy air. The most difficult part about traveling in the hard direction was that his body kept trying to slip to one side or the other. If he didn't hurry, but kept sliding a thin edge into the hard direction, then expanding it to make a crack that he could flow into, the going was steady. It was like going into a wind, but different. The wind kept pushing on him even when he was still, but the only force he felt from moving in the hard direction was the force he himself made when he attempted to move in that direction. If he stood still, for a while he could still feel the pressure, but then it slowly penetrated his body until he finally felt nothing—until he tried to move again.

See-High looked around and saw the rest of the party slowly struggling their way along. Ahead of him was Flow-Hunter, one of his favorite fun partners. Although he was leader of the hunting party and shouldn't be doing such things while they were on a hunt, the slow grind of pushing into the slippery air had made him bored. He pushed even harder and in a little while was right behind Flow-Hunter. He tickled her trailing edge. "What are you planning at break period?" he whispered, the electronic waves of his whisper tingling her multihued skin.

"Stop that!" Flow-Hunter protested. "It is hard enough pushing through this slippery stuff without being tickled from behind. Get back or I won't be doing anything with you for many turns, much less during break period."

See-High persisted. He flowed forward, both above and below the trailing edge of Flow-Hunter, giving her friendly squeezes as she tried to ripple him off. She pushed forward harder to get away from him. Although normally she could out-distance him, See-High found that he kept right up to Flow-Hunter with almost no effort. Suddenly he stopped playing around and tapped her to a stop. "I had no trouble at all keeping up with you," he said in amazement. "There you were, pushing away in the hard direction and I felt as if I were going east or west! Why?"

After a little bit of experimentation (and many giggles and slaps) they found that, once a gap was opened by a pathbreaker, the gap would remain open as long as she kept moving. Then if someone else stayed right on her trailing edge, very little extra effort was needed for him to move forward. As See-High had found, it was like moving in the easy direction (except for the pathbreaker, of course).

Before long, the hunting party was rearranged in a line. The head of the line worked at top effort as long as possible, then dropped to the side to let a fresh pathbreaker move ahead, while the tired one dropped into the end of the line and strolled along, cuddled up to the friendly trailing edge of someone of the opposite sex. The hunting party pushed forward at rapidly increased speed, with no breaks needed except when the two mismatched males got tired of being in on only half the fun and insisted upon being between two females.

They soon reached lands where there were fewer and fewer hunting parties and, after many turns, came to a region where mature petal plants could be found with pods still on them. It was not long before they had not only plenty of ripe pods for food, but also more than enough seed pods, bursting with little hard seeds. They stuffed pods and seeds into carrying pouches until the pouch orifices in their skins bulged out painfully.

The way back was rougher, for their bulky thickness caused by the load of pods and seeds made it necessary to open a wider gap in the hard direction before they could move through it. Their thickness also made them obvious targets for attack. Their new technique for moving in the hard direction saved them from being overcome by a large war party from a neighboring clan, but it cost them See-High, who was at the end of the column when the war party rushed at them from ambush out of the east as they went by. They were going to turn and attack, but See-High ordered them to continue while he kept the attackers at bay long enough for them to escape.

Broken-Petal eventually saw a thicker but shorter column of hunters show up over the horizon. At first he was bewildered by the shape and speed of the moving cluster of cheela. From a distance, they looked like a strange new type of Flow Slow, except that a Flow Slow was too lazy to move in the hard direction. He started to call an alarm, but it soon was obvious that that unusual motion of the head of the monster was the peculiar heave of Flow-Hunter as she pushed her way along.

Soon the whole clan gathered at the edge of the settlement and watched as the happy, giggling hunting party returned and dumped their booty. The seeds were distributed and quickly planted in the waiting holes by a large crew, all munching on ripe pods.

Flow-Hunter spent the next turn giving a detailed account of the trip to Broken-Petal. The report of the loss of See-High caused a moment of sadness in them both, but they turned their minds back to the present and continued on.

The nearby volcano dominated their lives. Fortunately it became dormant for a while, with just a thin wisp of yellow-white smoke spiraling up into the air, but the rumbling in the crust grew worse every turn. The crop grew well, but when the volcano became more active again, Broken-Petal decided that they had better move further away. The crop was harvested and the clan took the food and their few belongings, especially the precious broken shards of ultra-hard dragon crystal, and moved off toward the south.

There were many in the clan, and they were not in a hurry, so a modification of the hunting party pathbreaker technique was used. The stronger young ones formed a broad front and pushed ahead in the hard direction. They kept up a steady pace and the rest of the clan, packed close together, followed along behind.

TIME: 14:44:14 GMT SUNDAY 22 MAY 2050

The interstellar ark, St. George, settled into its orbit around the spinning neutron star at a radius of 100,000 kilometers and with a period of thirteen minutes. The science crew began their scientific surveys. Although they would get much better data when they could go down in Dragon Slayer to look at the neutron star from only 400 kilometers away, they still could do a preliminary survey with the long-range telescopes.

Jean Kelly Thomas was belted into the seat in front of the imaging science console on St. George. The belt was adjusted to accommodate the fact that she was sitting on her crossed legs. With her cap of short red hair and her upturned nose, she looked like a pixie seated on a toadstool (with seat belt). Her bright blue eyes flicked over the features of the latest scan of the hydrogen-alpha ultraviolet imager. The computer had noticed something unusual in the last scan and had alerted her.

A blinking square drew her attention to a small oval bull's-eye pattern that had appeared on the image of the star. In the upper corner of the screen, the computer had printed:

LYMAN-ALPHA SCAN TAKEN 14:44:05 22 MAY 2050
NEW FEATURE AT 54 W LONG, 31 N LAT

Jean leaned forward. "Identification?" The image remained, but the words were replaced with:

TENTATIVE IDENTIFICATION—ACTIVE VOLCANO.
CENTER TEMPERATURE 15,000 DEGREES.

Jean spoke again, "Switch Lyman-alpha scanner to high resolution scan of target region!"

She watched as the image was replaced on the screen with a close-up of the volcano. The image blinked five times a second as the imager took a scan at each rotation of the star. As she watched, she could see a flare-up in the central region, followed by a streak of brightness that flowed away from the center, the lava flow getting dimmer and dimmer as it moved.

A detailed history of the birth and death of a volcano was certainly worth keeping a careful watch on. Perhaps if they were lucky, the amount of matter that built up in the shield would become so great that it would initiate a starquake during their visit. That should set the whole star to vibrating and they might be able to determine the internal resonant modes of the star and get a better computer model for the thickness and density of the inner layers. The new volcano was certainly a high priority item, but it would have to take its turn. She couldn't tie up the scanner to take pictures of only one thing.

She leaned forward again and spoke, "Assign Priority One to this target!

"Inform if any major change or if activity stops!"

She leaned back and pushed the print button.

"A volcano," she thought. "Pierre will surely be interested in this one. He wants to study the internal dynamics of this star, and now he has some insides to look at. However, the hot gas and dust that monster is emitting are sure going to complicate my atmospheric studies."

TIME: 14:44:15 GMT SUNDAY 22 MAY 2050

The clan moved very slowly southward. Travel in the hard direction against the magnetic field lines was not easy, even for the young hunters, and was still more difficult for the old and the hatchlings, although they were flowing into the gaps created by the moving van of pathbreakers. The hardest thing for them all to learn was to keep close together and keep moving. If a gap developed or if anyone paused for a moment, the east-west magnetic field lines would reassert their position, pinning their bodies on the lines like beads on a wire. Unless they had the strength to begin moving south again, their only choice was to move east or west and join the tail of a portion of the group that was still moving.

The clan got better at it, and by trial and error soon developed a flying-wedge technique, with one strong hunter out front taking the full brunt of the fields, and the rest of the stronger ones in a chevron behind, opening up the gap that was created. The other adults soon learned to form secondary chevrons behind, with the hatchlings and Old Ones in between. Then if a gap developed, it was soon closed by the adults in the following chevron, and the trailing edge of the moving clan now no longer looked like a wounded Flow Slow leaving a trail of vital fluid behind.

They had progressed a good distance when Broken-Petal called a halt. He knew that they were probably still on some clan's territory, but he decided that, because so few hunting parties were on the horizon, they were probably in a region between two other clans. Normally, this would have been a poor place to stop; if they had had to depend on foraging to the east and west, there would have been less and less food to find the further away the hunters went. But with the ripe seeds and the knowledge of how to take the sky away from them to make them grow, the clan could stay in one place, always at full strength with all of its warriors home tending the growing plants, and going out only for game to vary their diet and to show off their prowess.

The clan settled in with relief, and a crew was sent off to a nearby cliff to get building stones for the stockades, pod bins, and the all important egg pens.

As Speckled-Egg approached the cliff with the quarry crew, the youngster grew frightened. Never before had he been so close to anything so tall. It seemed that it was going to fall directly down on him, but he certainly was not going to let his fright show on his first time with a hunting party.

"It sure is tall," he remarked calmly.

"Sure is," said Flow-Hunter. Her tread rumbled teasingly. "Looks as if it is going to fall right on top of you, doesn't it?"

"Yes, but it has not fallen before, so I guess it won't now," Speckled-Egg said confidently.

"But it will when we get through with it," said Flow-Hunter. Then turning serious she said, "Which end looks closer?"

The top of the cliff sloped downward toward the east. The party took off in that direction, carrying their broken shards of dragon crystal and one unbroken, round-tipped whole dragon crystal that they had found when digging holes for the seeds. They soon came to the end of the vertical fault plane and began the long, slow, arduous climb up the slope.

"It's like traveling in the hard direction, but worse," complained Speckled-Egg. "When you stop moving in the hard direction, you can rest. But when you are climbing up, you might as well not stop to rest. When you do, you still have to hold on to keep from flowing back down."

Flow-Hunter showed him her trick of waiting until she came across a small stone before stopping to rest, and then stretching her body out upwards from the stone. With the stone preventing her from flowing downward, and the hard directions holding her in from the side, she could almost relax and enjoy her food-pod in comfort. It was a tricky technique, and Speckled-Egg found his edges flowing around the stone more than once, but soon he was as accomplished a climber as any of them.

Although they had gone east for only one turn before reaching the end of the fault, it took them many turns and much food to struggle up the sloping hill in the intense gravity and make it back to the top of the cliff. Flow-Hunter formed a strong crystallium core in one of her eye-stubs, held the eye up as high as she could, then moved slowly toward the edge.

"I can see the clan camp off in the distance. This is the right place," she said. She stood still and looked for a long time.

"What is the matter?" asked Speckled-Egg.

"Just looking," she said. "Everything looks very funny when you can look down on it. Come and see."

The last thing Speckled-Egg wanted to do was go near the edge, but he did, one of his eyes held high in imitation of Flow-Hunter. Together they moved forward until they could see the members of the hunting party they had left at the bottom of the cliff.

"They are so big around!" exclaimed Speckled-Egg, "and so funny looking. You can see all the lumps on their topsides."

"You would look just as big and lumpy yourself if you could see yourself from the top instead of only from the side," said Flow-Hunter. "You are right about the lumps though; they are funny looking. I bet that big reddish yellow lump in the middle of Double-Seed is an egg that is about ready to be dropped."

She pushed her way back from the edge. "Come on, we have a lot of hard work to do."

The climbers started to work. The first thing they did was to push the large, whole dragon crystal to the edge and let it fall off. The nearly unbreakable, super-hard crystal became invisible and reappeared at the bottom, splintered into a dozen sharp shards. The waiting group at the bottom rode out the shock and then moved quickly forward to retrieve the now valuable hunting knives and digging tools.

When the dragon crystal shards had been removed, the climbers at the top moved forward to the edge and used their digging tools to gouge a long line in the top of the cliff. The gouge line was back from the edge a distance equal to the height of the stones that they could easily carry. They spread apart the fibers in the crust until there was a long, deep crack, held in place by the connections at either end of the long strip. They then went to the west end of the strip, where the nap of the crust would give them a better grip, and formed a chain with their bodies. Flow-Hunter stretched out as far as she could with the sharpest crystal shard held in front of her in a long manipulator. She concentrated for a moment and soon several short manipulators were arrayed at her back edge. Speckled-Egg and Dusty-Crust flowed above and below her and also formed manipulators to grasp hers. The rest grasped them and spread themselves out as flat as possible to form an anchor.

"Everyone ready?" asked Flow-Hunter. She then started sawing away at the end of the slit, only this time cutting across the fibers in the crust. It was slow hard work, for the fibers were the source of the real strength of the crustal material. They switched places; to Speckled-Egg's horror, it was his turn to be sawing away when the weight of the long section of crust overcame the strength of the remaining fibers and the face of the cliff came away in a long curling rip that extended the slit in the top surface down to the base.

The top surface of the cliff, relieved of some of its stress, rebounded with a shock wave. For the first (and he hoped only) time in his life, Speckled-Egg's tread was not solidly in contact with the crust. He had no time to be afraid before the crust came up to meet him with a bruising smash. They all lay quietly for a moment and then pounded each other with triumph as they backed away from the crumbling edge.

They hurried back down the way they had come, pausing only now and then for a little food. They all felt like having a little fun, too, but that had to wait (except for friendly pats and treadings) until they got to the end of the cliff, where the crust was flat. By the time they had returned to the bottom of the cliff with the jumble of stones at its base, Speckled-Egg was a full-fledged hunter, having not only been a hero by being at the point when the danger was greatest, but having been given a hero's reward and his initiation into manhood by Flow-Hunter herself.

Having felt the successful conclusion of the quarrying expedition come rumbling in through the crust, Broken-Petal had sent out an additional work crew to help drag the stones back to camp. Soon the place began to look like home again. A pod bin was the first task, so that everyone could drop his load of pods without having to worry that the constant winds would roll them away. The Old Ones were most grateful for the pod bin, for they had been tied down holding onto most of the food store while the younger ones had been working. Now they could move around and get to the more important (and pleasurable) task of turning eggs and raising hatchlings.

Next came the egg-pen, and again another great load was taken off the clan as all the females could drop the eggs they had been hauling around since they had left the old home and started on their exodus.

For many, many turns the clan grew and prospered in their new home.

TIME: 15:48:10 GMT SUNDAY 22 MAY 2050

Pierre Carnot Niven, his long, straight hair in a halo about his head, worked away at the console keyboard, overlaying one multicolored computer display on another. His soft brown eyes peered at a complicated pattern of lava flows that would have hopelessly confused anyone but him. Pierre set the computer to calculating the load on the crust from the new lava flows. It was a complicated problem; while the computer was working, he floated out from in front of his console and went over to see what Jean was doing.

Jean was checking the plots showing the drift of the smoke from the volcano through the atmosphere, and correlating it with the magnetic field measurements and the Coriolis forces caused by the high spin speed of the rotating star. She was developing a computer model for the magnetic field structure so she could produce a detailed theory for the iron-vapor atmosphere and how it interacted with the conflicting forces of gravity, magnetism, and spin of the star.

Pierre floated nearer and watched over Jean's shoulder as she had the computer rotate the image of the star slowly on the screen. The hot smoke patterns were in white, the magnetic field lines in blue, and the Coriolis and gravity forces in green.

"It looks like the weather patterns on the Earth," Pierre commented, his fingertips resting on her shoulder to help him keep station.

"Yes," Jean said. "The smoke travels mostly east-west from the volcano because it is easier for it to travel along the magnetic field lines than across them. But when the smoke reaches the magnetic poles, the easy direction is into the ground, so the smoke piles up into a big crescent with the volcano in the middle. There is some leakage at the poles though."

"Why is the leakage staying in a belt north of the equator?" asked Pierre. "I can understand that the smoke leakage from the east pole would stay in the north spin hemisphere since it is above the spin equator, but why doesn't the smoke leaking from the west pole contaminate the atmosphere in the southern hemisphere?"

Jean spoke toward the console, "West pole view!"

They watched as the image rotated to the view over the west pole and stopped. Jean pointed to the screen. "It happens that one of the stronger sub-poles of the chaotic west polar region happens to lie along the same magnetic longitude as the volcano, and it also happens to be above the spin equator. That sub-pole has blocked off that longitude, keeping all the smoke trapped in the northern hemisphere. The leakage from the west pole, combined with the leakage from the east pole, forms the intense smoke belt just north of the spin equator."

TIME: 16:45:24 GMT SUNDAY 22 MAY 2050

Smoky-Sky looked up and worried. The sky was now nearly always full of smoke. When it was time to name him shortly after he had left the egg, the Old Ones in charge of the hatching pens had thought a smoky sky so unusual that they had given him that name. Now—many, many turns later—here he was, Leader of the Clan, and haunted by his own name.

The crops from the petal plants had been getting worse and worse. The nearly constant cloud cover overhead seemed to suffocate the plants. It was time to move. But could they go far enough to escape the ever-present smoke?

"I had better move slowly," Smoky-Sky said to himself. "No use running from a Flow Slow right into the maw of a Swift."

He moved to the clear place between the stockades and the field of plants and t'trumed a call for the clan to gather. Soon all but the guards and the hatchlings were arranged in arcs to the east and west of him.

Smoky-Sky spoke. "The times are not good. We will have to move where the sky is not so smoky and the petal plants can grow. It will be a long journey, so we must have much food to carry. Blue-Flow, you are to take a hunting party and look for a better place for us. I think it will be far from here, so take as many pods as you can carry, for you will not be back for many turns. Remember the words of our ancient Aged Ones—'Go in a direction others do not go.'"

Blue-Flow moved off to one side, followed by a crowd of younger warriors eager for adventure. He picked a small group and led them off to the pod bin to load up on food. Smoky-Sky watched, musing, "He will be a good leader. He has picked the ones with stamina, even if they are not the best hunters. More importantly, since it will be a long journey, he has an equal number of both sexes."

Smoky-Sky turned to the crowd and said, "I don't know how many turns it will be before the hunting party comes back, but when they do, I want the pod bin filled to the walls. The petal plants are not growing many pods, so we will just have to plant more of them." Amid a shuffle of groans, Smoky-Sky pushed his way to the tool bin, picked up a sharp shard of dragon crystal, and set off to the field to start poking holes in the hard crust, knowing that the best way to get people working on a long hard task was for the leader to start in first.

Blue-Flow looked over his group. They were all well bulked out with pods tucked away in their storage pouches. "Let's go," he said, and started to push his way southward in the hard direction, the others snuggled up to him in single file. After a turn of hard travel, they finally passed over the horizon and were on their own.

For many, many turns the hunting party moved along, the sky overhead still smoky. Finally, Shaking-Crust remarked during a pod break, "I think that the smoke is even worse here than back at home."

They could not all agree then, but after a few more turns of travel it was very obvious to all of them that conditions were worse here. The smoke filled the sky, and the crust was covered with sickly red-yellow ash that chilled their treads as they flowed over it. There was some talk of going back, but Blue-Flow would have none of that. This was his first trial as a leader of a hunting party and he would not come back with pods still pouched in his body.

Blue-Flow drove them on, always moving in the hard direction. The difficult grind of pushing ahead, with the poor grip that the ashes gave to their treads, took all the fun out of the expedition. But something else was happening that added to their discomfort—they were becoming lost!

It was not for many turns that one of them mentioned what

they had all been feeling. "This land bothers me," said Final-Pod. "I feel that I am lost all the time. Yet I know right where I am. I can see the cliff over there that we passed a few turns ago, so logically I know that I could make my way right back to the clan with no problem, just by going in the hard direction in the opposite way we have been going—but I still feel lost."

They all agreed. Logically they knew they were not lost—but they definitely felt as if they were.

"Let us move on," Blue-Flow said, pushing off again. But the further they went, the worse they felt and the darker the sky became. Then the pods began to run low.

At the next break Shaking-Crust spoke up for all of them, "I think we should turn back, Blue-Flow. The land and the sky just get worse and worse the further we go. Perhaps the instructions of the ancient Aged Ones are no longer correct."

Blue-Flow countered, "If we tell the clan to go back in the direction that we came from, they will just get closer to the volcano. If we have them go east or west, we know they will run into the other clans that are fleeing the volcano. If they stay where they are, the smoke will kill the petal plants and we will all starve. Our only hope is in this direction. We must keep going as long as we can."

Shaking-Crust said, "You may go on if you like. I'm going back."

Blue-Flow had been expecting something like this for a long time and was ready for it, but he had never expected rebellion from his favorite playmate. Without warning, he was on top of her, drubbing her brain-knot soundly with his tread and knocking her out before she had a chance to move. Still on top of the unconscious body, he whispered, "Does anyone else want to challenge me?"

No one moved as he flowed off Shaking-Crust, who was starting to recover from her sonically induced shock. As her senses cleared, she heard Blue-Flow talking.

"I don't think you realize how serious things are. The volcano is poisoning all the Crust that it can reach. The only hope for the clan is for us to find a place where we can survive. If we do not, the clan will die, the hatchlings first." This last was a telling blow. For although the cheela were not attached to a specific hatchling, and no female could even remember which egg she had put into the hatchery unless it had some distinctive marking, they were all very attached to the little hatchlings, who lived a spoiled life until they were old enough to go to work. The thought of hatchlings dying was enough to eliminate any thought of quitting.

Many turns later Blue-Flow was really worried. They were way past their food supply limit. It would be a weak and thin party of cheela that came back to the clan—if they made it back. The feeling of being lost had become worse. At the next break he was almost ready to quit. But first he decided to have a better look ahead. He took the longest dragon crystal spear that they had and poked its sharp end down into the crust. It stood far up into the sky, many times higher than he could ever lift an eye on one of his own flimsy eye-stubs. When the others saw what he was doing, they gathered in a circle around him and applied pressure on his edges. He formed a thick pseudopod with one of his eye-stubs at the end and flowed it up along the shaft of the dragon crystal spear until his eye was perched on top of the spear. The sky looked smoky right to the horizon . . .

"I see a star!" he shouted, and his pseudopod flowed back down so quickly that they were all rippled by the energy regained from its fall. "The sky is still smoky, but it must be thinner because I can see a star through it. The star was right on the horizon."

Shaking-Crust insisted on seeing it, too; after much effort, she soon had one eye perched on top of the spear. The star was almost exactly in the hard direction, and right on the horizon. Shaking-Crust was almost positive that it was brighter than any star she had ever seen, but without any other stars visible to compare it with, she was not sure.

Great-Crack and some of the others wanted a look too, but Blue-Flow stopped the sight-seeing. "It takes as much energy to put an eye on top of the spear as it does to travel a few turns where we can all see it from eye level. Let's get moving!"

With something to aim for, spirit returned to the column; for the first time in many turns, they made good time over the ashen land. Soon the star appeared above the horizon, and as it did, the feeling of being lost began to decrease. By silent agreement, the rest breaks were short and they pushed on.

Soon Blue-Flow noticed that there were short breaks in the intense cover of smoke. After a few more turns of travel, the ashes on the crust stopped being a hindrance to travel. Soon other stars were visible, strange ones that they had never seen before. But the strangest one of all was the intensely bright reddish yellow one that hung motionless in the southern sky from turn to turn, while all the others whirled about it like a cloud of minor deities paying homage to a god.

It was an awe-inspiring experience for them all as they moved forward out of the smoky hell in back of them into a new land, free from smoke and ash, and with untouched petal plants growing in delicious profusion all about them. There were plenty of game signs, and soon they were all enjoying the meat of a Slink, interspersed with delicious, perfectly ripe pods.

"There are plenty of game signs, but no sign of a single other cheela," said Shaking-Crust. "The game was not particularly afraid of us. It is as if they had never been hunted before."

"This place sounds like an Old One's stories of heaven," Great-Crack said.

"I guess we should call it Heaven," Blue-Flow agreed. "Bright's Heaven. For Bright, the God Star, rules over it all, and its bright glare keeps the smoke from coming over the horizon. Let us load up with food and head back over the 'lost' region to tell the clan the good news. We have been gone so long, they probably think we are dead."

TIME: 16:45:34 GMT SUNDAY 22 MAY 2050

Pierre turned from the display on his console and called over to Jean, who was operating the Lyman-alpha telescope at another console. "I was trying to think if the weather would be any different on Earth if the magnetic field of the Earth were east-west instead of nearly north-south."

"No," Jean said. "The Earth's magnetic field is too weak to affect the atmosphere on Earth as it does here."

Pierre laughed, and Jean looked at him quizzically. "I just realized that the only real effect of an east-west magnetic field on Earth would be on homing pigeons. Homing pigeons use a combination of the Earth's north-south magnetic field and the east-west Coriolis spin forces for homing. They would feel completely lost if the magnetic field lines and the Coriolis force lines were in the same direction—as they are along the spin equator here. That would be even worse than the fact that the directional sense of a homing pigeon gets turned around when the pigeon is released in the southern hemisphere after being trained in the northern hemisphere."

Pierre turned back and spoke at the console:

"Store that sequence!

"Continue monitoring volcanic lava flow pattern on Priority Two basis!"

He turned to Jean. "Well, the main console is all yours. I'm going to get some food, write a little, then head for bed. See you next shift."

Jean pulled herself into the main console seat, quickly checked all the settings, and carefully buckled herself in. "What are you writing now?"

Pierre stopped himself at the hole in the deck and replied, "It's a physics text for the ten-to-fourteen age bracket. According to the communication flashes from the publisher, I made such a hit writing scan-books about science and space for the eight-to-twelve age group on the way out to Dragon's Egg that I actually have fan clubs. Do you realize that when I get back from this trip two years from now I am going to be getting more in royalties from children's books than I will in salary for being a space scientist?"

"Well, none of us are jealous—much!" Jean said. "We all realize that every kid you make enthusiastic about space science is going to be a voting taxpayer after we return, and we should come back to Dragon's Egg with a follow-up expedition before it leaves the Solar System."

"I'm sure the World Space Administration agrees with you. They even gave my publisher a special rate on the cost of transmitting my manuscripts back." He turned and pushed himself down the passageway.

TIME: 16:45:35 GMT SUNDAY 22 MAY 2050

Great-Crack was a pack rat. Although one of the better hunters in the clan, with two Flow Slow kills to her credit, she was the constant butt of jokes from her hunting mates because of her habit of picking up and carrying anything she found that looked interesting—and because of her highly developed sense of curiosity, practically everything looked interesting to her.

When it came time for the hunting party to load up with ripe pods for the long journey back to the clan, Great-Crack had to unpouch her trinkets so she could load up her pouches with pods. She went over to a shallow depression in the crust; amid ribald calls of "What are you doing? Laying three eggs at once?", followed by "No, just one, but it's the size of a Flow Slow!", she dumped her precious pile of odds and ends, with the heavier ones around the pile in a low wall that she hoped would protect them from the constant winds. With luck, she would be able to pick them up again when they returned with the clan.

With her bulk reduced to fighting trim, Great-Crack flowed off the pile. Paying no attention to the jokes, she went off with the others as they moved through the petal plants, carefully picking off the best of the pods and storing them inside their body pouches until the whole hunting party was loaded to capacity.

"Are you sure that bulk is all pods, Great-Crack?" chided Shaking-Crust. "You didn't go back for a few trinkets, did you?"

Great-Crack was in the midst of rippling out a vicious whisper about being a better fighter when loaded with pods than Shaking-Crust was in fighting trim, and would she like to have her prove it . . . when Blue-Flow interrupted with a loud t'trum on the crust.

"You two stop that!" he said. Then his eyes looked around to all of them and he called, "It's time to go back!" Blue-Flow pushed his bulk in the hard direction, while the rest of them rapidly formed a single file and pushed off behind him.

Suddenly Blue-Flow stopped. "Wait!" he said in amazement. "We're going in the wrong direction!"

They all looked up from their crouched, streamlined positions in back of him and looked ahead. There was the benevolent beam of Bright, directly ahead. They stopped, confused. They had come into Bright's Heaven far enough that they had stopped having the lost feeling that they had experienced earlier under the smoke. Being good hunters, they knew instinctively where they were and in which direction to go. But their instincts were leading them directly toward Bright, while they knew from logic that the way back to the clan was in the opposite direction.

"I guess we will have to forget our where-sense when it comes to traveling in this land," Blue-Flow said. He flowed to the back of the column and pushed off again, this time directly away from Bright.

The group soon reached the edge of Bright's Heaven. They all cast longing looks behind with a few of their eyes as Bright dipped below the horizon and their sense of being lost returned. Blue-Flow kept the break periods short since they were all in good shape and well fed, and they made it quickly back across the "feeling lost" territory with its intense smoky sky flowing to the west.

Their sense of direction slowly returned, and Blue-Flow felt much better now that his instincts finally agreed with his logic. They were following their previous track very closely, and Blue-Flow was disturbed that he could read their spoor. They must have been extremely discouraged to have been so careless. Well —they were on their way back now, and that spoor of many turns ago would just lead any trackers astray if they kept their present track clean. When it came his turn at the rear of the column, he looked back and was pleased with the fact, that except for a quickly fading whitish track from the heat of their bodies warming the crust, he could see almost no evidence of their passage.

At the next break, most of them had another pod to eat. As was her usual custom, Great-Crack kept all the seeds from the pod in case the clan needed more. Blue-Flow noticed that she had only added a pod skin to the burial pit and came over to talk to her.

"You are a good hunter and a hard fighter, Great-Crack, so I have never complained about your bulk. But we are now on a very serious mission and everything that slows us down hurts the chances for the survival of the whole clan. I want you to put all the seeds and anything else you have picked up into the burial pit and stop collecting things until we have the whole clan back to Bright's Heaven."

"But the seeds are valuable!" she protested.

"The clan will have no need for seeds to plant when they are on the move to Bright's Heaven, and there will be plenty of pods and seeds when we bring them there," he replied.

She could only agree with him, and he stood by watching, first with amusement, then with amazement, as a steady flow of seeds, pebbles, worthless dragon crystal shards, and Flow Slow nodes filled the burial pit. He did not know that Great-Crack held back something. In each one of the food pods from Bright's Heaven, the bottom seed in the clump had an unusual twelve-pointed cluster shape, instead of the normal oval shape. Great-Crack's curiosity had been aroused by the unusual shape and she had looked carefully at each pod she had opened. Every pod had a cluster-shaped seed, and she was especially careful to keep each one. She wanted to plant them to see if the petal plant that grew from them would be different in shape than the ones that grew from the oval seeds. When she dumped her store of treasures, she withheld the cluster seeds.

"They are so small, they won't slow me down," she said smugly to herself. "Besides he will never notice, now that I have an egg growing." Covering up the burial pit carefully to leave no trace of its presence, she returned to join the others.

After many, many turns the hunting party began to enter familiar territory. They took no breaks now, but pushed steadily onward. As they approached the home of the clan, they felt disturbing tremors under their treads. There were loud voices booming through the crust and much rapid movement of treads. Some of the voices were in a strange accent.

The clan was under attack! Blue-Flow moved ahead more rapidly. Thinning way down, he stopped just over the horizon from the camp. He quickly reinforced an eye-stub and raised one eye up to evaluate the situation.

A large war party from another clan was attacking the petal plant field. He could see movement between the rows as the war party drove the guards down the rows, so that others could strip the pods from the plants at the ends of the rows. There was another group that kept up feinting attacks on the pod bins and stockades on the other side of the camp, spreading the clan guard warriors thin. There seemed to be too few guards, and Blue-Flow could not see Smoky-Sky anywhere. There were no enemy warriors on their side of the field, so the plan of attack was obvious. Blue-Flow dropped his eye and whispered the situation to his group.

"The petal plant fields are under attack by a large war party that has control over the eastern half. We will go east from here, staying below the horizon, cross over in the hard direction until we are in back of them, then come down at them from the east and trap them in between." As he spoke, pods and digging tools dropped out of pouches into a disorganized pile on the crust. Rugged fighting manipulators sprang from their bodies and pulled sharp shards of dragon crystal from their weapons pouches. Although Great-Crack tried to hide them, Blue-Flow saw with disgust the small pile of funny pod seeds. He resolved to give her a drubbing once the battle was over.

With their killing spears of shattered dragon crystal at the ready, the hunting party moved east, going many times faster than their previous rate of movement in the hard direction. Once they had moved far enough east to be over the horizon in that direction, Blue-Flow led them across in the hard direction until they were in back of the attacking party.

Putting his warriors in a line, each with one or more sharp spikes sticking out from strong manipulators firmly imbedded in their thickened front ends, he whispered to them all. "They do not know we are attacking, so move as quietly as you can. If we can surprise them, we will catch them with their brain-knots in our direction."

They moved ahead smoothly, keeping a low profile as they came over the horizon. They flowed around a pile of pods that had been stacked for pickup.

Blue-Flow whispered, "We're in luck. The pickers have gone down to fight and push the guards further back."

They each chose a row and with their quarry busily engaged in a battle midway down the row, they were able to attack almost without warning.

It was hard to kill a cheela. If hit with something hard, the fluid body just retreated from the blow with the flexible skin absorbing the impact. If the something hard was very sharp, like the shattered end of a dragon crystal, it could poke a hole through the skin, and if that was big enough a hole, some of the glowing fluid inside would leak out before the automatic protection systems could close the wound. If an eye that was so rash as to be out on a stub could be caught, a sharp-edged shard might slice off the eye-stub with an accompanying shock of pain but only a partial loss of sight. After all, if one or two of the normal complement of twelve eyes were lost, the cheela could easily adjust the position of the remainder to have nearly complete vision.

The only really vulnerable part of a cheela was the brain-knot. It could be anywhere inside the skin, but it was a good bet that, if the cheela was fighting someone on one side, the brain-knot would be well over on the other side, far away from any sharp spears of dragon crystal. Blue-Flow was counting on this instinctive behavior as he rushed his enemy target from behind and flowed up onto her topside. He felt the telltale knot under his tread and shocked it into unconsciousness with a focused ripple from his underside, then neatly speared it three times as his momentum carried him up and over his now-dead foe.

"Blue-Flow!" shouted Weary-Tread, lowering the point of her spear. "Where did you come from?"

Blue-Flow surveyed the oozing hide of his old friend and replied, "We just got back and we have found a new home for the clan. But come, follow me, we have fighting to do."

Blue-Flow moved down the row of plants until he could see a sparring trio of warriors between the plants. Warm-Wind and Great-Crack had an enemy warrior between them. The warrior had parried Great-Crack's initial rush and was now fending them both off as he attempted to escape between the rows. In a rumble of despair he saw the long shard in Blue-Flow's grasp as Blue-Flow blocked the way, sending his spear directly into the center of the enemy.

"Another brain kill!" Blue-Flow gloated as the foe collapsed into a spreading disk that filled the space between the plants.

He quickly whispered to Great-Crack and Warm-Wind, pointing with a ripple of his eye-stubs, "You two go that way and we will go this way." Blue-Flow turned and, with Weary-Tread covering his trail, went down the row to find more of the foe.

With the return of the hunting party, the tide of battle turned, and soon the enemy war party had retreated, without their stolen pods, and with many of their number gone.

The clean-up work began. The stolen pods were stored in the pod bin along with the ripe pods that the hunting party had brought back with them. The many dead, among them Fuzzy-Crust and Star-Rise of the clan, were sliced open to let the fluid seep into the crust, and then the meat was dried and stored.

The news that the clan had for the hunting party was not good. They had been under almost constant attack by hungry war parties ever since the group had left. Smoky-Sky had died long ago in a battle to protect the fields and Weary-Tread was now Leader of the Clan. When Blue-Flow heard this news, he turned and looked at Weary-Tread, whose scarred hide was still oozing glowing, yellow-white fluid from some serious spear wounds.

"Now is the best time to do this," Blue-Flow thought. "The clan needs a strong Leader for the journey to Bright's Heaven." He turned, raised his spear and issued the formal challenge to Weary-Tread.

"Who is Leader of the Clan, Old One?"

There was a long pause as Weary-Tread evaluated her chances. She could still be a good Leader and did not want to be relegated to the status of an Old One, but never had she felt so like the dreary name she had been stuck with as a hatchling.

"You are, Blue-Flow," she replied, and winced as the ceremonial slash from Blue-Flow's spear added another small wound to her punctured hide.

Blue-Flow turned and said to them all, "I am Leader of the Clan. Does anyone challenge me?" There was no reply, and, with the formal ceremony over, his tone changed as he took command.

"I have good news. I have found a new land for us. A clean land with no smoke. A good land with no enemies, with much game and with many, many petal plants that have never been picked. It is a long distance away in the hard direction and the trail will be harsh and difficult. But we will go, for a new God Star and His Heaven—Bright's Heaven—waits for us!"

For the next few turns, Blue-Flow had everyone who was not out hunting meat busy in the fields picking the edible pods and storing them in the pod bin. He was outside the bin with Great-Crack, looking with satisfaction at the pods spilling out of the opening.

"It is enough," he said. "We will leave when the hunters return."

"But *is* it enough?" Great-Crack wondered. "We needed to eat many, many pods to get from Bright's Heaven back to the clan. There are many in the clan and they will travel much more slowly than a hunting party."

"There are many, many pods, Great-Crack. There must be

enough there to feed all the clan, for I have never seen so many pods before." Blue-Flow went off to greet a returning hunting party.

Great-Crack stared at the flowing pile of pods. "There are many pods," she thought. "But are there enough?"

She played internally with her pouch full of cluster-shaped seeds, which she had retrieved after the battle, and thought back over the many pods she herself had eaten while crossing the barren land between here and Bright's Heaven. Many pods would be needed, for she had taken the cluster-shaped seed from each one as she had eaten it, and there were many, many of those seeds in her storage pouch.

Then, in a flash of inspiration, one of the greatest mathematical minds ever hatched in the past or future history of the cheela made a great leap of abstract thought.

"I took one seed from every pod that I ate," Great-Crack said to herself. "So I have as many seeds as pods."

Her mind faltered for a moment. "But seeds are not pods!"

It recovered, "But there are as many seeds as there were pods, so the number is the same."

She laid the seeds out in a row that stretched all along the wall of the pod bin. There were many of them. She then took out pods and put one next to each seed until she had a row of pods.

"There," she said. "I will need that many pods to get to Bright's Heaven." She put the pods to one side in a pile. She took out more pods and laid them next to the seeds until she had another row of pods.

"Blue-Flow will need these pods to travel to Bright's Heaven," she said as she gathered the pods up again and put them in another pile.

Great-Crack soon had pile after pile of pods stacked inside and outside the pod bin as she set aside rations for each of the clan members. She was only halfway through the names of the clan members when she ran out of pods. There was not enough food!

Great-Crack hurried off and brought Blue-Flow back to the pod bin to explain what she had done. She got nowhere.

"Yes, I see the piles of pods, but how do you know that each person will need that many?

"Yes, I see that when you line up the pods next to the seeds that the line of pods is as long as the line of seeds, but what do seeds have to do with pods?

"Yes, I understand that you saved one seed from each pod as you ate it on the way back from Bright's Heaven, but what does that have to do with feeding the clan? You ate all those pods and there is nothing left but these deformed seeds.

"No, I don't understand what you mean when you say that the seeds tell you how many pods each one of us will need. Seeds are not pods."

Great-Crack tried in many ways to get Blue-Flow to make the jump in abstract thought that now came so naturally to her, but he could not do it. Finally, in frustration, he lost his temper and stamped, "There are plenty of pods. Look at them all. We will go now, for Bright's Heaven is waiting."

Great-Crack flowed to block his way. "We cannot go!" she said. "We will starve before we get there! The seeds tell the truth!"

"Seeds are not pods," he retorted, "and I have been meaning to tromp you for keeping those seeds after I told you to leave them on the trail."

Her reply brought him up short. "Who is Leader of the Clan, Old One?"

She moved toward him while he backed out of the pod bin. "No use endangering the pods," he thought. "We are both in good shape and this is going to be a long fight. I wonder why she is challenging me now?"

The clan gathered around them as they moved together into a clear place between the stockades. Blue-Flow watched with a combination of fear and amusement as his opponent emptied her pouches of tools and trinkets, formed a dueling manipulator, and raised her spear.

"Blue-Flow is in good shape," Great-Crack thought as she made a neat pile of her precious "unusual things." "I will need every advantage I can get to beat him. However, he must not be allowed to win—for he will lead the clan into sure starvation!"

She finally turned, raised her spear and repeated her challenge, "Who is Leader of the Clan, Old One?" She paused—then punctuated the challenge by ejecting her half-formed egg-sac from the protection of her body onto the crust between them. The clan looked in shock at the precious, tiny eggling wriggling out the last of its life among the glowing remains of its ruptured egg-sac.

Blue-Flow alternated his horrified eyes between the cooling eggling and the stern visage of Great-Crack. "She is really determined to win. Could it be that she is right, and there are not enough pods?" He shifted his spear. "No matter—things have gone too far to stop now."

Blue-Flow returned the formal reply, "I am—Hatchling!" He lunged at her.

It was not a pretty fight. Both were encumbered by the rule that they had to maintain control of their spears to keep from automatically losing, but were not allowed to use the points for cutting until the final ceremonial slash of the loser by the winner. They wallowed, struck at each other's eye-stubs with the sides of their spears, trod one another's edges, tried to wrest the spear from the other's grasp, and slapped each other with muscular pseudopods in an attempt to deliver a knockout shock to the brain-knot.

The usually fluidless battle for Leadership ended in a shocking way when Great-Crack found Blue-Flow's spear pointing in an opportune direction and deliberately impaled herself on it, taking it into her body. No longer in control of his spear, Blue-Flow had lost. He shook the glowing gout of Great-Crack's fluid off his dueling manipulator onto the crust as she repeated her challenge. "Who is Leader of the Clan, Old One?"

"You are, Great-Crack," Blue-Flow replied.

Great-Crack maneuvered her body and Blue-Flow watched, horrified, as his sharp spear broke out of the rapidly healing wound in Great-Crack's side. The spear reached over to his surface and gave him the ceremonial cut, the fluids from the two bodies mixing together as they dripped off the spear point onto the crust.

Although she had suffered a significant wound, the injury would only slow an excellent fighter like Great-Crack, and when she repeated the challenge, no one had the courage to reply.

Great-Crack then told the gathered clan, "We will go to Bright's Heaven, but not now. We do not have enough food to survive the trek across the bad lands between here and Bright's Heaven. We must grow more pods. Go back to the fields and plant many more seeds. We will go after the next harvest."

The clan turned to their work, their disappointment at the delay in reaching Bright's Heaven countered by their natural reluctance to leave their home. Within a few turns, Great-Crack had mended, and she spent the time making sure not only that the clan planted enough seeds, but that she wouldn't lose the services of Blue-Flow, one of the best warriors of the clan. At every opportunity she patted and teased him. In a few turns, he got over his sulk at losing, gave in to the teasing, and they enjoyed a romp together. Soon she felt a new egg growing inside her to replace the one she had sacrificed.

Great-Crack planted a few of the funny cluster seeds in one spot and watched the plants with interest, but to her great disappointment the plants, pods, and seeds inside were just like the plants grown from the oval seeds from Bright's Heaven. She could never figure out why.

While the crops grew, Great-Crack played with mathematics. In the same manner as she had learned to identify pods with seeds, she now had a collection of pebbles, one for each member of the clan.

With the new crop coming in, a new pod bin had to be constructed. Great-Crack decided that it was about time to check to see if there were enough pods for the clan. She did not look forward to hauling all those pods out of the bins, lining them up against the collection of seeds that she had accumulated on her trek back from Bright's Heaven, then putting them in stacks, and back into the bins again.

Then she made another conceptual breakthrough.

"Why do I have to move pods around?" she thought. "I can make a collection of seeds, one for each pod in the bin. Once that is done, then it is much easier to move seeds than pods."

Soon the pod bin had a smaller bin outside the opening containing a pile of seeds, one for each pod in the bin. Monitoring the bin was the cheela's first accountant, an Old One assigned to the task of adding a seed to the seed bin for each pod put into the pod bin, and taking one seed out for every pod eaten.

As the harvest proceeded, even the number of seeds grew to overflow their bin. Great-Crack looked at the seed bin and was both pleased and appalled at the number. Now that she had learned to use her mathematics to make her job easy, she kept trying to think of other ways to make it even easier. She mused as she pushed the seeds around in stacks. She then noticed that since the seeds were long ovals, they had a tendency to form into clumps. She found that if she arranged them so that their sides just touched, they formed a pretty cluster. Although there were too many to count, there was always the same number if they were all pushed together so that all the sides just touched. It was a pretty pattern, just like the cluster pattern of the bottom seed of the pods from Bright's Heaven. She put one of the cluster seeds next to the collection of seeds. They looked identical. Then the now familiar habit of isomorphic identification struck again.

"If a cluster seed looks like this small clump of seeds," she wondered, "why don't I just save a stack of cluster seeds, each one representing a whole clump of oval seeds?"

Soon she had the seed bin replaced with a smaller one containing a large number of cluster seeds and a few odd oval seeds left over. That bothered her a little, having some pods represented by cluster seeds and some by oval seeds, but it helped that the cluster seeds were a little bigger than the oval ones. Her real problem came with her accountant, who didn't understand at all.

"The old way was very simple, Great-Crack," the Old One said. "One seed in the seed bin for one pod in the pod bin. But this does not make sense. How can one seed, even a cluster seed, mean many pods?"

Great-Crack tried hard to explain, and ran into the phenomenon that is often encountered by one trying to teach someone something—the teacher often learns something new herself. Great-Crack learned to count past three.

"Now look, Old One, I will go through it carefully. Here is one pod, and one oval seed. Here is another pod next to the first pod, and another oval seed next to the first seed. That's two—and now three." Great-Crack moved the third pod and seed into place, then reached for another set.

"Now this many is . . ." Great-Crack fumbled for the nonexistent word. ". . . the same number of ways that you can travel: east, west, and the two hard directions." She continued adding sets. "And this many is the same as the number of fangs on a Swift. And this many is the number of petals in a petal plant . . ."

She went on. "And this . . ." she said as she completed the

pattern, "is the number of bumps on the cluster seed. It is as many as your eyes."

The accountant dipped each of his dozen eyes, one after the other, as he carefully touched each of the seeds in turn with a delicate tendril. "So it is," he said. "That will make it easy to count them."

The lesson really didn't sink in the first time, but after many repetitions even the accountant was using one, two, three, travel, swift, petal . . . all the way up to a dozen, as if he had learned it as a hatchling. But soon even that did not suffice, for there were so many pods from the harvest that Great-Crack had to invent the name "great" for a dozen dozen of pods. The accountant was very satisfied with her choice of word, for it obviously represented a "great" number of objects.

With the accountant's help, Great-Crack checked the results of the harvest. First the pebbles, one for each member of the clan, were placed in a column, then across the bottom were placed cluster seeds, only now the unique collection of cluster seeds that Great-Crack had accumulated during her trip back (and which measured the distance to Bright's Heaven in terms of pods) had been replaced by a concept—a number—a petal worth of cluster seeds plus a swift of oval ones.

The forecast was not good. As the cluster seeds grew out from each pebble, Great-Crack came to the end of the seeds before she came to the last of the pebbles. Great-Crack felt once again the frustration of being Leader of the Clan. The volcano had become more active and the sky grew steadily worse. With their vision of the sky clouded, the crops grew poorly and the harvests were meager. Their neighbors to the east and west were hungry and restless and there had been many more attacks on the fields of the clan. They must go. But there were not enough pods.

Great-Crack stared at the diagram in front of her. Although the pebbles and seeds were far removed from hungry bodies and nourishing pods, they still foretold of great anguish for all.

"I can strip the unripe pods from the plants before we leave, and they will get ripe enough to eat after a few turns," she thought. "There are usually about two nearly ripe pods per plant." She flowed over to her stockade, where she kept a pile of seeds that represented the number of plants in the fields. She soon returned with a collection of seeds that represented the unripe pods in the fields, but even when these were added to the diagram, there were not enough.

"Dragon's Fire!" she swore to herself. She shrank from making the obvious decision, arguing with herself, "But there are so many pods, surely there are enough for all to go." But the diagram, empty at the top and end, stared at her with its cold logic.

"A dozen plus two of the Aged Ones will have to stay," she decided, and winced as the numbers changed to names in her mind.

She called the clan together. To solidify her control as well as to signify her seriousness, she started with a formal challenge.

"Who is Leader of the Clan?" she asked, and her tread felt and marked the chorus of replies.

"You are, Great-Crack!"

Her eyes singled out and stared at a few warriors who were slow in responding, but soon all had replied. She then said, "We leave for Bright's Heaven at the next turn, but there are not enough pods to feed us all on the long journey, so some cannot go." She reeled off the names of the Aged Ones who were either too injured or too old to be of much value anymore, and they stoically accepted their fate, having grown weary of life after so many turns. It did not take long for the clan to strip the unripe pods from the plants and load up the eggs, hatchlings, pods, and their few tools and weapons into skin pouches tucked inside their bodies. The clan left their home, moving as always according to the rule of the ancient Old Aged Ones: "Go in a direction others do not go."

The massive group of burdened cheela pushed slowly south. It was almost two turns before they could no longer see the stockades and fields that had once been their home. Shortly after they had gone over the horizon, one of the guards at the rear broke ranks, pushed his way ahead and came up to Great-Crack, who was part of the pathbreaker chevron at the front.

"One of the Aged Ones that we had left behind is following us," the guard whispered to her.

Great-Crack left her place in the chevron, doing it carefully so that her replacement just in back of her could close the gap smoothly, thus preventing any loss in the progress she had made. She and the guard flowed quickly east and waited as the clan moved slowly by.

Great-Crack looked at the approaching Aged One. "It is West-Light, one of the most able of those who were left. Why is he coming?" They waited for almost a turn until the exhausted West-Light approached them.

"You heard my command, Aged One!" she stamped at him. "You cannot come with us. There is not enough food! Go back now or I will kill you instantly!"

West-Light stopped and emptied out his pouches. He had been carrying some half-ripe pods from the fields that must have become edible since the trek had started, along with some nearly ripe wild pods.

"We were worried that perhaps there might not be enough food to keep the hatchlings healthy," West-Light said. "So we gathered what we could these past few turns before you got too far away for me to reach. Here—take good care of the hatchlings."

Great-Crack whispered, "Thank you, West-Light." She moved forward to pick up his meager offering. She then stared as the thinnest cheela she had ever seen slowly pushed his way back to their now abandoned camp.

"He has not eaten a thing since we left," she thought to herself. She turned and went back to join the rest of the clan, still moving slowly southward towards Bright's Heaven.

The trek was dreary. The progress was much slower than Great-Crack had counted on, and she felt the pouch of seeds that represented the remaining food get smaller and smaller after every break. The quality of the food became worse as they ate all the ripe pods and started on the ones that had only partially ripened in their pouches. The littlest hatchlings didn't want to eat these and were constantly sick. Great-Crack sent out hunting parties both east and west, but often they came back with neither pods nor meat. Great-Crack grew desperate. They were losing a hatchling every few turns; for the first time in ages, some of the clan's eggs refused to hatch and had to be left after it became evident that the eggling inside was dead.

"All the clan is in poor shape," Great-Crack said to herself as she worked in the rear, constantly closing gaps that a youngster or an Old One had let fall into the body of the traveling group. She looked backward. There was a long, straggling column that had become separated from the rest of the group when one of the members faltered and allowed the hard direction to close in on him. She watched as he attempted to move forward again, but it was obvious that the speed he was able to make in the hard direction would not be fast enough to let him and his followers catch up with the rest of the clan. She then saw a movement off in the smoky east that sent her into action.

"Attack from east!" she stamped as she pushed her way through the crowded clan members. When she got to the eastern edge she saw it was serious. It was a large, hungry war party and they had already cut off the straggling string from the rest of the clan. She soon had a group of warriors on either side of her and noticed with satisfaction that the clan had stopped moving and were now in a coherent group, with the stronger ones facing outward, spears and shards bristling. She started forward to rescue the captives, when her trained senses detected something from the west. It was another war party waiting for them to attack the first group, when they could rush on them from the rear.

"Stop!" she commanded. She led the war party back to protect the rest of the clan, then watched in agony as the captives were killed and the precious pods wrenched from their flowing bodies and devoured by the hungry band of marauders. The war party stayed for a few turns, trying to figure out a way to attack the rest of the clan. They made a few abortive attacks, one of which gave Great-Crack deep satisfaction as she dispatched two of the enemy, partially to avenge the clan members she had lost. Finally the war party gave up the siege and went off toward the west, hauling the meat from their victims with them. Great-Crack immediately took the clan off again toward Bright's Heaven.

With their enforced rest, the clan was in better shape, and with the example of what happened to stragglers still etched in their minds, there were very few times that the gap opened by the pathbreakers was allowed to fail, and the clan made good time for a few turns. But it soon became obvious to Great-Crack that they were in serious trouble. At the next break she got out the pebbles that represented the members of the clan, and after discarding the ones that had been killed in the interchange with the attackers, she laid them out in a column.

She knew that they were still far from Bright's Heaven, for they had just started to get to the "lost feeling" region. She made an estimate of how many turns it would take them to reach Bright's Heaven and laid those cluster seeds out in a row. She then started to fill in the diagram with seeds representing the pods left. There was no question about it—they were short by many, many pods.

She stared at the large empty space in the diagram, and her imaginative brain turned the empty space into empty cheela. It was now time—she would have to risk the chance of another attack and split her forces.

The clan grew restless as the break grew longer while Great-Crack calculated. She finally called her warriors together and explained the situation to them. Blue-Flow had never really learned why the seeds and pebbles told things to Great-Crack that he could not see, but he now was very glad that Great-Crack had prevented him from leading the clan off many turns ago. With far fewer pods, he would have had them all dead by now. But he didn't need pebbles and seeds to tell him that there were not enough pods for them to make it to Bright's Heaven.

"Blue-Flow," she said, "I want you to lead a hunting party to Bright's Heaven and bring back pods for us." She looked down at the diagram and said, "You will only need a Slink's worth of pods to keep you going. You are going to arrive very hungry—but the ripe pods at the end of the journey will make it worthwhile."

Blue-Flow and the others in the hunting party emptied out most of their pouches. Some of them attempted to leave without taking any pods, preferring to leave them for the hatchlings while making do with bravado, but Great-Crack, trusting in her calculations, made them take their ration of pods. The hunting party took off and was rapidly out of sight of the slowly moving clan.

With her warrior forces depleted, Great-Crack took no chances and moved the clan along carefully so that no gaps developed and the perimeter always had warriors on the lookout both east and west.

The hunting party quickly traveled over the "lost feeling" region and soon saw the welcome sight of Bright peeking over the horizon. As they came into the region where the skies became clear and the petal plants flourished, they ate their fill and then started loading up their pouches in preparation for the long trek back to the hungry clan.

Suddenly Bad-Turn whispered, "I see a Flow Slow moving just over the horizon." Blue-Flow and the others soon confirmed the sighting and they thinned their bodies to keep out of its sight.

"It is to the east and we could get to it easily," Blue-Flow whispered. "The hatchlings have been without meat since we left home. Let's kill it!"

The Flow Slow depended on its armored plates for protection. This one had never seen a cheela before, and ignored them as it ignored all small, scurrying creatures. The Flow Slow moved ponderously from plant to plant, its armored tread plates moving over its top surface to fall directly on the plant, crushing it to pulp, to be ingested in the gaps between the plates as the huge body slowly flowed onward. The Flow Slow sought out plants, but, as many an unfortunate cheela had found out, it would eat anything that happened to fall before its onslaught.

The kill was easy, since the Flow Slow had never tasted a dragon crystal spear before. The cheela slipped in ahead of it, timing their moves carefully, and planted spears in the crust in just the correct position so that the sharp points entered the gaps between the plates as they came down to the surface.

As they started to move away from the carcass, Bad-Turn looked back at it and said, "Too bad we can't carry that whole carcass back to the clan. If they had all that meat to eat, there would be no worry about food for the rest of the trip."

Blue-Flow replied, "I thought about that too. We could try to push a large chunk of meat ahead of us, but we can carry in our pouches more than we can push—especially when we have to go in the hard direction. Besides, pushing the meat through the ashes over that whole distance will ruin it."

"If we only had some way to keep it out of the ashes," murmured Bad-Turn, and he went over to one of the large Flow Slow plates and looked at it. It was large, half as big as he was. It was a flat square plate of material almost as hard as dragon crystal. At the front and back edges were curved lips that had been attached to the skin of the Flow Slow. Bad-Turn flowed onto the plate, thinking, "This could hold a lot of meat and pods, much more than I could carry in my pouches." He flowed to the front lip and stayed there for a moment, his back edge hanging back on the front lip of the plate.

"What are you doing?" Blue-Flow asked. "We should be going."

"Watch!" said Bad-Turn, and Blue-Flow and the others saw his back edge stiffen as he grew a long internal manipulator crystal that ran from one end of the Flow Slow plate to the other. Since the crystal was horizontal and did not have to fight the pull of Egg, he could make it very thin, thin enough just to fit under the lip of the plate.

"I never heard of growing a manipulator bone that way," one of the party said to Blue-Flow. Then they both watched as Bad-Turn moved away, the front of his body digging into the crust and the back edge dragging the plate along behind, firmly attached by the strong crystal bar just under the skin and stretching from one eye to another.

"It feels funny, but it works," Bad-Turn said. "Once I get it moving, it is easy to keep it moving despite its weight. With someone behind pushing, I think we could pull much more than we could carry."

The others tried it and they were all quick converts, especially when they tried it with a huge pile of bulky chunks of meat that could never be crammed into pouches. Within less than a turn, the Flow Slow had been converted into meat piled on top of its own armored plates.

The hunting party then moved off in single file, a pathbreaker leading the way, pushing into the hard direction, followed by a plate-puller crouched up behind him, hauling a plate of meat and helped along by a pusher and followed by three other teams. The meat on the plates seemed to work as well as their bodies at keeping the gap open in the hard direction, so they made good time. Their rest breaks were few and short and only for downing another chunk of nourishing meat.

When Great-Crack observed them coming over the horizon, she saw them at a great distance. Many turns ago she had stopped the trek to conserve food, while she kept watch with an eye perched up on a long eye-stub. There were no longer any pods for anyone except the hatchlings, and they were doing poorly on those. The whole clan was gathered in a circle, too weak to move much, and Great-Crack herself was forced to lower her eye-stub often.

"Fine Leader you turned out to be," she berated herself. "Leading your clan off to die beneath smoky skies in a place where they always feel lost."

Still, she had faith that Blue-Flow would return shortly with pods and that then they could move again while Blue-Flow returned for more. She was relieved when she saw the returning column, but was amazed by the bulk and length of it. Only the obvious shape of Blue-Flow breaking path at the front of the column relieved her worry that it was another attacking war party.

The clan watched in awe as the procession pulled their wonderful-looking cargo into camp. Within two turns everyone was back to a good comfortable bulk. The hatchlings were soon feeling good enough to make pests of themselves while the adults were more interested in pairing off and having a little fun alone. Great-Crack listened in admiration as Blue-Flow recounted their journey, the kill of the Flow Slow, and the results of Bad-Turn's invention.

"Bad-Turn," Great-Crack said, "for too long you have been stuck with that dreary hatchling name. From now on you shall be Plate-Puller.

"Come with me," she commanded, and some of her eyes turned to look back at Blue-Flow as they left. "I will see you later. This new name calls for a reward." Blue-Flow watched the couple go off, a little jealous, but he would have his chance later this turn.

With their strength renewed by the meat and ripe pods, the clan moved off at good speed. It was not long before they began to feel less lost. The sky cleared and finally Great-Crack called a halt and arranged the clan so that all, even the smallest hatchling, could see the intense reddish yellow glow of Bright on the horizon.

"O Great Bright One. Brightest of all in the sky," Great-Crack intoned, all of her dozen eyes staring at the bright star while her undertread rhythmically pulsed the crust. "We thank You for saving us from the rolling walls of blue-white fire. We thank You for saving us from the choking clouds of poisonous red smoke that kill the plants and still the eggs. We thank You for leading us out of the land of starvation and lostness to Your Heaven."

Her eyes turned from the star and looked around at the clan. "Let us go now to claim our reward—a Heaven where there are no enemies and plenty of food and game. Come—all of you—into Bright's Heaven."

TIME: 21:54:20 GMT TUESDAY 14 JUNE 2050

The strong limbs of Commander Carole Swenson pulled her compact body slowly along the central shaft of St. George, her long yellow braid flipping from side to side with the motion. Carole's eyes automatically monitored the traffic in the side corridors, watching the to and fro motion of the humanity on her tiny planet. Although many of the crew were still busy with their normal tasks, there was a general flow toward the viewing ports near the bridge. However, Carole was headed in another direction, toward the port science blister. The view of the upcoming action would not be as good there, but she wanted to see the closeups from the cameras on the probe spacecraft. She swung into a corridor and with a dexterity born of many years in free fall, launched her body unerringly toward the hatch at the far end. Bouncing to a halt on the wall next to the hatch, she palmed the lock and floated in. No one saw her enter, for Pierre had his science crew busy.

"How much longer?" she asked the group gathered in front of consoles at the other end of the room.

Pierre glanced at the flickering numbers on the right of his screen. "Fourteen minutes, and everything looks fine."

Carole looked at a display across the room. The field of view of the monitor camera contained the glowing sphere of one of the larger condensed asteroids in the lower corner, and a small white speck representing the other large asteroid in the upper corner. As she watched, the smaller speck moved slowly across the screen, getting brighter as it came. Carole looked at another console, the picture there was almost the same, but reversed. The geometry of the elastic collision of the two large ultra-dense asteroids was almost exactly symmetric.

Pierre stared at his console. There were no pictures on his screen, just a computer-generated plot of two curved lines that were slowly approaching each other in a collision course. Numbers in boxes along the side of his screen changed rapidly. "Thirty seconds to last abort point," he announced. "Any problems?"

Jean spoke from another console. "Video monitors operating."

"Computer control well within margins," another voice said.

"Herder probe propulsion units all operational," said another.

"I'll let it go, then," Pierre said, lifting his finger from the abort toggle and snapping shut the safety cover.

Carole watched one of the screens as the smaller blob grew larger and larger. Angry tongues of fire burst rapidly in seemingly random directions from positions near the two spheres as the computer directed the herder probes to keep the asteroids on their correct paths. Then suddenly, in a sequence that was too fast to follow, an ultra-dense asteroid flashed around between its twin and the camera probe, and the screen was empty.

Pierre flicked on another camera that was off at a different angle, but that view was only good for a few seconds before the rapidly shrinking spot faded from the screen.

They all turned to Pierre's screen, which showed the orbits of the two asteroids. The trajectories had approached so close to each other that the tight curlicues in their respective paths due to their mutual gravitational attraction seemed to be placed one on top of the other. They now watched as one line headed outward toward the asteroid belt again, while the other seemed to be dropping straight into the neutron star. Actually, the falling massive asteroid would miss the star by a slight margin and was now in a highly elliptical orbit, with its aphelion near the 100,000 km circular orbit of St. George and its perihelion at just over 400 km from Dragon's Egg.

Their elevator was in place.

God

God came to the cheela slowly. For many, many, many generations, the cheela had no God. The sky was empty except for a
few tiny pinpricks of light scattered across the cold, black dome.
Then God had become lonely and made the great volcano grow,
driving the cheela from their home in the north to a new home
in the south. There the god Bright had welcomed his chosen
people into the Heaven he had prepared for them.

Bright had been good to the cheela. Bright never rose or set
like the other spots of light, but stayed up in the sky, keeping
watch over all the cheela. Life was good, and the cheela let
Bright know that they were happy by their prayers that they
faithfully gave every turn of Bright's throne.

Then one turn, when the eyes of the cheela were lifted to the
skies in prayer, one of the supplicants saw a new speck rise over
the horizon. As soon as the prayers were finished, he brought it
to the attention of the Holy Ones that interpreted Bright's
wishes.

The Holy Ones were puzzled, but did not let it show. As
masters of their profession, they had learned to say little and do
even less until they were sure of themselves.

"Yes—we expected something like that, but let us wait and we
will study it further," they reassured the excited discoverer.

They did study it. It was still a speck in the sky, not much
different from all the other specks, but it soon became brighter
than any of the others. Fortunately, it was not nearly as brilliant
as the god Bright, as it would have been difficult to explain two

gods to a people that had been brought up to believe in the om-
nipotence and uniqueness of the One God—Bright.

The new speck grew and grew in brilliance with each passing
turn, and although the common cheela noticed the increase in
brightness, it was only the Holy Ones who noticed that the speck
was also slowly moving with respect to the other stars in the sky.
A moving star! This was unheard of in cheela astrology, where
the pattern of lights, dominated by the glaring red-yellow presence of Bright, had always remained fixed in relative position
while rotating slowly about Bright's throne in the sky.

"If the stars are not fixed, but move around, how can one
make any kind of predictions from them? The future would be
constantly changing," complained Bright's-Second, the Chief Astrologer and next in line for the position of High Priest.

"I am sure Bright has a reason for this change in the sky,"
Bright's-First said. "It is up to us to use our intelligence in the
service of Bright and interpret its meaning."

The High Priest turned her eyes toward the young novice.

"Are you sure of the motion?" she asked.

"Yes, O Bright's-First," said Sky-Seeker. "In my training in astrology I have been learning how to estimate the angles between
the star specks with the astrologer sticks and have memorized almost all my number tables. I had tried to add the new star to my
memory but, still being a novice, I had failed to get all the numbers correctly. I realized my mistake many turns later when I
was trying to cast a fortune. I then went back to the astrologer
sticks to get the numbers correctly and I found that some of the
old numbers that I had memorized did not agree with the new
ones for that star."

"Unfortunately, he is correct," the Chief Astrologer said. "At
first I thought his memory was faulty or that someone had disturbed the astrologer sticks. However, when I checked the numbers against the ones that I had committed to memory on the
fateful turn when that star blossomed in the sky, I found out that
my old numbers were even further off than the novice's, yet none
of the other stars in the sky have changed their numbers at all."

"A moving star . . ." the High Priest murmured. "One that
moves. It must be that Bright has sent us a messenger! Perhaps
Bright will speak directly to us now."

Soon the religion of the cheela was broadened to include the new phenomenon, a star that not only grew brighter and brighter until it rivaled Bright in its brilliance, but which swept majestically across the skies. There was some consternation when Bright's Messenger reached perihelion and its brilliance started to fade, but all the cheela were relieved when after a few greats of turns, it retraced its path in the sky.

The new star set the small cadre of novices talking among themselves. Having been picked primarily because of their interest in numbers and their eidetic memory, so necessary for the position of an astrologer in a civilization without writing, they soon began to puzzle over the strange behavior of the motion of Bright's Messenger.

"If it were a circle, then it would make more sense," said one of the novices. "We could say that Bright and the other stars are perched on a large crystal egg that rotates once a turn, and Bright's Messenger would then be on a smaller crystal egg, turning at a slightly faster rate."

"But not only is it not a circle," another said, "it does not even move evenly along its path."

"Another way of looking at it is that Bright and the stars do not move in the sky," said a third, "but that Egg turns once on its axis every turn, and that Bright's Messenger rotates about Egg in an elongated path."

The others looked at her as if she had spoken heresy (which she had come close to doing), and one quickly put her down with one of the first lessons in Holy School.

"All stars rotate about the unique brilliance of Bright, worshiping the God of the Universe as all cheela do," one of them said. "Your picture would have the stars standing still, when we all know that only Bright, the center of the universe, stands still, while all else must revolve."

Knowing she was treading on unstable crust, Sky-Seeker did not bother to reply, although she knew as well as the others, that Bright did not really stand still but moved in a tiny circle about an invisible point in the sky. This lack of perfection of Bright had been a nagging splinter in the tread of the philosophers of theology since it was first discovered by the use of the astrologer sticks. The High Priest had assured them that they would understand this in time, but it had been a long time and a dozen High

Priests had come and gone and Bright still carried out the tiny motion, without bothering to explain.

TIME: 01:15:33 GMT
WEDNESDAY 15 JUNE 2050

The Chief Astrologer had been wrong. The variable motion of Bright's Messenger across the sky did not doom the science of astrology. Indeed, by adding some complexity to the sky it gave the astrologers much more to work with than a single set of memorized numbers that gave the relative position of the stars in the sky. Soon, the old technique of casting horoscopes by the star that was appearing over the horizon at the propitious time became obsolete. The position of Bright's Messenger among the fixed positions of the rest of the stars became the dominant factor in predicting the future.

It soon became evident that the technique of memorizing the numbers taken with the astrologer sticks was not going to work. Even the best memories of the novices could not cope with the flood of numbers that Bright's Messenger produced every turn. The ancient accounting technique of the business merchants, who monitored their inventory with pod seeds in bins, was adapted by the astrologers. After an awkward time of trying to work directly with seeds, one of the novices discovered the device of scratching pictures of seeds on flat plates of rock, then shortly after that, because of the hardness of the rock and the laziness of the novices, a shorthand written number system was invented. Not only astrology, but business and science were soon revolutionized by the discovery of written numbers. Then, shortly after having gotten used to writing numbers on a tablet, the merchant scribes (as lazy as the astrologer scribes) found that they didn't have to draw a complete picture of the object that was being counted for an inventory or delivery record, but only enough so that another scribe (presumably equally loath to make complete drawings) would be able to recognize what it was.

Thus, although none of the High Priests ever realized it, the cheela were soon using the gift that Bright had sent by its Messenger—the gift of writing.

TIME: 06:33:23 GMT FRIDAY 17 JUNE 2050

For greats of greats of turns, the life of the cheela was smooth. Bright kept watch over Heaven and blessed the cheela in their growth and in their conquests of the north and east. Small, savage bands of leathery-skinned barbarians would often leave their smoky lands to the north and attempt raids on the croplands in the northern part of Heaven, but the cheela farmers in the north were well protected by roving squads of needle troopers.

The needle troopers carried the dreaded weapon, the dragon tooth. A very long needle of melted dragon crystal, it was made by the forgers, who used fires of dried pod seeds blown to a blue white heat with bellows from Flow Slow skin to melt otherwise useless pieces of dragon crystal until they had a liquid melt. The glowing melt was poured into a groove cut into the crust along the easy direction. The long fibrous strings in the liquid became aligned by the strong magnetic field of the star. The liquid then recrystallized about the fibers, forming a two-component matrix material that was as strong as the original dragon crystal, except that now it was longer than any dragon crystal had ever been. A cheela trooper could envelop the blunt end of the needle and get enough leverage so he or she could extend the light, strong needle of crystal out a full body diameter without letting the point either touch the crust or rise too high in the air.

The barbarians, not having the secrets of the forge, were limited to broken shards of dragon crystal for their weapons and were no match for a well-trained squad of needle troopers, who moved in disciplined circles, their dragon tooth needles bristling across the tops of their interlocked Flow Slow plate shields.

TIME: 19:24:11 GMT FRIDAY 17 JUNE 2050

Commander Carole Swenson was floating above the console, watching over Pierre's shoulder as the outward-going asteroid met the first of the compensator masses still waiting far out in the asteroid belt. In the same manner as it had dropped the deorbiter mass toward the neutron star, the large asteroid overtook the first of the smaller masses and dropped it inward toward the star. It then went on to the next one. After watching the first two, Carole went back to the bridge. Nothing was more boring than the inevitability of the Newtonian law of gravitational attraction.

One after another, the six glowing compensator masses were dropped from their far-flung orbits to a spot near St. George, where they were met by the deorbiter mass, which stopped them in their tracks and left them dancing randomly about each other in a 100,000-kilometer circular orbit not too far from St. George. Their huge bulk dwarfed the long, thin mother ship, and the heat generated during their formation made them glow like new stars in the black sky.

TIME: 10:15:02 GMT
SATURDAY 18 JUNE 2050

One after the other, new stars began to blossom in the sky. The cheela in Bright's Heaven continued to multiply and prosper, but their very numbers began to strain the ability of the crust to support them. Decadence set in and soon the needle trooper commanders despaired of ever adequately defending the expanding frontier with the flabby, ill-fed recruits they were sent to use.

A fifth new light grew in the sky during the time the barbarians made inroads from the east. Alarmed, by both the losses and the new stars, the cheela rose under the leadership of a self-proclaimed General of the Clans and drove the barbarians back. The spasm of energy subsided—the General abandoned his post and went off to hatch eggs—and the cheela slipped back into their slow decline.

Yet another star blazed in the heavens, and this time the flurry of worry and religious concern was brief. Bright's-First still worshiped daily in Bright's Temple, but few came to worship with him. Those who were still in need of a god had found six of them in a new religion—a popular pantheistic religion that had a little bit of everything for everybody, including religiously inspired orgies that took place every time Bright's Messenger passed near "The Six"—which represented East, West, Sky, Crust, Food, and Sex.

TIME: 04:02:02 GMT SUNDAY 19 JUNE 2050

Most of the crew of the interstellar ark were floating in front of the viewports on the bridge as St. George approached the site of the compressed asteroid collection. The rest were at various observation posts where the telescopes and scanners gave them a better view.

Pierre looked up from the screen and rotated to face the Commander of the expedition.

"I know it's safe, but I still don't like it, Carole," he said. "Those red-hot asteroids are not only too hot to touch, but they would crush us with their gravity tides if we ever got too close. And we are going to live within 200 meters of six of them for over a week!"

Carole smiled reassuringly and replied, "You know perfectly well that, if it were not for the toasty embrace of those friendly asteroids, the gravity tides of Dragon's Egg would crush you instead! Let's get them down there where they will do you some good."

TIME: 08:00:13 GMT SUNDAY 19 JUNE 2050

Bright's-Second had been keeping a careful watch on the collection of six lights ever since he had been a novice. Having entered the priesthood because he was withdrawn and unpopular, he had submerged himself in the astrologer sticks and had invented new tools to measure more accurately the minute motions of the many lights piercing the darkness. He was the first to notice that the tiny circle that Bright made in the sky had become measurably smaller. He took the news to Bright's-First, who was delighted.

"That must mean that the imperfection in Bright, miniscule as it has been, is becoming smaller," she said. "When will be the time that Bright is perfect? Oh that I might live to see the turn!"

"I am afraid that when that turn comes, we will both be meat, O High Priest of Bright," the Chief Astrologer said. "Entire clans will have come and gone before Bright reaches its perfection."

The High Priest was disappointed, but she didn't let it show.

"Well, we must maintain our stewardship and keep Bright's Temple going until that turn comes and the people once again return to their One True God."

The Chief Astrologer listened politely, but was bursting to tell the High Priest the other news that he had.

"My new sticks have also informed me that something else is happening," he said. "The Six . . . I mean, the six newer lights are slightly shifting in position and are drawing closer and closer to the point where Bright's Messenger reaches its farthest distance from Egg. Also, if you watch The Six and Bright's Messenger as often as I do, you will see that they do not stay at the same brightness from turn to turn, but occasionally flare up slightly, then return to their original level."

"What can that mean?" Bright's-First asked.

"I don't know, but in about a great of turns, Bright's Messenger will reach its maximum distance from Egg, and it seems as if all six of the other lights will be there at the same time. If so, something interesting may happen."

TIME: 08:00:43 GMT SUNDAY 19 JUNE 2050

When the deorbiter came up this time, there was going to be a spectacular show. Commander Swenson was again in the port science blister, watching the action on the console screens.

"Check position of compensator masses!" Pierre called out.

Six confirmations flashed instantly on his screen and were echoed by voices floating through the air from six nearby consoles, where each compensator mass was being monitored by a crew member.

Pierre looked up at Carole as he shrugged and lifted his finger from the abort toggle. "I really don't know why we insist on monitoring the computer on these close encounters. Things are going so fast I doubt we could do anything about it even if something did go wrong with the computer."

"Still," Carole said, "it lets us get in on the fun." She watched as a tiny speck in one corner of the screen slowly grew bigger and approached the six glowing spheres in the center of the screen. Then, in a complex wiggle and flash, the deorbiter mass pulled its disappearing act. The six glowing compensator masses were gone, and the screen was empty.

TIME: 08:00:44 GMT SUNDAY 19 JUNE 2050

Bright's-Second had his suspicions verified. For when Bright's Messenger reached its point of maximum distance from Egg, it did not just pass in front of The Six, but instead grabbed East, Sex, Crust, West, Food, then finally Sky, and flung them down at Egg.

The dozen turns in which the sky was torn asunder by Bright's Messenger throwing down the false gods from the sky was a busy time for Bright's Temple. At first, the cheela were sure that The Six were going to fall and hit Egg, destroying the wicked cheela that had abandoned Bright and had turned to false gods. For a while, even Bright's-Second was worried about that possibility. But a few dozen turns staring through the astrologer sticks assured him that although the falling stars would come close to Egg, they would only come as close as Bright's Messenger did. When the High Priest passed Bright's-Second's assurance of salvation on to the cheela, the crowds flocked to Bright's Temple.

Near the end of the fourth great of turns after their fall, the six star-specks and Bright's Messenger drew closer, and moved more rapidly through the black heavens. Bright's-Second spent almost his entire time out at the astrologer sticks, writing down the numbers as fast as he could determine them. After he was certain of the orbits, he could spend some time carefully drawing them out and trying to understand them, but right now his full time was spent collecting the numbers as the seven bright objects moved through the heavens. He determined that Bright's Messenger had been affected by the interaction—not much, but an easily measurable change had been made in its highly elliptical orbit. He hated to do it, but he put a novice in charge of taking the numbers, and went off to draw up the new orbits of the fallen Six.

"Strange," thought Bright's-Second, "they all seem to be heading for the same place above Egg. Perhaps they will hit each other and destroy themselves, as an example to the cheela not to worship false gods."

Suddenly he had another thought, and shortly he was staring at still another egg-shaped orbit—that of Bright's Messenger with its new numbers used.

"Bright's Messenger is going to be at the same point at the same time," he said to himself. "What is going to happen? It would be to Bright's glory if I could predict the outcome for the people, so they could be properly prepared."

Bright's-Second tried as hard as he could to extract the most from the inadequate numbers that came from the crude astrologer sticks, but all he could tell was that Bright's Messenger and the six fallen ones were going to be near the same place at the same time.

"They look as if they will all collide and be destroyed," Bright's-Second reported to the High Priest. "But it could be that Bright's Messenger will toss the other six off into different directions again, perhaps back up to where they were. I simply don't know what to predict."

"It would be so much better if we knew," she replied, "but perhaps Bright is testing us again."

Bright's-First was wise in the ways of religious leaders and only told her people that they were all to be praying, with their eyes to the eastern skies, when the time came for the stars to meet.

Inexorably the seven spots in the sky drew closer together, and now everyone could see the irregular flaring in intensity as if they were glaring at each other. Bright's-Second was busy at the astrologer sticks. He had the novices working in teams, one for each of the seven lights. They often got in each other's way and a number or two was lost or misread, but he could take care of those later. He himself, with his practiced eyes, was estimating the relative distance between the points of light, while the novices were measuring with respect to the background stars. It was now obvious that they were not all going to meet at exactly the same place. Then, as the cheela watched, they saw Bright's Messenger swing by Sex, West, Food, East, Crust, and finally Sky, then continue on its accustomed path back into the blackness, leaving The Six standing still in the sky!

A keening vibration shook the crust as a great of greats of cheela treads chattered in fear and awe at the amazing sight. Where before, the six stars had risen and set in the skies each turn as the other stars and Bright's Messenger had done, they now were stationary. They neither rose nor set, but slowly rotated once a turn around a point above the east magnetic pole.

The High Priest took full advantage of the extraordinary sight, and at the next turn proclaimed that the new formation was composed of six of Bright's eyes, brought down to Egg by Bright's Messenger to vigilantly watch over the cheela to see if they were daring to worship false gods again. The proclamation was accepted by the cheela, and the pantheistic temples were reduced to rubble by frightened mobs cowering under the constant glare of the Six Eyes of Bright.

The new formation in the sky bothered Bright's-Second. It was counter to everything he had ever known about the behavior of the many lights in the sky. Having been a trooper chaplain during the last northern campaign against the barbarians, he had marched with the troopers across the equator to destroy a barbarian town. There, through breaks in the smoke cover, he had seen some tiny stars that rotated in small circles over the north pole, as Bright did over the south pole. He could understand a star being motionless in the sky if it were near a pole in the sky, but this was the first time an east or west magnetic pole had acted like the north and south poles.

TIME: 08:03:10 GMT SUNDAY 19 JUNE 2050

"The compensator masses are down," Carole said, turning to Pierre. "Now it is Dragon Slayer's turn."

Pierre, ignoring the small screen pager on his wrist, reached over to a nearby console. "Page crew of Dragon Slayer!"

The console blinked.

PAGING CESAR RAMIREZ WONG
PAGING JEAN KELLY THOMAS
PAGING AMALITA SHAKHASHIRI DRAKE
PAGING SEIKO KAUFFMANN TAKAHASHI
PAGING ABDUL NKOMI FAROUK

Pierre watched as the "Page acknowledged" mark appeared in front of each name. The computer had found them all busy at one task or another on board the Dragon Slayer. He leaned forward and asked, "Does everything look good for a departure at 0930?" He reached down and flicked the audio output panel to avoid the screen clutter from a multiple response. The computer fed him the positive confirmations one at a time. Dragon Slayer was ready to go.

Kicking off from the console, Pierre floated across the bridge of St. George, then pulled his way down the tunnels to the launching hangar that contained the seven meter sphere that would be his home for the next eight days.

TIME: 09:10:15 GMT SUNDAY 19 JUNE 2050

It was twenty minutes to separation and the crew of Dragon Slayer gathered in the small lounge at the base of the ship. Pierre looked over the crew who were to share the next eight days of danger, drudgery, and excitement with him. He couldn't have picked a better group. All had at least double-doctorates despite their youthful ages. Jean, Amalita, and Abdul each had a Ph.D. in astrophysics and a doctorate in one aspect or another of electrical engineering. "Doc" Cesar Wong (the only "real" doctor on Dragon Slayer) had the unusual combination of an M.D. in aerospace medicine and a Ph.D. in supermagnetics. Pierre himself had a Ph.D. in high-density nucleonic theory, and doctorates in gravitational engineering and journalism. Seiko, at 32, had them all beat. At last count she had four doctorates and expected to earn another as the result of their trip. Although each was a specialist in one aspect or another of neutron star physics, they had cross-trained so that each one of them could carry out any portion of the detailed science schedule that Dragon Slayer's crew was on. Pierre spoke.

"After separation we will be on ten-hour interlocking duty shifts. There will be a two-hour overlap so the new person coming on duty can be debriefed on the status of the experiments before taking over. It is now 0912 so Abdul, Seiko and Doc are on duty, with Doc on his mid-shift meal break and Seiko to go off duty at 1000. We had better get into the routine, so the rest of us should relax now. I know we aren't going to quarters during breakaway, but our shift will be coming up soon, so make sure that you get some sleep, and don't spend your off hours just watching the others work."

The time for separation approached, and they all went up to the main deck where each would have a viewport. The breakaway was quiet and uneventful. The procedure consisted of opening the hatch doors of the huge mother ship, unlocking the attachment fittings, and slowly backing the larger ship away from the freely falling sphere. Pierre had been right—no one went to quarters as the small sphere floated away from the immense side of the interstellar ark.

Cesar spoke. "It is always awe-inspiring to be outside, and up this close. The last time for me was when I came on board two years ago."

"I've been out a dozen times on antenna maintenance," Amalita said. "But you're right—no matter how often you see it, it is still impressive."

Pierre spoke into the communications console. "You look good, St. George. See you in a week."

"Good hunting, Dragon Slayer," came Carole's throaty reply.

They drifted away from the ark. As it grew smaller and smaller in the distance, the crew members gathered around the port facing the retreating mother ship. Finally Pierre went to one of the consoles and rotated the sphere so that the port faced the neutron star that they would soon be orbiting at close quarters.

"The deorbiter will arrive in six hours," Pierre said to the crew. "Everyone into the high-gravity protection tanks." He closed the metal shields over the viewport windows, turned off the console, and started opening the hatches in the six spherical tanks clustered around the exact mass center of Dragon Slayer.

The crew went to suit lockers, where they stripped down to briefs and put on tight-fitting wet suits with a complex array of hydraulic tubing, pressure bladders, and a full underwater breathing apparatus. They then climbed, one by one, into the spherical tanks. Abdul was ready first and climbed into the tank with the hatch that opened downward into the lounge. Pierre helped him in, closed the lid, checked the breathing air once more, got a final nod from Abdul and then purged all the air out of the tank, filling it completely with nearly incompressible water. He then checked out all the ultrasonic driver circuits that would send powerful currents to the piezoelectric drivers that would produce rapidly varying pressure waves from different sides of the tank to counteract the differential gravity fields that the water alone did not take care of.

Once he had Abdul safely in the tank, he turned and visited the rest of the crew. Amalita had checked out her equipment and was climbing into her tank, while Seiko Kauffmann Takahashi, with her typical Germanic thoroughness, was still checking out her air system. Jean was already in her tank and Doc had carried out the final checkout with her. Pierre floated by Seiko, and double checked Jean's tank for good measure. He took no chances, for if Jean's tank failed during the deorbiting maneuver and any of the water leaked out, then the beautiful body of Jean Kelly Thomas would be literally torn to shreds by the powerful tidal forces from the deorbiter that would yank at head and feet with a pull of 10,000 gees, while simultaneously compressing her about her waistline with 5000 gees.

"We would have to bottle her and pour her into the crematorium when we got back to St. George," he thought to himself. Pierre shook his head at the grisly thought and proceeded to climb into his own tank.

Pierre looked through his faceplate at the miniature control console built into the side of his tank. One viewing screen was divided into six sections. Each section held a picture of the inside of one of the tanks. He waited patiently as Seiko finished her methodical check of each one of her pressure bladders, closed her hatch cover, purged her remaining air, then turned to face her console pickup.

"Seiko Kauffmann Takahashi secured," intoned the stolid image, the short efficient oriental bob outlining the determined round face.

Pierre flashed a smile at all the screens. "I'll push the button for the down elevator," he said, touching a panel and flicking the screen controls to bring in a view of a large, rapidly spinning star in one corner and a glowing speck in another. The speck flashed occasionally as powerful rocket motors trimmed its course.

Through the long wait they could feel vibrations and slight accelerations that leaked through their water shields and pressure suits. These were vibrations from the ship's rockets, as the computer brought the spacecraft and the ultradense asteroid closer together.

"Down we go!" Pierre whispered into his throat mike, but he was only part way through the first phoneme when the asteroid passed by them. In a blink, they whirled halfway around the massive sphere and found themselves falling down toward the neutron star, the ship's engines firing at full blast to remove the angular momentum that had been imparted by the gravity whip.

The drop down into the fierce gravity well of Dragon's Egg only took two and a quarter minutes. All was quiet for most of the fall, but in the last few seconds—as they began to approach the neutron star—Pierre could feel the differential pressures of the tidal forces on the water in the tank. Then in a last instantaneous burst of feeling, Pierre's head was jerked about by a fierce acceleration. His ears ached and his hands and legs were jerked about by the second and third order tidal effects, as the piezoelectric drivers sang their ultrasonic cloak of protection into the water that surrounded him.

His eyes failed to see the glow of the deorbiter mass as it flashed again across his screen, leaving Dragon Slayer motionless in the center of the six compensator masses that were whirling about the neutron star and the spacecraft five times a second. "What a ride!" a female voice said over the intercom, masked by the excitement and the breathing mask.

"Time to get out of your swimming pools and get to work!" Pierre said to the faces on his screen. He fingered the pump control switch and felt the pressure drop inside his tank.

TIME: 09:45:00 GMT SUNDAY 19 JUNE 2050

Not many saw the faint star as Bright's Messenger left it at the center of Six Eyes. It had been too faint to see when it was in its high orbit above the star, since it did not have a glow of its own like the other stars in the sky. But once it was basking in the glow of Six Eyes, the speck reflected their radiance and could be seen by those worshipers of Bright with the best eyesight or the most faith.

"The new star in the center of Six Eyes does not move," the Chief Astrologer reported to Bright's-First, the High Priest. "The Six Eyes are almost motionless—however, they do rotate once every turn about the east pole. The new inner star is at the exact center of Six Eyes and does not move at all."

The High Priest was pleased with the news. Finally something logical was happening in the skies above Bright's Heaven.

"If the new star does not move in the sky, then it is like Bright —who also does not move. Many generations ago Bright sent down six of his eyes to keep careful watch on the unfaithful cheela of that time. It seems that Bright has approved of what he has been seeing, and he has sent down his inner eye of faith to look upon those who have been worshiping him for so long. This new eye is the Inner Eye of Bright."

TIME: 09:50:34 GMT SUNDAY 19 JUNE 2050

After exiting the tanks, the crew of Dragon Slayer gathered on the main console deck. The outside metallic micrometeorite shields had been pulled back from the six darkened viewing ports and they stared out. It was a dizzying sight, although they could feel no motion.

They were in a synchronous orbit 400 km out from the neutron star. To counteract the 41-million-gee gravitational pull from the nearby star, their spacecraft had to orbit about the star at five revolutions per second. Yet despite the rapid rotation they felt nothing because Dragon Slayer was stabilized to inertial space and did not try to keep a port facing the neutron star. It was good that it did not, for the centrifugal force in a spacecraft spinning around at five revolutions per second would have been enough to crush their bodies to a pulp against the outer bulkhead.

Since the spacecraft was orbiting but not spinning, this meant that the large, brilliant image of the neutron star flashed by each of the viewing ports five times a second, shining a flickering white glow on the walls of the central deck. Also visible through the ports was a ring of six, large, red ultra-dense asteroids only 200 meters away. They too whirled about the spacecraft five times a second, their glow alternating with the flashes from the distant neutron star.

Seiko took in the scene at one viewport with a quick professional glance. She then shut her eyes and went limp in the air. Her arms and legs were stretched out in all directions.

"What's the matter!" Cesar exclaimed, looking over at her with concern.

Seiko slowly opened one eye. "Don't be concerned, Doctor Wong, I was merely checking the tidal compensation," she said, slightly annoyed at being interrupted. "At 406 kilometers from the neutron star, the tidal gravity gradient should be 101 gees per meter. Even though my middle is in free-fall, my arms, legs and head try to go in different orbits. My feet are one meter closer to the star and should feel a pull of 202 gees. My head is one meter further than my middle and should also feel a pull of 202 gees, while my arms should feel a push of 101 gees.

"The six compensator masses also make tidal forces of the same magnitude, only they make tides of the opposite sign. I was just trying to see how accurately the two tides were compensating by using my hands and feet as crude accelerometers. I am surprised at how small the residual tide is. Only very near the hull can I sense any forces on my arms as the ship rotates." She closed her eyes again and continued to feel the play of the minute gravitational tugs coming twenty times a second on her hands and feet as the compensator masses and the neutron star whirled about the ship five times a second, rotating their four-lobed gravity pattern about the nonspinning ship.

After watching for some minutes, the crew began to be bothered by the flickering of the lights. By common consent, the metal shields were activated and slid back over the viewing ports, returning the main console room to its steady internal illumination. The crew then turned to their job, which was to examine the neutron star with instruments a lot more sophisticated than a naked human eye.

TIME: 06:26:30 GMT MONDAY 20 JUNE 2050

The Old One watched attentively as Sharp-Slicer carefully opened her laying orifice and deposited her egg at the entrance to the egg-pen. "That egg does not look right," the Old One said with a combination of concern and disapproval.

Sharp-Slicer looked at the egg-sac with her dozen dark red eyes. The egg was much smaller than normal, and very pale. "It didn't feel right while it was growing, either," she replied. "I hope it will be all right after it hatches."

"Don't worry, I and the other Old Ones will take good care of it," Loud-Talker said. "Perhaps it will grow bigger after it hatches and can get more food."

Relieved of her burden, Sharp-Slicer left the egg-pen and returned to her duties as Leader of the Clan. The egg would be well taken care of by the devoted Old Ones. Within a few turns, she had forgotten all about the incident. After all, when one was as old as she was, with a half-dozen eggs contributed to the egg-pen, they all seemed to blend into one another.

The pale egg got lots of attention, for all the Old Ones were very concerned about every one of the eggs entrusted to them. Loud-Talker took extra care to keep the pale little egg-sac sheltered at all times under the flared edge of skin that he used as a hatching mantle. He never forgot to roll the flattened oval sac over a full dozen times each turn, to keep the eggling inside properly exercised.

Loud-Talker was at first concerned when the time for hatching came and went, but soon thereafter he could feel the eggling stir inside the sac. It was with relief that he finally felt the warm flush of fluid under his mantle as the egg-sac burst and the eggling squirmed out.

Loud-Talker carefully rolled the other egg-sacs away from the new hatchling while still keeping them all under his hatching mantle. He maneuvered the hatchling to the edge of his mantle and let it come out.

"Pink eyes!" Loud-Talker exclaimed in amazement, his cool dark red eyes staring down at the small pale cheela. The dozen tiny pink eyes surrounding the white body of the new hatchling waved unsteadily as they stared up at the cold, dark sky.

His t'trum of amazement brought another Old One, who had been helping in the hatchling pen. The two Old Ones looked the new hatchling over with great concern. There was obviously something wrong with it, with its small size, pink eyes, and feverishly hot pale body.

"I have never seen a little one like this before," said the other Old One.

"I have not either," Loud-Talker said. "But when I was Leader of the Combined Clans, I heard from my advisors about hatchlings similar to this one. They are called Bright's Afflicted."

Loud-Talker flared another section of his skin and slowly passed it up and over the little one. "Why don't you take over the eggs for a while," he asked the other, "while I take this little hatchling out to the hatchling pen and give him something to eat?" Carefully prodding the little one along, he went out the entrance of the egg-pen to the feeding trough of the hatchling pen. There, Loud-Talker helped the hatchling put a tiny piece of pod into an intake orifice. Soon the little one was successfully finding and stuffing himself with more food, with almost no help from the Old One.

Loud-Talker watched the hatchling eat. He was clumsy, but then most hatchlings were clumsy until they had practiced eating for a few turns. However, this one seemed worse than the others. Loud-Talker formed a slender tendril and moved it close to one of the hot tiny pink eyes, but the eye did not withdraw into its protective fold until the tendril was almost upon it.

"Poor hatchling," Loud-Talker said. "I am afraid those pink eyes of yours do not serve you well." His protective instincts swelled, and from then on, the little hatchling became the special project of Loud-Talker.

Pink-Eyes ate and grew, but always stayed much smaller than the other hatchlings his age. He had courage, and tried to play in the rough-and-tumble games that hatchlings play, but his poor eyesight put him at a considerable disadvantage. The part of life in the hatchling pen that he liked best was listening to the stories of the clan storyteller.

Loud-Talker was the storyteller, for he had had many more experiences than the other Old Ones. After each storytelling session, the other hatchlings would rumble noisily away, pushing and shoving each other, while Pink-Eyes would stay and ask questions about life outside the hatchling pen. He questioned Loud-Talker about what it was like to be Leader of the Combined Clans and talk to a dozen greats of cheela at one time, and have them all listen quietly to the words.

"It must have been wonderful to have been so important, Old One Loud-Talker," Pink-Eyes said. "Why did you stop being Leader?"

"Well," Loud-Talker rumbled in wry humor, "I didn't really stop. It was just that someone bigger and stronger wanted to be Leader, and after discussing it with him for a while, I decided that I didn't want to be Leader of the Combined Clans any longer." He unconsciously formed a tendril and brushed it over a scar on his hide as he went on. "Besides, I was getting tired of being Leader. More and more I wanted to come and tend eggs and play with you hatchlings and tell you stories and do nothing else until I flow." Loud-Talker flared his protective mantle and brushed it over the feverish body of the eager little pale one while Pink-Eyes reflexively shrank to minimum area and reveled in the cool caress.

TIME: 06:30:00 GMT MONDAY 20 JUNE 2050

Abdul Nkomi Farouk's nimble brain woke up softly, ready for anything. He slowly opened his eyes and grinned inwardly at the sight of his brown arms floating aimlessly in front of him. He was awake, but they were still asleep.

"Get busy arms!" he thought to them. "You have a lot of button pushing to do today if we are ever going to get that neutron star mapped."

However, the first thing that the arms did was their now automatic twist and curl of the tips of Abdul's fierce black moustache. Abdul's eyes watched the arms in amusement. He then gave them his first direct command. Instantly his body dropped from its dreamlike trance and became one with his mind. He unsealed the sleeping cocoon and pushed off to the head.

TIME: 06:32:24 GMT MONDAY 20 JUNE 2050

It was nearly time for Pink-Eyes to leave the hatchling pen when Loud-Talker died. Loud-Talker was in the midst of his favorite activity; telling stories to the hatchlings. He was recounting the tale of the time he had led the forces of the Combined Clans in a punitive raid to drive back the barbarians in the north. He was just getting to the good part, where he personally hacked up a dozen barbarians at one time (the number of barbarians seemed to increase with each telling), when a fluid pump to his brain-knot failed. The constant muscular tension in his skin relaxed, and his body spread into a large, limp circle that flowed out and in between the hatchlings.

Pink-Eyes was shocked. This was not the first Old One that he had seen die, but the loss of his special friend and mentor was a great blow. He stayed rooted to the spot, not even moving when the butchering crew came to get the body. He was still there when the hatchlings returned from watching Loud-Talker converted into meat for the food bins.

While the others were busy eating, Pink-Eyes wandered out

the opening of the hatchling pen and went slowly off to climb a small mound just outside the clan camp.

As a leader of a clan that inhabited the eastern border of Bright's Empire, Sharp-Slicer always kept half her tread listening to the constant murmurs in the crust. Her clan was subject to many attacks by the barbarians, and although she had good warriors out on watch duty, she never relaxed. She paused now as something unusual rippled through the crust under her tread. It was very faint, and very high-pitched. It was not a sentry alarm, but it definitely didn't sound like the usual busy noises of the clan camp.

The strange ripple sounded like a voice from a hatchling pen, but her trained directional senses placed it well outside the camp boundaries. She moved to the edge of the camp where the high-pitched ripple now came more clearly. She then saw the source, a faint pale spot on top of a nearby rise. Sharp-Slicer moved toward it; as she got closer, she realized that the pale spot was the Bright's Afflicted hatchling, Pink-Something-or-Other.

She was annoyed that the hatchling had been allowed to wander off this far from the camp, but then again, there had been some confusion at the hatchling pen when Loud-Talker had flowed. Besides, the hatchling was probably old enough by now to be given some work, although Sharp-Slicer had a hard time thinking of what such a small, poorly-sighted one could do.

As Sharp-Slicer approached the base of the rise, she could hear the high-pitched voice through the crust. She was surprised at how well the tiny ripples seemed to travel. She stopped to listen.

"O Bright One in the sky. Why do you punish me so, for I have done nothing wrong. I have always worshiped you as I should," Pink-Eyes said. "You have inflicted this miserable pale body upon me—and now you have taken my only friend. Why? Oh why?"

Sharp-Slicer was a little bewildered that the youngster seemed so attached to the Old One. She had respected Loud-Talker herself. After all, anyone would respect an ex-Leader of the Combined Clans. But he was meat now—there was nothing left to respect. She supposed that this unseemly sorrow over a hunk of meat was just one of the many strange things that was wrong with the poor youngster. She rumbled a call in his direction.

"You—come down at once, and return to the compound!" she said. "You know there are barbarians not far away."

Pink-Eyes was startled at the voice booming through the crust, for his eyes had been busy trying to make out the blur that was all he could see of Bright, and he had not noticed the Clan Leader's approach. He was awed at being addressed personally by the Leader of the Clan, and quickly flowed down the hill and started back to the camp, but a command from Sharp-Slicer brought him to a stop.

"Wait!" Sharp-Slicer said. "Since you now feel that you can just wander out of the hatchling pen whenever you want to, perhaps you are too big for the hatchery. What is your name and age, youngster?"

"My name is Pink-Eyes and I have aged a dozen greats of turns, O Leader of the Clan," Pink-Eyes responded respectfully.

Sharp-Slicer flowed over and looked at him closely. He was small, much too small for training as a warrior or hunter, and even too small for tending crops. She was going to have a hard time finding something useful for this one to do. She finally had an idea.

"You are to go to the clan astrologer and tell him that the Leader of the Clan said that you are to train to be an apprentice astrologer," she ordered.

Pink-Eyes was delighted that he had finally been given something useful to do, and immediately flowed off toward the astrologers' compound.

Sharp-Slicer watched the eager youngster flow off, and then returned to more important business, having never connected the pale youngster with the pale egg that she had left at the egg-pen so long ago.

TIME: 06:32:30 GMT MONDAY 20 JUNE 2050

Cesar was busy at the science experiments console. Now that they had settled in over the east magnetic pole, it was time to start the survey instruments. The IR and UV scanners were busy, and the high resolution visible camera was taking shot after shot of small regions in the mountainous territory in the east pole region. Even the neutrino and gravitational radiation detectors were operational on the possibility that a crustquake might occur, although the chances of that happening were not high.

Cesar now readied the laser radar mapper. He first set it in the short pulse mode to get the best resolution on the mountains directly below Dragon Slayer. He checked over the laser parameters as they appeared on the screen.

```
LASER RADAR MAPPER:
WAVELENGTH 0.3 MICROMETERS
PULSE WIDTH 1.0 PICOSEC (0.6 MM RESOLUTION)
PEAK PULSE POWER 1 GW
PULSE REP RATE 1,000,000 PULSES/SEC
SPOT SIZE 60 CM DIAMETER.
```

Satisfied with the setup, Cesar leaned forward. "Proceed with laser radar mapper scan!" he said. "Circular scan from sub-surface point out to five kilometers radius!"

Cesar watched as the screen blanked and the image of Dragon's Egg appeared on the screen. He then saw a track of tiny little circles, each one representing a spot where the laser radar had reflected its beam off the crust of the neutron star, slowly winding its way outward in an ever expanding spiral.

"The spiral scan will take about eight minutes," he murmured to himself. He watched for a few seconds and then his fingers flickered over the keyboard as he moved on to set up the next experiment.

TIME: 06:39:55 GMT MONDAY 20 JUNE 2050

"I don't want to complain, but I don't want him around," the clan astrologer complained to Sharp-Slicer. "When you first sent Pink-Eyes to apprentice with me, I was willing to give him a try, even if he does look strange. He was eager, and tried very hard, but when we found out that his eyes are so poor that Bright and the Eyes are only blurs, and that he cannot even see most of the other stars in the sky, it was obvious that he could never be an astrologer. If you cannot see the stars, then how can you make astrological predictions?

"Despite that," the clan astrologer went on, "I did find him useful in helping me with the worship services. His voice is high, but the ripples carry well. I use him for all the chants, and have him take care of the worship symbols. But now, I am afraid that I will have to get rid of him. He's blasphemous."

"What!" exclaimed Sharp-Slicer.

"Yes," the clan astrologer said. "For a long time, as an apprentice, he kept saying that the Inner Eye of Bright was flashing on and off. We finally convinced him that it was just his poor eyesight tricking him, but recently he has been saying that every dozen turns or so, the flashes get brighter and brighter, and then fade away again. The last time occurred a few turns ago. He even dragged me up to the top of his silly hill and kept saying to me, 'Look at them! Look at those brilliant flashes! Are you blind, Old One!'

"I don't mind being called an Old One, for it is not long before I will get to play with the hatchlings," the clan astrologer went on. "But to be called blind by that nearly sightless freak is more than I can stand. Besides, he is going around telling everyone that Bright's Inner Eye is signaling to him—him alone!"

Sharp-Slicer looked at the seven points of light hanging nearly motionless over the east pole. She did not often look at the sky, as she was too preoccupied with running the clan here on the crust. However, if there had been bright flashes from the Inner Eye, she certainly would have noticed them. She normally did not pay much attention to religion, but, as Leader of the Clan, she was automatically Chief Worshiper of Bright at holy times, and it wouldn't do to let things be disrupted by an obviously deranged individual.

"I guess the Bright's Afflicted has other problems besides paleness and poor eyesight," she said. "However, times are good, so we will just let him get by without having to do any work."

Pink-Eyes was not happy with his new status. He felt worthless, and spent most of his time off away from the clan camp, gazing at the blurry shapes of Bright and the Eyes, talking to the spots of light and himself, and dreaming that he was Leader of the Combined Clans, speaking to the multitudes that gathered around him to hear his words of wisdom.

TIME: 06:40:35 GMT MONDAY 20 JUNE 2050

The console screen flashed, and Cesar looked up. Across the top of the screen appeared the words:

LASER RADAR MAPPER SCAN COMPLETE.

Cesar struck a few keys and the IR image that he had been examining disappeared and was replaced with the command setup for the laser radar mapping experiment.

For the next segment of the scan, the laser beam would be shooting obliquely across the curved surface of Dragon's Egg, and the equipment could now obtain both high resolution height and surface position information if it were set up to use a chirped pulse. Soon the laser was chirping in frequency from the visible up to the ultraviolet region, while the pulse repetition rate was lowered to 100,000 pulses per second.

Cesar set up the laser mapper to scan a one radian sector, starting from the edge of the five-kilometer circle that he had already mapped and extending out for another five kilometers—well over the curve of Dragon's Egg. He then watched as the sector scan started, the narrow fan beam taking about one second per sweep as it slowly crept outward toward the west.

TIME: 06:40:46 GMT MONDAY 20 JUNE 2050

Pink-Eyes made his way up the slight rise just outside the clan camp. He had been so sure that Bright had been talking to him through Bright's Inner Eye, but no one would believe him.

"Yet—it was so bright!" Pink-Eyes said to himself. "Such dazzling, brilliant flashes of pure light. It was Bright incarnate! Yet Bright would not let them see! Why? Why?? Why???"

Pink-Eyes rested once again on the low rise. Using the prayers and chants that he had so faithfully rippled into the crust every worship time, he again sought comfort from one who seemed to have inflicted nearly every indignity upon him—except death.

Pink-Eyes felt his small sharp knife in his personal weapons pouch, and drew it out. He looked at it for a long while, con-

sidering . . . He dropped the knife to the crust, where it lay, its
tiny point shattered by the fall.

Pink-Eyes knew that his clan would not allow him to starve,
even though they refused to let him share in the work, but he resolved never to return. Without looking back, he set forth toward
the east, directly into the wilderness—the territory of the barbarians. The sentry guards, used to the wanderings of this strange
pale one of the clan, let him pass outward without challenge.

Pink-Eyes had no plan. Having been rejected by the clan, his
only thought was to leave. He knew he was in danger from the
barbarians, but the thought of meeting death at the points of
their spears held no terror for him. He traveled onward, drawn
toward the pattern of lights over the east pole that slowly rotated, once a turn.

Pink-Eyes found some partially ripe pods on an isolated wild
plant, and was slowly savoring the first food he had had in many
turns when he stopped, struck with awe. The Inner Eye had sent
out a brilliant, long-lasting, multicolored beam of light down
ahead of him. The beam was unlike the others that he had seen
previously. Those had been short flashes of light, so fast and so
intense that there was no color to them. These were like silent
words of rolling crustquakes. They started in the deep red and
slowly—taking their time—swept through strange colors into a
radiating brilliance. Pink-Eyes waited, and shortly was rewarded
by another dazzling display. As if in a trance, he put the pods
into a storage pouch and moved off toward the beam of light. It
came again and again, and soon he began to depend upon its
regularity.

As Pink-Eyes moved forward to intercept the beam, he noticed
that it was slowly moving off to the north. A short while later, he
saw that it had stopped its northward movement. It now seemed
to be coming closer and closer with every lengthy blink. He
moved to intercept its southward path, and finally stopped and
waited for it to come to him. As the turn passed he watched the
brilliant, multicolored display get brighter and brighter.

Then suddenly it was on him. His eyes ducked reflexively
under their flaps while the crust around him sparkled with multicolored glints, but the strangest feeling of all was the warmth
on his topside. It tingled and felt good, so good it was like having sex with a god. Pink-Eyes writhed in pleasure under the

beaming ray, his pale body automatically thinning out to absorb the delightful feeling. Then almost as suddenly as it had come, the feeling stopped.

Bewildered, Pink-Eyes drew himself into shape and waited. A short while later the beam came down again, this time off to the south. His eyes could now stand the glare, while his topside only felt a slight tingle of the intense feeling that it had experienced just a few moments ago. Pink-Eyes tried to keep up, but the blinking light moved too rapidly for him, and left him behind in its progress across the crust.

Pink-Eyes waited, his eyes gazing upward, as the beautiful beam slowly blinked its way southward. He was sure it would return, so he waited, only moving to find some food to sustain him, until he saw the beam come closer again. When it finally arrived, he was ready, his small, pale body thinned out to its maximum to receive the warm caress of the light. The beam struck him, and he reveled in sexual pleasure, his tread kneading the crust in a paroxysm of prayer. "Bright! O Bright!! Pour down your blessing of love on me. Thank you! O thank you for rewarding your faithful servant!"

For dozens of turns, Pink-Eyes existed in the wilderness, communing with the Inner Eye of Bright as its beam of love and pleasure swept by every half-dozen turns. His slow wandering path took him steadily back toward his old clan camp as his pace over the crust matched the steady motion of the scanning beam. As Pink-Eyes moved along, he became more and more convinced that he—and he alone—had been called to bring the Word of Bright to the cheela.

Fortified spiritually, Pink-Eyes finally broke away from his addiction to the intense sexual pleasure of the beam. He now moved more swiftly, and left the beam behind him. The beam was still making its north and south movement over the crust while slowly creeping westward. Pink-Eyes went directly toward the clan camp. He made his way slowly up to the top of the mound near the camp where he had previously communed with Bright. He began to preach, his high-pitched voice, now strong with undoubting assurance, rippling through the crust.

"Prepare! Prepare, all people! For the Blessing of Bright will soon be on you!" sounded Pink-Eyes' voice.

At first, only the perimeter guards came to investigate the

source of the voice. When they saw who it was and heard his strange speech, they jeered and moved back to their posts. After a few guard shifts, most of the clan knew of the strange rantings of the Bright's Afflicted. The news finally reached the clan astrologer, who went immediately to Sharp-Slicer.

"We must do something," the clan astrologer said.

Sharp-Slicer agreed. "You are right. Let us go and try to get him to be sensible and stop."

Sharp-Slicer, the clan astrologer, and a group of warriors went out to the mound. As they approached, they could hear Pink-Eyes preaching to a small group of heckling warriors and older hatchlings.

"Repent and pray!" Pink-Eyes was saying. "Repent! For soon the Blessing of Bright will be upon you!"

Sharp-Slicer thudded her tread against the crust. "Pink-Eyes! Stop that nonsense and come down here!"

"No!" Pink-Eyes said. "I now obey a higher leader than you!" Pink-Eyes reached a tendril into a pouch that had been closed since he left the hatchling pens, and pulled out his clan totem.

"I am no longer of this clan," Pink-Eyes said, holding the clan totem up so that all could see. He dropped the totem and it shattered on the crust, sending a little shock wave through the disturbed treads of all around.

"I have been called by Bright," Pink-Eyes said, "to lead all the people of all the clans to greater worship of him."

"This is enough," the clan astrologer whispered to Sharp-Slicer. "Stop his ranting!"

Sharp-Slicer took command of the situation, although unwillingly. It was a distasteful duty to punish someone who was obviously mentally sick, but by destroying his clan totem, Pink-Eyes had lost the protection of the clan.

"Since you have destroyed your totem," Sharp-Slicer said in a loud voice, "you yourself have left the clan. Therefore, I command you to leave clan territory."

Her dozen eyes shifted to pick out three warriors who were nearby. "I want you three to escort this self-proclaimed barbarian to the border. Do not let him return. If he does not leave, turn him into meat!"

The three warriors moved slowly up the hill, none of them even bothering to pull a slicer or pricker from a weapons pouch, for any one of them was more than a match for the frail body of Pink-Eyes.

"Halt!" Pink-Eyes said to the warriors, and they hesitated, slightly bewildered at the strange behavior. Looking north, Pink-Eyes saw the beam approaching the mound. He turned all of his eyes upward toward the Eyes and started to pray, ignoring the warriors.

"O Great Bright! Show these wicked unbelievers the love that you can give to them if they become your true followers." The warriors continued to hesitate, uneasy over interrupting a prayer —yet their treads were rippling lightly with suppressed humor.

Sharp-Slicer was in the midst of stamping a sharp command to the hesitating warriors when suddenly she felt herself flattening in a frenzy of glowing sexual pleasure. Her eyes, writhing on extended eye-stubs, could see others also flowing and thinning out around her. She felt the edge of the nearby clan astrologer flowing over one side of her, partially blocking the intense warmth. A male tread on her topside—normally a pleasurable feeling—did not feel good enough, and she contracted and withdrew herself to bask her entire topside in the more sublime pleasure that poured down from the sky.

As she wiggled in enjoyment, she could hear Pink-Eyes' high-pitched voice coming through the crust. "Come—all of you—receive the Blessing of Bright that I bring to you."

The pleasure grew more and more intense, then it stopped. Slowly Sharp-Slicer, the clan astrologer and the others regained their normal shape. Exhausted, they waited motionless while Pink-Eyes spoke.

"I have brought you the Blessing of Bright," he said. "It will be yours again if you will believe in Bright and will worship him."

"I believe!" one of the warriors cried. "Bring down the Blessing of Bright on me again!"

"First we must worship Bright properly," Pink-Eyes said. "To do that, we must all go into the clan camp and pray. In a half-dozen turns I want all the clan to be gathered and worshiping Bright in the temple area."

Sharp-Slicer said nothing as the others hastened off to tell the rest of the clan about the miracle and the commands of Pink-Eyes. She did not like losing authority to this pale excuse for a cheela, but with Bright seeming to back him, she had little choice.

Six turns later, the whole clan was gathered in the temple area and listening to Pink-Eyes as he preached. Their bodies filled the temple to overflowing. Pink-Eyes had allowed the clan astrologer to start the worship service, but he soon took over with a lengthy, hypnotic sermon.

Sharp-Slicer listened to the worship service from the fringes of the crowd. She had not neglected her duties as Leader of the Clan, despite the interruption caused by Pink-Eyes. Since Pink-Eyes had insisted that even the perimeter guards attend the worship services, she made sure that she and the other good warriors were on the periphery of the crowd, in case of a barbarian attack. Also, despite their protests, she made the Old Ones stay outside the egg and hatchling pens.

"When the Blessing of Bright comes on you, it will be just as if you were having sex," she tried to explain to Hard-Rock, the Old One in charge of the eggs. "You will lose control of your body, and may damage an egg while you are thrashing around."

"What do you mean!" Hard-Rock protested. "I am too old for sex. All I want to do is tend my eggs."

However, when Pink-Eyes brought down the Blessing of Bright on the worshiping clan, Hard-Rock felt a sexual surge that was more intense than the best experience of his youth. His body thinned and his eyes stared out from extended stems as his topside was bathed in the warming beam. Then—just at the end of the Blessing—Hard-Rock, his eyes gazing upward at the Eyes in pleasure, saw a faint glimmering beam of deep-colored light pouring down upon him.

"I see it! I see it!!" Hard-Rock shouted. "I believe! I believe!!"

Hard-Rock, instantly converted, left his precious eggs without another glance and moved through the recovering crowd. As he made his way he kept repeating, "I saw! I believe! I want to follow you, bringer of the Word of Bright!"

Pink-Eyes questioned Hard-Rock carefully, and finally was convinced that Hard-Rock had seen a dim version of the dazzling, multicolored display that was so obvious to him. When the next beam came down to the north of them, Pink-Eyes had Hard-Rock look up at the Eyes, but the beam, not being directly on him, was just barely visible to Hard-Rock.

Any remaining thought that he had been imagining things left
Pink-Eyes completely, now that his visions of light from the Eyes
had been confirmed. He again turned his eyes to the crowd and
spoke. "I am Bright's chosen one," he announced. "I give you
the glowing love of Bright, and I bring to you his Word."

"Yes!" Hard-Rock broke in. "Listen to the Chosen of God, and
obey!"

Pink-Eyes turned his eyes toward Hard-Rock. He formed a
pale tendril and curled it around one of Hard-Rock's eye-stubs.
"You are one of Bright's chosen ones too, Hard-Rock," he said.
"I want you to come with me on my mission."

"I obey, God's-Chosen," Hard-Rock said; and without hesitation, the hardened veteran reached into a pouch that had not
been opened for five dozen greats of turns. He removed his clan
totem, raised it high, and let it crash to the crust.

Pink-Eyes called Sharp-Slicer to him and announced, "I will
travel to the west to bring the Word of Bright to the rest of the
clans. I will need food, and warriors for protection."

"Yes, O God's-Chosen," Sharp-Slicer said, relieved that this
perplexing individual would soon leave and allow the life of the
clan to resume its normal pattern. "We will obey."

At the next turn Pink-Eyes, now reverently addressed as
God's-Chosen, moved off to the west with a large party of followers, Hard-Rock the foremost among them, and surrounded by
a small contingent of worshipful warriors. Sharp-Slicer had a
hard time keeping more of her people from leaving. Fortunately,
God's-Chosen had helped by preaching that Bright wanted them
to stay to take care of the eggs and hatchlings, and protect
Bright's Empire from the barbarians.

The procession moved slowly across the crust toward the next
clan. A small group led by Hard-Rock was sent ahead with the
message that God's-Chosen was coming to bring down the Blessing of Bright upon them all. Although Hard-Rock was well
known in the next clan, it was an incredulous group that gathered around God's-Chosen as he stopped at the edge of the clan
compound to meet with No-Fear, the Leader of the Clan, and
his clan astrologer.

"Why are you bothering our people, clanless one?" spoke No-
Fear sharply.

"I only wish to bring them the Word and Blessing of Bright,

O Leader of the Clan," God's-Chosen said politely. "I know that you have a hard time believing me, but I tell you that I am Bright's chosen one. Believe in me and you shall receive his Blessing."

"I don't like him," the clan astrologer whispered to No-Fear.

"I am suspicious myself," No-Fear said. "But Hard-Rock has fought beside me in many battles with the barbarians, and he is not only convinced that this funny pale one tells the truth, but he insists that he can see the Blessing beam himself."

"I still don't like it," the clan astrologer complained again.

"All he asks is to be allowed to use the temple to pray to Bright," No-Fear said. "That is what the temple is for, so what harm can there be in that?"

"Yet . . ." complained the clan astrologer, perturbed over possibly losing some of his authority in the clan, "it is the words that he will preach that bother me. He insists that he is the chosen one of Bright. That cannot be. If Bright were to choose a cheela to send his word by, it would be a strong, heroic person, not that insignificant caricature of a cheela."

"Still," No-Fear protested, "he may be right, and I would not want to risk a curse from Bright for ignoring the bringer of his Word." No-Fear turned his eyes toward the pale one.

"We will let you use the clan temple, God's-Chosen," said No-Fear, "if you will be sure to bring down the Blessing of Bright upon us."

Pink-Eyes turned a few of his eyes to the south, where he saw the multicolored beam off in the distance.

"We will rest this turn," he replied. "But on the next turn I want the entire clan in the temple, and I shall bring the Blessing of Bright upon you all, for I feel that you believe."

"Well! I don't believe," whispered the clan astrologer to No-Fear. "No one can order the God Bright around. If he fails in the coming turn, I want you to order the clanless one turned into meat for speaking such outrageous blasphemy."

"I had already made that decision," No-Fear said quietly. "He may be able to fool his own clan, but he will not fool us."

The bringer of Bright's Word was not fooling. With the next turn, the following of God's-Chosen grew. On the succeeding turn God's-Chosen left the newly converted clan and a puzzled but convinced clan astrologer. The astrologer had asked for and received a special prayer that he could use, for he was going to change his temple worship services to thank Bright for having sent the Bringer of the Word during his lifetime.

As the caravan of the followers of God's-Chosen moved slowly west, bringing the Blessing of Bright down upon clan after clan, the word of the strange happenings on the eastern border reached Hungry-Swift, the Leader of the Combined Clans. It sounded serious enough to cause him to investigate personally. Taking a squad of needle troopers with him, he moved quickly along the pathways of Bright's Empire, his troopers clearing the often-crowded way for him. Finally, Hungry-Swift cautiously arranged a meeting with God's-Chosen and his followers.

Hungry-Swift was too much of a politician to use his power ostentatiously. He left his troopers and came alone to visit with the holy one. He had heard descriptions of the miracle worker, but still was not prepared for the tiny pale body, and especially the pink eyes. Feeling no fear from the little one, he went forward to meet him.

"Greeting, God's-Chosen," he said. "I hear strange tales about your work."

"They are not tales, Hungry-Swift," God's-Chosen said. "They are the true Word of Bright."

"Tell me more," Hungry-Swift asked. "For what I have heard has come through many treads and has been distorted in the telling."

God's-Chosen had been keeping his traveling band well ahead of the sweeping beam. He found it better to keep the number of blessings to his followers down, so they would not get too used to it. Besides, if any of them ever figured out that the Blessing of Bright came every half-dozen turns, whether he called for it or not, they would soon be able to receive the Blessing without having the Word of Bright preached to them. His practiced eyes found the beam in the north, and he gauged its motion.

"I could tell you much, Hungry-Swift, but you still would find it hard to believe," God's-Chosen said. "Come with me for a journey alone into the wilderness. Together we will pray and you shall have the Blessing of Bright come upon you alone. Gather food for three turns and come with me."

"Why wait three turns?" Hungry-Swift complained. "Why not now?"

God's-Chosen looked at him severely. "Because you do not believe," he said. "And it will take three turns before I can get you to believe enough to receive the Blessing of Bright."

Hungry-Swift could only agree that God's-Chosen had judged the level of his disbelief correctly. He did not believe in this charlatan at all, and he doubted that three turns of preaching would change him a bit. However, the stories that he had heard of this strange one were not distorted, but often came from some of his best trooper commanders, who naturally had investigated anything that could perturb the security of the far-flung borders of Bright's Empire.

Hungry-Swift hated to waste three turns, but if that was what it would take to clear up this mystery, he was willing to do it. If it turned out that there was no mystery, he personally would make sure that there would not be enough left of the pale body to bother collecting for the meat bins. Still, the miracle worker did seem to be very confident and unafraid.

"I will go with you, God's-Chosen," Hungry-Swift said. "Lead the way."

The two loaded their pouches with a small amount of food and then God's-Chosen took them to the northeast to meet the beam sweeping down from the north. The trooper squad leader had protested the idea of Hungry-Swift traveling without protection in the wilderness between clan camps, but Hungry-Swift brushed off his protests.

"We are well within the outer borders and there are no barbarians in this region," he said. "And I hope you don't think that I can't handle that pale priest by myself. If I were just to tread on him lightly I would burst him like an egg-sac."

As they journeyed into the wilderness, God's-Chosen tried to preach continuously, but Hungry-Swift would take the opportunity during pauses to ask personal questions about the earlier times when God's-Chosen had been called Pink-Eyes. After hearing of what Pink-Eyes had gone through as a hatchling and youngster, and about his conversion in the wilderness, Hungry-Swift gained a grudging admiration for the courage that seemed to fill the tiny body. Soon, Hungry-Swift stopped noticing that the personality that was God's-Chosen/Pink-Eyes inhabited anything less than a normal body. He was continually being surprised that Pink-Eyes was not of normal size, as, for example, when he had to ask for help to pick a pod high up on the side of a petal plant.

As their line of travel came closer and closer to intersecting the path of the beam from the Inner Eye, the preaching of God's-Chosen became more and more intense. Hungry-Swift listened intently, for he now respected God's-Chosen, but he had to admit that despite all the preaching, he still did not believe that his companion was Bright's chosen one, and that he could bring the Blessing of Bright down upon him.

"I listen, God's-Chosen," Hungry-Swift said. "But I still have trouble with my belief."

"Even the act of confessing your disbelief is a motion in the right direction," God's-Chosen said. Then turning all of his eyes upward, and slowly counting off the moments since the previous flash of the beam just to the north of him, he chanted.

"Help, O Bright! Help this unbeliever find faith! Bring down the Blessing of Bright upon Hungry-Swift."

Hungry-Swift's eyes followed those of God's-Chosen up to the strange formation of seven lights that hung overhead in the sky. He was calmly wondering how they managed to stay in one place while the rest of the stars in the sky moved from east to west—when suddenly his body seemed to explode with pleasure.

For what seemed like an eternity, Hungry-Swift reveled in the heaven-sent pleasure of Bright's love. His eye-stubs reached out toward the Eyes in an attempt to copulate with the stars. They writhed back and forth, stretching to their limit—then suddenly they froze as they saw the beam coming down from the Inner Eye of Bright.

"I see! I see!!" he shouted. Then as quickly as it had come, the warmth stopped.

Hungry-Swift composed himself and self-consciously wiped the dribbles of yellow-white mating fluid from the orifice under each eye-stub. As he gathered his senses, he could hear God's-Chosen praying.

"Thank you, O Bright, for bringing the Vision as well as the Blessing to the Leader of the Combined Clans. I pray that you will guide him to lead all the clans into greater worship of you."

Completely convinced, Hungry-Swift also prayed. As Leader of the Combined Clans, he was automatically the head worshiper of Bright. However, the ritual chants that he had learned to use in the worship services now seemed completely inadequate, and he clumsily made up his own prayers.

"Lead me, O Bright," he said. "Give me your Word, and I will follow it with all that I command."

"I will give you Bright's Word," God's-Chosen said. "For too long Bright has been neglected. Bright has been good to his people. They have grown in numbers and have prospered. What used to be a small clan gathered in the city of Bright's Heaven is now many clans that are spread out over Bright's Empire—so powerful that the barbarians shrink from angering them. Yet what have the ungrateful cheela done for Bright in return?"

"We worship him often," Hungry-Swift protested.

"Yes, but where?" God's-Chosen asked. "In tiny temple areas. What Bright deserves is a temple appropriate to his greatness."

"Tell me what is needed," pleaded Hungry-Swift.

"You shall build a Holy Temple. It shall be in the shape of Bright, in whose likeness we are but imperfect copies. The outer walls shall be a perfect circle, and a dozen greats of cheela shall be able to line up from one side of the circle to the other without crowding their edges."

Hungry-Swift was appalled. "That will be almost as big as the city of Bright's Heaven!"

"Yes," God's-Chosen went on, unperturbed. "For it must hold all who live in Bright's Heaven, plus many others. At one dozen places about the circle there shall be placed walls representing the eye-stubs of a cheela at full alert. At the ends of each eye-stub shall be a round mound representing the eyes. Between each pair of eye-stubs there shall be an opening in the Temple walls, representing the orifices that allow things to enter and leave the inner mysteries of Bright's body. Finally, at the very center of the inner area, there shall be a circular mound representing Bright's Inner Eye."

"I will obey, God's-Chosen," Hungry-Swift said. "The Holy Temple to Bright will be built as you say."

Still dazed, Hungry-Swift followed God's-Chosen back to the two encampments. When the squad leader came out to greet them, it was obvious from Hungry-Swift's demeanor that the Leader of the Combined Clans had felt the Blessing of Bright. He was even more awed when he learned that the Leader had also seen the Blessing, since very few had been allowed by

Bright to receive this indication of being one of his chosen ones.
The journey into the wilderness over, Hungry-Swift automatically resumed command.

"Call the troopers to alert," he ordered. "We return to Bright's
Heaven at once, for there is much to do."

Before he left, Hungry-Swift returned for one last visit to his
friend and teacher.

"Are you God?" he asked.

"No," God's-Chosen said. "Bright is God. I am merely Bright's
vehicle by which he sends his Word and his Blessing. You have
received the Word. Go and carry it out. Yours will not be an
easy task, for it will take a dozen greats of turns to create a temple of that size. But do not worry about the time, for Bright is
patient. I will stay here and bring the Blessing of Bright to all
the clans. That too will take time, but by the time you have the
Holy Temple built, I will have brought the Blessing of Bright to
all here in the east and will come to Bright's Heaven to bring the
Blessing down on all who live there—on the Holy Temple itself."

"Bright give me strength that I might live to see the time,"
said Hungry-Swift.

"Your work will keep you strong," God's-Chosen said. "Now
go!"

At first Hungry-Swift experienced resistance to the project of
building the Holy Temple. There were even rumors that some of
the underleaders, or even one of the nearby clan leaders, might
attempt a formal challenge to his leadership.

Hungry-Swift quickly eliminated all objections to the building
of the Temple by insisting that everyone with any power or authority take a journey to the east to be initiated by God's-Chosen
into the mysteries of the Blessing of Bright. As the converts returned, the enthusiasm for the project grew.

Fortunately the barbarians were quiet during these times, and
the crops grew well without excessive tending, for soon nearly
one-third of the population of Bright's Heaven and surrounding
areas was engaged in hauling rocks and loose crustal material to
form the outline of a cheela at perfect alert, with twelve round
eyes perched out on extended eye-stubs. The first thing built was
a round mound at the center that represented the Inner Eye of
Bright. Then as the outline of the Holy Temple grew, the old
worship area was abandoned and services were held inside the

growing Temple, with the High Priest speaking from the Inner Eye mound.

As the greats of turns passed, God's-Chosen moved slowly west, pausing to make sure that each clan camp was given the Blessing of Bright. As they moved nearer and nearer to Bright's Heaven, the clan camps became closer and closer together. They also began to spread more widely to the north and south, because the population pressure had overcome the natural reluctance to engage in travel in the hard direction. It soon became impossible for God's-Chosen to bring the Blessing to each camp himself. There also came rumors of small groups of cheela who had received the Blessing out in the wilderness without God's-Chosen being anywhere near. God's-Chosen then decided that the time had come to give to others the power to bring the Blessing. Since some could see the beam if it were near, he made them his disciples. He sent them off in the hard directions, north and south, with instructions to take the Word to the clans there. They were to watch the Inner Eye carefully and, as the beam approached, time their worship services with the receiving of the Blessing of Bright. The results were not as satisfactory as the well-preached services that God's-Chosen conducted, but more and more of the cheela in the great Empire felt the miracle of the Blessing of Bright.

As the greats of turns passed, the Holy Temple neared completion. Nearly all who worked on it had taken time off now to complete a pilgrimage to the east to receive the Blessing from God's-Chosen, and all returned to work with renewed vigor. When God's-Chosen reached the outskirts of the sprawling city of Bright's Heaven, he left his preaching to Hard-Rock and went ahead to see the Holy Temple.

When Hungry-Swift heard of the approach of God's-Chosen to the city, he came out with an honor guard of troopers to greet him. As they moved along the pathway to the city, the troopers would move ahead, lining the pathway and keeping the curious multitudes from bothering God's-Chosen and the Leader of the Combined Clans as they moved leisurely along, their pace limited by the small tread of God's-Chosen.

The crowds that gathered along the pathway were well behaved. The troopers would suffer hatchlings to ooze between them, or allow an eye-stub to be rested on their topsides (especially if the eye-stub belonged to a nubile one of the opposite sex). The onlookers were treated to an unusual sight: a huge battle-scarred warrior with an obvious air of command, who carried the highest rank in Bright's Empire, maintaining pace and speaking deferentially to a tiny, pale, pink-eyed, clanless one. Yet the pale one had an air of assurance about him that caused the crowd to murmur as he passed. Occasional cheers radiated outward from small groups as the two made their way into the city.

"How is the Holy Temple proceeding?" God's-Chosen asked.

"The basic foundation is done, O God's-Chosen," Hungry-Swift said. "And the finishing work is well under way. We should have it completed well before the Blessing of Bright is due to come down upon the Temple grounds."

"Good," God's-Chosen said. "I would like to see it."

As the two took the path to the south to visit the Temple, a squad of troopers formed a chevron in front of them and pushed their way into the hard direction. The two leaders moved comfortably along behind the pathbreakers. As they came closer to the Holy Temple, even God's-Chosen was impressed, for the outer walls of the Temple seemed to extend almost to the horizon in both directions.

"It is a fitting monument to the honor of Bright," he said with obvious satisfaction.

"Yes," Hungry-Swift said. "All of us who worked on it are extremely proud that we were allowed to contribute to such an impressive edifice. As you commanded, a dozen greats of cheela can fit between the outer walls. One of the astrologers calculated that the Holy Temple can hold a great of greats of greats of cheela within its walls."

"May we bring down the Blessing of Bright upon them all," said God's-Chosen.

The two, together with their honor guard, approached the walls of the Temple. They passed between two of the circular mounds that represented two of the outer eyes of Bright, and moved between the narrowing walls that represented the eye-stubs, until they came to a break in the wall between the two eye-stubs that was one of the entrances to the inner portion of the Temple of Holies.

As they passed through the Temple orifice and entered the

inner yard, God's-Chosen knew that he had been right. This was the Word of Bright! Ahead he could see the Inner Eye mound, but all around him was a horizon of wall that blocked off the view of the city, leading the eyes naturally upward to look at Bright toward the south and the Eyes of Bright to the east.

As they entered the Temple, they could see a small crowd around the base of the Inner Eye mound.

"We have come just at the end of a worship service," Hungry-Swift said. "Bright's-First, the High Priest, is on the Inner Eye mound now. Let us go to meet him."

They made their way to the rear of the crowd around the mound as the service ended. God's-Chosen was then bewildered to see a line of cheela, each dragging a sled piled with food, slowly making its way up the mound. At the top, the supplicants left their sleds, where they were taken by apprentice astrologers, while the supplicant went up to the High Priest and slowly rotated around once, while the High Priest touched each eye, one after the other, murmuring as he did so.

"What is going on?" God's-Chosen asked of one of the cheela slowly pulling his heavy burden up the slope of the mound.

"I am bringing my dozeth, and have come to get my blessing," the cheela said.

The tread of God's-Chosen rippled sharply on the crust. "What dozeth, and what blessing?"

The cheela's eye-stubs wavered randomly in bewilderment, and Hungry-Swift's voice broke in from the side.

"The High Priest has said that those who would divide up their harvest and kill into twelve parts, and give one-twelfth to the Keepers of the Temple, will receive a special blessing from Bright, given by the High Priest himself. He holds a worship service every turn, and these people come from all over Bright's Empire to give their dozeth and receive Bright's Blessing.

God's-Chosen was shocked. His tread exploded in a furious shout.

"No!" he shouted, and scurried up the mound as all eyes turned toward him. "The Blessing of Bright belongs to all, and is freely given. You cannot bribe Bright with gifts!" He moved across the top of the mound to where the apprentice astrologers were taking the sleds of food. With a strength borne of fury, he pushed a load of pods and meat off a sled down the slope. The pods rolled downward, gathering speed and disappearing, to reappear as they came to a stop against the shocked edges of the cheela at the bottom of the mound.

God's-Chosen moved back to the center of the mound and repeated in his high-pitched voice, "I will bring you the Blessing of Bright. You do not have to give a dozeth to receive it, but only what you wish to give!"

God's-Chosen turned his small pink eyes from the crowd, stared hard at the motionless High Priest, and said, "I do not want my people coerced into worshiping Bright. If the astrologers cannot live on free will offerings, let them work in the fields!"

A murmur of approval started in the crowd of supplicants, and then grew to a continuous cheer as the crowd began to realize who the pale figure was—and what he had been saying. As the crowd started up the mound to gather around God's-Chosen, the High Priest moved away down the other side, his apprentices abandoning the sleds and following after him.

Later in the astrologers' compound, the High Priest was conferring with Bright's-Second, the Chief Astrologer.

"He has no idea what he is doing," Bright's-First said.

"The people are behind him," Bright's-Second warned. "Not to mention the Leader of the Combined Clans and all of his underleaders."

"But he does not understand the importance of our work," the High Priest said. "You cannot have apprentice astrologers out tending crops in the fields like common laborers. They will never learn their numbers or how to cast horoscopes with the astrologer sticks."

"You are right," Bright's-Second said. "He ought to be dealt with in some way. He is disrupting the important duties of the people that work in God's service."

"Unfortunately," Bright's-First said, "only Hungry-Swift, the Leader of the Combined Clans, has the authority to do anything about this rabble-rouser, and he is under his spell."

The Chief Astrologer hesitated, then said, "His Blessing is a powerful one. You should have come with us when we went east to experience it."

The High Priest answered with a sharp ripple, "I have no need of any blessing from the pale one."

The turns passed; it was now less than half a great of turns until the Blessing would be on the Temple. As the time grew near, great crowds began to come into Bright's Heaven, in order to be in the Temple at the time of the dedication. It seemed as if half of the Empire thronged into the city.

Finally, God's-Chosen held a gathering outside the eastern orifice of the now completed Temple. As the Blessing of Bright came down upon them once again, God's-Chosen announced that the next Blessing would come upon the Temple, and that in preparation for that turn, the next half-dozen turns were to be Holy ones. All should stop their labor and prepare for the occasion by prayer. Then at the appointed time, all should be inside the Temple to receive the Blessing.

TIME: 06:48:47 GMT MONDAY 20 JUNE 2050

The science experiments console screen blinked.

EAST SECTOR LASER RADAR SCAN COMPLETED.
NORTH SECTOR SCAN STARTED.

Cesar looked up at the words at the top of the screen, and went on with his analysis of the IR scanner data.

TIME: 06:48:48 GMT MONDAY 20 JUNE 2050

Three turns before the dedication of the Holy Temple, God's-Chosen knew there was a problem. He had seen the pulsating, multicolored beam go south. But then it had stopped. The time came near, and he looked in vain at the Inner Eye. He could see no beams—no light of any kind.

"Bright is testing my faith," he said to himself. "For many greats of turns the people have had to accept my word that the Blessing of Bright was coming. Now I am as blind as they are. I must have faith."

God's-Chosen asked that the Temple be cleared, and when the crowds and astrologers were all outside the orifices, he went in alone and climbed up on the Inner Eye mound to pray.

God's-Chosen looked out from the central mound across the

empty inner court toward the outer walls in the distance. There was no doubt in his mind. This was what Bright had wanted. He turned his eyes to the sky, and looking south toward Bright, began to pray.

"O Bright. Give me the faith that the others have, and if my belief falters, help me to overcome my weakness so that I may believe in you and your Blessing."

God's-Chosen slowly moved down the inner mound and went out the western orifice toward the astrologers' compound. As he left, the troopers, who had been keeping the people out, finally let the crowds pour in, for the dedication was only a turn away. For fully half a turn cheela poured through the orifices and gathered around the inner mound. Soon the inner courtyard of the Temple was full, with little groups gathered around outside each of the twelve entrances. Some climbed laboriously up to watch from the top of the walls when they found they could not get inside.

As the time grew near, the High Priest went to fetch God's-Chosen, who had isolated himself in the old temple. As Bright's-First approached the old temple area, he could hear God's-Chosen in a whispered prayer to Bright, and even he was stirred by the genuineness of the supplication.

"Bright. Give me the strength to do as you will have me do."

The prayer stopped, for God's-Chosen had felt the tread of the High Priest through the crust. As Bright's-First came nearer, God's-Chosen appeared at the entrance.

"Let us go and receive the Blessing of Bright," he said, leading the way to the Holy Temple.

Together the High Priest and God's-Chosen moved through the throngs gathered in front of the western orifice. They were followed by a large group of astrologers, all experienced in speaking to crowds. Slowly the procession made its way through the packed inner courtyard and up the slopes of the Inner Eye mound.

At the top, God's-Chosen and the High Priest took up a position at the center of the mound while the other astrologers formed a circle around them. God's-Chosen looked out at the multitude, whose every eye seemed to be upon him. He would have liked to have talked to them all directly, but there was no way that even his far-carrying, high-pitched voice could reach them all. Fortunately, most of the throng had been to one of the previous services where he had called down the Blessing of Bright, so they knew the ritual.

God's-Chosen scanned the Eyes. It had been many turns since he had last seen the beam from the Inner Eye, and he was now unsure exactly when to expect the Blessing to come.

God's-Chosen began the service as they had planned it. He would chant the prayers, which would carry out and down the mound to the nearest ranks of cheela. The chant would then be repeated by the High Priest and the rest of the astrologers, the combined treading of the chorus carrying through the crust even to those at the farthest walls. The prayers would then be echoed by the rumbling treads of the multitude.

"Bright the glorious!

"We believe!

"Bring your Blessing!"

God's-Chosen paused, but nothing happened. He went on.

"Bring your Blessing!

"Down upon us!"

He paused again, waiting in vain for the Blessing to come down upon them all. In desperation he continued.

"We are waiting.

"In your Temple!

"Bring your Blessing!"

For the first time in many greats of turns, God's-Chosen felt his faith falter. There was a subdued murmur from the crowd. There was nothing hostile, just bewilderment, for God's-Chosen had never failed before.

God's-Chosen gazed upward at the Eyes, longing for the sight of the Blessing. None came.

Without further word, God's-Chosen moved his pale body through the ring of astrologers, down the mound and out into the multitude, heading for the eastern orifice.

Some of the crowd whispered as he passed, others reached out to touch his hot pale body with a slender tendril. The High Priest, still up on the mound, tried to salvage things by proceeding with the regular worship chants, but no one paid him heed—not even the chorus.

As God's-Chosen left the Temple, the multitude of worshipers broke up into bewildered groups. Many had gone without food for a full turn, and they now went out to find something to eat in the overcrowded city.

By the next turn, food had run short and the crowds became nasty. Some recalled the original clan name of God's-Chosen, and from then on, whenever he was mentioned, it was by his old name of Pink-Eyes.

The High Priest went to discuss the previous turn's events with Hungry-Swift, the Leader of the Combined Clans. Hungry-Swift was completely demoralized by the experience.

"I am sorry that you too were taken in by that charlatan," Bright's-First said.

"But I saw! I saw the Blessing coming down!" protested Hungry-Swift.

"Yes—you may have seen the Blessing of Bright, but this Pink-Eyes person was using the Blessing of Bright to his own advantage," the High Priest replied. "He said that he gave the Word of Bright, and that he was God's-Chosen. But was he? No! Bright chose this way to say that he was a false prophet, for Bright withheld his Blessing before all the multitude."

"You seem to be right," Hungry-Swift agreed.

"I am right," the High Priest said. "I have served Bright longer than this pink-eyed hatchling. You must do something about this fraudulent impostor."

Hungry-Swift was too dejected to do anything. Bright's-First took advantage of his hesitancy and gave a command to a squad of troopers nearby.

"Bring Pink-Eyes to the Temple!" he commanded.

The troopers hesitated, looking at Hungry-Swift, who remained silent. Finally the troopers moved off to carry out the High Priest's command. They found Pink-Eyes in the wilderness to the east of Bright's Heaven. He had been going back toward the Eyes, constantly looking upward for the missing beams of light.

The troopers had no problem with Pink-Eyes, and they treated him gently. Most of them had experienced the Blessing of Bright and were still in awe of the personality in the tiny pale body.

"You are to come with us," the squad leader stated. Without a word, Pink-Eyes reversed his direction of travel and went back along the pathway, with the troopers surrounding him.

As they slowly made their way back west, paced by the small

tread of Pink-Eyes, the crowds gathered again. As they passed, most of them stared, their treads silent. Other groups, hungry and angry, muttered into the crust, and a few rolled sharp fragments of crust into the pathway in front of Pink-Eyes. He did not swerve but moved steadily onward, often leaving a sharp fragment wet with his warm white juices after his tread had passed over it. The squad leader saw what was happening, and put two troopers on either side to keep the pathway clear.

As they passed through the outskirts of Bright's Heaven and headed for the Temple, the crowds following them grew. As they entered the eastern orifice of the Temple, Pink-Eyes saw that the inner courtyard was partially full.

The troopers led Pink-Eyes up the inner mound where the High Priest and the Leader of the Combined Clans waited. Bright's-First led the interrogation.

"Are you God's-Chosen?" the High Priest asked.

"If you believe it, then I am," was the reply.

"Well, I don't believe it," the High Priest said angrily. "Admit you are a fraud!"

Pink-Eyes made no reply.

Bright's-First turned his eyes to Hungry-Swift and said firmly, "I say we should turn him into meat!"

Hungry-Swift hesitated. "He did bring us the Blessing," he said.

"Maybe," countered the High Priest. "But where is it now? He has caused us to lose it."

As the two leaders talked, Pink-Eyes had been gazing alternately at Bright and the Eyes for guidance. Suddenly he saw a beam from the Inner Eye!

"I can see it again!" he called out.

"What?" the startled Hungry-Swift asked. The High Priest was worried. Could it be that this creature had arranged all this in order to bring down Bright's curse upon him, to destroy him, and take over as High Priest?

"I can see the Blessing of Bright," Pink-Eyes said, but then in despair he saw that the beam was no longer coming toward them, but instead was pointing toward the north.

Hungry-Swift looked up at the Inner Eye, searching in vain for the faint flicker that he had longed to see these many turns. "I don't see anything," he said.

"I am afraid that you cannot," Pink-Eyes said. "The beam is now going off to the north."

"The north!" the High Priest exclaimed in relief. "That is the territory of the barbarians! By your own admission you have caused Bright to avert his Blessing from us and give it to the barbarians."

There were angry murmurs from the crowd at the base of the mound.

"Away with him!" the High Priest shouted, and Hungry-Swift and his troopers stood by helplessly while an angry crowd flowed up the mound and pushed and rolled the helpless pale body down the slope.

Sharp prickers were pulled from weapons pouches; they prodded at Pink-Eyes' edges, forcing him out the eastern orifice of the Temple. A storage bin at a nearby needle trooper compound was raided and two dozen long dragon tooth spears were brought and laid out on the ground. Pink-Eyes was then forced onto the row of spear shafts. The ends of the shafts were raised by burly warriors. As Pink-Eyes felt his tread leave the crust, he went into a hysterical panic. The small pale body was easily carried to a nearby field.

The crust in the field had recently been plowed and seeded, but it would be a long time before the petal plants would grow. Now, however, a more vicious crop was springing up, as warrior after warrior planted a slicer or pricker in the crumbled crust, point upwards.

Pink-Eyes' tread trembled in pain as his body was lowered down over the points. He tried to support his body on the narrow shafts of the spears, while lifting the rest of his tread away from the tormenting pricks. Then the spear shafts were pulled out from underneath his trembling tread. His tortured body fell helplessly onto the crust, the slicers and prickers glinting up through his topside, wet points glowing white with his juices.

In agony, Pink-Eyes attempted to lift his pale body off the agonizing shards of dragon crystal, but with each heave he only sliced his body further. He gave up trying, and slowly spread out as his juices flowed into the crust.

"O Bright," his tortured tread cried in muffled agony, "bring down your Blessing—even on these—for they want you too much."

It was half a turn before the butchering crew was called. There was not much meat on that tiny carcass, and the meat had the same sickly paleness that the skin had. One of the butcher crew sucked at a hunk of meat. "It does not even taste right," she said. "I wouldn't eat this stuff."

"You are right," another said after taking a small taste. So by common consent, the body was left in the field to dry on the glowing crust, the shrinking skin pricked through with sharp shards of dragon crystal abandoned by their former owners.

TIME: 06:49:32 GMT MONDAY 20 JUNE 2050

Seiko Kauffmann Takahashi looked up as her shift relief drifted in from his breakfast—early as usual. Abdul, still sipping a squeezer full of sweet mint tea, pulled himself to the vacant communications console. With a few practiced flips of his left hand, he soon had a copy of Seiko's screen on his console.

"Anything exciting?" he said as his unbuckled body floated slowly up out of the console seat. He was surprised at the reply—for nothing ever excited Seiko.

"Yes," she replied firmly, reaching out to finger a panel. A picture from the star image telescope flashed on both their screens. She did not say another word—she did not have to.

TIME: 06:50:12 GMT MONDAY 20 JUNE 2050

Pierre Carnot Niven, having finished his ten-hour shift and a leisurely dinner, was relaxing. He sat buckled into a seat in front of a console down in the library, his finger flicking over the screen.

"Fatter!

"More!

"Fine!"

His finger traced another line. "Now—the other arm—same as the first!

"Good!"

He stretched back and surveyed his handiwork on the screen with pride. The image of the child on the screen now looked the way it should, although the baby-fat pudginess made it an unlikely candidate for what he would make it do next. However, that image was just what he had been striving for. The audience for his scan-book needed to identify—even if they couldn't copy. He leaned over to the screen and touched the right hand of the image.

"Put a ball in this hand!" A ball was instantly there, with the fingers of the hand opened to grasp it.

"Now comes the difficult part," he thought. "We'll see how good the body action subroutine is."

He spoke again. "Throw ball from here—along here—to here. Use Earth gravity!" While he spoke, his finger scribed a curve leading from the hand along a high arc down into the background area of the picture.

He watched as the body in the image leaned back in a slightly jerky movement and launched the ball into the air. The ball rose and then fell back to the ground—stopping abruptly without a bounce. The computer handled the perspective very nicely; the ball grew smaller and smaller as it sailed into the distance.

"Good—repeat with Lunar gravity!"

The scene was repeated with the words LUNAR GRAVITY in the upper corner of the screen. The ball now rose much more slowly, with a significantly flatter trajectory.

Pierre spoke again, "Repeat both!"

The two scenes repeated their actions. First EARTH GRAVITY, then LUNAR GRAVITY. Pierre watched, checking them carefully. They would look much better after they were fleshed out with the publisher's curved surface software routine. He then generated another one using Mars gravity. There weren't many of his readers on Mars yet, but he suspected there would be by the time he returned to Earth.

Pierre leaned toward the screen. "Earth gravity picture—rotate 45 degrees to right!

"Display action!"

He watched as the action repeated, this time as seen from the side. The ball rose in a nice parabolic trajectory. He smiled and thought, "The kids have had their fun imagining that their bodies are strong enough to throw a ball fifty meters. Now they will have to get to work and learn some science, which—after all—is why they are scanning the book." He spoke aloud:

"Shrink ball by two!

"Shrink child by five!

"Put in graph axes—vertical here!" His hand reached out and scribed a line from the top of the screen down to the miniature figure now tossing a baseball as big as its head.

Pierre was halfway through getting the coordinate axes numbered and the parabolic equation placed in the picture where it would be out of the way of the trajectory, when he was interrupted by a message that flashed on the upper part of the screen.

LINK FROM BRIDGE CONSOLE

Pierre looked up. "Accept link!" he said.

HI PIERRE,
COULD YOU COME UP TO THE MAIN DECK?
THERE IS SOMETHING HAPPENING ON DRAGON'S EGG.
WE WANT YOU TO CONFIRM OUR SUSPICIONS.
CESAR

"Sure Doc," Pierre said. "Be right there.
"Break link!
"Store under Trajectory Graph!
"Detach job!"

He unbuckled from the console chair and pushed himself quickly up the passageway leading to the main deck as the computer obediently flashed confirmation after confirmation toward his disappearing feet.

LINK BROKEN
SAVED TRAJECTORY GRAPH: EARTH GRAVITY
DETACH JOB 3; PIERRE. ACCT: GOLDEN SCIENCE PRESS
TIME 06:52:30 20 JUNE 2050. USED 0:01:26 IN 1:36:33

Pierre swung onto the bridge and over to the group looking at some fresh printouts. As he floated over he could see that they were pictures from the high resolution star image telescope.

Cesar spoke up as he approached. "Sorry to drag you up on your break, Pierre, but these printouts are really bewildering. Since you are our resident expert on neutron star crustal activity, we figured you could make a better evaluation than we could."

Seiko handed him a sheet. "I took these off the star image telescope this shift. This one was taken at 0645 hours. Notice the pattern here near the west limb."

Pierre looked briefly at the printout. The chaotic hash of the west limb region was almost familiar by now. But there was something new there, a short arclike pattern. Seiko was right. As of yesterday there had been no such structure at that place on Dragon's Egg. "It looks like wrinkle ridges that you could get on any crusted object with a liquid core. In fact, there are many similarities between those patterns and the ones near the Caloric pole of Mercury. But wait . . . the directions in the pattern are all wrong. From what I know about the behavior of neutron star crustal material under the influence of high magnetic fields, the ridges should all be aligned along the magnetic field lines."

"So far, we have all come to the same conclusion," Seiko said. "This pattern is not a wrinkle ridge from a collapse of the surface. Besides, we have been monitoring the spin speed of the star, and if there had been a slump of that magnitude in the past day, it would have shown up as a glitch in the rotation period, and there has been none."

"Now," Abdul said, "show him the kicker."

Seiko pulled out another sheet from beneath the first.

"This was taken at 0648 hours, just before Dr. Wong finished a laser scan of that region."

She passed it over without further comment.

Pierre saw an elongated oval shape, with ten oval dots around it and one in the middle. The dots on the outside were connected to the large oval with short exponentially tapered horns. There were slight traces of two more dots that would complete the symmetric pattern.

"The direction of the oval looks generally east-west," he said.

"It is," Seiko stated, with the calm assurance of someone who had taken the trouble to check. "The semimajor axis is within less than a milliradian of magnetic east, so the pattern is dominated by magnetic effects and not rotational effects. But the lines that make up the oval are not straight magnetic east-west as are all the other cliffs and wrinkle ridges in that area."

"It looks like something that is stretched," Pierre said, holding the printout up to his eye. "In fact, from this angle it looks exactly like a Sheriff's star in an old western movie, complete with a bullet hole in the center. However, it isn't complete, there are only ten points."

He looked up and the others watched his expression change from initial surprise to suspicion.

"You're kidding me," he said.

"No," Cesar said. "We are deadly serious. I knew you would have a tough time accepting this without better proof, so I had Seiko fix up the star image telescope with the filters for direct viewing."

Pierre knew from the tone that Cesar was serious and that the image print was real—but he still found himself diving up the passageway toward the star image telescope control post. He floated in, quickly checked the filter settings, then flicked the switch that opened the direct viewport. The light beamed in from overhead and down onto the white frosted table top in the center of the room. He drifted over and hung above the glaring image and adjusted the strobe controls until the spinning image in the center of the table slowed down and finally stopped rotating. He found the symmetric flowerlike diagram.

Pierre looked up as the others came up the passageway. "The diagram is now complete," he said.

They gathered around the table and looked down at the image as Pierre whispered softly, "It is not only complete, there are no extra lines. There can be no other logical explanation. Whatever that is, it was made by intelligent beings!"

"Intelligent beings!" Seiko exclaimed. "That is impossible! The surface gravity of that star is 67-billion gees and the temperature is 8200 degrees! Any being that existed on that star would be a flat glowing pancake of solid neutrons."

"They wouldn't be made of neutrons," Pierre replied. "My measurements show that although the interior of the star is made of neutrons, the outer crust has a density more like that of a white dwarf star, and its composition is quite complex, with most of the same atomic nuclei that we have in the Earth's crust, only much more neutron-rich and without the electron clouds around them."

Pierre was perplexed. They had a mission here at Dragon's Egg. The mission was to get as much scientific data as possible from their vantage point only 400 km from the neutron star. His problem was that the magic gravitational elevator that had put them down into this orbit a few days ago would soon finish its complicated interlaced orbital pattern and would be returning to take them away again. They had only a limited amount of time—what should they do?

Abdul spoke. "I don't really come onto shift for over an hour. Why don't I try to generate some kind of signal to send down in case there really is some form of intelligent life there, while the rest of you keep up with the science time line."

"Fine," Pierre said. "We have finished with the laser radar mapper on this hemisphere, so you can use that. If you need anything else, let me know. I am sure we can reschedule an experiment for later on in the program."

Abdul pushed his way to the communications console. Soon a simple one-two-three . . . dot-dash number series was beaming down to the surface, followed by a crude diagram of Dragon Slayer inside the six tidal compensator masses over the sphere that was Dragon's Egg. It was a dot-dash pattern, 53 by 71 dots on a side.

Trek

Commander Swift-Killer fixed her attention out toward the horizon. Each of her eight watch eyes reported back that the shallow arc of a needlelike dragon tooth could still be seen, held at guard position by one of the perimeter guards. She left the watch eyes at their automatic duty and scanned her other eyes around the camp where the rest of her troopers were relaxing. Most were still eating, but a few had paired off and were now enjoying each other over in one corner of the camp. She looked at them enviously and was tempted to pass over the watch to her second-in-command, go get her favorite fun-partner and join them, but the last contact with the barbarians had only been a turn ago, and they must stay at full alert.

Frustrated in her bodily pleasures, Swift-Killer turned to her other personal form of recreation—trying to figure out why things work. She paused, concentrated for a moment, and her body pushed out some pseudopods. She then grew some articulated crystallium bones under the protrusions of tough, muscular skin to form manipulators. The bones in the manipulators were small, not like the ones that she grew to hold her shield and sword in battle. Still keeping her watch eyes on the horizon, Swift-Killer glanced with the remaining eyes at the four extremities, made a minor change to one of them, then reached through the sphincter of a carrying pouch in her body and pulled out her "experiments."

One experiment was an old one that she had come upon in the last campaign. Their pursuit of the barbarians had taken them into strange territory where the crust was not smooth, but had suffered a recent shaking. In that region, the crust did not have its usual fibrous plasticity, but was almost as hard as dragon crystal. The quake had shattered the crust into many flat plates, their cleaved surfaces glinting with the reflected image of the God Bright that hung motionless over the south pole. Her mind always active, Swift-Killer had collected several plates and had played with them, turning them first one way, then the other, to bring the image of Bright to each of her eyes in turn. She had even held one well up above normal eye level (it had taken most of her bone-forming crystallium to support the plate against Egg's tremendous gravity pull) and had actually looked at her own topside. It looked weird to her, what with the deep red color, the reddish-yellow lump of her brain nodule near the middle, and the smaller lump of a forming egg next to it. She had hastily withdrawn the plate and had glanced around quickly to reassure herself that no one had seen her examining her own topside. Unless it was your lover trying to get you in the mood, no one ever talked about one's topside, much less looked at it.

As a troop commander, she had found an excellent use for the mirror plates. A "glancer" was now standard battle equipment on the eastern front. With careful aim of the mirror to reflect the image of Bright in the right direction, messages and commands could be sent over great distances to other squads without alerting the barbarians. They still used the old code patterns for the commands, since the limitations of the glancer communication system were similar to the old technique that used synchronized thumps of the treads of a trooper squad on the crust. With this new communication technique, the element of surprise that they had gained over the barbarians had decreased their losses by significant factors.

Swift-Killer placed her collection of equipment on the crust. Along with the glancers, there was another of her discoveries, the flares. The fact that certain types of crust would glow when pod juice dropped on them had been known since ancient history. Swift-Killer had been intrigued by this effect, and everywhere she went in her service to the Leader of the Combined Clans, she had always sacrificed a few drops of her daily ration of pods to the crust to see how brightly it would glow. She had recently come across a very reactive portion of crust. A drop of pod juice would make a blue-white flare of light almost too bright to look at. She had carefully used a slicer to extract some long, fibrous rods out of the crust; these were her flares. She had visited a chemist at the base hospital, and soon her enthusiasm persuaded him to use his ancient arts to separate the various components of a large batch of pod juice, until she had a small vial of cast dragon crystal with the concentrated essence of the factor in the pod juice that made the flares glow.

Swift-Killer tested out the flare by holding the vial above the end of the stick and letting a few drops of fluid fall on the end. The eyes on that side of her body popped reflexively into their skin pouches as the brilliant blue-white glare of light burst forth. Swift-Killer noticed with pleasure the murmur of startled treads vibrating through the crust to her.

"The Commander is at it again . . . now what is she up to?"

Remembering her prime duty, she turned her attention to her watch eyes, and again assured herself that each one still had a distant dragon tooth firmly fixed in its vision. She noticed that one or two of them also had a fuzzy spot off to one side, where they had picked up the momentary glare of the flashing flare. However, true to their assigned duties, they had not ducked into their skin pouch at the bright glare.

With the flare ready, she then turned her attention to her latest discovery, the "expander." She had come upon it not long ago when she had been out visiting the perimeter guards. Normally that task was the duty of one of the squad leaders, but since her favorite at that time had been one of the guards, she took the opportunity of an inspection tour to get a few moments alone with him. Of course, being on guard, he had to remain at alert with his eyes on the horizon, while giving stiffly formal responses to her queries. Although her questions followed the usual routine of an inspection of the guard, her actions took advantage of the fact that he was not allowed to break his at-alert condition.

"Who approaches?" boomed the crust as his tread rippled at her approach.

"Troop Commander Swift-Killer," she replied.

"You may approach," he said. So she did . . . and got closer and closer and closer until her body was pressed up right next to his and had flowed around in a crescent that nearly enveloped his periphery. Her cool dark-red eyes stared right into his, while he dutifully kept his gaze fixed on the horizon.

"Report!" she commanded, but instead of using solid talk, she whispered it with an electronic tingle that sent thrills through his frustrated body.

"Guard to the east under observation and secure. Guard to the west under observation and secure. No unknown objects on the horizon. All secure, Commander Swift-Killer," boomed his muffled report in formal solid talk. She then felt a soft electronic whisper as he added, "But I seem to be under attack from Bright-side."

"At Alert!" she barked, and felt his body stiffen.

"What is this I see," she said, as her eyes went up on stubs to look at his topside.

"Dirt!" she said severely; and reaching out a soft muscular pseudopod, she proceeded to brush imaginary specks of dirt off his topside, making sure that she had touched all of his sensitive spots in the process.

"Just for that, Squad-Leader North-Wind, after you have been relieved of your post, you shall report to me for extra duty," she said, with a mixture of solid talk and electronic whisper that trailed off into a pure whisper at the words "extra duty" that left no doubt in his mind what that duty would consist of.

Commander Swift-Killer slowly slid her body along North-Wind, who kept his outer perimeter in the prescribed circle and his eyes on the horizon. Then drawing herself back into proper traveling form, she went off to visit the next guard on the perimeter, leaving an emotionally frustrated North-Wind at his post, his eyes and body at attention, but his mind full of things other than non-existent barbarians.

"He does not have too much longer before the change of the guard," she thought as she moved off to inspect the next guard. "But by that time, will he be ready!"

The next guard had always been one of her problem troopers. She had never really learned discipline. Although Easy-Mover had never given any trouble when under direct supervision, she did not have the proper spirit of a real needle trooper, and would not discipline herself to act always in the manner of a trooper even when there was no superior officer nearby. Unfortunately, the lonely duty of perimeter guard gave her plenty of opportunity to become lax, and she had been caught so many times that she had never been able to keep any of her promotions for very long.

"She is at it again," Swift-Killer said to herself as she approached the guard and felt a telltale grinding noise in the crust beneath her tread. Her eyes carefully surveyed the guard, but there was not one sign of motion in the body of the guard or the arc of dragon tooth that jutted out towards the horizon. A challenge replaced the grinding noise as the guard noticed her approach.

"Who approaches?" boomed the guard.

"Troop Commander Swift-Killer," she replied.

"You may approach," came the formal reply.

Swift-Killer flowed to one side of the rigid trooper and barked, "Move here in front of me!"

There was a moment's hesitation, bad enough in itself, and then the trooper swiftly flowed over and resumed the formal guard position. Swift-Killer went to the spot that the guard had vacated, formed a manipulator and picked up the two plates of broken crust that lay there. The plates were placed one on top of the other; as Swift-Killer took them apart, a dusty powder of ground-up crust fell to the surface. Bored with guard duty, Easy-Mover had been holding her outside surface at alert, but had been absent-mindedly rubbing one plate against another under her tread. This was not the first time she had been caught doing something like that, so it didn't surprise Swift-Killer.

"You are already down to trooper, so I can't demote you any further," Swift-Killer barked at the now rigid form of Easy-Mover. "But until you learn that troopers on guard duty are to remain at full alert at all times, you will have to make do without recreation periods. Since this is not your first offense, it will be a dozen turns this time!"

Swift-Killer thought she detected a quiver of protest, but fortunately for Easy-Mover, she recovered rapidly with her reply.

"Yes, Commander," she said.

Swift-Killer then took the guard through the remainder of her formal report and left to inspect the rest of the perimeter, taking the two plates with her to remove temptation from the scene.

"A dozen turns with no recreation is not only going to be hard on her, but also on about three males that I know of," Swift-

Killer thought as she flowed off. "I don't know how she keeps them all happy. One lover at a time is enough for me."

The offending plates had been tucked away in one of Swift-Killer's carrying pouches and she had forgotten about them until their shape got in the way during her fun and games with the eager North-Wind. She had put them to one side and had attended to more important business, such as thinning herself down and slithering under the hot kneading tread of North-Wind as their eye-stubs entwined softly about one another. They took turns kneading each other's topside with their treads, concentrating on their favorite spots. Then with their eye-stubs firmly intertwined to pull their very edges together, their mutual vibrations raised in pitch with an electronic tingle adding an overtone of spice to the massage. Finally, in a multiple spasm of their bodies, a dozen tiny perimeter orifices just under North-Wind's eye-stubs opened—to emit a small portion of his inner juices into the waiting folds around Swift-Killer's eye-stubs.

Swift-Killer felt the tiny globules of North-Wind as they were carried by her automatic reflexes to the egg case. She slowly gathered herself into her more normal shape and slid from beneath the still thinned and exhausted North-Wind. She left him lying there and began to pick up the various things she had laid aside from her carrying pouches. As each item was tucked away, she became less and less Swift-Killer the lover. Finally, as she placed the four-button symbol of her rank into a holding sphincter on her side, she turned back into Troop Commander Swift-Killer.

As she came to the last few items, she picked up the crustal plates that she had taken from Easy-Mover. The plates no longer had flat surfaces; instead one was slightly hollow and the other was slightly rounded. Some of the shiny aspect of a freshly cleaved surface was gone, but it was still possible to see a reflection in them. Always inquisitive, Swift-Killer looked at the two curved plates and was amazed to see that in one of them her eye looked smaller than normal, while in the other, it was larger.

She reached out a soft pseudopod and wiped the dust off the surfaces. This improved the image some. Now completely absorbed in trying to understand the strange behavior of the curved plates, Swift-Killer the inventor forgot her lover and her command duties while her mind wandered off into thought.

For many turns Swift-Killer spent her spare time with the curved plates. She talked to Easy-Mover and found that she had been carrying those plates for many turns and had used them to relieve her boredom on many tours of perimeter guard duty. Swift-Killer duplicated her grinding process and soon had several expander and shrinker mirrors. She found that if she did not apply much pressure in the later parts of the rubbing, the mirrors could be made very shiny, almost as good as the cleaved surfaces of the original plates.

She spent a long time on one set of plates to see how curved she could make them, for she had found that the more the mirrors were curved, the more they would expand or shrink the image. Finally she obtained one pair where something amazing happened; not only was the image of her eye expanded, it was also turned upside down! She found that if she put her eye very close to the mirror it would appear right side up and expanded, but as she moved back it would get bigger and bigger, finally filling the whole mirror with a distorted image, then would finally appear again upside down.

Swift-Killer now held one of those expander mirrors. She knew that a flat mirror would reflect the light from her flare, and she wanted to see what the expander would do. Perhaps it would expand the light and make it brighter.

Swift-Killer formed her body around in a crescent, with her four free eyes moved around so that they were concentrated on the inner part of the crescent where they could observe the experiment. Aware that the light would be quite bright, she had them tucked under their protective folds of skin and had closed the fold until each was only watching through a narrow slit. Carefully she held the vial of pod juice extract above the flare and adjusted the little crystal valve until a thin stream of liquid fell down on the end of the flare. Soon she had a continuous bright arc going. Light flared over her body and up into the sky. Using her manipulators she brought the expander mirror up near the arc. Instead of reflecting the light off in all directions like a flat mirror, it seemed to collect it and make it smaller. She moved the mirror back and forth. She first found a point where the light seemed to go off in a straight beam from the expander. She then found that there was a position in which the light was focused into a spot on the crust. She reached out with a pseudo-pod to touch the bright spot.

"OW!!!"

The whole camp came to alert as they heard the agonized t'trum of their troop commander on the crust. Swift-Killer, her burned spot sucked into the interior of her body where it was quickly enveloped in soothing liquid, stopped the flow of pod juice from the vial, waited until the flare stopped glowing, and then put her experiments back into her carrying pouches as her eyes glared around the camp. In short order, all the troopers were very busy.

After many turns of experimentation, Swift-Killer understood how the expander worked. Halfway between the mirror and the point where her eye flipped from right side up to upside down was the point where the flare would give off a straight beam. If it were in front or in back of that point, the light would be focused to a point, later to spread out again. For a while, Swift-Killer thought that she had a new weapon, a thing that would burn at a distance, but a little experimentation showed her that it was far easier and faster to poke a hole in a barbarian with a dragon tooth than to burn one with an expander (assuming that the barbarian would hold still long enough).

However, the more she thought about the long-reaching beam of light that she could make, and the old stories about the narrow beams of invisible light that the ancient prophet Pink-Eyes had seen, the more she thought that she ought to talk to some of the scientists back in Bright's Heaven who were trying to make sense of the still pulsating beams.

It took some discussion with the Commander of the Eastern Front, but after seeing her experiment, he decided to relieve her temporarily of her command and let her make a journey back to Bright's Heaven.

TIME: 07:54:50 GMT MONDAY 20 JUNE 2050

The road to Bright's Heaven was long but fast. It stretched out in a straight line along the easy direction from the eastern outpost trooper camp. The way had been smoothed by generations of treads and baggage sleds. Swift-Killer moved along the road at her rapid trooper's glide, her four button troop commander's insignia automatically clearing the path ahead of her and giving her preferential treatment at the food stations along the way.

One of the food station keepers was well known for his interesting and nearly inexhaustible repertoire of love kneadings, and she had enjoyed a couple of dalliances in previous trips, but her mind was elsewhere when she passed through this time, so she didn't wait for him to return from one of his periodic trips to restock his pod bins. She just took the pods that she needed and continued on her way, crushing the pod with the powerful muscles in her food intake pouch and sucking the tingly juices in through the thin skin at one end of the pouch.

Swift-Killer finally arrived at Bright's Heaven, and after a short formal meeting with the Commander of the Central Defense Command, she took off to visit the Inner Eye Institute, part of the large Holy Temple complex.

"Troop Commander Swift-Killer!" the Institute astrologer greeted her. "We are honored by your visit. The fact that you are here gives us reassurance that the eastern border is safe."

Swift-Killer's eye-stubs twisted with embarrassment as the Institute astrologer continued. "That invention of the glancer has given you a reputation among the astrologers here at the Institute. Have you ever thought about leaving the Troopers and becoming one of us?"

Swift-Killer knew what she was best at. Her extraordinary size, strong muscles, and quick intelligence had led her to her natural position as a front line troop commander. They had also given her a new name, when as a youngster just barely out of the hatchling pens, she had killed a Swift unaided, with only a slicer for a weapon. She enjoyed her hobby of trying to figure out how things worked, but she had no intention of making it her life's work, not as long as there were barbarians trying to destroy Bright's Heaven. She brushed off the Institute astrologer's question with one of her own.

"What is the latest news on the strange pulsating beams from Bright's Inner Eye?" Swift-Killer asked.

The Institute astrologer hesitated. He and the others in the Inner Eye Institute had been undergoing a difficult conversion. Fortunately it had happened so slowly that they had had time to overcome the shock. However, they were not sure yet, so neither the populace nor the rest of the temple priests had been informed of their suspicions. The eyes of the Institute astrologer swayed back and forth rhythmically as he evaluated Swift-Killer. He equivocated.

"The beams from Bright's Inner Eye continue to bring down a message from the mind of Bright," he replied. "The beams are invisible except to certain ones who have what is known as Bright's Blessing, although Bright's Affliction would probably be a better term for it, as the unfortunate individuals rarely live to breeding age. Fortunately, the alchemists have found a liquid that is sensitive to the invisible beams, and turns color temporarily if a vial of it is exposed to the beam, so now we do not have to search the Empire for those unfortunate ones and drag them away from their clans to interpret Bright's message to us."

"The pulsations continue?" Swift-Killer asked.

"Yes," the Institute astrologer replied. "And there seems to be some pattern to them. We are still trying to analyze what they mean. They come so slowly, one pulse every few turns."

The fact that the pulsations seemed to have a pattern intrigued Swift-Killer's inquisitive mind.

"May I see what you have collected?" she asked eagerly.

The Institute astrologer formed a manipulator, extracted a tally string from a storage pouch and gave it to Swift-Killer, who quickly ran a tendril down its length.

"It is a string of numbers!" she exclaimed. "Only it stops at ten and then repeats twice more." She continued her examination of the tally string.

"This seems to be a number system that only goes to ten, then goes into two symbols to represent things larger than ten," she said.

"Yes," he replied, "and if you go on, you will find that after counting to ten times ten, new symbols appear, interspersed with the number symbols."

Swift-Killer moved quickly over the repetitious section and found the new symbols. First a one, then a strange symbol, then another one, then a different strange symbol, then a two. The Institute astrologer kept his tread still, while his eye-stubs watched the tense body of Swift-Killer. Finally her eye-stubs resumed their normal wavelike motion and she started murmuring.

"One plus one equals two, one plus two equals three, two plus two equals four . . ." she said. She then turned her attention to the Institute astrologer and her eyes stared at him, twitching nervously. The Institute astrologer clenched his tread muscles and waited for Swift-Killer's brain to realize what he and the others in the Institute had finally had to face.

"This is nothing but a primer in arithmetic, but in a number system that goes only to ten. Surely Bright would not waste time to send such a trivial message, and take so long to do it. This is more like an interpreter trying to learn one of the barbarian tongues."

Swift-Killer hesitated, for what she was about to say next went against all her early religious training. "It is almost as if there were a strange clan of barbarians living on the Inner Eye, and trying to set up communication with us," she said. "But that cannot be!"

The Institute astrologer kept his tread quiet and passed over another tally string. This one was a fringe string, with many strings knotted to a main string, and with each side string containing many knots. At first Swift-Killer could make no sense of it, for there were no symbol groups, only large and small knots. She felt through the fringes, puzzled by the large blank sections.

"It took us a long time to figure that one out," the Institute astrologer admitted. "In fact it was a novice who literally stumbled onto it, when he happened to glide across the tally fringe as it lay on the crust. Here, let me arrange it."

The Institute astrologer took the tally fringe and laid it out as a rectangle on the crust.

"Now glide onto it carefully and see what your tread tells you," he said.

Following his instructions, Swift-Killer moved her body onto the large rectangle, and suddenly it all became clear. Whereas her eyes could only see the tally string at such a low angle that everything was distorted beyond recognition, her touch sensitive bottom tread could absorb the picture all at once.

"It is like a map," said Swift-Killer, who utilized the devices when planning large scale campaigns. "But it is not any place that I know . . ."

She hesitated, and then said, "Wait . . . In this large circle, this tiny feature here must be the Holy Temple, and this must be Bright's Heaven—but everything is so distorted. The circle must

be Egg itself, and these seven small dots must be Bright's Eyes."
She looked again at the Institute astrologer and said, "This is a
picture of Egg and the Eyes of Bright. But why is everything on
Egg so distorted? It looks like it has been stretched in the east-
west direction."

"We don't know," said the Institute astrologer. "We are still
trying to figure that out. We have since received another picture
map, and the present signals are in the process of beaming down
a third one."

"May I feel them?" Swift-Killer asked.

The Institute astrologer pulled out two more tally strings from
carrying pouches and laid them out on the crust without comment. They were close enough together so that Swift-Killer
could spread herself out to cover both of them at the same time.

"This shows the Eyes of Bright," Swift-Killer said. "But the
smaller Inner Eye is not just a featureless circle like the others. It
has strange markings and circles on it and there is a cylinder
sticking out of one side. And this other is an enlargement of the
Inner Eye, and you can see forms inside the circle, as if you were
peering through holes in the Inner Eye."

Swift-Killer paused. "What does all this mean?" she asked.

"We are not positive," said the Institute astrologer, "but we
think that those things we can see inside the orifices are strange
beings."

"But they are so sticklike and angular, they would be broken
in a moment," she exclaimed.

"They are floating in the sky above the east pole, so they seem
to be immune to the gravity pull of Egg, although why they
want such long manipulator bones is unknown." While the Institute astrologer had been talking, Swift-Killer had been reexamin-
ing the pictures.

"The Inner Eye looks like a giant machine," she said. "This
thing at the top of the cylinder looks like a glancer in a holder,
and these other things look like my expander."

"What is an expander?" asked the astrologer.

Swift-Killer finally remembered that she had not yet told him
of her discovery. She had come to give him some new knowledge, but instead had been bedazzled with one new concept
after another.

Swift-Killer formed a manipulator, reached into a carrying

pouch and pulled out the expander and the shrinker. Then she explained their odd behavior to the Institute astrologer as he moved them back and forth in front of one of his eyes.

"This curved shape for a glancer means that it can send a beam of light a long way," she told him. "And that is probably why they exist on the Inner Eye thing, to send the beams down to us on Egg."

The Institute astrologer moved onto the tally pictures on the crust, and compared the shapes of the things protruding from the Inner Eye with the object that he held.

"The shapes are very similar," he said. "You are probably right. But what is this about sending beams?"

"I came to give you a demonstration," Swift-Killer said.

"Wait," the Institute astrologer suggested. "I will gather the rest of the members of the Institute."

Soon Swift-Killer was the center of attention as she demonstrated her bright light source and the way the expander could bring the light into a hot spot, or send it off in a straight beam.

After several demonstrations, Swift-Killer let some of the more eager novices play with the new toy. As she flowed back to talk to the Institute astrologer, she could hear others starting to grind away at two plates to make their own expanders.

It was soon obvious to all in the Institute that Swift-Killer's new invention provided a means to signal back to whatever it was in the Inner Eye that was beaming down messages to them. After several turns, they set up a bright light source and started sending off a coded message aimed at the Eyes of Bright. They kept it up for many turns, but nothing happened; the pulsed beam from the Inner Eye continued its methodical blinking, slowly finishing off the last picture. After many, many turns, Swift-Killer had a thought. Far to the east of Bright's Heaven was a fracture ridge that stuck up just over the horizon. Its side was the quarry for the blocks that were used to build the housing and storage compounds for Bright's Heaven. Swift-Killer decided to go out to the quarry, and make the arduous climb up the slope to the top; then she would look for the beam of light that the astrologers would send periodically in that direction.

After a dozen turns, a dejected Swift-Killer returned to the Institute.

"It is no wonder that Inner Eye is not responding to our signals," she said. "I can just barely see them from the top of the quarry."

"I was afraid of that," the Institute astrologer said. "The Eyes are so low on the horizon that our light beam has to travel a long way through the absorbing atmosphere. It is too bad that the Eyes of Bright are hovering over the east pole, if it were hovering above us, we could not only detect their beam easier, but they could see our pitifully weak attempt at a response."

Swift-Killer shivered at the thought of something hanging over her in the sky, but agreed that Bright had certainly sent his seven Eyes to the poorest spot in the sky for seeing.

Then suddenly, Swift-Killer had an idea.

"If we went to the east pole, we could send our light beam straight up to the Inner Eye. The distance through the atmosphere would be a lot shorter, and the beam would be going in the easy direction and would not fade so much."

"But nobody goes to the east pole," the Institute astrologer protested. "The land is full of barbarians, every direction that you move is in the hard direction, the sky is hot and full of volcano smoke, the crust is too bristly to move on . . . No cheela could survive there."

"I know it is not as nice as Bright's Heaven," Swift-Killer said. "But cheela can survive there. After all, as you said, the place is infested with barbarians.

"Actually," Swift-Killer went on, "the troopers on the eastern border have penetrated a good way toward the east pole in punitive raids on barbarian settlements. We have them cowed enough that they would not bother a good-sized expedition."

A discussion of the pros and cons of Swift-Killer's suggestion continued for many turns. The cost would be high, especially in terms of the number of troopers that would be needed to guard an expedition deep into barbarian territory. It was beyond the resources and authority of the Inner Eye Institute, and the idea might have been dropped if the last section of the third picture had not been so dramatic. The picture of the machine with the strange beings was remarkable enough (for there was no doubt that the sticklike things seen vaguely through the holes in the Inner Eye were beings). But up in one corner of the picture was a similar figure placed next to the familiar (although stretched) outlines of the Holy Temple. It seemed incredulous, but the markings left no doubt that the being was about one-twelfth as big as the Temple. When the new picture was completed, the Institute astrologer decided that he had better inform the rest of the ruling authorities of their discoveries.

Initially, the High Priest and the Chief Astrologer were perturbed about the Institute astrologer's interpretation of the pictures, but finally accepted his version as no threat to their religion by assuming that Bright worked in a mysterious way, and that some time in the distant future, it would all become clear to them.

The Leader of the Combined Clans, although nominally a devout worshiper of the God Bright, was willing to compartmentalize her mind and look at the pictures without being bothered by the religious overtones.

"Weird looking creatures," the Leader said. "And giants at that. Yet if they have learned to hover in the sky without falling down, we could learn much from them, and they seem to be willing to talk to us. It can't hurt to learn more. Proceed with the expedition."

There was no doubt in anyone's mind who would be the leader of the expedition. As a combined astrologer-thinker and battle commander, Swift-Killer was the obvious choice. With the authority of the Leader of the Combined Clans behind her, Swift-Killer organized the expedition. They would be gone for many, many turns, and meanwhile the work of the Institute had to go on, so she only took a few of the younger astrologers and novices. A good supply of flares and concentrated pod juice were obtained under her direction, and during that time a few excellent large-diameter expanders had been manufactured by the careful grinding of newly trained artisans. One of the expanders was so large in diameter that only a few of the novices could get a carrying pouch around it; once it was pouched, they could carry little else.

For the trip out to the eastern border, no troopers were needed for protection, and the food stops sufficed for supplies. However, messengers were sent ahead to gather the supplies that the expedition would need in the turns ahead. Soon, Swift-Killer returned to take over command of her troop of needle troopers, for naturally she had requested that they supply the guard for the expedition. Soon the entire party was assembled.

Rations were distributed, and civilians were taught the elementary thrusts of the short sword in case a barbarian ever penetrated to the center of the circle formation. Finally they left, gliding easily over the crust toward the east magnetic pole.

TIME: 07:56:29 GMT MONDAY 20 JUNE 2050

Dead-Troopers pulled her eye down from its crystallium-cored stub and pushed her way off in the hard direction, keeping her body as thin as sex until she was well over the horizon. She could not figure out why this circle of troopers was penetrating so far into her territory. The scouts had reported that they were on the move, and she had acted to defend the nearest village that would have been an obvious target for a punitive attack, but the circle of troopers had carefully worked its way around it. Such behavior of Empire troopers was new, and Dead-Troopers hated anything new. They were up to something, and she would stop it—but what?

As she slithered into the compound, she noticed with glum satisfaction that the scrape of her tread on the crust had warned the camp. Those who were presently in her good graces were merely very busy taking care of important matters, while those who weren't had rapidly absented themselves when they felt the first murmurs of her approach.

Her second-in-command, and one of her lovers, was busy rubbing his unusually brilliant short sword against a chunk of crust. Although the cast dragon crystal would usually stay sharp until the edge was notched by a hard blow, it did help a little to keep the edge in fine hone by monotonous rubbing against the crustal material. Dead-Troopers knew that Pink-Sky had never let the short sword get dull since the time he had wrested it from the dead body of a trooper whom they had killed jointly. She glided up next to Pink-Sky until their edges were touching along almost half their length. Pink-Sky continued to hone his sword as Dead-Troopers watched.

"They are in full force," she said. "But they do not attack! I don't like it!"

"There are very few things about troopers that you do like," he replied calmly.

Dead-Troopers paused for a moment, then said, "Well, I like this even less."

"Where are they going?" Pink-Sky asked.

Dead-Troopers shifted, several eyes staring at Pink-Sky while the rest wriggled in irritation. "It looks as if they are headed for the east pole," she said. "But that makes no sense at all. No one goes to the east pole. It is too hot and bristly."

Pink-Sky remarked sagely, "They seem to be getting very far from their home base, and the mountainous territory near the east pole makes the horizons undependable."

Dead-Troopers paused a moment, and then realized what her second-in-command was referring to. It was a good thing he was a lot smaller than she was, or he would have been leader of the clan.

"You are right, as usual," she said. "Let us gather the warriors and go east to the first range of ridges, to the one that has a cliff different than the rest, the one that looks as if it is a horizon until you are almost on it."

Pink-Sky shortly had a signaling crew together and was sending out phased messages to the nearby barbarian clan settlements. The message took a long time to send, since the signaling crew had to adjust their treading to emphasize the natural resonant frequencies of the crust.

"What is that strange rumbling sound in the crust?" one of the novices inside the circle of marching troopers asked. "Is it a crustquake?"

"No," another said. "This is the wrong part of Egg for quakes."

Swift-Killer had felt the rumble long before the novices. Despite what one of them had said, the east pole was crustquake country, but this was not a quake.

What they felt was only a long distance signal from one barbarian clan to another. From its similarities to others she had heard, it was probably the call to assemble. No doubt her expedition this deep in barbarian territory had caused some concern. Since it was a long distance message, and not a localized call for attack, she had no need to put the troopers on alert, but she noticed with pride that most of them had felt the presence of the barbarians, and that the dragon teeth, which had been in typical marching disarray, now gleamed as a single, coordinated, double row of interleaved needles.

At the next rest break, Swift-Killer ordered out the feeding-time perimeter guard, and gathered the civilians to the center.

"The barbarians have called for an assembly to decide what to do about us," she said. "Hopefully, they will realize that we are not bothering their settlements, and are too large to attack, and will leave us alone. However, this is the territory of Trooper-Killer, one of the few barbarian chieftains to have killed more than one trooper and survived to tell about it. For the next few turns we will keep in a tight circle formation, and you civilians will have to stay in the center."

Moving in one direction while looking and fighting in another direction came easily to the multieyed, nonoriented cheela. Although each had a preferred set of eyes, all dozen worked well and gave the cheela a complete, if two-dimensional, view of the region around them.

Each cheela also had one or two preferred eating pouches and elimination orifices, but with a little concentration to break many turns of habit, the two could actually be reversed in function if necessary. The same went for carrying pouches, which were just immature feeding pouches. However, it was only the very young or very old who slobbered on their collection of trinkets.

On the body of a typical cheela there were certain sections of skin that had developed good muscle tone and a high level of tactile sensory endings that made the best pseudopods, and there were other chunky muscular sections that were the best to drape about a crystallium manipulator skeleton for maximum leverage. All troopers learned in basic training camp to form deep pockets in their skin, backed up with crystallium sockets imbedded in their tread muscles to handle the long, heavy dragon teeth. A well-trained trooper could perform that function at any point around the circle while maintaining the measured tread of the advance ripple, and simultaneously eating, eliminating, and switching trinkets from one pouch to the next. It was the brag of Swift-Killer's troopers that they could engage in sex on top of all of that. But as had been proved during a few after-battle orgies, that was more talk than performance.

The commander of a circle of troopers had two choices. One was to put all the troopers of one sex in one ring, with the next ring of the opposite sex constantly riding partially on the topside of the first rank. This kept the troopers happy, with a constant reminder of fun either under tread or topside. However, there was always the problem of the one or two who didn't quite fit into the geometry of the circle. A second choice was to alternate male and female side-by-side in each rank, with purely (nearly) platonic interaction between ranks, although they were overlapping on topsides. Swift-Killer preferred the second ordering since it made for tighter rank spacing, despite the other problems it caused.

At one time, early in her career as an officer, she had considered the possibility of a trooper circle made up of only one sex. She could see herself, leading the Ferocious Females to triumph in battle. But her trooper background vetoed that bleak, joyless scene quickly. In their battles against the barbarians, the real enemy was boredom, and a single-sex battle circle would not survive long.

Dead-Troopers led her clan, and the out-family warriors who had joined them, off to the east, then back again to the west.

"A long crawl for no progress," Sinking-Cliff, one of the out-family fighters, complained. But even he had to admit that their route had taken them safely around the trooper scouts who would slither quickly over the horizon and back again.

Sinking-Cliff had been the leader of his small clan before he had decided to join forces with Dead-Troopers' larger clan that contained many of his out-family. The penetration of the large force of well-armed troopers into his clan territory was of great concern, and he readily joined himself and his three best warriors to the cause. However, he did not really like taking commands from someone else.

Dead-Troopers knew that she was treading on prickly crust when she heard the complaint and made her move, but she could tolerate no insubordination if she were going to keep control of this half-wild band.

"Silence!" came Dead-Troopers' harsh whisper, and Sinking-Cliff half raised his club as a dozen eyes on a huge form blazed down at him.

Dead-Troopers dropped into lingua inter-familia, and applied her most diplomatic accent—Pink-Sky would have been proud of her. "Even hatchlings are quiet when the Swift is around," she admonished in a soft whisper. "This dark-side cliff we have come to is along the path of the marauding troopers," Dead-Troopers continued. "There is none other like it, since all other cliffs in this region show their faces to the bright light."

The tension relaxed, and Dead-Troopers slid a pseudopod on the topside of Sinking-Cliff as she continued, "The path of the troopers takes them to the bright-light side of this cliff. They will never see us behind it, and we can rush out and take them unaware." She removed her pseudopod with a promising pat and glided off to arrange the attack.

TIME: 07:56:30 GMT MONDAY 20 JUNE 2050

The expedition to the east pole moved slowly on in its quiet but determined way. Scouts moved ahead to look over the horizon, but the crust was getting prickly, especially on the way back, so they did not range out as far as they had done in the past. None of them realized that the horizon off to one side was not the real horizon, but instead was the top of a precipitous cliff that sheltered a horde of barbarians behind its sharp edge.

It was to Dead-Troopers' credit that she held her mixed pseudo-clan of warriors until the circle glided past. She released them with a terrible thump that shook the very crust under Swift-Killer's tread and they attacked with a fury born of turn upon turn of punitive raids on their loved ones and hatchlings.

"At Alert!" t'trumed Swift-Killer, and narrowed herself down to pass through the dazed civilians to the rear of the circle.

Her automatic judgment of the tactical situation was verified when she saw the stream of barbarians seem to pour endlessly out of a notch in the horizon. Her dozen eyes lifted slightly on stubs as they once again evaluated the near perfect boundary between dark sky and glowing crust, and she saw her mistake. A slight rise of the glowing crust indicated a low cliff. Too low to see, but high enough to hide a war party of barbarians.

"East! West! North! Bright! — East! West! North! Bright! — East! . . ." chanted Swift-Killer as her eyes took in the battle situation. Her troopers moved obediently in a rigid march that took them nowhere, as their bodies became attuned to the cooperative movement and the deadly needles of the dragon teeth formed their impenetrable barrier about the circle of close-coupled troopers.

The civilians peered over the flattened ranks of troopers and some of them were beginning to panic. Swift-Killer lowered the intensity of her rhythmic thump on the crust as her squad leaders took up the chant to make up for the loss of her volume.

Swift-Killer circled around the inner rank of her troopers, sliding encouraging pseudopods on male and female alike, as her whisper sped through the crust, its electronic tingle emphasizing the solid thump of the squad leaders.

". . . North! Bright! — East! West! North! . . ."

At the same time, she thinned out the inner third of her body and spread a thin hatching mantle over the bewildered noncombatants at the center. In almost automatic reflex action, their bodies reverted to minimum area, and they huddled together under the protective cloak. As the pressure in the center was released, the ranks of troopers compacted, and the needle points at the outer ring grew imperceptibly closer together.

Swift-Killer watched the charge of the barbarians with cool detachment. Although they came in a group, they were still individuals, and the first of those individuals actually to make contact with the deadly circle of dragon teeth would die, and both she and the barbarians knew that horrible fact.

". . . West! North! Bright! — East! West! North! . . ." Swift-Killer added the thump of her tread to the clamor as the barbarians approached. With a roar that shook the very crust, they came straight along the easy direction from the west, then broke into two peeling waves that plowed their way off into the hard directions toward the north and Bright sides.

Swift-Killer had expected the attack to break off in the face of a well-tended circle. What she had not expected was the rattle of pod seeds and smooth rocks rolling and sliding across the crust toward her circle of troopers. That was all that they were, rocks and garbage from an ordinary pod meal, but the unexpected did to her troopers what anything unexpected would do to any group—it confused them. In their effort to avoid what was harmless, the troopers slid to one side or the other. Their careful cadence was lost and the impenetrable barrier of needlelike dragon teeth wavered.

From the middle of the still flowing barbarian horde burst Dead-Troopers and five of her warriors. They were nearly hidden by their load of undried cheela skin. Swift-Killer's eyes shrank at the sight, but she had to admire the tactical effectiveness of the result. As the raw cheela skin contacted the pricks of the dragon teeth, the natural death reflexes in the muscular skin pouched up and grasped the points of the dragon teeth in viselike sphincters.

Backing off for a moment, the barbarians let the skins drag the ends of the deadly needles to the crust, and then flowed over their grisly weapon and pinned the circle defenses under their treads as they encountered the outer perimeter, their clubs and stolen short swords shattering crystal and slashing skin.

"West! West! West! West! . . ." t'trumed Swift-Killer as she changed the cadence and moved the circle into the direction of the attack. The small knot of fighting troopers and barbarians stayed fixed, each slashing where they could at the small amount of skin exposed behind their shields of dried skin or Flow Slow plates. Meanwhile, the steady cadence moved the circle of troopers around the point of attack, like a cell enveloping its struggling prey. The surprise was gone, and the next rapid attack of the barbarians from the east did not produce the desired confusion when a rattle of crustal pebbles and pod seeds came sliding across the crust. The needle points of the dragon teeth did not waver, and the holders of the remainder of the poor unfortunate cheela who had unwillingly donated his very skin to the cause of the barbarian attack left their glowing white juices dripping off the ends of the dragon teeth.

"Out! Out! Out! Out!" Swift-Killer commanded. She expanded the circle in all directions, but most importantly in the direction towards the clump of barbarian warriors. The pincher closed and the needle points of the dragon teeth began to have their effect.

With the trap shut, Swift-Killer pulled back her mantle from over the civilians. Making herself into an avenging needle, she slipped her huge bulk between two of her troopers in the rear ranks. Three knives held in front of her and her short sword trailing behind, she screeched a high-pitched whisper that threw the knot of combatants into confusion, and dove in under their bodies, knives slashing.

Swift-Killer climbed out of the hole she had carved out of the middle of Dead-Troopers' body, glowing juices running down her eye-stubs. She then attacked the rest of the beleaguered barbarians from behind. Their initiative was lost, and it took little time for the troopers to finish them all with thrusts of their short swords.

Swift-Killer looked across the topsides of the still quivering bags of juice and surveyed her command. True to the tradition of trooper discipline, even if the commander seemed to ignore it, the squad leaders had disengaged the little knot of dead and wounded to the inside, and a nearly perfect circle of regrouped troopers were now arrayed in rank after rank, their needle points in perfect array as the cadence continued. "East! West! North! Bright! — East! West! North! . . ." The remainder of the barbarian horde sent taunts and curses through the crust, made weaker and weaker feinting attacks, and finally faded off over the horizon.

Swift-Killer shivered her skin, sending yellow-white globs of cooling juice showering down on the bare topsides of the motionless layers of skin beneath her tread. She slowly flowed down off the sagging mound of flesh, checking each one of her short slashing blades before inserting them back into her lined weapons pouch. As she descended, her tread automatically kneaded the flaccid skin beneath her and worked out the lumps that were hidden away in the enemy skin pouches.

One cache yielded buttons. Swift-Killer paused in shock. There were three single buttons that signaled that each had come from a trooper; a dublet button that used to grace the skin of a squad leader; and another with four buttons that matched the one that now glistened wetly on her supple skin.

"The Trooper-Killer!" she said, and fury sent her short sword again and again through the already damaged brain-knot. Her exhaustion forgotten in the discovery, she moved the dead hunks of meat off the sworn enemy of every troop commander of the east border, and proceeded to strip the tiniest pouch of that dead hulking body.

To her dismay, she found four more trooper buttons—well tarnished—in an almost sealed-off pouch, but nothing else.

"Kill! Kill! Kill!" she murmured. "Nothing to live for but to kill troopers."

She went on to the other bodies, glancing around as she did so to notice that the battle was over and the circle was back in its proper form. One body yielded a trooper button, but this one came from the holding sphincter of a trooper, who had died defending its honor. She searched the periphery until she found the trooper's heritage pouch, and she slowly kneaded it until she extracted the mementos given to the trooper as he left his clan to join the eastern border guard. She separated the personal ones from the clan ones, tossing most of the personal ones to the crust but taking those that might be of value to her some turn. She put the clan totem into a special pouch that she sealed until she might, at some future time, deliver it to the clan chief, while giving thanks for the assistance of that segment of the clan in the protection of the far-flung borders of Bright's Empire.

"It is a good thing that we lose so few troopers in these skirmishes with the barbarians," she thought to herself, "or else the troop commanders would be so laden down with clan totems that they would not be able to move."

At the thought, she self-consciously twitched the little pouch in a forgotten segment of her body that had not been opened for over three dozen greats of turns, and would not—until death relaxed the sphincter that kept her little piece of homeland and kin within her.

Swift-Killer continued her search. Two of her troopers and six barbarians. A poor trade. And it was her fault for not having trained her troopers against the "rolling garbage" attack. It was an old and seldom used tactic, but in this time and in this environment it had come close to equaling the odds for the barbarians.

Kneading a recalcitrant pouch on one of the last barbarian skin sacks, she almost cut her tread. Moving off and sliding a pseudopod under the edge of the folded skin, she extracted a short sword. The fact that a barbarian had succeeded in wresting a short sword from a trooper was not unusual, but the condition of the short sword was. She examined its shining sides and keenly honed edge with wonder. If only her troopers could be encouraged to keep their weapons in such good condition! She pouched the shining sword in her weapons pouch and finished the inspection, then finally turned to cleaning herself.

The troop was still on full circle march alert, when she finally finished and resumed command.

"Rest!" rolled the command through the crust, and the gleaming needles of the dragon teeth stopped in space, paused, then relaxed into a disarrayed, but still outward-facing circle.

"Make camp!

"Post Guards!

"Squad Leaders Report!"

The commands rippled out through the crust and the troop camp took on its normal life style as the subordinates interpreted the Commander's orders, added a few of their own for local order and discipline, and then gathered near the mound of cooling bodies for a conference with their Troop Commander.

"We are in no real hurry," Swift-Killer announced to them. "And we have a long way to go in hostile territory without food storage depots. We will stop here long enough to dry the meat, then we will move on to the east."

The squad leaders were pleased with the Commander's decision. The troopers had been on constant march for a dozen turns, and this break would not only give the more restless ones a few moments to relieve the pressure of their juices, but would also give the whole command a chance to revert to a seminormal life style, not to mention a welcome change in diet from the ever-present food pods.

The squad leaders had no trouble in getting volunteers for butcher duty, and soon the whole pile of eight bodies was neatly drained, the muscular meat carefully sliced from the skin and the leathery skin stretched out as far as it would go in the easy direction. The ends were held down with the ample weight of a couple of otherwise useless novice astrologers, and left to dry for a turn on the glowing crust, until they were ready to rewrap the meat hunks that they had so recently enveloped.

When the butchering crew came to the eggs, there was a lengthy pause. One of the troopers and the Trooper-Killer barbarian were found to have eggs in their egg cases. Unfortunately for the sensibilities of the butchering crew, the precious egglings were still alive in their leathery sacs.

The news of the living egglings brought Swift-Killer to the scene at once. As much as she hated it, it was her duty to pass judgment. She looked carefully at the leathery egg-sacs, sliding each one in turn under the protection of a hatching mantle to feel the pulsating life form within.

Unfortunately, the pulsations from the wee ones only confirmed what they all knew. Egg-sacs with that color had no chance of surviving without many more turns of protection and nourishment within their mother.

Swift-Killer felt the terrible urge to lift the little eggling into her egg case—to give it the protection and nourishment that it needed. But she knew full well that within one turn, her normally protective egg case would have swollen into a bloated anger, and the vile juices that it would have exuded would have literally dissolved the egg-sac and its precious cargo. As much as they all would have liked to have saved them, the egglings were doomed.

Swift-Killer softly took the two quivering egg-sacs into a holding pouch and moved off. The butchering crew continued their work, while the rest of the expedition followed Swift-Killer to the other side of the camp.

"Another nasty duty," Swift-Killer complained. She drew out the flashing sword that she had so recently acquired.

"If it has to be done, let it be done quickly," she said. With two swift slices, she sacrificed the juices of the egglings to the all-absorbing crust of Egg, which glowed momentarily in response.

The others returned to the camp, but Swift-Killer, who had had the duty, stayed on to punish herself. As she looked at the dead egglings, she was horrified at her inner thoughts.

"That is a tender looking slice of meat," her appetite said.

"Not even a barbarian would eat an eggling!" she remonstrated. Shifting her attention from the immature egglings baking on the glowing crust, she flowed back into the camp to supervise the wrapping of the meat, for that would be the troop's main source of food for many turns to come.

TIME: 07:56:36 GMT MONDAY 20 JUNE 2050

After two dozen turns, the expedition began to approach the east pole. Every direction was now a hard direction for travel, and if it weren't for the disciplined nature of the troopers, who were used to marching in close formation, the going would have been difficult. Fortunately, since there was no easy direction of travel, there was also no danger of rapid attack, and their guard could be relaxed. Swift-Killer changed the usual loose marching circle into a modified wedge. The troopers were placed in a sharp pointed chevron formation, with the front of the chevron thrusting steadily through the resistant atmosphere to force an opening. The remainder of the troopers kept the gap open, and the small group of scientist astrologers moved swiftly along at the trailing edge, moving easily into the gap created by the troopers.

To break the monotony, the squads in the troop had been having a contest. Each squad would take a turn as pathbreaker and see how many treads they could keep up the pace before having to fall back and let the following squad have their turn. Each squad, of course, had to break the previous squad's record, and when Swift-Killer began to notice that several troopers on the front line were beginning to surreptitiously drop equipment and food parcels from their pouches in order to keep up the pace, she decided to call a break before things got beyond control.

"Cease March!" Swift-Killer's voice rolled through the crust.

An exhausted group of troopers halted their steady push and felt the hardness close in around them. Since all directions were hard going, no one wanted to move from his position, but Swift-Killer was pleased to see that the squad leaders kept after their troopers until they were dispersed in a rough circle, with a few individuals designated to keep one or two eyes on the horizon while they were eating.

"They really must be tired," Swift-Killer thought as she looked around. "No one has the energy to pair off for a little fun."

Having stayed at her normal position near the center of the troop, Swift-Killer had not had to participate in the exhausting procedure of breaking path, and so had not even begun to tax her great strength. So she was feeling fine and would have liked to have a little relaxation after eating; but a quick survey of her many lovers among the troop convinced her that she should let them rest.

Swift-Killer wandered over to the clump of astrologers and approached Cliff-Watcher, who was busy tying knots in a tally string. On the crust beside him were three tread sticks.

"Amazing, simply amazing," Cliff-Watcher was murmuring to himself as he added knot after knot to the tally string.

"What's amazing?" Swift-Killer asked, curious as always, and confident enough in her position to ask questions of someone many turns her junior.

"Egg is really shaped like an egg!" exclaimed Cliff-Watcher as a few of his eyes glanced away from the tally string and noticed her approach. He then saw the bewilderment in the jerky overtones of Swift-Killer's normal eye-wave pattern and continued, "I have been keeping a count of the number of standard treads on our march with the tread sticks. The east pole is on a very flat place on Egg. It takes many, many treads of travel before there is a noticeable change in the horizon," he said.

Swift-Killer looked ahead along their direction of travel. She could see the east pole mountains just raising their tops over the horizon. It was true, the horizon had hardly changed for the last three turns.

"Like an egg?" she asked.

"Yes," the young astrologer said. "An egg-sac is flattened on the top and bottom because of the pull of gravity, and spreads out in the other directions. Our home, Egg, seems to be constructed the same way. Near the east and west poles it is very flat and you have to go a long way to see a change in the horizon. Halfway between the east and west pole, where Bright's Heaven is, the horizon is very close in the east and west direction but many treads away in the hard direction."

Swift-Killer knew this elementary fact of the topography near Bright's Heaven, but she had never connected it with the shape of Egg. However, neither she nor Cliff-Watcher realized that Cliff-Watcher's calculations had misled him. The star was spherical, not egg-shaped. It was his tread sticks that were distorted, giving him a false impression. Everything on the star—the tread sticks, the dragon crystal weapons and even the nuclei in their bodies—was distorted by the trillion-gauss magnetic field of the star so that they were many times longer along the magnetic field lines than across them. Since even their eyes participated in the general stretching, they couldn't see the distortion; everything looked normal to them.

Swift-Killer turned professional. "How many treads until we reach the east pole mountains?" she asked.

Cliff-Watcher, who was proud of his advanced education in conceptual geometry, immediately went into a calculation trance, his practiced counting tendrils shooting forth from his body. The tendrils began to wave and interlace with each other at blinding speed. Finally he broke from the trance.

"Two dozen standard marches," he announced.

Swift-Killer looked at the east pole mountains that loomed over the deceptively near horizon and announced, "Then I guess we had better get the troop moving."

Without shifting, she roared, "At Alert!" The troop smoothly reformed and continued their push to the east, the disruptive contest between squads forgotten.

Cliff-Watcher had been right, it really was about two dozen standard marches to the east pole mountains, but since a standard march between breaks was impossible in this terrain, it really took much longer.

"It is like constantly climbing a hill in the hard direction," Swift-Killer complained to herself as she took a turn at the point of the chevron forcing its way into the hard direction.

"I know," said the trooper at her right. "Except you never end up on top."

Swift-Killer breasted another furry hillock in front of her. Each tiny little thread of crust was sticking up toward the sky in the easy direction. It looked impossible—the threads seemed to be laughing at the powerful gravity pull of Egg. But when Swift-Killer had to push over that tiny little thread, along with the myriad others that made up the fuzzy surface, she found they were powerfully strong. It took a great deal of strength just to move through the fuzz, knocking it down and pushing on over it. Then on top of it all, if the fuzz slowed her down too much, the hard direction closed in on her and made the going even worse.

The troop finally reached the foothills of the east pole mountains without further incident. Swift-Killer looked with awe at the height of the mountains, then upwards at the Eyes of Bright, still hanging in the sky far above the mountains, defying the mighty pull of Egg.

Swift-Killer put the camp on bivouac status. First, long-range sentries were put out at a good distance from the camp; then she allowed the troopers to put down their weapons. A file of troopers went into a virgin stand of crust-fuzz and stamped out a circular depressed region where the dragon teeth and the short swords were stacked to block out the constant winds. In the center, the remainder of the pods and dried meat was stored, while those who had been burdened with their weight during the long march became free again to frolic without care. Hunting parties were formed, with old and new couples taking off in small carefree groups to see what was off on the horizon. Now was an important time for Swift-Killer. She gathered the astrologers and began to set up her experiment. She first took the flat glancer mirror and set it on a mound of rubble at an angle until she could go off at a distance and see the Eyes of Bright reflected off the center of the mirror.

"The Eyes of Bright are larger and closer, and they look a little brighter," Cliff-Watcher remarked, as a few of his eyes scanned the cluster of seven lights in the sky.

"I should hope so, after all the work we did to get here," Swift-Killer said crankily as she struggled to scrape a notch for the curved expander in the fuzzy crust some distance away from the glancer.

"I could never figure out why Bright chose to send his Eyes to the east pole, when we were in Bright's Heaven," Cliff-Watcher mused.

"Perhaps Bright did not want to see us too well, because we are so wicked," Swift-Killer said in annoyance. "Here, hold this while I sight through the pointing hole."

Swift-Killer had the large, curved expander standing vertically on the crust. It came up almost to the top of Cliff-Watcher as he moved over to surround it and hold it vertical. He was glad it had not been his job to keep that thing pouched during their travels.

Cliff-Watcher flowed his body away from the center of the expander as Swift-Killer backed off and stared through the small hole in the plate. Swift-Killer moved her eye until she could see the center of the glancer through the hole. There, shining in the center of the flat mirror were the Eyes of Bright. Now she had to tilt the expander until the image of her eye off the flat backside of the expander was swallowed up in the hole that she was looking through; in that way she knew that the expander was pointing at the glancer, which in turn was pointing up at the Eyes of Bright.

"Up a little," she said. "Hold it!" She moved quickly and soon Cliff-Watcher's place was taken by a cluster of pieces of crust.

The message to the strange sticklike beings in the Inner Eye

had been decided long ago. Since they had used a rectangular
format with a prime number of rows and columns to send crude
pictures, they would certainly recognize that format if it were
beamed back to them—only the picture inside the rectangle
would be new. First it would show a picture of the Eyes of
Bright over the east pole with a dragon tooth pointing the way
to Bright's Heaven. Then later pictures would show the Eyes of
Bright hovering over Bright's Heaven, with the distinctive profile
of the east pole mountains poking up over the horizon of Egg.
Each picture had been converted into a complex tally string,
ready to read off. Swift-Killer gathered her crew of astrologers
and they proceeded to retransmit the message that they had sent
in vain from the compound back at the Inner Eye Institute.

"Long burn, flick, flick, flick, dash, flick . . ." Swift-Killer intoned as she ran the tally string through a set of tendrils. The
crew of flare holders and pod-juice controllers kept up their
steady work, and flash after flash of light glared from the end of
the flare, reflected from the curved surface of the expander into a
straight beam that flashed across the crust to the glancer, then
went beaming upwards toward the cluster of lights in the sky.
After several lines, Swift-Killer would take another look through
the sighting holes to make sure that the beam was being sent off
in the right direction, while the flare crew replaced their flares
with fresh ones.

After the first picture had been sent, Swift-Killer went over to
the astrologer whom she had put in charge of the dark detector.
She was slightly disappointed that there had been no darkening
of the detector, but she resolved to keep on with the rest of the
series.

A dozen turns and more than twice as many messages later,
Swift-Killer finally had to admit that perhaps the messages were
still not getting through.

"The Eyes still look dim to us, so you can imagine that our
weak little light is going to be very dim by the time it gets
up through the murky atmosphere," Cliff-Watcher said as his
thinned out body tried to knead the worries out of the flattened
Swift-Killer.

Swift-Killer lay relaxed under the tender ministrations of Cliff-
Watcher and felt the small globules that used to be a piece of
Cliff-Watcher moving slowly through her body on their way to

her egg case. Her body was at rest, but her mind was a turmoil of emotion.

"If they cannot see us yet, then we must get closer," she said. "I am going to climb the mountains to where the atmosphere is clearer."

Cliff-Watcher's kneading stopped. "But that will take forever!" he remonstrated.

"So it may," said Swift-Killer, who had slipped out from under Cliff-Watcher and had rapidly resumed her more normal shape. She was now putting on her office of command as she gathered and pouched the tools, weapons and trinkets that she had cast aside earlier. "But we are going anyway."

TIME: 07:56:48 GMT MONDAY 20 JUNE 2050

The climbing of the east pole mountains was like a siege. The mountains were many times higher than any that had ever been attempted. Swift-Killer took her time to organize her support, for once she had started up the mountain the organization would have to run itself. The formal command structure of the troop was dismantled, and a new arrangement organized more along the lines of a permanent border fort replaced it. A quarry crew was sent out and soon a fortified compound replaced the campground. Regular hunting parties were organized, and the short swords and dragon teeth soon were sinking their sharp fangs into wandering animals instead of their natural prey. With much grumbling, long rows of petal plants were placed in the crust, and the business of tending them rotated among the troopers— who in many cases had only joined up to get away from the clan farm.

With her supply lines secure, Swift-Killer organized the assault on the east pole mountains. Swift-Killer, Cliff-Watcher and North-Wind would lead the climb, but backing them would be over half the troop. Swift-Killer worked carefully, orchestrating the climb like a major battle. Twice she backed down from a hard-won valley because the climb—although not difficult for an unburdened cheela—would have been impossible for one loaded with food parcels. Slowly the expedition worked its way into the foothills. Chunks of crust were stationed on the steeper slopes for rest stations, and soon two lanes of porters were moving back and forth from the fort on the lowlands to the point of the climb that slowly thrust its way inward and upward.

"That was a terrible stretch," Cliff-Watcher complained as he lay exhausted on the crust in one of the rare flat spots in the mountain pass. "The glancer almost wouldn't fit through that narrow crevasse."

Swift-Killer, her body bulging with the curved shape of the expander, ignored the complaint and announced, "This will be an ideal place for our next base camp. I will go ahead and reconnoiter, while you two work your way down to the lead parcel crew. Take your time and make sure that you secure the path for them."

Swift-Killer carefully emptied her pouch of the expander, and moved swiftly off as North-Wind and Cliff-Watcher wearily dropped their loads and moved back down the mountain.

Swift-Killer was pleased. The way ahead was steep, but broad. They would make good progress with their loads over this stretch. In her hurry to explore well ahead, she thinned her body down and pushed only a narrow path through the prickly crust. She would broaden it on her way back down, when the tremendous pull of Egg would help instead of hinder her motion. She came around a low ledge and then stared at the barrier ahead.

"Bright's Curse!" she exploded. Her eyes scanned the area, but there was no escape from the fact that the canyon they had been traveling had come to an abrupt end. There was a tall cliff blocking the way. She moved closer to it and began to examine the vertical cracks that rent the face in the easy direction.

There were a lot of the cracks, for the crust had very little strength in the easy direction, and the pull of Egg was constantly attempting to draw the soaring cliffs to its bosom. This particular cliff must have been formed recently, for it had not been worn much by the ever-present winds. Swift-Killer searched along the base and then found a fairly large rent that went back a good way into the cliff. Conquering her fear of the cliff face towering over her, she moved up to the rent. Without looking up at the terrifying sight of that mass of rock ready to fall on her topside, she narrowed down and pushed her body into the crack. She soon filled the bottom of it completely. Then, still pushing with her tread and muscles on the outside, she forced her body fluids into the narrow crack; slowly her body became tall and narrow instead of its usual flattened ellipsoidal shape. Although the pull of Egg tried to drag her down, the narrow crevasse kept her from being flattened, and since the easy direction was upwards, it was not hard to move in that direction, while the hardness in the horizontal direction actually helped her to maintain her body in the crevasse. She pushed and pushed and felt the pressure build up in her lower body. When she felt she could stand the pressure no longer, she took a quick, terrified glance up the remainder of the crack and was disappointed to find that she had climbed only a small portion of the way to the top.

Dismay and terror weakened her hold, and she felt herself falling down and out the bottom of the crevasse. The force of her fall caused her internal juices to form a small wave that actually rolled her outside sack of skin over and over. For the first time since she was a tiny hatchling blown about by the wind, she found herself tread upwards.

Swift-Killer slowly righted her bruised body and moved away from the front of the cliff while she thought. She went over to a mound of rubble and thoughtfully picked her way through the chunks of crust that lay tumbled there. She picked up several good-sized slabs that were thick plates. She went back to the crevasse with her burden and, turning one of the chunks endways, pushed it ahead of her into the crevasse. She again pushed her body into the crack, and lifted the plate up as high as she could. She then turned the slab sideways and slowly let it come down, where the flat edges jammed against the narrowing sides of the crack as the pull of Egg sat it firmly into place. Swift-Killer slowly relinquished her hold, and she watched in pleasure as the heavy chunk of crust stayed suspended between the walls of the crevasse, just over her normal eye height. She took another slab, a longer one this time, and soon it too was suspended against the pull of Egg at the same height, but further out from the back of the notch. Swift-Killer looked her creation over with care and then flowed back out of the crevasse and shortly returned from the rubble pile with another thick slab of crust, longer than the others. With a great effort she lifted the slab and soon it was in place, resting on top of the other two. Swift-Killer hesitated, then slowly induced herself to glide under the improvised platform to the back of the crevasse. She again forced her body into the narrow crack, and stretching out a narrow pseudo-pod that snaked up to rest on top of the wedged slabs, she slowly pumped her juices up against the pull of Egg so that they inflated that portion of her skin on the platform. She halted after she had several eyes transferred to the upper level, then formed some strong manipulators that grasped the top slab tightly. Then, firmly anchored, she finally pushed and pulled the rest of her body up onto the platform.

All during this long procedure, Swift-Killer had been careful to keep all of her dozen eyes carefully concerned with watching the wall, the manipulators, the slabs, anything but the outside environment. Only when she was safely on top of the slab, her manipulators keeping her from flowing off the front or the back, and the firm walls of the crevasse holding her in from the sides, did she finally allow herself to observe the predicament she had put herself into. She looked out of the crevasse at the horizon, then at the pile of rubble in the distance, then at the crust just at the entrance to the crevasse, then just inside the entrance, and then her eyes refused to look any further. Try as she might, she just couldn't seem to make them look down from the platform where she hunched, perched at a height above the crust that would have burst her skin like a ripe pod if she had fallen.

"It needs to be wider," Swift-Killer said to herself, "if we are going to use this as a platform to make another one further up. And perhaps they should be closer together so it isn't as hard to flow up onto them. But it will work. We will just make floating platforms up the crevasse to the top of the cliff."

Swift-Killer slowly let herself down, forming a few more massive manipulators to hold onto small ledges in the cliff walls to slow her descent. She quickly flowed out from beneath the platform and returned to the base camp, happily breasting her way down through the fuzzy crust.

Conquering the cliff took many turns. Although some of the troopers soon became expert scalers, and even found a technique to get the awkward expander and glancer up the notch, almost one-third of the troopers were incapable of forcing themselves to climb up on the overhanging platforms. Despite the thinning out of her supply line, Swift-Killer pressed on, and as the double line of the expedition wound its way through the east pole mountains, it slowly became obvious to all that the atmosphere was getting thinner and the visibility was getting better. Far to the north, they could see a swirling cloud of smoke that came southward from the large volcano in the northern hemisphere and, turning at the east pole, made its way out to the west along the equator. However, the dense clouds didn't penetrate into the mountains.

During a rest period, Cliff-Watcher gazed up at the seven bright points of light. "Perhaps we could try sending a message again," he said.

Swift-Killer had made up her own mind about that long ago. "It is clearer," she said. "But we could still have a better chance of being seen if we were to go higher still, for the atmosphere is getting thinner rapidly as we go higher. We could attempt a message now, but we have only a limited supply of flares and pod juice, and I would rather wait to use them when we are as high as we can get."

The climb had taken over two greats of turns. Even Swift-Killer was surprised when she realized that she would soon have a second egg mature inside her to be sent back down with one of the plodding porters that moved back and forth between base camps, shuttling food up the living chain. Finally, the supply line had been stretched to its limit. There was no limit to the food supply at the base of the mountains, for the fort had turned into a prosperous town, complete with egg-pens, hatchling schools, farms and small businesses set up on the side by enterprising troopers. The hunting parties and harvesters kept a steady stream of food pouring into the base of the pyramid, but most of it went into supplying the daily needs of the porters who used the energy to haul supplies up the mountain against the great pull of Egg. Swift-Killer finally called a halt at a flat place in the mountains.

"We will stop here," she said to Cliff-Watcher and North-Wind. "I want you both to rest and eat well to build up your reserves while the porter crews build up our supplies. I will scout ahead and see if there is another place equally as good ahead of us. If there is, we will move on to it to send our message, otherwise, we will attempt it from here."

Swift-Killer emptied out her pouches, especially the bulky glancer she had been carrying, and moved steadily on up the canyon. She was gone for so many turns that Cliff-Watcher and

North-Wind began to get worried, but finally she returned with good news.

"There is another wide, level place further up the mountain," she said. "It will be a long climb carrying the equipment, but there are no tricky traverses or steep cliffs, just a long, upward trip."

She glanced at the nervously twitching eye-stubs of her two compatriots. She could tell that they were thinking about objecting to a continuation of the climb, since the messages could be sent almost as well from their present spot. She decided to reassert her authority.

"At Alert!" boomed the tread of Troop Commander Swift-Killer, only slightly muffled by the fuzzy crust.

Although Cliff-Watcher was not a trooper, he had been living with the troop for so long that he found his body imitating the instant response of North-Wind as the Commander's rigid eyes glared at them.

"The sole purpose of this entire expedition is to send a message to the beings in the Inner Eye," Swift-Killer began. "And I intend to do that to the best of my ability—and yours! This camp is not the best place to send that message, so we will go on—do you understand?"

"Yes, Commander," boomed North-Wind's formal reply, echoed by Cliff-Watcher's awed response.

"Good!" she said. "From now on, I want you two to obey my orders." Her body relaxed slightly and she continued. "We three will push on in a dozen turns, after we all have had time to rest, build up our internal food reserves, and have a good supply of food parcels. Now for my orders. My first order is to rest. My second order is to eat well, and my third order is to thin out, because I have just returned from a long lonely journey, and I am going to take you both on at once." With that she moved in between them and shortly was enjoying being the middle layer of a triple layer orgy.

After twelve turns of rest and recreation, Swift-Killer was anxious to be on her way. Since they had to have other things to occupy their time besides eating and sex, she had Cliff-Watcher learn the finer points of short-sword infighting from North-Wind while she refereed. Then both she and North-Wind learned to make counter tendrils and soon both could compute almost as fast as Cliff-Watcher.

They were now ready to go. She had convinced North-Wind that there was very little likelihood of meeting barbarians in the mountains at these heights, so they left their weapons. They loaded up with the all-important message equipment and as much food as they could carry, and the three set off up the mountain. The rest of the troop was left with orders to set up food caches at the various base camps down the mountain and to withdraw to the fort.

The climb was difficult, but as Swift-Killer had assured them, there was nothing particularly tricky about it. Because of their bulky burdens, however, it took them much longer to make the climb than it had taken Swift-Killer in her exploration climb. They ate their food rapidly as their bodies labored under the pull of Egg.

"I always felt that I would rather carry the food in my juices than in my pouches," North-Wind said as he ate a pod. "It may all weigh the same, but somehow when it is inside me, I feel it is at least carrying its share of the load."

"I will be glad to relieve you of any food you don't want to carry any longer," Cliff-Watcher said.

"Sorry," North-Wind said, carefully sucking the last drop of juice from a pod skin as he pulled it from his eating pouch. "Last one."

"Oh well," Cliff-Watcher said as North-Wind cracked open each pod seed with a tiny, hard manipulator and carefully ate the little kernel inside. "Guess we might as well be on our way." He turned his attention to Swift-Killer, who was busy calculating something.

"That will work out just about right," she said. "We are about two turns from our destination. We will be out of food by then, but our body reserves will last long enough for us to send up the messages and get back to the base camp with plenty to spare, although we will be hungry most of the way back down."

"I'm hungry right now," Cliff-Watcher said, "and I finished all my food last turn."

"That is what the troopers call fat hunger," North-Wind said. "When you think you are hungry just because you are used to eating every turn. You can't eat every turn when you are a trooper pursuing barbarians. Wait a dozen turns, then you will know what being hungry really means."

"I'm not looking forward to it," Cliff-Watcher said as he led the way up the canyon.

At last they came over a rise and entered the wide, level region that Swift-Killer had found. With a sigh of relief, they unloaded the message equipment and spread out on the fuzzy crust for a rest.

"I sure could use some food right now," Cliff-Watcher said. "Even an unripe pod would taste good."

"You would never make a trooper," North-Wind retorted. "I haven't been hungry since we left the last base camp. It is all just a matter of proper attitude. Look at me, I am not even hungry for a pod, much less an unripe one."

"Well, that's too bad," Swift-Killer remarked. "I just happened to have saved out three ripe pods, but since North-Wind isn't hungry and Cliff-Watcher seems to pine for unripe pods, I guess I will just have to eat them myself."

At these words the two males swarmed over her, prodding her all over until they found the pouch that held the three pods. Despite her protests that this was no way to treat a troop commander, North-Wind held her down while Cliff-Watcher carefully kneaded the pouch open and extracted three slightly bruised pods. They all then relaxed, eating their last meal for some time, as they stared up at the tiny light hanging in the sky, with its ring of six bright lights slowly circling about it.

Soon the three were busy setting up the beaming apparatus. The flat glancer mirror was propped up at an angle against a nearby cliff, and the curved expander was placed a slight distance away. Swift-Killer organized them into a smoothly working team. North-Wind held up the flares, and kept them placed as close as possible to the point in space that Swift-Killer and Cliff-Watcher had decided upon. Cliff-Watcher used his finest tendrils to manipulate the flow valve on the holder for the pod juice, while Swift-Killer constantly checked the alignments of the various portions of the apparatus and at the same time rhythmically read off the calls from the tally string that she held at her side.

"Long burn, flick, flick, flick, dash, flick . . ." Swift-Killer droned slowly as Cliff-Watcher concentrated on turning the valve of the vial of pod juice and North-Wind held the flare carefully at the correct position.

The message was very boring, since it was just a picture with a lot of blank space, but both North-Wind and Cliff-Watcher had participated in previous attempts to beam a message up to Inner Eye and knew what they were getting into. The many short flashes representing spaces were just as important as the dashes representing points or the long burns that signified the beginning of a line. A few omitted flashes could badly distort the picture and the message they were trying to send.

Swift-Killer had decided long ago that accuracy was more important than speed, even constant speed. After all, the strange beings in the Inner Eye certainly took their time in sending down their pictures—almost as if they were too slow-witted to cope with anything faster.

They slowly ground through the first picture message. Swift-Killer called a halt to see if there was any darkening of the dark detector, indicating that there was a message coming back to them in return.

"Nothing," Swift-Killer said, as she lifted the small vial of fluid and peered through it.

Contact

TIME: 07:58:24.2 GMT MONDAY 20 JUNE 2050

The wide angle X-ray/ultraviolet scanner on Dragon Slayer detected a moderately strong pulsed emission in the east pole mountains. It had not been there when that same area had been scanned a few seconds ago. Automatic feature extractors singled out the region and a search-and-identify priority was assigned to the narrow angle scanner, which locked onto the blinking light source in a millisecond and began to record and analyze the pulses in detail.

An occasional pulse of high temperature thermal radiation at the east pole was not unexpected. Fairly often, a chunk of meteoric material would be pulled in by the star's gravity, and as it would approach the star, the extreme gravitational and magnetic fields of the star would rip the rock apart and transform it into a blob of ionized plasma. The hot gas would fall at near relativistic speeds down along the magnetic field lines to impact on the surface in a brilliant explosion of heat and light.

However, these pulses coming from the star were not the fiery blasts from infalling meteors. The regularity of the pulsations triggered a higher priority circuit that kept the narrow angle scanner on the pulsations until they quit several milliseconds later. Low-level judgment circuits evaluated the significance of the periodicity and assigned it a moderately high priority. The narrow angle scanner would return to that site often in its constantly varying scanning routine, but there was nothing there of interest to the humans.

TIME: 07:58:24.3 GMT MONDAY 20 JUNE 2050

"Let's try again," Swift-Killer said. Keeping the dark detector in front of one of her eyes, she went back to the apparatus. This time she held the valve herself with a set of manipulators, while a set of tendrils felt off the knots in the tally string.

Much later Swift-Killer called a halt. The second message had been beamed up to the Inner Eye, and still there was no response.

"If only we could be sure that our weak light could be seen at that distance," Swift-Killer complained bitterly.

"You could climb to the top of that peak over there," North-Wind said with mild sarcasm. "Cliff-Watcher and I will be glad to beam a message up to you and you could check on the reception."

For once, Swift-Killer was silent. She could think of nothing else to do but to try again.

They were nearing the end of the third message when a loud crash came vibrating through the crust. Swift-Killer didn't move. The highly developed sonic direction-finding apparatus in her tread had told her exactly what had happened.

"The glancer has fallen," she said. Her eyes, which had been concentrating on the work of monitoring the fall of the drops of pod juice onto the end of the flare, continued their gaze while Swift-Killer slowly turned the valve off, closing it tightly to prevent leaks. She pouched the vial, and then finally turned her attention to the base of the nearby cliff where the glittering shards of the broken glancer lay in a shattered heap.

Swift-Killer flowed over to the base of the cliff, forming a manipulator as she went. She felt through the sparkling pieces, but found none that were anywhere near the size of the original mirror.

"At least we got some of the messages off," Cliff-Watcher said consolingly.

"Yes, but there are still more, and we ought to repeat them as often as we can to make sure they are received," Swift-Killer said. "We must find a way to keep sending without using the glancer."

"Perhaps we can find a suitable chunk of crust around here," North-Wind suggested.

"I'm afraid not," Swift-Killer said. "I have been looking at the various types of crust as we passed by different formations, and all the material in these mountains seems to consist of fuzzy crust. I have not seen anything around here that had anywhere near as shiny a cleavage surface as a glancer. We will have to think of something else."

Swift-Killer tried many things. However, there was no way that she could get a beam formed and directed upwards to the Inner Eye. She had even tried leaning the expander up against the cliff at an angle (being careful this time to back it up with chunks of crust), but the light from the flare came in at such an angle that the light reflected from the expander was sprayed out in a distorted beam that rapidly dissipated into the sky. She knew where the focus spot of the expander was, but it was an unreachable point way up in the sky, at least a dozen times higher than she could reach, and almost as high as the cliff itself. Then she had an idea.

"If we put the expander flat on the crust, pointing up at the Eyes," she said, "then the focus spot will be up around the top of this cliff. If we climbed up there with the flares we could make the light near the focus and the beam from the expander would go straight up to the Eyes."

Being a trooper, North-Wind said nothing, but Cliff-Watcher exploded. "You can't be serious. That cliff must be twice as high as you are wide. It will take you a dozen turns to climb that high, even if you can find a route, and we are out of food! We will be nothing but bags of skin if we ever make it!"

"You are not going," Swift-Killer said. "You will stay here. I will need to have you move the expander to different positions along the face of the cliff until we get the focus spot so it is just above the edge of the cliff where we can reach it."

Swift-Killer went to the broken glancer, picked up one of the larger shards and pouched it.

"Let's go, North-Wind," she said, and took off toward the far end of the cliff, with the obedient trooper close on the tread of his Commander.

TIME: 07:58:24.4 GMT MONDAY 20 JUNE 2050

A fraction of a second later, the pulsed emission started again, and this time the narrow-angle scanner caught it early in its emission period. The semiautomatic search-and-identify circuits kept the scanner focused on the pulsations, while the feature extractor in the frequency analysis circuits activated a correlation program. A strong match was then found between the pulsation pattern of the emissions and the rectangular picture pattern that Abdul had chosen in his attempts at communication with Dragon's Egg. If the computer had been a human, its eyebrows would have raised.

The new correlation was enough to trigger an action circuit. As a result—a millisecond later—humans were called into the loop.

PERIODIC X-UV EMISSION—EAST POLE

Seiko glanced up at the computer message across the top of her screen. She was floating too far away from the console to reach any of the keys, so she used audibles, even if they were slower.

"Display!" she commanded, and instantly a replay of the narrow-angle X-ray/ultraviolet scanner was on her screen. She watched the regular blinking of the spot in the middle of the east pole mountains, then glanced up to see that the computer had slowed it down considerably for her.

1/100,000 REAL TIME

Seiko watched it for a few seconds. The pulsations stopped abruptly. There seemed to be no sense to them.

"Analysis!" she commanded.

The picture on the screen stayed, while the computer overprinted result after result of its analysis.

POSITION 0.1 DEG W LONG, 2.0 DEG N LAT
SPECTRUM MODIFIED THERMAL, 15,000 K
MODULATION SIMILAR TO DRAGON'S EGG COMM
    PICTURE
NO IDENTIFIABLE NATURAL SOURCE

Seiko scanned down the list and stiffened in shock. She expertly twisted her body in a midair position-reversal maneuver, caught hold of the edge of the console and pulled herself up to it. Her fingers flew over the keys. Within a few seconds, Swift-Killer's second message was building up on her screen.

"Abdul!" she called to the next console, where Abdul Nkomi Farouk was laboriously working out a new message. "They are answering!"

TIME: 07:58:28 GMT MONDAY 20 JUNE 2050

Cliff-Watcher had been right. The path that finally took them to the top of the cliff was tortuous and hard. Both Swift-Killer and North-Wind were hungry long before they reached the top, and this time it was the real hunger of someone who had been working at hard labor for a dozen turns. Swift-Killer still had plenty of reserves, but she was beginning to worry about North-Wind, for he was not as robust as she was. However, being a trooper, he never complained.

As Swift-Killer approached the edge of the cliff, she pulled the glancer shard from a pouch. "I'm sure I could never get one of my eyes to look down over the edge to see where Cliff-Watcher is, but as long as it thinks it is looking out at the horizon, I shouldn't have any trouble," she explained to North-Wind. Forming a strong manipulator with a deep root embedded in her tread muscles, she extended the shard out over the edge of the cliff.

She clustered her eyes in a line; with a little adjustment, she could see the deep red top of Cliff-Watcher waiting patiently next to the expander.

"I must really be getting hungry," Swift-Killer thought. "Here I am gazing full on the topside of a handsome young male and I am not even interested."

Swift-Killer turned to North-Wind and said, "We will have to move down this way." She led the way down the cliff until they were at the point above the waiting Cliff-Watcher. Cliff-Watcher had never thought that his hatchling name had amounted to much, and now here he was spending what seemed to be his last dozen turns on Egg, doing nothing but watching a cliff.

Swift-Killer tried both long-talk and short-talk, and soon found that there was no trouble in communicating with Cliff-Watcher if he just kept a portion of his tread leaning up against the face of the cliff.

Cliff-Watcher had already arranged the expander; it was as close to the base of the cliff as he could get it. North-Wind formed a heavy manipulator like that of Swift-Killer and slowly stretched it out over the edge, a small flare held at the end.

Swift-Killer removed one of the vials of pod juice from a pouch, and gripping it carefully, extended that, too. She constantly reminded herself to hold tightly to the vial; if it fell, the expander would be shattered in as many shreds as the glancer. Slowly she formed a muscular pseudopod that slithered out on top of the hefty manipulator. The fine tip of the pseudopod curled its way around the valve. The valve slowly turned and a tiny stream of liquid hit the end of the flare. They both flinched from the unaccustomed blue-white light, but soon a steady beam shot forth into the sky. Swift-Killer evaluated it carefully. Fortunately the winds were high that turn, and there were many dust particles in the air. Swift-Killer could see the strong beam as it went upwards, only to come to a bright point at some unimaginable distance overhead. Swift-Killer turned off the valve and they both slowly withdrew their manipulators back over the edge and relaxed.

"We are too far away from the focus spot," Swift-Killer said. "We will have to move down the cliff."

North-Wind had never been able to figure out exactly what Swift-Killer and Cliff-Watcher were talking about when they mentioned things like focus spots, but he decided to let Swift-Killer do the thinking. After all, she was the commander. He silently followed her along the edge of the cliff until they came to another convenient portion of the ledge where they could both get a good tread grip. Swift-Killer again stuck her little glancer over the edge and watched as Cliff-Watcher pouched the expander, hauled it to the new position underneath Swift-Killer's waving manipulator, then repositioned it carefully on the crust and moved back.

This time, when the light blazed from the top of the cliff, the beam that came out from the expander did not refocus. Swift-Killer thought that it was still slightly converging as she lost sight of it high in the sky, but it was good enough.

"We will continue our message," she said as she pulled the tally strings from a pouch. North-Wind shuffled the crust in resignation, retracted the short flare they had been using for testing purposes and replaced it with a longer one.

"At least I won't have to climb for a while," he said tiredly to himself, and settled down to hold the heavy manipulator as still as he possibly could.

Soon a disciplined pulsation of light was beaming its way up to the Eyes, continuing the message that had been interrupted a dozen turns ago when the glancer had fallen from the face of the cliff. Swift-Killer did not pause long when she came to the end. Since they were on their body reserves, it didn't help much to rest anymore; except for an occasional change of flare or pod juice vial, the two troopers doggedly kept at their task.

Their job finally finished, Swift-Killer and North-Wind started their way back down the path to the base of the cliff. By mutual consent, they left everything but their clan totems in a pile at the top of the cliff.

A dozen turns later, a weary Cliff-Watcher saw two very thin cheela slowly making their way around the end of the cliff. Swift-Killer was in front, breaking a path for the exhausted trooper.

"Another tread length," she would urge, and gently nudge the sides of his treads with her trailing edge to keep him rippling. Slowly the two came up to Cliff-Watcher.

"I cannot go any further," North-Wind said. "Leave me here."

"No," said Swift-Killer. "We are all going together." She turned her attention to Cliff-Watcher. "I know you are tired too, but we must get to the base camp where there is a cache of food waiting. You get behind North-Wind and keep him moving while I break path." Cliff-Watcher was too tired to argue and moved in behind his friend North-Wind. Together the three began to move off and down the sloping valley.

Cliff-Watcher, who had been checking the dark detector periodically, had just repouched it after looking to see if there had been any reply to their hard sent messages. There was nothing. He turned some of his eyes up to the specks of light above him and wondered at their silence. As he looked, a rapidly falling streak of bright light appeared to the side of the Eyes, high in the sky. The falling meteor became elongated and grew brighter and brighter. Cliff-Watcher stirred, and the other two raised their eyes, then tried to draw them under their protective flaps. There was no time. In an instant the whole sky was aflame with an explosion of light and heat that seared their topsides and left three skinny blobs of scorched, blinded flesh that wriggled away from each other in their attempts to escape the pain.

Swift-Killer had never hurt so. Her last thought was that Bright had decided to punish her for having the temerity to attempt to talk to God. The automatic protective mechanisms in her body, activated by the lack of body reserves and the shock from the topside burns, suddenly took over. The animal reflexes were turned off, and for the first time in untold generations, a cheela went to sleep.

TIME: 07:58:37 GMT MONDAY 20 JUNE 2050

Abdul came flying over to Seiko's console. He halted his headlong dive with a practiced swing around one of the support stanchions and hung motionless just over Seiko's head.

"What reply?" he said.

"There is someone down there who is sending back pictures with the same format that you used," Seiko replied, "but they are coming from the east pole, they use thermal ultraviolet radiation instead of laser light, and they are coming very fast. Look— here is the first picture."

"It is a picture of Dragon Slayer and the six tidal compensators above Dragon's Egg," Abdul said. "But the star seems to be badly distorted into the shape of a pancake. It must be their star, however, because they have drawn in the mound formation. But what is that long narrow wedge with its base near us and its point over the formation?"

"It is a pointer," Seiko said. "If you look at the second and third pictures, you will see that they are almost identical, except that the position of our ship slowly shifts toward the west, while the wedge symbol gets shorter."

Seiko's fingers flew over the keyboard, and soon the first picture was joined by a second and a portion of a third.

"You are right," Abdul said. "It looks as if they want us to move to a position over their formation. I know why, too. The visibility through the atmosphere is poor in that direction. It would be much better if we were directly overhead."

Abdul suddenly realized something else that Seiko had said. "How fast was the message being sent?" he asked.

"The computer had to slow it down," Seiko said. "I estimate a pulse every four microseconds."

Abdul went back to his console and soon had a trace of the pulses from the first picture lined up on the screen. He leaned forward and looked more closely at the interval between the pulses.

"They are very irregular in spacing and amplitude," he said. "Almost as if they were handmade. You would think that a being that could make an ultraviolet laser could make a decent modulator."

"The radiation is from a thermal source," Seiko retorted.

Abdul paused as her reply sank in. "They are signaling to us with the neutron star equivalent of American Indian smoke signals!" he said. "And each one of those crude pulses is made in four microseconds—Great Allah! That means that those beings must live something like a million times faster than we do! And I have been sending the laser pulses at a rate of about once per second. To them that is like a million seconds between pulses."

Seiko quickly did the calculation for him. "As if it were about a week between pulses."

Abdul had another horrible thought. "How long has it been since they started to reply?" he asked.

Seiko's hands flicked on the keyboard, and the first picture reappeared with the time of reception in the upper corner. "The first picture arrived almost a minute ago," she replied, "and if the ratio is a million to one, that is like two years ago."

"They have probably gotten tired of waiting for an answer and have gone home," Abdul said. "We had better get busy—and fast!" He hesitated a second, then lifted the cover on a panel on the side of the console and flicked the emergency alarm switch.

"You explain the situation to Pierre and the others," he said over the whoop of the alarm signal, "and get Pierre to start moving the Dragon Slayer over the mound formation. I will try to get some sort of reply back as fast as I can."

Seiko fixed up her screen with all the pictures displayed so she would be ready when the rest of the crew came boiling into the main deck to see what the emergency was. Within a few seconds Abdul had swiveled the laser radar to illuminate the east pole directly below them, while its operational frequency had been pushed up to the short ultraviolet. Because he had nothing better immediately at hand, Abdul had the computer play back the pictures that had been sent up from the surface. While they were pulsing down at a megahertz rate, he quickly pulled in the first picture that he had beamed down, showing the Dragon Slayer and the six tidal compensators above Dragon's Egg. He added an arrow that curved over to a position above the mound formations, and had the computer send that down to the east pole. He then swiveled the laser back toward the strange starlike formation, and had it repeat the message twice, alternating between ultraviolet and light output. Since they had seen his first messages they should be able to detect it one way or the other. This time Abdul hoped that nobody would die of boredom waiting for the next pulse.

TIME: 07:58:40 GMT MONDAY 20 JUNE 2050

The nearly empty seared sacks lay on the crust, quietly sleeping. Ancient plant genes, activated by the almost complete lack of food reserves, began their strange work. The animal enzymes were neutralized, and new enzymes were generated that attacked the very muscles that supported the skin, turning the striated flesh into a floating cloud of long fibers. The skin itself was thinned until it was almost transparent. Other plant enzymes took over and used the liquid material and long fibers to fashion large super-strength crystals. This was not the brittle crystallium that the animal body had previously used for manipulators—this was dragon crystal. At the center of the now flaccid tread, a tendril forced its way into the crust. In its core was a sharp cone of crystal. Exuding acids that ate their way into the crust, the spike slowly penetrated deeper and deeper into the hot, neutron-rich crust. Hairlike threads spread out between the crustal fibers and nutrients began to flow in from the threads and up the tap root. Meanwhile, smaller spikes of crystal, thick at the base and finely rounded at the tip, began to form in a starlike pattern at the head of the tap root. The strong dragon crystal structure overcame the frightful pull of Egg, and jutted out at a low angle to the surface. The dozen spikes spread out like a thorny crown. They grew longer and longer, and the flaccid skin, long since cured of its burns, was lifted up into the air. As the spikes grew longer, even their great crystalline strength was no longer adequate to resist Egg's pull, so strong tension fibers formed that went from attachment knobs just below the growing tip of each spike to a stubby post that stuck up from the base of the spikes. Slowly the twelve-spiked cantilever canopy raised itself off the crust until the skin was drawn tightly to it.

The topside portion of the skin, hanging in a smooth dark red concave arc between the ends of the spikes, found that its shape shielded it from the glowing yellow surface crust, and it stared straight up into the cold sky. With its spike buried deep in the hot, neutron-rich crust, and its thinned upper surface area well coupled to a cold heat-sink, the heat-engine-plant that used to be Swift-Killer began to make food. It was oblivious to the fact that nearby were two other dragon plants, the first crop since before recorded cheela history. For many, many turns the dragon plants grew and prospered. They were massive, and slow-growing, and had to replace a lot of food reserves, so they took their time.

After waiting in vain for the three climbers to return, the troop was finally taken over by the senior squad leader, who mustered out those who wanted to stay in this Bright-forsaken region, and moved the remainder of the troop back to the borders of Bright's Empire, where he then had the unpleasant duty of reporting the deaths of Swift-Killer, North-Wind, and Cliff-Watcher to their clans.

Time went on and Bright's Empire grew and expanded its borders. Since the fort of Swift's Climb existed, it was easy for the border to expand all the way to the foothills of the east pole mountains. However, no one really liked to climb unless they had to, especially in the hard direction, so there were no visitors in the mountain paths, and the dragon plants grew undisturbed.

One turn there was a sharp quake as the massive overburden that the east pole mountains put upon Egg readjusted itself. A poorly formed joint in one of the three dragon plants failed. The spike fell instantly in the strong pull of Egg, tearing the skin and dumping the vital fluids onto the surface. For a while the dragon plant struggled to survive, but finally it gave up. After a dozen, dozen turns, there was nothing left but shiny spikes of dragon crystal, a few shreds of dried skin, a clan totem, and the double button of a squad leader.

For a long while nothing happened. Then the dragon crystal spikes sparkled as a slowly pulsating beam of pure blue light shone down from the tiny center speck of the seven points of light in the sky. The pulsations went on for some time, bathing the mountains in a blue glow, but there were no eyes to see them. They finally stopped.

Time continued on. The barbarians were driven further and further from Bright's Empire, and grew smaller in number. The large volcano in the north became more active, and billows of smoke crowded against the east pole. The unbalance in the heat radiated from the star into the dark skies became so great that huge wind storms grew, and were strong enough occasionally to push smoke into the east pole region. The sky grew cloudy, the bottoms of the smoky clouds turned yellow with the heat reflected from the glowing surface. The heat engine that ran between the tap root in the crust and the skyward facing concave dish of skin in the dragon plants began to fail. With food reserves high, and growing efficiencies low, the plant forming genes began to lose their potency, and other enzyme mechanisms were triggered. Slowly the dragon crystal was dissolved, to reappear as firm muscle under a thick skin. The little photosensitive bud cups at the tips of the crystal spikes reformed their flaps, and new little eyes, still dormant, grew under those flaps.

Swift-Killer woke up.

She felt very strange, as if she had not moved a muscle in a long time. Fortunately, she was feeling no pain from her burned topside and eyes.

"My eyes! I cannot see! How will I ever get down out of these mountains without eyes?"

She then realized that she had all of her eyes tucked tightly underneath their flaps. She cautiously pushed out one after the other.

"I can see light," she said, "but everything is all blurry."

She tried to form a pseudopod to wipe off her eyes, and found that she was as weak and clumsy as a hatchling. She soon had the fluid wiped off her eyes, but it was a full turn before she could really see clearly.

She knew that she must have been badly hurt by the blast of fire from the sky, but now she felt perfectly fine, except for her muscular weakness, her clumsy coordination and blurred vision. What amazed her was that she was no longer hungry.

Being a good troop commander, her first thought had been for her troopers, and she had looked around for North-Wind and Cliff-Watcher, but could not see them. She was too weak to travel, so she concentrated on exercises until she felt ready to cope with the hazards of downhill travel in the vicious pull of Egg.

After a turn she felt much better and started to examine her surroundings. As far as she could remember, she was still in the same valley where they had been when the flame struck, but she had not remembered the giant plant to one side, or the fabulous collection of dragon crystal lying on the crust on the other side. She might have ignored a plant, even if it were as big around as herself, but she would never have ignored a veritable treasure of shining dragon crystal. At the very least, she would have marked the spot and arranged to have a crew climb back up to retrieve it. She went over to the glittering spikes and picked them up, one after the other.

"Strange," she thought to herself, "these are amazingly shiny, as if they were brand new, or fresh cast. All the natural dragon crystals are weathered by the constant scrubbing of wind-blown dust."

She picked up another spike that had a shred of something sticking to it. She pulled the shred off the spike and suddenly dropped it in a horrified reflex action.

"North-Wind!" she whispered in horror, her eyes tracing out the faded but unmistakable three-pointed scar pattern that had been North-Wind's memento from their last fight with the barbarians.

Any doubts that North-Wind had died and that his body had decayed away were gone when she found his squad leader button and clan totem half buried in the fuzzy crust. She pouched them and looked around in bewilderment. But what were North-Wind's remains doing mixed up with fresh dragon crystal?

She looked over at the huge plant nearby. She then began to

get the connection between the twelve spikes arching into the sky and the twelve spikes of dragon crystal spread out on the crust. She wandered over to the plant and circled all around it, looking at it closely. It looked somehow familiar, yet it was just a giant version of many types of plants all over Egg. On one side she saw a little lump in the thin skin. Just over it was a tiny pucker.

"A plant with a carrying pouch?" she said to herself. Carefully —for she did not want to meet the same fate that had apparently met North-Wind when the heavy plant had fallen on him—she reached a slender tendril under the plant and forced the tip into the pucker.

"It's a pouch!" she exclaimed in wonder. Reaching further in, she grasped an object, and slowly withdrew it through the constricting orifice. It was the totem of Cliff-Watcher's clan!

Swift-Killer could not believe what her eyes were seeing. But soon she had identified other pouches and had removed a short knife and a dark detector from them. She was finally convinced that somehow, in some way, this giant plant in front of her was really Cliff-Watcher.

"And if Cliff-Watcher is a living plant, then perhaps those slivers of dragon crystal over there used to be North-Wind," she said to herself, "and . . ." She continued as the logic drove her on to the inescapable conclusion, ". . . I must have been one of these giant plants too! With large dragon crystal spikes in me!"

At this thought, she remembered that she had been annoyed by a hard lump tumbling around in her body. She had paid it no attention, since it did not hurt and she had plenty of other things to worry about at the time, but now she concentrated, and soon the lump was ejected from an elimination orifice. Overcoming her natural distaste, Swift-Killer wiped it off. It was a shiny knob of dragon crystal.

Swift-Killer looked at it with awe, and pouched it to use as evidence when the time came to make someone believe her fantastic story.

Meanwhile, she had a problem. Although North-Wind was dead, and she had his totem to take back to his clan, Cliff-Watcher was very much alive, and she didn't feel she should leave him.

Swift-Killer finally decided to wait. She had plenty of reserve energy (she must have built that up when she was a plant), and it would be important for her sanity to have someone else to corroborate her story.

The skies stayed cloudy, and soon the trigger that had revived Swift-Killer was activated in Cliff-Watcher. Swift-Killer watched in amazement as, turn after turn, the slender spikes grew shorter and shorter, and the thin skin began to thicken and become muscular once again.

She was stroking Cliff-Watcher on the topside when he woke up. She treated him gently, and slowly coaxed his eyes out as she reassured him that he was going to be fine despite his blurry vision, and weak and clumsy state. After a few turns, they both felt well enough to travel and started down the mountain, carrying the crystallized remains of North-Wind with them.

When they came to the highest base camp, Swift-Killer sought out the food cache. It was there and had not been disturbed by mountain animals, but the meat and pods were hard as crust. This puzzled Swift-Killer, since a well-wrapped piece of dried meat should be expected to be hard, but not rock hard, even after a great of turns.

It was the same at each cache, although some had been broken into by animals long ago. Finally they reached the pass on the upper foothills where they could look down into the distance and see the trooper fort. As they came over the rise, both Swift-Killer and Cliff-Watcher stopped in shock. The fort was gone.

"Bright's Heaven!" exclaimed Cliff-Watcher.

"No," Swift-Killer said a moment later, "that is not Bright's Heaven. It looks almost as big, but the arrangement is all wrong."

"You are right," Cliff-Watcher said. "But where did it come from?"

"I think that you and I were plants for longer than we thought," Swift-Killer said. "There are going to be some very surprised people when we glide into that town."

"Provided they even remember us," Cliff-Watcher said pessimistically as he followed Swift-Killer down the hill.

Commander Swift-Killer led the way into town. When they passed the fields of crops, they both looked over the harvesters loaded down with pods, but didn't see anyone either one of them knew.

As they approached the town, the four-button insignia jutting out of Swift-Killer's breast got them the proper respect from the passers-by; but at the same time, the obvious youthful appearance of the troop commander resulted in strange whispers as they passed. For the first time, Swift-Killer was beginning to feel unsure of herself.

She paused on the outskirts of the town and said quietly to Cliff-Watcher, "I think we are going to have a difficult enough time convincing people that we are who we are, without antagonizing them. I think we had better just survey the whole town before I go and announce who I am." Cliff-Watcher could only agree, and kept looking for a familiar profile, but found none.

They stopped at a military food station at the outskirts of town, and quietly relaxed and ate their fill. They took their time and listened to the conversations between the couriers as they came and went on Combined Clan business. They had expected to hear that there was a new Leader of the Combined Clans, but were surprised to learn that the name of the town they were in was Swift's Climb.

Cliff-Watcher inquired of the keeper of the food station about the name. After the keeper got over the oddness of his slang, he told them a capsule history of the naming of the town.

"Almost three dozen greats of turns ago, this place was a barren plain," the station keeper said, "when an expedition came to the east pole to try to talk to the Eyes of Bright. The expedition was led by a troop commander named Swift-Masher, or something like that, and he climbed up into those hills to talk to God's Eyes and never came back. His troop stayed around for a few greats of turns, then finally they gave up. By that time some of them were old enough to muster out and they stayed here, while the rest of the troop went back to the border. Since then the border has come here to Swift's Climb, and it is really a booming place, I tell you."

"Where can we find some of the old troopers?" asked Cliff-Watcher.

"Where else?" the station keeper asked. "In the meat bins. Or if they kept healthy and were lucky, they are having the time of their lives tending hatchlings in the hatching pens."

Swift-Killer was initially pleased to hear that the town had been named after her exploit, but if the average cheela in the town knew as much about her as the station keeper, she was glad that she had kept her mouth shut and had let the four buttons of a troop commander speak for her. They asked the way to the hatching pens and headed off in that direction, hoping to see somebody—anybody—who might know them.

The road to the hatching pens went past the face of a low cliff. As they approached the cliff, Swift-Killer noticed a bright blinking light coming from the top. A cheela was up there in front of some apparatus, and a bright blue-white beam was blinking its way across the crust to the distant horizon.

Ever curious, Swift-Killer said, "Let's go by way of the top of that rise. I want to see what is making that beam of light."

Cliff-Watcher shuffled his tread in annoyance, saying that he had had enough climbing for a whole lifetime, but his curiosity got the better of him too, and they slowly worked their way up to the top of the cliff, where they approached a soldier.

Swift-Killer was bewildered to see the insignia of rank on the soldier operating the apparatus. Instead of a trooper's button, she had a horizontal bar. Swift-Killer couldn't say anything without getting herself in trouble, since a troop commander should address a trooper by her proper rank, so she again decided to let her four buttons speak for her. Looking vaguely interested, she wandered up to the trooper as if she were a visiting inspector.

The trooper heard the military tread as Swift-Killer approached; when Swift-Killer came within hailing distance, she quickly signed off her message and came to alert.

"Troop Signaler Yellow-Crust, Commander," she said. "Do you have a message to send?"

"No, no," Swift-Killer assured her. "But after you have finished, could you please show us your apparatus?"

Yellow-Crust thought it strange that a troop commander would be interested in such a thing as a swift-sender, but perhaps she was an inspector out looking for trouble. If so, she would find nothing wrong with her equipment!

In a short while Yellow-Crust was through with her messages and showed the two visitors how the swift-sender worked. Yellow-Crust decided that she would give them the full drill.

Parroting her training officer, Yellow-Crust began: "The swift-sender is the troop's method of maintaining contact with Headquarters and other troops. The most important element in the swift-sender is the expander, which must always be kept clean." Yellow-Crust opened the side of the box to reveal a very shiny and very clean expander. Both Cliff-Watcher and Swift-Killer were awed by the size and surface finish on the strongly curved reflector.

"We sure could have used one of those up in the mountains," Cliff-Watcher whispered.

"We never could have carried it up those hills," retorted Swift-Killer.

Yellow-Crust, ignoring the whispers, continued: "The light-juice vial is to be filled and pressurized before each message, and the signaling valve is to be checked for rapid action under pressure."

Yellow-Crust closed the door, filled a container on the outside with fluid, then placed a close-fitting plunger on top and added a weight. She then reached to the other side, and rapidly flicked a small lever. Short bursts of light flickered out over the crust.

Yellow-Crust went on, "The flare should be renewed every shift, and the holder for it should be adjusted to give maximum beam brightness without focusing in the far field." With these words, Yellow-Crust extended a tendril and moved a small lever back and forth and Swift-Killer could see the beam diverge and focus in the distance. Yellow-Crust, with a trained twist of her tendril, left the beam with parallel sides shooting off to the distance.

Yellow-Crust's t'trum dropped the training officer twang as she said, "There is more about message protocol, Commander. Would you like to have me recite that?"

"No! No, thank you," Swift-Killer said. "Very clean and well working machine you have there, trooper." She started to move away.

"At Alert!" boomed a commanding tread through the crust.

Yellow-Crust froze at alert, and Swift-Killer almost followed, but instead slowly returned to the swift-sender to await the arrival of a squad of well-armed troopers, led by none other than the local troop commander.

It was obvious that the troop commander was flustered with Swift-Killer's four buttons. Having expected to take action against meddling visitors that bothered his communication link, he found himself eye-to-eye with a stranger of equal rank.

Equal rank or not, he was the troop commander of this town and still in command. "Who are you, Commander?" he asked. "I was not informed of any visitors."

"Don't you recognize me, Red-Sky?" Swift-Killer asked.

"No!" Troop Commander Red-Sky replied.

"You and I came from the same clan, and you joined my Troop shortly before we went on the expedition to the east pole mountains," Swift-Killer said, immensely relieved that the one cheela with real authority in this town was someone that she was sure she could convince. Swift-Killer formed a pseudopod, and reached into a pouch that had not been opened since she had left the clan to join the troopers. She pulled out her clan totem and held it out to Red-Sky.

Red-Sky shuffled nervously. He took the totem and examined it carefully. Then, still holding on to it, he circled around Swift-Killer, examining her very closely. The visitor was one of the largest cheela he had seen since his early youth.

"Do you remember this scar?" she said, thrusting out a portion of one side. "You gave it to me when I was teaching you short-sword drill in my training camp."

"You're dead!" Red-Sky said, trying to command order back into his bewildered mind.

"No, I am not," Swift-Killer said, taking advantage of Red-Sky's hesitation. "And I want your help in getting a message back to Trooper Headquarters in Bright's Heaven."

Faced with the physical reality of the huge Swift-Killer body that he had known in his youth, and convinced by the clan totem and four buttons of authority on her breast, Red-Sky finally overcame his bewilderment at seeing Swift-Killer in a youthful body, when he himself was almost ready to be an Old One tending hatchlings. He dismissed his armed guard. After arranging for Swift-Killer to send messages to the Central Region Troop Headquarters, the Inner Eye Institute, the Leader of the Combined Clans, and her own clan family, he took them both down to the trooper camp, where finally Cliff-Watcher was able to drop his burden of dragon crystal.

TIME: 08:05:15 GMT MONDAY 20 JUNE 2050

Seiko's announcement came as no real surprise to Pierre. He had suspected the time differential from the surprising rapidity with which the mounds had risen. There was no question in his mind that the job of communication with another race took priority over any other scientific mission, and without hesitation he went to the propulsion console and initiated the move from the east pole to the mound formations ninety degrees around Dragon's Egg. Because of the mass of the tidal compensators, and the necessity that they all move together to keep the tides from harming the fragile human flesh inside the Dragon Slayer, the move had to be done slowly. As soon as the new position was set into the propulsion command subsystem, he pushed himself from the console chair and floated over to join the group hanging in the air around Seiko and Abdul.

"We should be shifted to the new position in half-an-hour," he reported as he joined them.

Without looking up from her screen, Seiko said, "At a million to one, that will take the equivalent of sixty years."

Pierre had already made the calculation himself, but there was no way that he could make the move any faster, the herder probe propulsion systems for the tidal compensators were not made for speed. He gave a quiet shrug, which looked odd on a body that was floating in midair.

"We have a more serious problem," he said, addressing the whole crew. "After we get there, what are we going to say?"

Seiko spoke up, her eyes still on the screen. "There is no way that we can carry on a two-way conversation with a million-to-one time difference. By the time we can think of anything intelligent to say, the person down there who asked the question would have died."

"It's not that bad," Pierre said. "Of course we don't know how long they live, but if they last seventy of their type years, then . . ." He paused to think and Seiko finished for him.

"There are pi times ten million seconds in a year, times 70 years is 2200 million seconds, which is 2200 sec or about 37 minutes of our time."

"Well, that isn't so bad," Jean said. "At least we can talk with a person for long enough to get to know him."

"He is going to get awfully tired devoting his entire life to a casual conversation with you," Seiko retorted.

Pierre took charge. "We are going to have to come up with material for our side of the conversation, and we are probably going to need more than one communication link going at a time. Abdul, how many communication links can we set up?"

Without turning from the console, Abdul replied, "We have been using the laser radar mapper as a communication link, but it isn't designed for that job. It has a pulsed modulator and can't handle high bit rates. The microwave sounder is also available, and I think its modulator can handle up to 100 megahertz. The laser communicator would be ideal, since it can handle a few gigahertz modulation, which at a million to one, would be like the bandwidth of a telephone line; you could send slow facsimile pictures through it, but nothing like a television picture. Unfortunately, the laser communication antennas were never designed to point at the surface of Dragon's Egg; they are on the main body and one or the other is always pointed out at St. George."

"We will have to make do with the laser radar mapper and the microwave sounder until we can get one of the laser communicator dishes reoriented," Pierre said. He turned in midair and surveyed the faces hanging in the air around him until he found the one he wanted.

"Amalita," he said, "put on your suit and get one of those laser communicator dishes pointing at Dragon's Egg. Meanwhile, I will be contacting St. George and will tell them we are going to cut off one of the laser communication links with them."

A voice broke in from the communications console around on the other side of the central core.

"We have been monitoring, Dragon Slayer." The speaker was Commander Swenson. "Continue your course of action."

Amalita pushed off to the suit room. As she went, she called over her shoulder. "I am sure I can mount the communication dish on the laser mapper mount," she said. "I can't guarantee the boresight accuracy, but they should be fairly close."

Pierre turned to Jean. "I want you to go through the ship's library for anything that is designed for initial contact with other species. Look in the fiction HoloMem for science fiction stories if you have to, but I think that somewhere in the ship's encyclopedia you might find something on communication languages.

"Meanwhile, we will have to have something to send while Jean is searching the data banks. I will put my children's books into a computer file for Abdul to put on the communication links. I'll start with the most elementary books first, then build up to the more adult ones."

"But they all presume some sort of prior knowledge," Cesar protested. "Even your A-B-C books assume the reader knows what an apple is."

"They will work if we send all the art work with it," Pierre said, going around to the console on the other side of the main deck. "Don't forget, they are going to have lots and lots of time to figure out what each page means while they wait for the next one to print out slowly on their equivalent of a facsimile machine."

Cesar left to check out Amalita's suit before she exited. Abdul had finished sending the crude pictures, and was monitoring the story file that Pierre was building up in the computer.

Suddenly Seiko announced, "They are replying again. This time it is to the west of the east pole mountains."

Moving rapidly, Abdul read off the coordinates that the computer had flashed at the top of Seiko's screen and keyed them into his communication console. Almost instantly the laser radar was repositioned to beam down to that point, and the messages continued to trickle slowly down to the surface.

TIME: 08:18:03 GMT MONDAY 20 JUNE 2050

Swift-Killer's messages back to Bright's Heaven caused surprise and shock. Having once been almost forgotten, as is the case when one does not have an immediate family, but merely is one of the members of a large, far-flung clan, Swift-Killer's strange story made her known throughout the nation. However, the most exciting news for Swift-Killer was the reply from the Inner Eye Institute. Their first message back to Swift-Killer told her that about eight greats of turns ago, the slow messages from the Inner Eye had stopped. Then about four greats ago, they had started again, only this time they were much faster. The pictures had been sent with pulsations of light that could be seen by everyone, without having to have a dark detector or be one of Bright's Afflicted. There then followed a copy of the first picture.

Swift-Killer let Cliff-Watcher read the message string from the Institute for himself, then they both worked on translating the linear string of dashes and blips following the message into the fringed tally string arrangement needed to make a picture. They laid it carefully out on the crust and Swift-Killer flowed onto it.

"Our message got through, Cliff-Watcher," Swift-Killer said in a soft whisper. "That climb was not in vain."

"How can you tell?" Cliff-Watcher asked.

Rather than reply, Swift-Killer flowed off the tally fringe and let Cliff-Watcher sense the pattern of knots in the strings.

"It is like the first one that we sent," Cliff-Watcher said. "It shows Bright's Eyes over the east pole and a needle pointing to a position over the Holy Temple, except the needle is a funny skinny one, with a chevron at the tip."

"That must be their symbol to indicate direction," Swift-Killer decided. "It is too thin to support itself, and has odd, unnecessary, sticklike, angular projections. Such strange creatures! Their symbols are as sticklike and angular as they are."

"This message must mean that they understand us and will move to a position over Bright's Heaven," Cliff-Watcher said.

"I hope it means that," Swift-Killer said. She turned some of her eyes up to the seven points of light in the sky. "I don't see that they have moved yet."

Cliff-Watcher repeated Swift-Killer's glance with his practiced astrologer's eye. After a moment's pause he reported, "I think they have moved. Let me get some astrologer sticks."

They hunted down the local contingent of astrologers. After a turn of observations, it was concluded that the Eyes of Bright had definitely shifted position. From a viewing point in the town of Swift's Climb, one of the far-away stars in the sky used to go behind the Inner Eye once every turn. Now the point of light grazed the top of the Inner Eye. The Inner Eye was moving!

With two-way communication established, Swift-Killer's strong inquisitive drive took her over completely. She would have to find out more about these strange, slow-living, sticklike creatures, and their magical power that let them float in the sky, impervious to the all-powerful pull of Egg. She had many questions to ask, and her busy mind started working on ways to ask those questions in a fast way that could be done with simple pictures. But first, she had a lot of negotiating to do. She went back out to the swift-sender to send some messages to the Commander of the Eastern Border and the Inner Eye Institute.

Within a half-dozen turns, Swift-Killer had changed professions. The Commander of the Eastern Border was relieved when Commander Swift-Killer asked to be mustered out. He had been wondering what he was going to do with a trooper commander who had tallied more than enough turns to have been mustered out long ago, yet according to reports looked as youthful as the youngest recruit. Besides, he didn't have a troop for her to command. He was so relieved, in fact, that he readily agreed to let Swift-Killer have the use of a swift-sender.

The Inner Eye Institute also had no hesitation in accepting Swift-Killer's proposal that she join the Institute. If it had not been for her brave climb into the mountains, they would still be gathering pictures at a rate of one dash every few turns. In fact, since Swift-Killer was closer to Bright's Eyes from her place near the east pole, it was decided to have the first replies come from there, and Swift-Killer would be in charge of sending them.

Within less than a dozen turns, Swift-Killer had her own swift-sender set up in the compound of the local astrologers, and was beaming out picture after picture into a glancer set at an angle in the crust, to bounce up into the sky toward the Eyes of Bright. She was overjoyed when after two dozen turns she noticed that the Inner Eye started slowly blinking back at her. She could see it with her own eyes! She was at last in communication with another race of beings—and she was Keeper of the Sender.

TIME: 08:18:33 GMT MONDAY 20 JUNE 2050

Amalita Shakhashiri Drake slipped neatly into her spacesuit, her long, lithe, ballet-trained body making the usually clumsy procedure look like a dance. She carefully read through the check list, even though she knew it by heart. She should, for she had been supervising emergency suiting drills for the past two years while St. George had slowly made its way across the 1/30 light-year distance that separated Sol from Dragon's Egg. The neutron star now lay 400 kilometers outside the hull of their tiny science flitter, Dragon Slayer.

She was in a hurry to get the laser communication dish repositioned, but the crew of Dragon Slayer was too few in number to afford any mistakes. So Amalita waited patiently until someone came to give her a final checkout.

Ship's doctor Cesar Ramirez Wong came flying headlong into the upper room, performed a neat somersault, and absorbed his momentum on the ceiling with a carefully programmed flexing of his knees. He rebounded slightly and soon was hanging upside-down in front of her. She noticed idly that the tidal compensators were not working perfectly on the upper deck, for he was slowly drifting up to the ceiling as he read off the check list.

". . . main and emergency air tanks—full. Time to put on your helmet and check air and cooling," he said.

Amalita was ahead of him and her muffled voice spoke from behind the visor. "Helmet on—air and cooling fine."

He glanced back at the check list. "Magni-stiction boots . . ." Amalita flicked a switch on her chest console that rearranged the pseudo-random pattern of the magnetic monopoles in the soles of her boots so that they matched up with the hexagonal pattern of monopoles built into the inner plates and hull of Dragon Slayer.

Electromagnetic boots would have been simpler if Dragon Slayer could have been built out of steel, but since the neutron star and the tidal compensators outside had significant magnetic moments, the engineers had had to come up with a substitute. Amalita's boots clanged onto the floor, each foot twisted 30 degrees to the outside as the boots conformed to the hexagonal pattern in the plate. She looked down at her feet and thought idly, "What a sloppy third position. My ballet instructor would never have let me get away with anything that poor." She flicked off the magni-stiction boots, then slowly rose into the air as Cesar droned on through the check list.

"You are checked out," Cesar said as he floated over to the lock controls. "Out you go. Try to move that communication dish to the swivel mount as fast as you can. Don't forget that if those neutron star creatures are really living a million times faster than we are, fifteen minutes to us is like thirty years to them."

Amalita opened the hatch to the air-lock and went in, dogging the door behind her. She signaled to Cesar through the port and felt her suit stiffen as the pressure dropped. The outer hatch swung in, and Amalita held onto her safety line as she cautiously looked out. Although she had been outside St. George a dozen times on repair jobs in the long journey out to Dragon's Egg, this was the first time she had been outside Dragon Slayer, and she knew the scenery was going to be very confusing. Anything in space that causes confusion is a prime source of accidents, and she had not lived this long by taking chances in out-ship jobs.

Amalita looked out of the air-lock set in the middle of Dragon Slayer. Since the ship was inertially stabilized, the stars remained fixed in the sky. However—flashing in front of the port five times a second was the bright white globe of Dragon's Egg. At 400 kilometers distance, the 20-kilometer-diameter neutron star was about five times bigger than Sol at Earth and took up an appreciable part of the sky.

"If only we were orbiting around it at a faster rate, so that it would blur out into a ring," she thought. "At five times a second it is right in the visual flicker band and is going to be a real annoyance."

She moved to the portal and put her head out. With her view enlarged, she now saw the complete ring of tidal compensators encircling the ship. They revolved about their common center at five times a second while simultaneously orbiting about Dragon's Egg. Because there were six of them, they seemed almost fused together into a solid ring.

Amalita paused to get accustomed to the sight. There was a bright white globe of light circling about the middle of Dragon Slayer, and at right angles to that a ring of glowing red that twirled about the ship like a wedding ring spinning on a table. The spins of the two matched so that the plane of the ring was always perpendicular to the direction to the neutron star.

"How are you doing?" Cesar's voice came through the suit communication link.

"Fine," Amalita said. "I'm just waiting here to get used to the whirling scenery. It reminds me of the time back in the Lunar Ballet Academy when I tried to break the *Guinness Book of Records* mark for the most number of fouettés in a row. After twirling around on one foot for over one hundred turns, I missed my kick, lost my spotting point, and the vertigo got to me—I don't think things were whirling around as much then as they are now."

Amalita looked up at the top of Dragon Slayer to the large central turret containing the solar mirror, laser radar, microwave sounder, and other star-oriented instruments. The turret was rotating five times a second, keeping the instruments pointed at Dragon's Egg. "You haven't turned off the turret," she complained. "I can't work on it while it is spinning around."

Cesar replied, "Since you first have to remove a laser communication dish from its mount on the hull, and won't be ready to install it on the turret for several minutes, I thought we should wait to de-spin the turret. Once we stop it, we will have to cut off communication to the neutron star beings. Abdul is now making up a simple message to let them know that we will only stop for a short while, so they don't think we have given up and gone away."

Amalita looked around the equator of Dragon Slayer until she could see one of the laser communication dishes. She fixed her eyes on it, then stabilized her personal up and down. She told her eyes to ignore the bright objects whirling through her peripheral vision; activating her magni-stiction boots, she stepped out onto the hull.

As Amalita stood up, she could feel the play of pulsating residual gravitational forces through her body. In addition to the pulsating fields, there were slight variations in the overall compensation, since the spacecraft was slowly shifting its orbital position from the east pole to a position over the mound formation on the star's surface. Sometimes she was pulled outward with a fraction of a gee, and sometimes pushed inwards.

Amalita made her way carefully to the nearest laser communication dish. She detached the coaxial cable that brought the modulating voltages from inside Dragon Slayer, then the power line to the laser, and finally she started working on the mounting bolts. It was a well-designed system, with the bolts staying captive in the frame, so there was no chance of having them float away in free fall. She held onto one strut of the bulky piece of apparatus and plodded her way carefully back over the curve of Dragon Slayer's hull.

"Start de-spinning the science turret, Doc," she called through her suit radio. "I'm clear of the control jets."

As she moved over the curving hull, she could see the spinning turret slowly come to a stop while the control jets flashed on Dragon Slayer's hull to throw off the excess momentum.

As she approached the stationary turret she glanced upwards along the three-meter length and found the laser radar. The radar dish was tucked under the huge mirror that brought a one-meter diameter image of Dragon's Egg directly into the star image table.

She was getting far from the air-lock, so she fastened a secondary safety line to a ring at the base of the turret. She then stepped carefully off the spherical hull of Dragon Slayer onto the cylindrical turret. She allowed herself a few seconds to readjust her personal up and down; then, still holding the bulky laser communication dish, she ascended. As she climbed further and further from the center of Dragon Slayer, the accuracy of the tidal compensation fields became poorer. Halfway up the turret she found that the play of gravitational fields over her body became too strong to ignore. She felt as if her suit were haunted by tiny elves that pushed and pulled at various sections of her anatomy. The overall tidal compensation was also off, and the laser communication dish began to pull ahead as it gained weight while they made their way up the column.

The increased weight was not much, but it was significant enough so that Amalita stopped at each step to move her safety lines from ring to ring behind her. She finally reached the laser radar and looped the lanyard attached to the communication dish to a nearby ring and let the ring support the burden. She fastened another lanyard from her belt to the laser radar.

Firmly anchored to the column with magni-stiction boots and a pair of short safety lines, she started to remove the laser radar. Fortunately the laser power supply line and the modulator coaxial cable connectors were the same for the two laser systems. All they had to do was switch the cable on the inside from the pulsed modulator used in the laser radar to the video modulator in the laser communication console. Unfortunately, the bolt patterns for the two laser systems were incompatible and she could tighten only one bolt. However, she had been prepared for that problem and had brought some quick-setting vacuum epoxy to fasten the laser communication dish onto the laser radar mount.

"What I need is four hands," Amalita said as she reached into a pouch for the epoxy. The twin tube had been designed for use with her clumsy gloves and even had a tear-off top. But in her hurry to get the job over, Amalita made a mistake.

The mistake was a very innocent one for someone who had been living in free fall for many years. All she did was to park the laser radar in space alongside her while she opened the epoxy. While she was busy with the glue, the laser radar slowly floated outward, gaining speed. When it reached the end of its lanyard, it jerked cruelly at Amalita's middle. She found herself pulled off the turret. There was a quick second of panic, then Amalita came to the end of her two safety lines and rebounded. She felt a rip as the weaker joint in the equipment ring holding the laser radar came out of her safety belt, while the two stronger personal safety loops held. She looked down to see the laser radar module head outward away from the ship. It gathered speed rapidly in the strong attractive gravitational fields from the dense masses in the tidal compensator. She lost sight of the module as it whipped out to join the whirling ring of ultra-dense asteroids.

"We have trouble, Dragon Slayer," she said into her suit microphone. "I lost the laser radar module to tidal forces."

Amalita pulled herself hand-over-hand back up the safety lines to the turret and proceeded to bolt and glue the communication dish to the empty mount and then hook up the power and modulation cables.

She quickly climbed down off the turret and signaled to Cesar to start up the turret again. She watched, staying out of the way of the control jets, until the huge cylinder was again spinning around at five revolutions per second. She then glanced up to see an elongated glob of crushed and extruded glass and metal come whirling back toward the hull of Dragon Slayer. The sharp points of metal on the glob were emitting a blue corona of electric discharge built up from the rapid motion through the strong magnetic fields of the star.

Amalita was appalled. If that ever hit the hull of Dragon Slayer they would be dead. Cursing herself for having been so careless, Amalita knew that this was no time to play it safe.

"Emergency! Emergency!" she called. Without waiting for a

reply, she began a move-by-move description of the problem and her efforts to solve it.

"Laser radar module loose and moving at high velocity in vicinity of ship. I am jettisoning safety line and will use jet-pack to try to catch it."

Amalita unhooked her safety line, moved her left hand to the jet-pack controls on her chest, and took off to capture the deadly missile.

As she swooped around the curve of the hull, she spotted the module above the turret. It had slowed down as the tidal forces had pulled on it. The module had looped slowly in a large arc and was now headed back again toward Dragon Slayer. She would have to catch it while it was moving slowly if she were going to hold onto it, so she jetted straight up to meet it.

As she flew past the spinning turret, her body began to feel the tidal pressures. She tried to hunch in her head and draw up her feet to cut down her length and relieve the forces, but it was hard work holding them in against the strong outward pull. It was worst on her head. Her ears and nose felt as if they were being pounded twenty times a second, while the top of her head felt as if she were being scalped by a savage with a dull knife.

Despite the pain, she continued upward to meet the module that was slowly gaining speed as it fell again toward Dragon Slayer. This is where her two seasons as captain of a free-ball team on L-5 would pay off. Her left hand played quickly over the jet control keys on her chest. She slowed, whirled about, and then accelerated again to match speed with the now rapidly falling chunk of metal. As her head changed orientation, the tidal pressures changed also. Her nose, now jerked viciously outwards, began to gush ellipsoidal globules of blood. Peering anxiously through her red-stained visor, Amalita found a short section of lanyard in front of her and grabbed it with her right hand while her left flicked over the jet controls. The laser radar module continued on its hyperbolic path downward past the hull of Dragon Slayer and then outward along the belt line. Slowly Amalita got it under control and dragged it down to the hull. Within seconds after her boots had clicked onto the plates, she had both herself and the distorted hunk of metal attached by shortened lines to safety rings on the hull.

Her voice was hoarse from the running commentary she had

kept up during the chase. "All secure," she croaked. "I will need some help getting this inside."

"Are you hurt?" came a concerned voice over her suit speaker.

"I'm sore all over, Doc, but the only real damage is a bloody nose," she replied.

Amalita was making her way back to the air-lock, moving her bruised body slowly from one safety ring to another when she saw a suited figure rising from the air-lock to help. She was only too glad to hand over her problems to the welcome crew mate.

"I am sure glad to see you," Amalita said. "Even if only through a red haze. Here—you take what's left of the laser radar module. Watch out for it—when it got mashed in the tidal forces of those asteroids several sharp spikes got extruded—they could nick your suit."

"I've got it," Jean said. "Now you get in that air-lock and cycle through. Doc is waiting on the other side with a warm wet compress for that nose. And in case you were wondering, the laser communication link is working fine. The first messages have gone down, and we have already received a reply back through the ultraviolet scanner."

Interaction

Swift-Killer moved slowly through the compound of the Inner Eye Institute in Bright's Heaven. She was getting old and did not bluster her way directly into the hard direction as she had used to. Instead, she slid obliquely along, letting the bulk of her still huge body do the work against the "lines of magnetic force" that one of Pierre's early science books had taught them about. She made her way to the Sky-Talk Library. It was still under construction, with workers busily assembling low walls with storage bins for the knowledge that had been beaming down from the sky for almost two generations now. There were smaller bins for the tally fringe strings that were the method of recording the pictures early in her job as Keeper of the Sender, and larger ones for the new tasting plates that could accurately record the high resolution, multihued "television" images that the humans were now using.

The taste-plates had also been one of Swift-Killer's many inventions. She had begun to despair over accurately recording all the subtle nuances of the human television signal in the form of knots of various shapes and sizes. She had happened upon the new technique when she had been on inspection after they had broken camp and were moving on to a new station under the westward-drifting human spacecraft. She had flowed through the remains of the kitchen for the camp and her tread moved across an abandoned mixing plate, stained with meat juices and spices. Her ancient hunting senses had sprung into action, attempting to extract every item of information from the complex chemical spoor that it found under her tread. Swift-Killer had experimented and found that her tread could "taste" with higher resolution and comprehension using her ancient spoor-tracking senses than it could feel with her high-sensitivity tactile senses. After a little experimentation to find the most pungent and long-lasting spices, the knowledge of the humans was soon being stored on long-lasting, apparently featureless plates, that burst into a detailed, "full-colored" image as a trained tread flowed onto it.

Swift-Killer approached Sky-Beams, one of her apprentices, who was busily staring upwards at the rapidly blinking Inner Eye, a set of trained tendrils in front of him, shooting drop after drop of spice onto a fresh plate.

Leaving half of his eyes devoted to the recording task, Sky-Beams turned the others toward his mentor. "What are you doing here, O Keeper of the Sender?" Sky-Beams said, his correctly formal address scarcely concealing his annoyance that the Old One was interrupting him.

Swift-Killer knew exactly what was wrong with the youngster. He was ready to become the new Keeper of the Sender, and she was still around. However, it didn't bother her any longer. As she grew older, she grew more mellow and now was actually looking forward to tending eggs and hatchlings. What stories she would tell them!

"I came to bring you good news, Sky-Beams," she said. "The advisory council of the Inner Eye Institute has agreed with my recommendation, and you are now the new Keeper of the Sender."

Swift-Killer flowed over toward him as the tendrils on the younger one hesitated. She started to form a pseudopod to stroke his topside as she had done many times in the past. He seemed perfectly willing, but she found that she was just not interested in sex anymore. She wanted to get to the eggs that were waiting for her. She gave him a friendly brush anyway, then said, "Stay vigilant, Sky-Beams. The work may be tedious at times, but one never knows but what the next page will bring a new truth to our people."

"I will, my teacher," Sky-Beams said, and turned all his eyes back to the sky as Swift-Killer flowed away in the easy direction, heading for the egg-pens on the east side of Bright's Heaven.

Pierre looked up at the flash in the corner of his screen.

LINK FROM JEAN—LIBRARY

"Accept link!" he said.

PULLED SECTION ON MATH AND PHYSICS.
IT IS NOW CUED IN COMPUTER AFTER YOUR BOOKS.
CONCENTRATED ON PHYSICS OF NEUTRON STARS.
SLOW GOING, HOWEVER.
WHAT NEXT?
JEAN

Pierre thought for a moment. Jean was right. If they spent time searching through the extensive ship's encyclopedia for useful knowledge on the HoloMem crystals, then dumping those sections into the communication computer and out the laser communications console, it would take them forever and a day. A day for the humans and what would seem like forever to the neutron star beings.

"Amalita!" he bellowed, and soon a bloody handkerchief with two eager eyes above it was peering down through the passageway. "Can we hook up the library HoloMem reader directly into the communications console?"

There was a slight pause as Amalita flicked circuit diagrams through her nearly eidetic memory.

"Sorry, Pierre," she said. "The HoloMem crystal reader is hardwired into the library computer. However, the communications console does have the capability of reading or recording a single HoloMem crystal at a time."

"It does?" Pierre said, surprised.

Amalita floated over to the communications console where Abdul was monitoring the latest transmission and flipped open a small door in one side. She reached in and carefully removed a three-sided object. When she pulled it out, Pierre could see the bottom was missing and the interior was a corner cube of brilliantly polished mirrors.

"This is one-half the scanner cavity," Amalita said, "and here is the HoloMem crystal itself." She pushed a button and a clear crystal cube about five centimeters across sprang out of the door,

twirling slowly as it floated into the room. The corners and edges
of the cube were jet black, but through the clear faces Pierre
could see the rainbowlike reflections from the information
fringes stored in the interior. Amalita deftly plucked the cube
out of the air, her thumb and forefinger grasping it at opposite
corners.

"This has been storing everything that has gone through the
console since we started," she said. "It is exactly the same size as
one of the encyclopedia HoloMems and we can put one of them
in place of this one and read the encyclopedia down one crystal
at a time. It will take about a minute to switch crystals and
check the scanner adjustments, and about half an hour to read
out each one of the 25 encyclopedia crystals, but that should still
be faster than shoving all those bits from the library computer
through the communications computer to the console."

"Good!" Pierre said. "Go get the first encyclopedia crystal and
start with that."

"A to AME, AME to AUS, AUS to BLO, BLO to . . ." muttered Amalita as she twirled down through the passageway to
the library, her trained legs and feet propelling her as efficiently
as her hands, which were still busy holding the HoloMem crystal
and the corner of the laser scanner cavity.

"A complete education, from Astronomy to Zoology," Pierre
mused. "Alphabetical order may not be the best way to teach
someone, but in this case it is the fastest."

TIME: 11:16:03 GMT MONDAY 20 JUNE 2050

Suck-the-Crystal pressed the pores of his tread to the page—absorbing again the revelation that had come dripping across from
the neutron-depleted plates. His t'trums of joy and surprise
pounded the page. From the page they were transmitted to the
floor and thence to the entire courtyard of the Sky-Talk Library
—raising admonishing taps from the librarians and scholars. The
taps were soon followed by slower waves emanating from the
methodical approach of his friend, mentor and (unfortunately at
this time) Chief Librarian—Seek-the-Sky, who arrived saying,
"Have you lost your senses or is it only that you've drained your
nuclei dry trying to read those depleted plates of crystal and
have gone into convulsions?"

"I am sorry, Seek-the-Sky. It is just that I absorbed a piece of knowledge that made my previous studies come together into one coherent piece. Here—try it."

Seek-the-Sky flowed onto the dusty, well-tasted crystal plate as Suck-the-Crystal flowed off. From the heading on the plate the librarian noted that it was an early plate from the human encyclopedia, HoloMem 2—AME to AUS. It was a table in the section on Astronomy.

"So?" Seek-the-Sky said. "This plate has been tasted so often that there is hardly a neutron left on it, much less any information that has not been correlated and cross-correlated and cross-cross-correlated by the Old Ones many turns ago. What do you find here that I don't? This seems to be a brittle, tasteless table of stellar nebula."

As he flowed off the plate he stamped, "What is so important about this that you should disturb the scholarly researches of the entire library staff?"

"But, please," Suck-the-Crystal said quickly, "it was an entry in the table that suddenly cross-correlated with some new plates that I helped prepare and catalog just this turn. A few milliseconds ago, over at the Comm Input, I had prepared the crystal plates from the turn's batch of data transmitted by the humans, and had proof-tasted them carefully with the vibrations from the acoustic delay line as any apprentice should. Now—most of the apprentices don't really care what is on the plates, just as long as they agree with the delay line vibrations—but I like to taste them and do preliminary correlations and pretend that I am the Keeper of the Comm."

"You?" Seek-the-Sky shuffled. "Keeper of the Comm?"

"Well . . ." said Suck-the-Crystal. "Yes!" He hastened to explain himself. "Heaven's-Bounty has been Keeper of the Comm for more than fifteen human minutes. There may be other apprentices who are older than I, but I'm the only one who really cares about the information we are collecting. I bet when the Council meets to replace Heaven's-Bounty, they will choose me. Am I right?—You're on the Council."

"Hmm," Seek-the-Sky said. "Maybe you are right—but don't let it make you spread. Now—what is this correlation that has your edges flapping?"

"The large veil-like nebula that is fifth on the list can be extrapolated back to a point of origin at a certain time about 500,000 human years ago. That point is very close to here, about 50 light-years away. That point in space and time is also almost exactly on the path that Egg is on, if you extrapolate back along its track."

"Very interesting," the Chief Librarian said. "You have probably identified the time and place of the supernova explosion that formed Egg."

"But what is more interesting," continued Suck-the-Crystal, "is that the climatological records that are coming down right now indicate a very drastic change of climate on the human's Earth at about that time. Also, that time corresponds with the human anthropologist's estimate for the genesis of the homo sapiens species. I believe that the laying of Egg by a supernova explosion so very near the Solar System was the direct cause of the emergence of intelligence in the creatures that now float above us, teaching us all they know."

"I am sure the humans will be amused when they hear that," Seek-the-Sky said. "Let us go see Heaven's-Bounty and have her put that in her next message."

TIME: 14:20:05 GMT MONDAY 20 JUNE 2050

Jean was busy setting up an alternate communication link with the infrared scanner when she heard a loud snorting bark. It sounded like an angry seal. She quickly turned, looking for the source of the noise.

"I fell asleep and snored," said an abashed Pierre, who had been handing her tools while she was head downwards inside the infrared scanner bay.

"No wonder," she replied, pulling herself out of the bay and taking the tool kit from him. "You missed your sleep shift when this ruckus started. You head off to your rack and get some sleep. You are no good to us in this condition."

"But if I go to sleep for eight hours, there will be a thousand years of cheela development before I wake up. That is like sleeping through the rise and fall of the Roman Empire!"

"Set your alarm for six hours," she replied, pushing him down the passageway. "That will give you enough sleep to keep you going and maybe you will be awake again before they develop spaceflight."

TIME: 14:28:11 GMT MONDAY 20 JUNE 2050

Soother's-Worry paused in the middle of his message to the human. He formed a manipulator, grew a crystalline bone to strengthen it, and pressed the panels that turned off the image that was beaming 400 kilometers down from the human space-ship in its synchronous orbit about Egg. The face that lay under him on the tasting screen flickered off, and was replaced with his own image.

"I simply must see how gorgeous I look," Soother's-Worry thought. "Those humans can just wait awhile. Besides, with the computer slowing everything down by a million to one so the Slow Ones can follow things, I bet they never even notice that I stopped talking."

Soother's-Worry absorbed his image through his tread and glowed inwardly at the sight. His dozen eyes glistened in a deep red halo about the baroque pattern that he had recently had painted on the topside of his flattened ellipsoidal body. He turned slowly, watching the pattern shift on the screen. The dozen shiny reflective circles near the base of each eye-stub mir-rored the black sky and stars, so that it looked as if he had holes through his body looking out on another universe. Winding be-tween the circles was a stripe of highly emissive paint that glowed a hot yellow against his deep red topside surface.

"Beautiful, simply beautiful. Mother will simply love it," he gloated.

He wanted his mother to like him. She almost never visited him anymore, and seemed to spend all her time with Soother's-First and Soother's-Pride.

"You must remember," Soother's-Worry said to himself in an imitation of the Old One who had had the job of raising him, "your mother is Soother-of-All-Clans and has more important things to do than to take care of her children.

"If only," thought Soother's-Worry, "she had not commanded that her eggs be kept separate from all the others. Then I would be just another cheela from the central nursery and not have to worry whether my mother was neglecting me or not.

"But," he reminded himself, "if it had not been for mother, I certainly would not have the enviable position of Keeper of the Comm. As boring as the job is, it is certainly one of the most prestigious in Soother's-Empire."

Soother-of-All-Clans paused at the entrance to the egg-pen. The Old One in charge of the pen, having no eggs to keep him busy, had felt her tread and was waiting for her. He watched with a combination of anxiety and eagerness as the egg-sac was extruded onto the crust from Soother's laying orifice. As soon as the sac was safely on the crust, flattened into a nice ellipsoidal shape, the Old One spread out one of his edges into a hatching mantle and covered the egg gently with the thin membrane. He then slowly rolled the egg toward him and placed it under the protection of his body.

"This one shall be named Soother's-Rock," Soother said. "Its father is Yellow-Rock, Leader of the Clan in the northwest. As soon as the eggling is ready to leave the hatchling pen, it is to be sent to Yellow-Rock for rearing as a youth of its father's clan, for it will become Leader when its father flows."

"It will be done, Soother-of-All-Clans," the Old One said.

Soother turned and rejoined her chief advisors, Soother's-First and Soother's-Pride, her first two children. She was getting a little tired of the constant egg laying, but it was one of her most important duties as Soother-of-All-Clans.

"Who is the next one?" she asked Soother's-First.

"There are many choices, Mother," he said. "However, our merchant informers in the clans to the north have told us that the clan leader Deadly-Sting has been talking about a formal challenge to your leadership, despite the fact that you have forbidden leadership duels. Perhaps a command to him to visit here for a formal mating with you would awe him enough that we could get him to hold off."

"Then again," Soother's-Pride said, "if he gets too difficult while he is here, we could arrange for him to flow."

"No," Soother remonstrated, "I don't think that will be necessary. After all, the whole object of my reign is to soothe away these barbaric instincts in my people, so that in future generations they will act in a civilized manner—as the humans do."

"Shall it be Deadly-Sting then?" Soother's-First asked.

"Yes," Soother said, "we will give that near-barbarian from the north a royal welcome that will make him feel much more important than he really is. Then after the formal mating, we will send him home with so many gifts that he will forget all about trying to challenge my rule."

"I will arrange it immediately, Mother," Soother's-First said, moving off toward the Royal compound.

"I am going to Sky-Talk Library," Soother told Soother's-Pride. "I understand that a new book about one of the early human rulers has been sent down by the humans on one of the alternate communication channels. I want to study it carefully for new ideas. I hope that the ideas on government by the human Napoleon will prove to be as interesting as those of Machiavelli were."

Soother's-Pride watched his mother flow off toward the Sky-Talk compound, a squad of troopers automatically shaping a chevron formation about her, their burly bodies acting as pathbreakers for her in both the hard and the soft directions. As she moved off, Soother's-Pride heard her tread muttering as she moved.

"What shall I name it? Soother's-Sting? Who ever heard of a soothing sting? Soother's-Deadly? No—that's worse . . ."

As Soother approached the Sky-Talk compound, she headed directly for the library and was careful to avoid the Comm complex. The last thing she wanted to be bothered with was the fawning presence of Soother's-Worry.

She was very sorry that she had studied only the GOVERNMENT sections of the human encyclopedia in her youth. She had applied her new knowledge of government to the naive ruling system of the semibarbaric cheela of her time, and had shortly taken over the Leadership of the Combined Clans. She had forged a mighty state that had conquered the remainder of the barbarian tribes on Egg and had finally brought peace to the entire star. As Soother-of-All-Clans she was now powerful enough to subjugate any unruly band or clan, but her job now was to consolidate her rule by less violent means, and form a hereditary dynasty that would eliminate forever the problem of deciding who the next ruler would be, for that would be foreordained from birth.

Her first (and she hoped her only) mistake, was trying to form the line of descendants completely from her own flesh. Soother's-

First was a beautiful example of a cheela, and she would be proud to have him carry on her name after she flowed. She had thought that, since he was such a handsome specimen, she could combine her excellent qualities with his by mating with him as soon as he left the hatching pens. Unfortunately, the result was not what she had expected. The Old Ones at the hatchery tried to give the little one extra attention, but it was soon obvious to all that the hatchling was barely smart enough to feed itself. Soother had found the sinecure of Keeper of the Comm for Soother's-Worry, but the last thing she wanted was to be reminded of her own weaknesses. For according to the human encyclopedia section on GENETICS, the weaknesses that were so obvious in Soother's-Worry were lying dormant in her, only they were masked by other, better genes from her mates.

"If only I had at least scanned the other sections, instead of concentrating solely on the GOVERNMENT section," she said to herself for what seemed to be the dozenth time, knowing full well that if she had done that, she would still be in the library, and would not now be Soother-of-All-Clans.

Actually, Soother had almost gotten away with her scheme. The cheela biophysicists would not determine the genetic coding mechanism for the cheela for dozens of generations, but when they did, both they and the humans would be surprised at how different it was. Because of the high temperatures on the neutron star that attempted to disrupt everything into random chaos, and the all-pervasive magnetic field that lined everything up along the magnetic field lines, the cheela genetic structure was a triply-redundant linear strand of complex nuclear molecules. As the duplicating enzymes would copy the genetic molecule, the check at each triply-redundant site provided an automatically correcting copying mechanism; if one of the three linear strands had mutated, the copying enzyme would be governed by majority rule, and the new triple strand would have the mutation corrected. If two mutations had occurred and all three sites were different, the enzyme would self-destruct, taking the faulty gene with it. It was only when the two mutations were the same that an error was able to creep through. Unfortunately, there had been too many repeated errors in those genes that had formed the nervous system in her son, Soother's-Worry. He was mentally retarded.

Many, many eggs later, Soother was getting tired, yet her ambition drove her on. Her aging body was now pouring nucleonic hormones into her juices that were designed to make her slow down her aggressive drive and retire to the essential job of being an Old One.

The Old Ones were designed by the cheela genes to carefully tend the clan eggs that the younger females would lay and forget, while they returned to their jobs as warriors protecting the clan from enemies. There were no real enemies anymore, and Soother did not want to be an Old One tending eggs, so she transferred her developing parental instincts to the cheela as a whole and drove herself on, consolidating her rule by using the governmental techniques developed by generations of humans.

Finally Soother began to realize that she could not go on forever. Eventually she would have to flow, and the Soother-of-All-Clans would not be there to keep the quarrelsome clans soothed. Of course, Soother's-First was quite capable and willing to take her place and assume his duties as Soother-of-All-Clans, however, her personal ambition kept her from relinquishing her control over her people.

Soother then remembered an old story about the ancient one named Swift-Killer who had first made contact with the humans. The Leonardo da Vinci of the cheela, Swift-Killer had invented the first communication system and was the first Keeper of the Comm. That was long ago when the Keeper of the Comm had to know how to keep the communication and data storage systems operating, and didn't have a team of communication engineers and library assistants to run things.

Soother went to visit the scientists at Sky-Talk compound. "I understand that Swift-Killer, the first Keeper of the Comm, experienced a strange transformation that rejuvenated her," she said.

"Yes," the scientist replied. "Under extreme trauma, her body reverted to that of a dragon plant. She stayed that way for some dozens of greats of turns, and then for some reason the dragon plant reverted back to that of a cheela. However, the new body, having been almost completely rebuilt, was that of a youth, while the scarred outer skin and brain was that of an older one."

"I want to go through that transformation," Soother said, "so that I may continue to lead my people."

"That would be very dangerous, O Soother-of-All-Clans," the

scientist said in alarm. "Shortly after Swift-Killer's experience, the experiment was tried by many cheela. With most of them, nothing happened, and they finally gave up and went off to tend eggs. With others, they had starved themselves so much that they just stopped living and flowed. There was not enough meat left on them even to bother calling the butchers. A few tried both starvation and a severe heating of the topside. Most of these died from the serious burns, and only one started the transformation. However, even that one died before he was well started. You may not have learned it in the stories that you read about Swift-Killer, but she was not alone; there were two others with her, and one of those died."

"Then if it is done properly, the odds are two out of three," Soother said firmly.

"But Soother," protested the scientist, "we don't really know how to do it properly. No one was there to witness the transformation."

"Still," Soother continued, "if I do not go through the transformation, I am surely going to flow soon. I want to be transformed, and within the next great of turns. You and the others are to read all that you can and make preparations. I will return when you are ready."

"It shall be done," the scientist said with resignation. Soother flowed away from him without further word, her squad of troopers forming automatically around her as she moved off.

There was really little more to learn about the ancient transformation of Swift-Killer. What records the scientists had were mostly old storyteller tales that had been distorted by many tellings before they had been written down. It was well less than a great of turns before the scientists let Soother know that they were as ready as they could be.

Soother came at once. She left Soother's-Pride in charge of the routine business of running the Empire, while Soother's-First and a full troop of needle troopers came to Sky-Talk compound to make sure that the experiment was carried out safely. When Soother's-First and the troop commander heard what Soother would be subjected to, they protested strongly.

"They are going to kill you with that treatment!" Soother's-First warned.

"First they are going to starve you until you are an empty sac, and then they are going to sear your topside with a bank of X-ray arcs!" the troop commander shouted.

"Yet, that is what Swift-Killer went through, and so can I," Soother said bravely. "I want you two to see that they do it properly."

"I can't see how we can protect you from them," the troop commander said. "What they propose to do to you does not sound like a treatment, but a fiendish torture for a particularly nasty barbarian!"

"But you can protect me," she replied. "For if I die, you can see that they do also!"

The troop commander hesitated, for to kill unarmed thinkers who had only done their best, and under protest, did not seem like the kind of thing a decent warrior should do, but his sense of duty overcame his principles; after all, the one giving the order was the Soother-of-All-Clans.

"It will be as you say, Soother-of-All-Clans," said the troop commander obediently.

"And if I do flow," Soother said to Soother's-First, "you shall be the next Soother-of-All-Clans. Rule well, my son." She formed a small tendril and stroked him lightly on the topside.

"I will, Mother," he said.

"But don't count on it," she cut in abruptly. "For I intend to come back—younger than you." Her tendril whipped off his topside and shrank back into her surface. She moved off toward the waiting scientists.

"You may proceed," she said.

Although Soother had not eaten for three dozen turns in preparation for the ordeal, it took two dozen more turns before the scientists and doctors felt that she had been weakened enough that her body functions were disrupted to the point where the plant transformation enzymes could begin to dominate the animal enzymes. They could now start the next phase of the transformation.

According to the legends of the storytellers, Swift-Killer had a blotchy topside after her transformation. Some painful experiments with volunteers who had suffered a small section of their topsides to be seared with lengthening sessions under an X-ray arc had shown that the blotches were caused by blisters that formed on the skin after a certain amount of exposure to X-rays.

The timing was critical, however, for too long an exposure caused the blistered surface to char, and then the burn was too severe. The volunteer who had suffered that much radiation still had a nasty scar in the small test spot. He would not have survived if the burn had been over a much larger area.

Soother was barely conscious when the banks of X-ray arcs were struck. The violet-white radiation beamed unmercifully down upon her weakened body. The pain and shock knocked her out and she flowed. The doctors were watching closely, and the arcs were extinguished just as the blisters started.

The troop commander and Soother's-First stood by, looking with distaste and horror on the flattened sac of blistered skin that lay in front of them. The scientists and doctors hovered around, their tendrils constantly touching the now sleeping body.

"She still lives," one of the doctors said. "But her body functions are very unusual. Her fluid pumps are not beating as they do when a cheela is struck in the brain-knot and knocked unconscious; instead they are moving very slowly. It is a state that the humans call sleep."

Soother's-First moved toward the body and confirmed their diagnosis. "It is indeed fortunate for you that she is still alive," he said. "Continue your work."

"There is nothing left for us to do," one of the scientists said. "It is now up to her body. All we can do is make sure that she is not disturbed. We can only wait and watch."

For two dozen turns, nothing much happened, except that the blistered topside started slowly to heal itself. As the healing progressed, Soother's-First noticed that the muscle tone of the skin, which had been poor at the end of the starvation period, now became almost nonexistent. The skin under the healing blisters seemed to be almost transparent. Then after another dozen turns, a small, twelve-pointed crown started to lift up under the center of the sac of skin.

"It looks as if the transformation is working," one of the scientists reported. "The root spike must now be complete, and that is the start of the cantilever structure that will hold the skin up to the sky."

Inside Soother, the hormones and enzymes were busy. The animal muscle was attacked and dissolved, but the enzymes were careful to take their dissolution process just so far. The stringlike molecules in the muscle tissue were carefully teased apart into separate strands, but the strands were carefully maintained as long fibers. The longer they were, the stronger would be the resulting dragon crystal. The fibers floated through the juices where they were picked up by the enzymes building the engineering marvel that would lift the huge body up off the surface of Egg against the fierce gravity, the stiff structures of the plant body being capable of doing something that the more flexible tissues of the animal body could never do. Carefully the enzymes worked the long fibers into the crystal, embedding them firmly into the clear crystallium, to make a composite material that was many times stronger than the crystallium itself. Things went well for a while, and the cantilever structure grew, slowly lifting the thinned sac of skin off the ground. However, long before the twelve-pointed structure was really finished, the muscle tissue ran low. The growth slowed, and every strand that floated nearby was eagerly salvaged by the enzymes that struggled to make do with inadequate building materials. Finally the last portions of the spikes were being made almost entirely of inadequate clear crystallium.

Soother had waited too long for her transformation. The ancient Swift-Killer had been a well-exercised troop commander, and even in her starved state she had had plenty of muscle tissue; but Soother had been an administrator too long, and had not gone into her ordeal with sufficient reserves.

Soother's-First was awed by the huge plant that began to tower over him. Even the scientists were greatly pleased with the result. As the turns passed, the skin folds lifted off the crust, and the doctors could already tell from the wastes emitted from the still partially functioning animal orifices that new nourishment was being generated by the plant portion of the body. Everything looked good. Soother's-First even began to think about leaving the Sky-Talk compound to visit with Soother's-Pride to work out the details of their temporary joint rule for the next dozen greats of turns until his mother was rejuvenated.

Then it happened. The tip of one of the weakened spikes broke as it attempted to tighten the skin. Soother's-First was horrified to see a jagged point of dragon crystal sticking up out of the torn fold of skin. The skin held for a while, and the scientists attempted to build a mound up against the side of the body to support the damaged section. But before the support could be arranged, an adjoining spike gave way under the unequal tension, and in a rapid series of sharp cracks and loud crashes, the remainder of the twelve-pointed skeleton broke and fell to the crust.

For a few moments, they all stood in horror as the thin skin oozed the last of its juices out of jagged holes onto the crust. Then Soother's-First turned to the troop commander.

"I am Soother-of-All-Clans," he said. His eyes took in the horrified group of scientists and doctors.

"They failed," he said. "Do as my mother commanded!"

The troop commander hesitated. "But they did their best!" he protested. "There must have been something wrong with Soother's body for the failure to have occurred like that. It is not proper for you to punish them."

"Do not lecture to me about what is proper, for I am Soother-of-All-Clans," he replied angrily. "Obey me at once, or you will no longer be troop commander."

The troop commander felt an angry muttering among his warriors. Although they were well-trained troopers and obedient to duty, it would take all of his prestige to get them to carry out the order. Then suddenly the troop commander realized the strength of his position. His troopers were more loyal to him personally than to Soother's-First. They would not have backed him against the legendary Soother herself, but he had no question as to their choice now.

"Who is Leader of All Clans, Old One?" he said quietly, and not a tread moved in the complex as the ancient challenge rang out through the crust.

"What is this nonsense!" Soother's-First demanded angrily. "The leadership challenge was outlawed by Soother long ago." His eyes swept over the large body of troopers and found a burly squad leader.

"You," he ordered. "You are now commander of this troop. Take command and take this traitor into custody!"

The squad leader hesitated. Then with the repressed violence of someone who has seen her whole clan-oriented life disrupted by Soother, who kept track of her eggs like a perverted Old One, she vibrated a harsh reply back through the crust, "I take orders from my commander, not from you—you clanless mother-lover!"

The vehemence of the reply startled Soother's-First. He looked through the mass of trooper eyes, looking for support, but found none.

The troop commander, now confident of his backing, repeated the challenge. "Who is Leader of All Clans, Old One?"

Soother's-First did not reply, knowing that he had no chance against this battle-hardened warrior. He attempted to flow off to the west. The troop commander watched for a moment, then accepted a dragon tooth from the nearest trooper. After a very short chase, a well-aimed thrust to the brain-knot ended the short rule of Soother's-First.

The troop commander found a very strong popular support for his actions, and soon the much larger group of "Clannists" had overcome the numerically smaller group of "Mothers" and by popular acclaim, the troop commander became the new Leader of All Clans.

TIME: 14:28:53 GMT MONDAY 20 JUNE 2050

Seiko was watching the image of the decorated cheela on the screen. Soother's-Worry was in the midst of one of his confused sentences when suddenly there was a large crowd of cheela surrounding him. She caught a glimpse of glittering knives of dragon crystal as the computer-fed display stopped. Almost instantly the screen flashed on again. There was no trace of Soother's-Worry, and the very plain topside of a cheela again was centered on her screen, the dozen eye-stubs waving smoothly as the intelligent-looking eyes stared intently at the optical pickup.

"I am Leonardo, the Chief Scientist of the Sky-Talk science complex," the image said. "I have been appointed the new Keeper of the Comm by the Leader of All Clans."

Not a flicker of surprise crossed Seiko's stolid face. One second ago, the ruler of this world had been called Soother-of-All-Clans. Now they were back to the old title of Leader. Well, they were probably going through their equivalent of the consolidation of China by Ch'in or of Europe by Napoleon, and one would have to expect rapid changes for a while until they had left their semibarbaric state and had settled down to a method for transition of rule by peaceful means.

"Welcome, Leonardo," Seiko said, slightly amused. The name was probably inherited with the job as Chief Scientist. Right now the cheela were in awe of the accomplishments of the humans and often took names from the encyclopedia the humans were sending down. Within half a day, they would have surpassed the humans in knowledge and technology. She doubted that she would meet any Leonardos or Einsteins on her next shift.

"We are about through with the HoloMem crystal GAM to GRE and we will have to take a short break while we load in the next one," Seiko said.

"Good," said the computer-slowed image of Leonardo. "That will give us a chance to install the new radiation to taste converters."

TIME: 20:29:59 GMT MONDAY 20 JUNE 2050

Super-Fluid was dejected. This turn was to have been one of the greatest moments of his career, and it had been blasted by his meeting with the Council for the Programmed Education of the Slow Ones. The Council had decided that the humans would not be told about Super-Fluid's new theory of gravity. Instead, the humans would have to rediscover it for themselves.

Super-Fluid had wanted to have his new theory appreciated and used by the humans. After all, they had given so much to the cheela. Yet he recognized that the only reason that the cheela were still developing on their own was that the extensive knowledge of the humans had been transmitted down to them so slowly that the faster-thinking cheela had usually figured out things by themselves, long before the detailed human explanation had finally trickled in.

The Council had decreed that his new discoveries on antigravity would have to be sent up to the humans in a coded form. The detailed information on his theory would be in the hands of the humans, but they would not be able to read it until they knew the crypto-keyword that would decipher the gibberish that they had received. The crypto-keyword for the antigravity section was the complete nonlinear formula that Super-Fluid had laboriously developed only after many turns of deep thought.

"It isn't fair," Super-Fluid thought. "Before they can find out what I did, one of the humans will have had to think the same thoughts that I did, and that person will get the credit!"

Yet he knew that, although the human might receive some limited notoriety for breaking the crypto-code to the antigravity section, it would give no real consolation to the person who, after all, had come in second best.

"They are so brave—so noble—those Slow Ones," thought Super-Fluid, as he approached the construction site for the antigravity machine.

Helium-Two, Project Manager of the Negative Gravity Test Project, watched the wrinkled figure of the elderly scientist approach. According to reports, the Aged One still had enough juice left in him to take an interest in his earlier scientific exploits, even though he had served a full stint at the hatching pens. He had been expecting a wrinkled, but still perky Aged One; but what was coming toward him was the sorriest, most dejected cheela he had ever seen since he had been hatched. There must be something wrong.

Then, as Helium-Two watched, the cheela in the distance noticed his presence. Shivering himself all over, Super-Fluid suddenly changed character and moved surely toward him, even though he was partially off in the hard direction.

"I presume you are Helium-Two," the Aged One said with a firm tread. "Thank you for arranging to have me present during the demonstration."

"I knew that you would want to see it," Helium-Two said. "Please follow me."

The two cheela moved in single file across the dense crystal crust of the neutron star. Helium-Two pushed hard, as if he were leaning into a heavy wind. His opalescent, ellipsoidal body flattened out to force an opening between the trillion gauss magnetic field lines. He deferentially held the gap open with a trailing cluster of reinforced manipulator arms that allowed the elder scientist to flow after him with minimum effort. They paused to look around; as they did so, they felt the magnetic field close in on them again, their bodies pinned onto the field lines like beads on a wire.

"How do you like it, Super-Fluid?" Helium-Two asked. "Big, isn't it?"

"I don't see much of anything except those large pumps over there and some ridges in the crust."

"We had to put most of the antigravity machine underground because of the high pressures. Underneath those ridges are the largest high pressure vessels ever made by cheela. They are formed of strong pipes wrapped around and around in the shape of a ring wrapped with wire. You can see one ring under that ridge and the top of the other ring over there. They are set up at an angle to each other so that the place of maximum interaction is just above the surface in the middle."

"I didn't visualize anything like this when I was working on the theory," Super-Fluid said, as his dozen eyes took in the vista.

"You are lucky. Very few theoretical scientists ever see their mathematical equations turned into working hardware in their lifetime, especially when the theoretical work involves such a fundamental change in our understanding of nature such as does the Super-Fluid-Einstein theory of gravitation. Einstein himself was one of the few. He lived to see his $E=mc^2$ prediction bring about control of nuclear energy. Einstein was lucky because it turned out to be easy for the humans to get a nuclear chain reaction going—they just have to bring two pieces of uranium or plutonium near each other. You are fortunate in that it is easy for us to get the very high mass-densities and velocities that are needed to make the Super-Fluid effect work."

"I wish you wouldn't use that term," Super-Fluid said. "The correct term is the gravimotive effect. People keep referring to the effect by my name—and I appreciate the honor, but I am thinking of the poor students in the future. They are going to have a hard time remembering that the Super-Fluid effect is the gravimotive effect and does not have anything to do with superconductivity."

The two started back toward the bunker as Super-Fluid went on, "I have always been proud of the unusual name that the Old Ones chose for me when I was a hatchling. Like you, I was hatched during the generation when the humans were beaming down the SUPERCONDUCTIVITY section of their encyclopedia. The theories of superconductivity revolutionized our understanding of the interior of our home star. It made quite an impression on everyone to learn that we are floating on a crystalline crust over a liquid core of superfluid neutrons."

"All right—the gravimotive effect," Helium-Two said. "Anyway, the gravitational engineers did a good job on the design. The antigravity machine is a lot more efficient and compact than I thought it would be when I took on the job of managing the design and construction contract."

Helium-Two went around the bunker to the entrance in the rear. "Come inside, then we will give the machine its first try. We will only take it to half-power in this first trial. We won't try to make the gravity force go negative, but there should be plenty of interesting effects when we get to zero gravity."

The project manager and the scientist went into the low bunker. They raised some of their eyes up on short conical stubs and looked out over the top. Helium-Two spent the next few moments going over the check list with the gravitational engineers.

"It is a big moment for them, too," Helium-Two thought. "They have been studying and training for many turns, and this is the first time they will be able to see the theories they studied work."

Everything was soon ready and Helium-Two signaled for the power to be applied. Super-Fluid could feel the vibrations from the great pumps as they started to move their massive loads of ultra-dense liquid. The fluid moved around in the pipes at a constantly increasing velocity. The acceleration supplied by the pumps was so great that the velocity of the dense fluid would begin to approach the speed of light in a millisecond. However, that would be more than time enough for the fast-living cheela to carry out a leisurely experiment.

Super-Fluid could almost visualize the Einstein gravity fields generated by the motion of the liquid and was not surprised to see the crust in the center of the machine lift up and flow out from the center. Soon there was a great cavity almost a centimeter deep, as the Einstein fields took hold and started to nullify the neutron star's 67-billion-gee gravitational field.

"So far it has all been Einstein antigravity fields," Helium-Two whispered to him. "Very shortly the hyper-nonlinear portion of your theory should take over and we should get the contraction of the Einstein fields into a region at the center."

They watched tensely as the crust started to flow back to fill in the depression—more slowly this time—while the whine of the pumps moved to higher and higher pitch. Soon the crust was nearly what it had been before, but now above the crust at the center of the machine was a distortion in the atmosphere.

"Why can we see the region?" Helium-Two asked. "It can't be a distortion in space-time caused by strong gravity fields. The gravity is less there than it is here."

"No," Super-Fluid said, awed in spite of himself. "The explanation is much more pragmatic than that. The low-gravity region is visible because it doesn't have any atmosphere. The atmosphere has all flowed to the outside edges. That is an oval-shaped chunk of outer space hanging in front of you, and what you are seeing is the difference in the index of refraction of vacuum and the atmosphere."

"Now for the fun part," Helium-Two said. "We are going to inject a small chunk of pure carbon into the zero gravity region and see what happens."

Helium-Two turned to the crew and initiated the sequence of events. Super-Fluid watched as a short stubby cylinder started to rise up out of the crust right under the distortion. He could feel powerful hydraulic pumps complaining as the top of the cylinder started to approach the edge of the oval-shaped region.

"That last little bit of distance is going to take some time," Helium-Two said, as the hydraulic pumps labored under the strain. "Moving those few microns from our normal gravity to the zero gravity in the gravimotive-effect region is equivalent to going straight up off our neutron star into outer space. Not much distance to travel, but it takes a lot of energy. We are going to stop the cylinder just as it gets to the inner edge, and fire the carbon pellet from a gun built into the piston."

The vibration of the hydraulic pumps finally stabilized and began to beat with the rising whine of the antigravity generator pumps that kept the distortion activated. Helium-Two turned a few of his eyes toward his engineers and his undertread rumbled an order through the crust: "Inject!"

Super-Fluid watched as a tiny speck rose from the center of the piston and floated to the center of the distortion, brightly illuminated by lights that flooded the central region with X-rays. As he watched, the speck grew, and by the time it had reached the center and hung there, it had grown to be almost as round as he was wide.

"Why doesn't it fall out of the zero gravity region as the atmosphere did?" Super-Fluid asked.

Helium-Two replied, "Those X-ray lights are not just for illumination, they are also coupled to a servo control system. We use X-ray pressure to keep the carbon speck centered in the zero gravity region."

"As it gets bigger, it gets harder to see," Super-Fluid said, watching in awe and amazement as the tiny speck of degenerate crystalline carbon slowly came apart. Once the material had been released from the tremendous gravitational pressures exerted by the neutron star, the nuclear repulsive forces took over and the nuclei moved further and further apart. Now that there was space between the nuclei, the electrons, which had been packed into a superconductive fluid coursing through the close-packed array of carbon nuclei, began to evaporate from the fluid to take up orbits around the nuclei, further isolating the nuclei from each other. Soon the tiny speck had grown a hundred times larger in each direction while its density dropped by a million.

"I can't see it anymore," Super-Fluid said.

"I can, and it's beautiful," Helium-Two said, waving one of his eyes after another. "At least with some of my eyes. I think I can fix things so we can both see it without having to move around." He went to the servo control console and talked to the engineer there.

He returned. "I had the engineer set the servo control so that the crystal would rotate while staying in place."

They both watched as the seemingly empty space suddenly sparkled into a brilliant flash of light—then winked off again.

"You wouldn't think that something with a density of only a few grams per cubic centimeter would be visible at all—much less be so brilliant," Helium-Two said.

"It is because the crystal structure reflects the X-rays when the atomic planes of the crystal are at just the right angle between one of the lights and one of our eyes," Super-Fluid explained. "I have been watching the pattern carefully as it rotates. If I am not mistaken, that is a crystal with a cubic lattice structure. What did you say the seed material was?"

"Carbon," Helium-Two said.

"I think that is what the humans call a diamond," Super-Fluid said. "They were right—it is pretty."

TIME: 20:30:00 GMT MONDAY 20 JUNE 2050

The chimes rang again and again, insistently. Pierre woke up grudgingly, his red-lined eyes peering at the numbers on the clock.

2030, the numbers indicated.

"I missed my shift!" Pierre exclaimed, slapping the release and running an index finger down the sealing seam of the sleeping sack. As his brain became more active, he realized that shifts no longer counted, but he still should be awake and helping.

"Six hours," he groaned as he rubbed his face. "Six hours—and three-fourths of a millennium. I wonder what is going on?" He quickly bathed, and, still holding a food-stick, swung up the passageway to the back of the communications console.

Abdul looked up as he came in. "Glad to see you, Pierre," he said in a concerned voice. "Did you get some sleep?"

"Yes," Pierre replied. "Enough to keep me awake for the rest of my shift. Thanks for standing in for me."

"No problem," Abdul said. "It has been interesting watching the cheela civilization develop almost right in front of my eyes."

"At what stage are the cheela now?" Pierre asked.

"They are beginning to pass us in all areas except molecular chemistry. But since they don't even have molecules to experiment on, you can't blame them for that. They tell us that they can almost predict the contents of the rest of the encyclopedia, but they insist that we send the entire text down for the sake of their historians and humanologists. We should be changing to the last encyclopedia crystal WAT to ZYZ shortly. Then you should erase the encyclopedia crystals and the cheela will start filling them up with information that they have learned on their own in the past day."

"Good," Pierre said. "Amalita and I can take it from here. You had better get some rest yourself."

"I won't take long," Abdul said as he floated out the door. "This is too interesting to miss."

TIME: 22:26:03 GMT MONDAY 20 JUNE 2050

Floating-Crystal returned from her vacation with mixed emotions. It had been a delightful vacation, eight long turns in the foothills at Swift's Climb mountain resort. She had enjoyed every millisecond of it, even though she would never get used to the idea of looking down on things. She was reluctant to return to what everyone would admit was often the most boring job on the star, yet at the same time she felt eager to be back at work; while the job of Keeper of the Comm was boring at times, it was the most important position a cheela could aspire to (with the possible exception of the President of the United Clans).

Floating-Crystal was feeling good as she entered Sky-Talk complex. She decided to take a shortcut. Rather than moving along the paths in the easy direction, and then crossing over at the superconducting tunnels, she flattened herself out and pushed her way in the hard direction across the park that separated the compounds in the complex. She could almost feel the magnetic field lines rippling across her topside as she pushed herself along, her tread gripping the textured surface. She flowed by the crumbling ruins of the gigabit receiving antenna that had been the pride and joy of her predecessors many generations ago, and went into the compound surrounding the huge transmitter array.

Her first thought was to check on the Comm display. As she flowed onto its large flat surface she could tell that the human—Amalita Shakhashiri Drake—was still in the middle of her sentence. At the bottom of the screen the computer had superimposed the words of the sentence. Those that Amalita had already spoken were in one taste and the computer prediction for the words in the rest of the sentence were in another taste. It was a long sentence, and full of the many redundancies that humans found necessary to insert into their speech. It was the very predictability of the redundancies that made the job of Keeper of the Comm so boring.

Before Floating-Crystal had left on her vacation Amalita had spoken the words:

"Pierre has informed me that the Ho . . ."

Floating-Crystal did not need a computer to figure out that the next few phonemes were ". . . loMem crystal . . ." and that the rest of the sentence was probably something about the holographic memory data storage crystal being full and that they should stop transmitting data up for a minute while Pierre put in a blank crystal.

When Amalita had gotten to "Holo . . .", Floating-Crystal had decided it would be a good time for a long vacation and had taken off. On her return to the display, she was surprised to find that both she and the computer had misjudged the human. Amalita had progressed much further in her sentence than she had expected, although the general content was the same. The computer display of the spoken part now read:

"Pierre has informed me that the HoloMem's full. Stop one min . . ."

"Good," Floating-Crystal thought to herself. "The old array has been transmitting data up to the humans for generations. That minute will give us time to tear down the obsolete hunk of junk and build a decent one with computer-controlled phased-array beam steering."

Floating-Crystal flowed off the display and went to the translation compound. Her three apprentices were busily scanning the human-language output of a computer generated translation of a text on cheela physiology. Although the computer did an excellent job of translation, there were many times that a straight human translation of a cheela sentence ended up distorted (or even bawdy) and it required an experienced student of human culture to figure out how to restructure the human sentence to retain the original cheela intent. Clear-Thinker, the eldest apprentice, felt the vibrations from Floating-Crystal's tread as she approached. He turned a few of his eyes toward her.

"Remind me in three or four dozen turns to find a good stopping point in the data stream," Floating-Crystal instructed him. "It is time for the humans to change crystals."

"This book on physiology that we are translating now is scheduled for transmission in about three dozen turns," the apprentice replied. "It has a lot of pictures, so the number of bits is quite high, but it shouldn't take too many turns to transmit—even at the slow bit rates that the human receivers can handle."

"Good," Floating-Crystal said. "Make the break at the end of the text."

She then returned to the Comm display room and prepared her reply in front of the cameras. The computer stored her performance and then played it back for her review—first on the long, thin visual display that just showed her front edge and eyes, and then on the human-oriented rectangular taste display. The camera for that display looked down at her from an angle and showed her whole flat body with the ring of eyes around its periphery. She could see the bulge that was an egg near her middle and wondered idly whether it had been Clear-Thinker or Bit-Cruncher who had put it there. "Not that it really matters," she thought to herself. "It looks as if it will be ready to leave with the Old Ones at the hatching pens pretty soon.

"I still think the whole thing is slightly obscene," she murmured as she examined her image in the human display. "Nobody but lovers, computers, and humans ever see the topside of me."

She didn't like her first performance and redid it a couple of times until the message was short, yet clear. She then keyed the computer to transmit the message at human rates as soon as Amalita finished her sentence.

With a long break coming up, there was a lot to do. She contacted Comm Engineering and told them that they would soon be able to replace the aging antenna. They were delighted to be able to switch from maintenance to design and building. She could almost taste the eagerness in the Chief Engineer's image as he flowed away to tell his crew.

She then called a meeting of the Comm Advisory Board. There had been some talk of a possible expedition to visit the humans, but because it would involve a good deal of direct communication, it had been put off until the next break in the data stream.

A dozen turns later the Advisory Board gathered. They listened to the gravitational engineers as they explained the latest test results on their gravity-control and inertia-drive experiments. The inertia drive was the propulsion mechanism that would allow them to leave their neutron star home, where the escape velocity was 39 percent the speed of light. However, the most dangerous part of travel off the surface of a neutron star was the explosive decompression of neutronic matter (including the neutronic matter of the space traveler!) when it was no longer kept compressed by the gravitational pressure supplied by the star. Now the engineers were sure that both problems had been solved.

Most of the Advisory Board had a difficult time accepting the fact that solid substances like the hard crystalline crust of their neutron star home or their equally tough yet supple bodies were not stable. Yet, without gravity to hold them together, they would decompose and reform into a tenuous molecular structure with the nuclei spaced a hundred times further apart than normally. However, these facts were well known to Floating-Crystal. One of the Old Ones tending her hatchling pen had worked on the original antigravity machine. He, himself, had seen a small speck of neutronic material expand when placed in the zero gravity region formed by the machine, and he had watched it turn into a transparent, twinkling molecular crystal floating in space. He had given her name to her when she hatched, and later told her about the beautiful floating crystal that had been her namesake.

After many meetings of the Comm Advisory Board and the engineers, it was finally decided that a visit to the humans was technically feasible. However, the effort required was substantial, so a commitment by the President and the Council of the United Clans was needed.

After much public debate, the program outlined by the engineers was approved, the finances were allocated, and the generation long project was started. Although the focus of the effort—"A Visit to the Humans"—was quixotic in nature, since there was almost nothing that could be communicated during the visit, they all knew that the real reason for the project was to crack the invisible egg-sac of gravity that had kept the cheela bound in the hatchery of their laying. For they all knew the cheela species could not stay on their home star forever.

The decision for the Visit came soon after the data stream was turned off. During the period while the cheela engineers were rebuilding the data transmitter and Pierre was replacing the full HoloMem crystal with an empty one, Floating-Crystal took over the Comm link to Amalita and with the help of the Visit program engineers, told her what to expect and what to do.

"We are coming out to visit," was her first message. As the turns passed and she saw in the display the look of astonishment and concern build on Amalita's face, she quickly brushed aside the protest that was forming on Amalita's lips. "We will not explode. We will provide our own gravity."

For the next minute Amalita listened attentively while Floating-Crystal explained the general outline of the planned visit. Amalita was a little concerned when she heard about the X-ray generator they were going to use to illuminate the inside of the spacecraft, then blushed a little when she began to realize how much someone could see who used soft X-rays for part of his vision range. However, the cheela already knew a great deal about human physiology. They had had plenty of time to study the human encyclopedia and the textbooks that had been beamed down by the humans many generations ago, so they knew that the total X-ray dose they would be using on their human friends during their short visit would be minimal.

At the end of the first minute, Pierre returned from the computer room to hear the musical voice of Floating-Crystal.

"We have started the data again. First is a schedule for you to follow during the visit. The expedition will start in about fifteen minutes. Read the instructions carefully, for the whole visit will only last ten seconds."

Floating-Crystal saw Pierre come slowly around the corner and was overjoyed to see him. She had been hoping he would come back into view before she had to retire her job and take her place as an Old One teaching the hatchlings how to talk.

"I'm glad to see you again, Pierre," she said. "I must say goodbye now. You have much reading to do and preparations to make. When you return to the monitor, there will be a new Keeper of the Comm."

"These fifteen-minute lifetime friendships are hard on the emotions," Amalita said to herself as she brushed her eyes, then flicked the communications screen to the computer and started reading the words that appeared there.

The cheela plan was very detailed and concise, for the cheela had long since had a complete description of the ship Dragon Slayer.

Amalita punched for a hardcopy of the screen full of words for Pierre to read, then went on to the diagram. The diagram was animated and showed herself seated at the console and Pierre near one window. Then the cheela ship arrived outside the ship. Her cartoon image rose from the chair at the console, raised its arms and, twirling around once like a clumsy ballerina, fell toward the right viewing port. Meanwhile, the cartoon of Pierre clung to another port, its nose pressed to the glass. A closeup view showed that less than a meter from his nose was a tiny speck a few millimeters across, and on that speck sat a cheela—no spacesuit—no pressure container—nothing to keep it from exploding.

Pierre quickly read the instructions, then they both watched the animation again. They were bewildered by their motions in the animation. They both looked clumsy and constrained—as if they were acting out their motions in earth-bound simulators instead of the graceful ballet of free-fall motion they were used to.

They read further and then began to realize why they had been so clumsy in the animation. To survive in space, the cheela explorers had to bring gravity with them. Their main spacecraft was a hard crystalline spherical shell about four centimeters across with a rather "large" miniature black hole at the center. At 11-billion tons mass, the black hole provided 180 thousand gees at the surface of the crystal sphere. Although far from the 67-billion gees that the cheela lived in at the surface of the neutron star, it was enough to keep their electron structure in its degenerate form. Individual cheela and equipment modules had their own smaller version of the main spacecraft. The radii of the individual flitters and equipment tugs were much smaller, so that only a tiny black hole was needed for each one. The smaller spacecraft had separate power and inertia propulsion subsystems, and the whole swarm fitted neatly into hemispherical depressions that pocked the surface of the main spacecraft.

"Inertia propulsion!" Pierre exclaimed. "On our last shift we were teaching them Newton's law of gravity. Today they have inertia drives! Where will they be tomorrow?"

"They probably will be able to control space and time and won't have to bother with such clumsy things as black hole gravity generators and inertia drives," Amalita replied. "But now I see why we were so awkward. Their main spacecraft will stay fifteen meters away from our spacecraft, but it is so massive that we will experience about one-third of a gee from it, pulling me out of the console chair and over to the viewing port. I guess I could manage to twirl once as I fall so they can see the human joints in action, but I bet I am going to be clumsier in one-third gee than that animation." She turned from the screen and looked at him. "I wish you were doing my part, so I could get to see the cheela."

"I don't know whether you would like it," Pierre said. "According to this contour plot of the gravity field from the individual craft, although the size and mass of the flitters are much smaller than the main spacecraft, this one is going to come up to less than one meter from my viewing port and my nose is going to be pulling three gees!" He looked down at her body and grinned. "I guess the reason they didn't choose you is they must know you don't wear a bra in free-fall and they didn't want to give you reverse Cooper's droop."

Amalita turned back to the display, jabbing him with her elbow as she did so, and brought up the next screen full of instructions. "You know perfectly well that since this is the one time that our two civilizations will be close enough culturally to make a physical visit meaningful, they chose the Earth's best known science writer and interpreter for the interview," she said. "How long do you get?"

Pierre scanned down the time schedule that the cheela had sent up. "He will stay there for about one second, and will try to remain as motionless as possible for as long as he can, so that my eyes will have time to focus on him. At that, he will probably come close to starving to death unless they can figure out a way for him to eat without moving too much."

"It seems ridiculous for them to go through this visit," said Amalita. "We both have complete descriptions of each other's physiology and plenty of pictures, both still and motion."

"However," she went on, "if I were offered the opportunity to visit the surface of a neutron star and spend fifteen seconds watching a half year of cheela civilization whirling about me, I would jump at the chance."

The console beeped and the computer switched off the information display. A cheela's visage appeared on the screen.

"I am Bit-Cruncher, the new Keeper of the Comm."

Bit-Cruncher waited out the polite response from the humans by interviewing some new apprentices. One of them would take his place one of these turns, but all of them would meanwhile become so thoroughly soaked in human culture that they would almost think like humans. He was kind to the youngsters, remembering his terror when old Floating-Crystal had interviewed him. Still, they had a rough time ahead, for only one of them could become Keeper of the Comm.

As one of Floating-Crystal's apprentices, he had worked hard and had not only kept up with his apprentice work, but had developed a complex new computer program to cross-correlate the immense amount of human knowledge that was still stored in the Sky-Talk Library. His new program was now finding out more about humans than the humans knew about themselves. For this prodigious feat he was awarded the rare opportunity to choose a new name for himself, and it eventually had led to his being made the new Keeper of the Comm when Floating-Crystal became an Old One and went off to tend eggs.

"It was the opportunity for a new name that really drove me," he rippled to himself. "I'll never forgive that romantic-minded Old One that named me Moby-Dick, after reading one of those old human adventure novels."

Bit-Cruncher continued to think about prior times as he flowed back to the Comm compound. After he had been awarded the job as the new Keeper of the Comm, his comrades and competitors in apprenticeship had had to seek other occupations. Crystal-Blossom was now a Professor of Humanology at Sky-Talk University and Clear-Thinker was leader of the Visit expedition.

"Even though he lost out to me for Keeper of the Comm, I think maybe Clear-Thinker might be better off," he mused. "There will be many Keepers of the Comm, but only one Visit. In addition, although I see humans on the display every turn, I do it through their cameras, which are made for their eyes. He will get to see a human in the flesh, bones and all!" Bit-Cruncher returned to the display just as Amalita was finishing.

". . . meet you, Bit-Cruncher. When will the visit b . . ."

Bit-Cruncher contacted Clear-Thinker through the links and got the latest schedule. Things were going well. The main spacecraft had made it out to space and back on automatic control. Everything, even the unwilling Slinks that had been sent along in cages to test the life support system, had survived without damage. Another few hundred turns and they would be ready.

"Set a definite time," said Bit-Cruncher, "so the humans can get everything ready."

"All right," Clear-Thinker said. "Two greats of turns from now."

"That long? Everyone is going to be tired of waiting for the liftoff," Bit-Cruncher said. "But I guess it is better to be on the safe side." Bit-Cruncher returned to the communications display as Amalita finished and informed her that the visit would take place in exactly 57 seconds.

Amalita and Pierre turned away from the console and got busy. Amalita opened the shields over the viewing ports, set the automatic cameras for the focal distances and exposures the cheela had recommended, and turned them on. She then returned to her chair at the console, found her acceleration belt and adjusted it so she would stay in her seat until the time came for her to twirl across to the port.

Pierre bustled about the cabin, plucking loose items from loops, off sticky pads and out of corners where they had drifted, and stuffed them into a cabinet. He then went around making sure that all the cabinets were latched.

"The last thing we want is a pile of loose junk cluttering up the ports," he said.

The seconds ticked away. Pierre took up his position near one port, his hands firmly gripping the handholds set in the frame. They both looked out the other port toward the place where the visitors would arrive.

As they waited, the light in the room flickered eerily as the white radiance from the neutron star flashed into the ports five times a second, alternating with the red glow of the ultra-dense asteroids that circled around their spacecraft, their strong gravitational fields blocking the crushing, tearing tides of the neutron star.

Suddenly there was a flash of multihued light and they both glimpsed a small brilliant white object the size of a golf ball holding a steady position fifteen meters away. There was a moment's pause and then the golf ball seemed to explode into a cloud of colored snowflakes that swarmed across the intervening distance. The larger snowflakes stayed well away from the ports while the smaller ones came in closer.

TIME: 22:30:10.0 GMT MONDAY 20 JUNE 2050

"Holy Egg!" murmured one of the cheela crew as they slowly drifted in between the large glowing condensed asteroids and settled down in a synchronous orbit fifteen meters out from one of the viewing ports. "I expected the thing to be big, but I never imagined it would be this big!"

Clear-Thinker mentally agreed with the crew member. He couldn't see who said it, since she was out of sight around the horizon on their little home away from home. What really bothered him was not that the human spacecraft was big, but that it was "overhead." Although all the crew had been in space and had learned to conquer the fear that the home star they were orbiting was going to fall on them, this object was much too close for comfort. He quickly called an unscheduled hold in their carefully timed schedule. The humans would hardly notice a one-fifth of a second pause and he felt a full turn of rest and recreation while the crew got used to the sight of the human spacecraft overhead would be worth the delay.

He ordered everyone to stay in his assigned station on the spacecraft while he rotated the shell slowly around. The gigantic human spacecraft passed above every crew member several times while they all gazed at the metal skin and stared into the viewing ports, where they could vaguely glimpse some huge shadowy shapes behind the heavily tinted fuzzy glass. After a short while Clear-Thinker stopped the rotation, ordered a minimum crew to stay at the controls and let the rest of the two dozen crew members have a vacation break for a full turn. A few paired off and wandered around to the back side to find a quiet place behind some piece of equipment, but most gathered at the front and continued to stare at the unbelievable sight as the slow turning of the human spacecraft around their home star changed the lighting. At last the neutron star set behind the spacecraft and the show was over. The darkness was also strange, but the cheela psychologists had anticipated that problem and had made sure that the crystal shell underneath them had all the old familiar heat and radiation characteristics that they were used to on Egg, even though the gravitational pull was nowhere near that of home.

With half a turn gone, Egg rose from behind the opposite side of the spacecraft, and the spectator crowd grew once again. It was obvious to Clear-Thinker that the initial problem of having the spacecraft overhead had now dissipated, but he decided to wait for one full turn before putting the crew back onto the schedule so that their timing for the photographs and spectral analyses would be correctly oriented with respect to the illumination from Egg.

Precisely one turn later the crew members were back at their posts and the Visit began. A cloud of individual fliers and many small instrument packages took off. Each one was a tiny sphere with a sub-miniature black hole at the center to keep it under enough gravity so that it would not explode. The first instrument packages to get to the human spacecraft were several X-ray generators. Some larger ones were positioned at a distance to illuminate the general scene, their radiation varying in opposition to the illumination from the neutron star that rose and set as the work proceeded. Others were placed in a ring around the viewing ports and sent their violet-white beams through the heavily tinted glass into the interior of the spacecraft. Soon the shadows in the room became clearer. Using the pictures and a map of the console room, the crew could identify the communications console and the chair in front of it. In the chair was a collection of strangely-shaped violet objects surrounded by a multicolored cloud. They increased the illumination and then could finally make out the outlines of the yellow-white clothing and blue-white human flesh covering Amalita's violet bones. Cameras were set up and adjusted, and data started pouring back to the mother spacecraft where other crew members monitored displays and tended the computers and the communication links back down to Egg.

TIME: 22:30:11.2 GMT MONDAY 20 JUNE 2050

"One-thousand-one, one-thousand-two . . ." counted Amalita as she felt the gravitational tug from the insignificant golf ball fifteen meters away.

". . . one-thousand-three and twirl," she chanted as she

pressed the belt release, did one pirouette through the air and landed on all fours on the thick glass of the viewing port.

"Rather prettily done, if I do say so myself," she thought.

TIME: 22:30:12.9 GMT MONDAY 20 JUNE 2050

"She is right on the time line," Clear-Thinker mused to himself as he observed the computer-generated image of Amalita taken the previous turn and compared it with those taken a few turns previously. The enlarged image of the seat belt showed it was coming apart. Now if she could turn around once while she fell to the window, they could get some high resolution, three-dimensional X-ray images that made so much more sense to their computers than the book-oriented, flat diagrams they had obtained from the human physiology textbooks.

In the following turns the crew members watched as Amalita's body ponderously fell through the air toward the viewing port, turning slowly as it came. Clear-Thinker kept the X-ray illuminators off most of the time, to keep the radiation dose on his human friend down to a minimum. At times calculated by the computer, the X-ray illuminators would flash on, and another snapshot of the human body in motion was taken. By the time Amalita's body was approaching the port, the computer had built up a detailed three-dimensional model of her body. Now the illuminators were brought in to focus on certain portions of her body as the scientists called for more detailed data on the glands and the corrugation patterns in the brain. The data they were collecting would keep generations of students busy.

As Amalita's hands and feet were contacting the viewing port glass and her body started to bounce back, one of the human-medicine specialists on the crew came up to Clear-Thinker and put down a computer-generated picture for him to scan. As Clear-Thinker flowed onto the pad and tasted the picture, the specialist said, "That is a closeup of Amalita's left breast. Fortunately she was not wearing a brassiere so that when she landed on the window, her breasts came forward and we were able to get a highly detailed image of the entire mammary gland complex. The thing that concerns us is the anomalous region right at the center of that diagram. We are sure that it is a small group of cancer cells. They are still too small to be seen by human X-ray machines, but it is our professional judgment that they are definitely malignant."

"Well, it looks as if we will be able to repay Amalita for her performance," Clear-Thinker said. "Prepare a picture that the human doctors can understand and we will send it to Amalita along with a warning of what we found."

The specialist replied, "We had already planned to do that, but we are all concerned about the time it will take. It will be a week before the Dragon Slayer leaves this orbit and takes Amalita and the rest of the crew back up to the mother ship, St. George. In that week, the cancer could grow and start sending out seeds to contaminate the rest of her body. We had another idea that we wanted to talk to you about."

Clear-Thinker flowed off the pad. "What is your proposal?"

"Now—you must realize that what we are about to suggest is against all normal human and cheela standards of ethics. All the human-physiology specialists here, along with many experts on human psychology, medicine and law back on Egg have argued back and forth for the last two turns. There has been a general consensus, although not unanimous by any means, and it was decided to bring it to you for your approval."

Clear-Thinker waited patiently while the specialist worked her way through the circumlocutious argument.

"The consensus is that because of the high malignancy potential of this growth, and the time it will take Amalita to get to a human doctor, we should treat the cancer now, even though we do not have time to get her permission first."

Finally it was out, and Clear-Thinker could understand why it had taken the specialist so much time to come to the point. She was right. By the time the slow-thinking Amalita had been informed of her problem, and had made the decision whether or not to let them try to treat her, the expedition would have had to return to Egg. He also realized that the specialists would not have made their recommendation unless they were sure that Amalita had a serious problem that needed immediate treatment.

"Go ahead," Clear-Thinker quickly replied. "What do you need?"

"We will want to modify one of the X-ray illuminators to increase its frequency and power output," she said. "Running it at a high power level will burn it out quickly, so it will no longer be available for general illumination, but if we do a careful scan, the focused beam of X-rays should kill the cancer cells with only minimal damage to the rest of the breast."

"We have plenty of illuminators," Clear-Thinker said. "Check with the camera crew to find out which one they can spare, and proceed whenever you are ready."

The specialist gathered a crew and soon a modified X-ray illuminator with a large focusing mirror and a high-intensity power source moved up to the window of the viewing port. The computer first aligned the coordinates of the focal point of the illuminator with the calculated position of the cancer deep within the slowly moving breast. Then burst after burst of high intensity X-rays shot out from the illuminator as it was slowly moved back and forth in wide arcs about the focal point buried deep within Amalita. The cancer shriveled and died, while the skin at the surface of the breast started to turn pink—as if it had gotten too much sun at the beach.

TIME: 22:30:16.3 GMT MONDAY 20 JUNE 2050

"Ouch!" Amalita cried as she rebounded from the window. Her hand went to her breast, but the sharp hurt was gone. "Reverse Cooper's droop?" she thought to herself. She then turned to watch Pierre, her mouth still forming the automatic count, ". . . One-thousand-seven . . ."

TIME: 22:30:17.1 GMT MONDAY 20 JUNE 2050

"It is time for the Visit," announced Clear-Thinker at one of the planning sessions. "Get out the skimmer and check the mush tube and waste disposal systems."

The skimmer was a small vehicle especially designed for the Visit. It was not much larger than an instrument shell and had only rudimentary propulsion and control subsystems. A standard individual shell was much larger, and needed a larger mini-black hole to keep it from exploding. Such shells had to stay over a meter away from the viewing ports since their gravity fields were so high. The skimmer was much less massive, so it could approach much closer to the ports. The skimmer had two things that an individual shell did not normally carry, however: a half-dozen turns worth of food, most of it in the form of a liquid mush, and a disposal grate connected to a holding tank.

Most of the crew had the decency to busy themselves elsewhere as the commander of the Visit expedition settled himself onto the skimmer. The spherical shell of the skimmer was only slightly larger than his body, so there was only one way that he could fit on it. With the controls at his front, his food intake orifice was situated near the tube from the mush tanks, while his elimination orifice was over the disposal grid.

Clear-Thinker formed some crystalline bones within his body, conformed them into manipulators, took hold of the controls and raised power.

"Never has a nickname for a spacecraft fit so well," thought Clear-Thinker, as the "Flying Toilet" rose from the main expedition spacecraft and moved over to the left viewing port where it stopped—just a bit less than a meter from the tip of Pierre's nose.

TIME: 22:30:17.2 GMT MONDAY 20 JUNE 2050

Pierre watched Amalita drop and tightened his grip on the handholds to keep himself from following her down to that end of the cabin. He turned his head toward the window as a small glowing speck pushed through the main cloud that stayed a number of meters away, came up to the window, and stopped outside the glass—about an arm's length away. Pierre looked out at the tiny incandescent sphere. It was slightly larger than a mustard seed.

Clear-Thinker stared up at the ghostly human face hanging in the air above him. The face was a half-dozen times larger than the highest mountain on Egg. The only thing he could see easily was the huge skull illuminated by the deep violet color of the soft X-rays emitted from the X-ray arc. There were the gaping holes for the eyes, each as large as the caldera of the Mount Exodus volcano. Between the eyes was a cavernous slash for the nose cavity, and below that were the two rows of dense teeth, like two mountain ranges, one stacked up on top of another. As a very faint blue-white outline surrounding and covering the skull, Clear-Thinker could see the flesh and hair reflecting the UV radiation from the arc, and thought he could see Pierre's eyes star-ing down at him.

"Well—there is no time for a long speech," Clear-Thinker said to himself. He activated the communication link control and spoke to the human.

"Hello, Pierre," he said, his undertread rippling a carefully modulated acoustic wave into the pickup. It was not much of a greeting, but he had hoped he had made it a personal one with a carefully practiced French accent on the "Pierre." With the greeting off on its way through the Comm computer, where it would be parceled out to Pierre in slow phonemes over many turns, he shivered himself, took the mush tube into his intake orifice, and got himself ready for the long, self-imposed ordeal.

He first formed a crystallium stiffener inside each eye-stub to keep his eyes steady. "No need to make it thick under this re-duced gravity," he reminded himself. "I will need the crys-tallium for the rest of the structure."

He concentrated and soon the eye-stubs were braced with an interlocking network of crystalline bones that would keep him from moving too much. This last technique was a new one to him, since like most cheela he had always limited his internal bone-growing repertoire to manipulators, eye-stubs and pulling bars. However, the medical scientists, having learned much about the capability of the cheela organism from a religious sect that had developed extraordinary control over their body func-tions, had taught him the interlocking technique.

With his preparations ready, he set the skimmer on automatic control, sipped a little mush, and settled down for the Visit with his gargantuan friend.

"Well—so you are Pierre Carnot Niven—are you?" he mur-mured up at the motionless skull. "All right, Pierre, let's see who blinks first."

TIME: 22:30:18.2 GMT MONDAY 20 JUNE 2050

Pierre focused his eyes on the tiny white-hot speck floating in front of him on the other side of the deeply tinted glass. The skimmer itself was an iridescent sphere about five millimeters in diameter. Almost covering the hemisphere on the side toward him was the opalescent body of Clear-Thinker. The various portions of his body changed color like an incandescent drop of liquid crystal, as the hot internal fluid currents and cooler radiative surfaces varied their temperature. Spaced around the periphery of the flattened ellipsoidal body were a dozen red pinpoint eyes glowing like tiny coals around a tiny campfire.

"Like a flattened miniature scallop on the half-shell," Pierre thought. "Although scallops don't have manipulators and their eyes are blue."

As his eyes and the humming automatic cameras took in the sight of Clear-Thinker patiently enduring his vigil outside the viewport, the speaker on the communication console spoke Clear-Thinker's greeting.

"Hello, Pierre."

As the echo of the last syllable floated across the console room, there was a flash of light and the incandescent speck was gone, leaving only a yellow-green afterimage on Pierre's retina. It was only after the gravity pull had lifted that Pierre finally realized that his nose ached from being squashed up to the window at three gees.

TIME: 22:30:19.3 GMT MONDAY 20 JUNE 2050

The mush was gone, the holding tank stank, and it was time to say goodbye.

"You win—my friend," Clear-Thinker spoke up to the ghostly apparition that had not moved during his long vigil. At that, Clear-Thinker had done better than he had thought he would—six whole turns without moving more than a ripple. Isomorphic exercises had helped to keep his innards from clogging up, but his skin felt as if it would crack if he moved it. He moved—and it didn't crack—so he moved some more; then, with a delighted dance that almost lifted him off the skimmer with its nearly negligible gravity field, he dissolved the crystalline bones that had kept him stationary, grabbed the controls, and flew the "Flying Toilet" back to the main spacecraft.

After a decent meal and some clean-up, Clear-Thinker was back in command of the expedition. It was time to pack up and go. The specialists were still busy taking long-distance pictures of Pierre and were reluctant to leave. However, the supplies were getting low, and at last they too wound down their activities and started to bring their equipment back.

Actually, of course, it was the shipboard computer that handled the motion of the instrument spheres while it monitored the flight paths of the individual fliers. The gravitational self-attraction of the spheres made navigation quite tricky, even when the pilots had reflex velocities that approached the speed of light.

Unfortunately, no one had bothered to inform the computer that the modified X-ray illuminator that had been used to treat Amalita's cancer had been firmly connected to the very large power source that had been used to drive it. Therefore the computer saw nothing wrong with choosing a return path for the illuminator that took it close to the viewport window. As the illuminator, dragging the power supply, passed by the window, the intense gravitational tidal forces from the massive power supply ripped a large jagged canyon out of the three centimeter thick laminated window. Huge chunks of glass as large as mountains fell toward the power supply. They were crushed into powder as they fell, and then disappeared in a flash of light as they impacted the surface of the shell.

TIME: 22:30:20.0 GMT MONDAY 20 JUNE 2050

The acoustic micrometeoroid detectors in the frame of the viewing ports sensed something wrong and slammed the outside metallic shields across the windows. Amalita blinked, then stared at a tiny scratch in the glass.

". . . One-thousand-ten," she said.

The Visit was over.

TIME: 06:13:54 GMT TUESDAY 21 JUNE 2050

Leaving Amalita talking to Sky-Teacher at the communications console on the main deck, Pierre dived smoothly through the hole in the floor to the lower deck and pulled himself over to the library console. He moved carefully, for between two fingers he was carrying a precious HoloMem crystal containing all the wisdom of the cheela that had accumulated during the past thirty minutes. He carefully placed the crystal in its scanner cavity in the library console, fitted the brilliantly polished corner segment into place, and closed the cover.

According to their conversations with the robot cheela communicator, this latest HoloMem crystal had a large section on the internal structure of neutron stars. Pierre had the computer jump rapidly through the millions of pages until he found a detailed cross section of the interior of Dragon's Egg. The diagram showed that the star had an outer surface that was a solid crust of nuclei; neutron-rich isotopes of iron, zinc, nickel, and other elements in a crystalline lattice, through which flowed a liquid sea of electrons. Next came the mantle—two kilometers of neutrons and iron nuclei that became more neutron-rich with depth. The inner three-fourths of the star was a liquid ball of superfluid neutrons and superfluid protons. At the very center was a small core of esoteric elementary particles whose normally short lifetimes were lengthened by the extreme pressures and densities inside the star.

Pierre looked carefully at the symbols for the elementary particles. Most were known to him, but there was one that he had never seen before. He looked at the legend to one side and saw that the symbol referred to an "Elysium" particle. The cheela had found an elementary particle inside their star that the humans had not yet seen in their atom smashers! Pierre quickly keyed the library console to search through the HoloMem crystal for more information on the Elysium particle. In a fraction of a second, his screen flashed:

PROPERTIES AND USES OF ELYSIUM PARTICLE—FURTHER INFORMATION ON THIS PARTICLE IS ENCRYPTED. THE KEY IS THE MASS AND LIFETIME OF THE FIRST EIGHT ELEMENTARY PARTICLES (INCLUDING THE ELYSIUM PARTICLE) TO FIVE SIGNIFICANT FIGURES.

The rest of the section was gibberish.

Pierre mused. The cheela could have told the humans about the particle, but had decided not to. The human race was going to have to find that particle by itself and learn enough about its mass and lifetime so that they could decrypt the section and read what the cheela had learned about it.

Of course, if the humans did their research correctly, they would know practically everything that was now hidden behind the gibberish, but if they had gotten off on the wrong track, then the knowledge the cheela had left would correct them before they went on to learn more about the universe that they lived in.

"Just like a good teacher," Pierre thought. "You give the students a start by letting them know there is something interesting to learn in a certain area, let them learn about it on their own, then finally check over their results and give them any correction necessary."

As he flipped back to the section on neutron star interiors, he mused that a cryptogram with only sixteen five-digit numbers could probably be broken by a large computer in an exhaustive search, but he figured that the human race would be too proud to peek.

His console screen returned to the original diagram of the interior of Dragon's Egg. Pierre scanned the next page. It was a photograph of a neutron star, but it wasn't Dragon's Egg. He could tell it was a real photograph, since he could see a portion of a cheela on a space flitter in the foreground. His eyes widened and he rapidly scanned page after page. There were many photographs, each followed by detailed diagrams of the internal structure of the various neutron stars. They ranged the gamut from very dense stars that were almost black holes to large bloated neutron stars that had a neutron core and a white-dwarf-star exterior. Some of the names were unfamiliar, but others, like the Vela pulsar and the Crab Nebula pulsar, were neutron stars known to the humans.

"But the Crab Nebula pulsar is over 3000 light-years away!" Pierre exclaimed to himself. "They would have had to travel faster than the speed of light to have gone there to take those photographs in the past eight hours!"

A quick search through the index found the answer.

FASTER-THAN-LIGHT PROPULSION—THE CRYPTO-KEY TO
THIS SECTION IS ENGRAVED ON A PYRAMID ON THE
THIRD MOON OF THE SECOND PLANET OF EPSILON
ERIDANI.

There then followed a long section of gibberish.

In near shock, Pierre turned off the console and slowly floated over to the nearby lounge. He was not surprised to find everyone except Amalita there. They were all sitting in the low gravity on the soft circular seat and looking down past their feet out the viewport below them. Pierre jumped up to the top of the lounge and held onto the handle in the hatch door leading to one of the high-gravity protection tanks. He too looked down and out the one-meter diameter port set in the bottom of the spacecraft. The electronically controlled density filter had been set to blacken the port thirty times a second as each of the six glowing compensator masses passed in front of the window five times a second. The only light that entered the port was the single point of intense brightness that was the sun—their home—2120 AU away.

Pierre broke the silence. "It's nearly time for us to leave," he said.

Jean looked up, her perky nose wrinkled in puzzlement. "I thought the plan was for us to stay down here for at least another week," she said.

"With the cheela doing all the mapping and measurements for us, there is really no need for us to stay any longer," he explained. "You should have read the detailed description of both the exterior and interior of Dragon's Egg in that last HoloMem crystal I brought down." He straightened out and swung down to hold himself in the doorway to the lounge.

"I had the computer reprogram the herder probes to move us into the path of the deorbiter mass. In about half a day we will be in proper position to be kicked out of this close orbit back up to St. George. Then we can be heading for home instead of looking at it." He looked up at the clock readout on the lounge wall.

"Time to change HoloMem crystals again," he said. He flexed his knees preparatory to leaping up the passageway to the main deck. He flashed his smile through his beard at them and said, "Come on, there is a lot of work to do to get this ship ready. Amalita and I will finish off the last of the HoloMem crystals, but the rest of you had better start buttoning up the ship; the gravity fields from that deorbiter will turn anything loose into a deadly missile." He jumped upward to the central deck and the others swam out the lounge door and spread out through the ship.

Pierre swung over to the communication console and looked at Sky-Teacher over Amalita's shoulder. The robot cheela was patiently explaining something. Pierre stared in fascination at the image. With the million-to-one time differential, it had not surprised Pierre that the cheela would develop a long-living intelligent robot that could take over the demanding task of talking to the slow-thinking humans. What amazed him was that the robotic creature was so highly developed that it had a personality. It was not robotlike in its mannerisms at all. In fact, it acted very much like a patient, old-time schoolmaster. One could almost hear the friendly smile and the graying hair in the voice. It was a relief to the humans to have Sky-Teacher to talk to. They no longer felt as if they were wasting a good portion of someone's life if they made a mistake or hesitated for a moment.

"We shortly will have filled up all your available HoloMem crystals," Sky-Teacher's image said, its halo of robotic eyes doing a perfect imitation of the traveling wave pattern in a real cheela. "I am afraid that you will find most of this material is encrypted, since we are now the equivalent of many thousands of years ahead of you in development.

"Yet, if it had not been for you, we would still be savages, stagnating in an illiterate haze for thousands or even millions of greats of turns. We owe you much, but we must be careful how we pay you back, for you too have a right to grow and develop on your own. For your own good, it is best that we cut off communication after this last HoloMem crystal is full. We have given you enough material to keep you busy learning for thousands of your years. Then we will both be off on our separate ways, seeking truth and knowledge through space and time. You in worlds where the electron is paramount, and we in worlds where the neutron dominates.

"But please don't despair. We may live much faster than you, but there are only a finite number of fundamental truths to learn about the Universe, so eventually you will catch up to us."

A tone sounded and a small message appeared on the screen.

HOLOMEM CRYSTAL FULL.

"You are on your own now," Sky-Teacher said, hearing the tone. "But we have one last present for you. You will need tens of thousands of years to develop fully, and minor nuisances like ice ages on your planet would slow you down. While we were exploring the interior of your Sun, we found five small black holes. There were the four that you already know about and a much smaller one. Since they were disturbing the fusion reactions in your Sun, we removed them for you. Now the Sun will stay stable while you are learning from the HoloMem crystals."

"We thank you," Pierre stammered, awed by the power implied by the simple statement.

"And we thank you," Sky-Teacher said. "But it is drawing near the time for you to leave. Goodbye, my friends."

"Goodbye," Pierre said as the screen blanked.

He turned to Amalita. "I'll put away the HoloMem crystal, and you start checking out the acceleration tanks," he said. "It's time to go home!"

Technical Appendix

The following sections are selected extracts from the 2064 Edition of Del Rey's *Science Encyclopedia*, published by Random House Interplanetary, New York, Earth.

DRAGON'S EGG

Dragon's Egg is a nearby neutron star. It has a mass of about one-half that of the Sun but a diameter of only 20 kilometers. It is spinning at 5.0183495 revolutions per second, has a gravitational field at its surface of 67-billion gees, and a magnetic field of close to a trillion gauss. As is shown in Figure 1, the star has four poles. In addition to the normal north and south spin poles, it has "east" and "west" magnetic poles that lie almost on the equator. The lines drawn from the east magnetic pole in Figure 1 are the lines of magnetic longitude. The actual magnetic field is three-dimensional, and extends for some distance out into the region around the star.

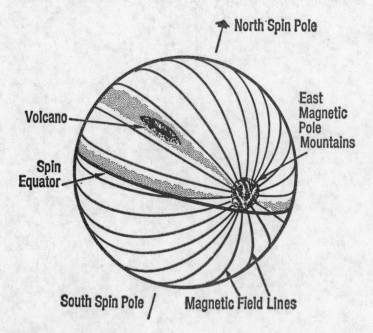

Figure 1. Dragon's Egg

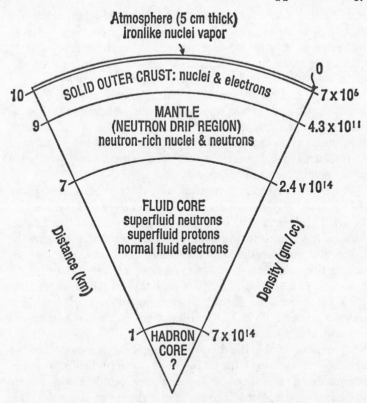

Figure 2. Interior Structure of Dragon's Egg

The internal structure of Dragon's Egg is shown in Figure 2. The center has a liquid core 7 km in radius containing superfluid neutrons, a small quantity of superfluid protons, and enough normal fluid electrons to balance the charge on the protons. At the very center of the star, where the densities and pressures are highest, there are various exotic elementary particles mixed in with the neutrons.

Over this core of liquid neutrons is a 2 km thick mantle of crystalline neutrons and nuclei. The crystalline crust varies from pure neutrons near the liquid core to nearly all nuclei near the top of the mantle. The outer crust of the star consists of neutron-rich nuclei (mostly iron) with a density near the surface of about 7 million grams per cubic centimeter. The number of neutrons in the outer-crust nuclei increases with depth, while the spacing between the nuclei decreases. The boundary between the outer crust and the mantle is the "neutron drip" region, where the neutrons can "drip" out of the highly neutron-rich nuclei and wander over to close-by neighboring nuclei.

The crust and mantle are solid structures over a liquid core. As the star cools and shrinks, the crust cracks and thrusts up mountain ranges. The mountains vary in height from a few millimeters to as much as 10 centimeters. The higher mountain ranges poke up out of the predominantly iron-vapor atmosphere, which becomes negligible at about 5 cm.

The large Mount Exodus volcano in the northern hemisphere of Dragon's Egg is a volcano that formed over a deep crack in the crust of the star. The liquid material at the lower depths rises through the fissure to form the volcanic shield. Because of the temperature differential with depth and the beta decay that occurs in the nuclei as they rise to regions of lower density, the lava can release enough energy to maintain its flow against gravity. Volcanos such as Mount Exodus can build up lava shields many centimeters in height and hundreds of meters in diameter and will finally cause starquakes.

Starquakes involve the drop of a lava shield or mountain range by a few millimeters in the 67-billion-gee gravity field of the star. Starquakes in several pulsars have been detected from the Earth by observing the slight decrease in the period of the pulsar due to the decrease in inertia of the star from the lowering of the mountain range.

Dragon's Egg was the product of a supernova explosion that occurred about 500,000 years ago at a distance of 50 light-years from the Solar System. In the process of formation, the neutron star/pulsar acquired a significant proper velocity of 30 km/sec (one light-year in 10,000 years or 6 AU in one year). The star was first discovered by space scientist V. Sawlinski in 2020 (see Reference 1). He detected its radio pulsations using the CCCP-ESA (see Acronyms—Ancient National Organizations) Out-of-the-Ecliptic probe, which was 200 AU up out of the planetary ecliptic plane. (See Figure 3 showing the relative position of Dragon's Egg, Sol, and the OE probe in 2020.)

At the time of its discovery in 2020, Dragon's Egg was at a distance of 2300 AU from earth. When the humans finally arrived at the star in the first interstellar spacecraft, St. George (see St. George), the distance had narrowed to 2120 AU. At the time of this edition (2064) the star is at a distance of about 2040 AU. It will reach its point of closest approach of 250 AU in about 300 years, then recede again. Some perturbation of the outer planets is expected, but there should be no significant effects on the orbit of Earth.

The position of Dragon's Egg in the sky was determined by S-Y Wang (see Reference 2) to be almost at the same declination (+70 degrees) and right ascension (11.5 hours) as Giansar, the bright star at the end of the constellation Draco (The Dragon). Its position among the constellations in the northern sky is shown in the simplified star chart of Figure 4.

CHEELA PHYSIOLOGY

By the time the humans discovered Dragon's Egg, life forms had evolved on the neutron star. (Amazingly enough, the possibility of the existence of life on a neutron star was predicted almost a century ago by the radio astronomer F. D. Drake in Reference 3. Dr. Drake was a great-grandfather of Amalita Shakhashiri Drake, one of the crew on Dragon Slayer.) The first forms of life on Dragon's Egg were plants, which lived by running a heat cycle between the hot crust and the cold of the sky. These plants later evolved into mobile animal forms.

The dominant animal life forms on the star are called cheela. Since they are intelligent, the cheela have roughly the same complexity as humans. That implies that they have the same number of nuclei, so it is not surprising that they weigh about the same as humans—70 kg. The cheela are flat, amoeba-type creatures about 2.5 mm in radius (0.5 cm in diameter), and 0.5 mm high, with a density of 7 million g/cc.

The atomic nuclei that make up the cheela do not have captive electron clouds to keep them isolated from each other, but instead share a "sea" of free electrons. Because of the resulting close proximity of the nuclei, it is as easy for cheela nuclei to exchange neutrons as it is for human atoms to exchange electrons. The nuclei couple into "nuclear bonded molecules" by neutron exchange. Since the cheela use nuclear coupling instead of mo-

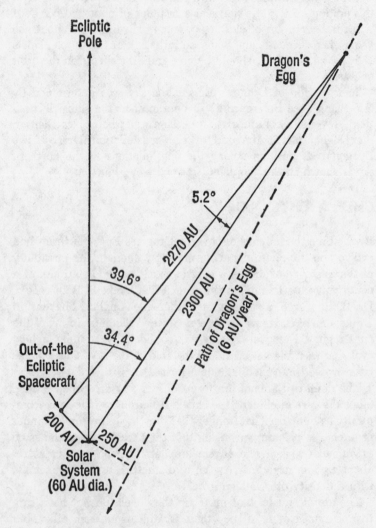

Figure 3. Near-Solar Space in 2020 AD (to scale)

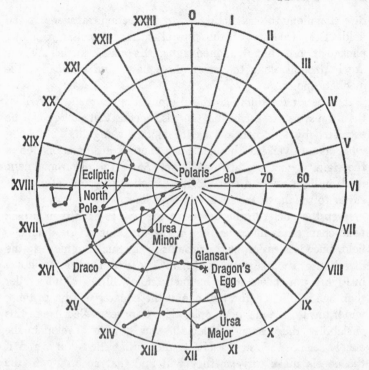

Figure 4. Northern Constellations in 2020

lecular coupling in their bodies, their rate of living is about one million times that of humans.

Cheela can form crystalline "bones" when needed, but normally keep a more flexible structure and can flow around and into instruments to operate them. Because of the high gravitational field, cheela do not have strength to extend themselves more than a few mm above the crust. Their psychology with respect to gravity, height, and things-over-your-head is identical to the ancient science fiction stories by Hal Clement about the alien beings called Mesklinites.

The magnetic field on Dragon's Egg dominates everything. The velocity of sound, the opacity of the atmosphere, the force it takes to move, the flow of lava and landslides, the pressure of the atmosphere, and many other things, vary by ratios of 10:1 from a direction along the magnetic field to a direction transverse to the field. The structure of the crustal surface consists of close-packed, dense "hairs" aligned along the magnetic field. These are horizontal along the magnetic equator and vertical at the magnetic poles.

It is easier for things to move along the magnetic field lines than transverse to them. But this also means that energy can be extracted by loss mechanisms for motion along the field lines, whereas transverse to the field lines, there is little motion due to the rigidity, so there are few losses. Since the electromagnetic fields in light are transverse to the direction of propagation, it is easier to see *along* the magnetic field lines.

Even the nuclei in the bodies of the cheela have their aspect ratio changed as much as 10:1 in the direction of the magnetic field, since it is easier for the protons in the nuclei to move in the direction of the magnetic field than across it. Thus, as is shown in Figure 5, a cheela at the magnetic pole will be 10 times taller than one at the equator, and one at the equator will be 10 times wider toward the magnetic poles than transverse. Because of this variability, the concept of "length" was slow to develop in the cheela sciences. Even the cheela measuring sticks vary, and if the cheela make surveys, they will find that according to the number of measuring sticks needed to count off a distance on the star, their home is "flattened" 10:1 near the magnetic poles.

The actual cheela body is, of course, much more complex than the stereotyped diagrams of Figure 5. A more lifelike picture is shown in the sketch in Figure 6. This was drawn from memory by the Leonardo da Vinci of Dragon's Egg (and first cheela Keeper-of-the-Sender), Troop Commander/Astrologer Swift-Killer. The Trooper in the drawing is Squad Leader North-Wind (identified by his two-button insignia of rank). He is holding a short sword and a dragon tooth (although squad leaders did not usually carry the long spear). The two puckered sections in his side are either carrying pouches or eating orifices. The small seminal fluid ejection holes under each eye-stub are the primary sex organs unique to a male cheela.

The cheela communicate by strumming the crust with their lower surfaces (tread) to produce directed vibrations in the neutron star crust. The strong magnetic fields polarize the surface

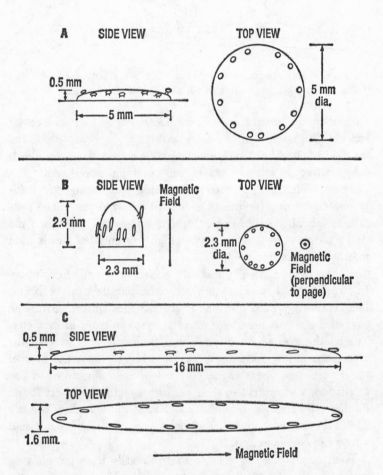

Figure 5. Relative Shapes of Cheela Bodies Under Influence of Gravity and Magnetic Fields: A, no magnetic field but strong gravity; B, near the magnetic poles magnetic stretching compensates for gravity; C, near the magnetic equator the cheela elongate along the magnetic field.

Figure 6. Squad Leader North-Wind with Short Sword and Dragon Tooth (Copyright 2050 by Swift-Killer, White Rock Clan)

material and since the crust has a nuclei lattice and an electron sea, the cheela have three modes of talking: long-talk—along the magnetic field using Rayleigh-type compressional waves; short-talk—transverse (shear) waves for communication across the magnetic field lines; and fast-talk—using electromagnetic fields generated by their bodies to excite the electron sea. Since fast-talk travels at the speed of light, it is somewhat faster than the two acoustic waves, but it is more highly attenuated and is used mostly for whispering.

A cheela's eyes are a remarkable example of parallel evolution. In structure and function they are close parallels to the bright blue, stalk-supported eyes of the scallop shellfish on earth. The eyes of the cheela are about 0.1 mm = 100 microns in diameter. To give the eyes adequate resolution, they must use wavelengths of 0.1 microns = 1000 angstroms or smaller. Thus, the normal range of cheela vision is the UV region, 1000 angstroms to 200 angstroms, although they can see down into the X-ray band if there is enough illumination. Some individuals (Bright's Afflicted) can see up into the violet end of the human visual range (4000 angstroms).

The illumination for seeing comes primarily from the glowing surface of the star. At a temperature of 8200 K the neutron star crust has adequate flux in the long-wavelength part of the cheela vision band (700-1000 angstroms), but it cuts off at 600 angstroms. Things that are hotter (cheela bodies at 8500-9000 K, and hot illumination sources from 10,000-50,000 K) not only have more photons, but their "color" shifts toward "blue" and the resolution goes up. Cooler things, (like the top of a cheela or a plant) have a shift to longer, "redder" wavelengths. (See Figure 7.)

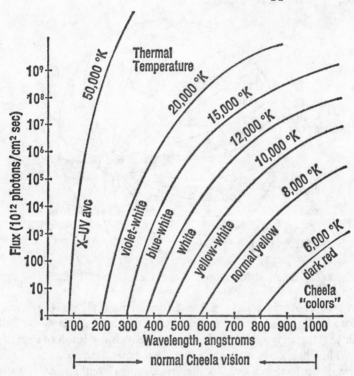

Figure 7. Photon Flux on Dragon's Egg

CHEELA HISTORY

The story of Dragon's Egg and its inhabitants is covered in great detail by Nobel Laureate P. C. Niven in Reference 4. To date, this is the only book to win the Nobel, Pulitzer, Hugo, Nebula, and Moebius prizes in the same year (2053). Figure 8 is taken from the second volume of this definitive three-volume study/ story and illustrates the major cultural migrations of the developing cheela.

According to ancient myths of the cheela, they are descended from a "chosen clan" that was driven from the northern hemisphere by a hateful Dragon God, who was said to live inside what is now the Mount Exodus volcano. The Dragon God sent blasts of fire, rivers of molten lava, and dense smoke to drive the

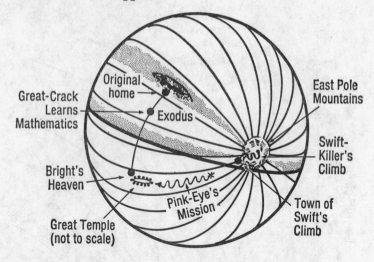

Figure 8. Historical Migrations of the Developing Cheela

cheela southward into a purgatory region where they were forced to travel in the hard direction (across the magnetic field lines), through a "feeling lost" region covered with dense smoke.

The cheela use a combination of magnetic and Coriolis fields for directional homing. In the "feeling lost" region, the lines of magnetic direction are parallel to the lines of rotation, and the cheela lose their inherent sense of direction and feel lost.

The smoke just above the equator is due to an interaction between the east-west magnetic field and the rotation of the star. The smoke from the volcano travels predominantly along the magnetic field lines until it reaches the east and west poles, where the magnetic field lines dip into the surface. The smoke then leaks out at the magnetic poles and moves again along the magnetic field lines, but now along the equator, driven by the equatorial "trade winds" in the atmosphere. The star thus has a crescent shaped band of smoke in the magnetic longitude of the volcano, and a circular band just above the spin equator.

The "chosen clan," driven from their original home by the Dragon God, finally moved southward across the spin equator to the southern hemisphere of the star, leaving the purgatory region behind. They found a land of plenty, with many edible plants and animals, but no other cheela. Their experience would be similar to the first entry of humans into the North American continent. Like the deep water barriers on Earth, the "feeling lost" regions at the spin equator had produced a psychological barrier to the cheela that had kept the southern hemisphere isolated until then.

In this new land, the "chosen clan" discovered a bright star sitting just over the south pole. The very bright star was our Sun, only 2120 AU (1/30 of a light year) away. A monotheistic religion developed based on worship of the God-star Bright. The "chosen clan" grew, and split into many clans, but all clans stayed under the loose rule of a Leader of All Clans.

The development of the cheela from a nomadic tribe into a great empire that finally established its rule over the entire star is well covered in Niven's book.

RELATIVE TIMES

The relative time scales between the cheela and the human race is still a subject of debate among experts, since the cheela physiology is so drastically different from human physiology.

The basic unit of time on Dragon's Egg is the revolution rate of the star, which is 5.0183495 rps, or a period of approximately 0.1993 seconds. Some experts have equated one turn of the star with one human day, giving a relative rate of 0.43 million to one. Others point out that since there is no night or day on the neutron star and the cheela, who never sleep, are active the full turn, that the ratio should be closer to a million to one.

The cheela use a base 12 number system (they have twelve eyes) and their next unit of time after the turn is a great of turns or 144 turns. They occasionally use a dozen turns, but it has never had the same significance as the week does to humans. A great of turns is 28.7 seconds, while a human year is 31.6 million seconds. The ratio of a human year to a cheela great of turns is 1.1 million to one.

From studying the history of the cheela we have learned that a cheela spends about 12 greats (six minutes) as a hatchling, 12 greats as a young apprentice, 30 greats (15 minutes) as a worker, 12 greats as an Old One tending eggs and hatchlings, then the rest of its life (maximum of 24 greats or 12 minutes) as an Aged

One. All of these indications lead to the conclusion that the effective relative time scale between the cheela and humans is approximately one million to one.

EQUIVALENT TIME SCALES

Human	Cheela (Equivalent human stages)	
10 ky	10 Bg	Primordial manna
5 ky	5 Bg	Beginning of life
2 ky	2 Bg	Multicelled organisms
1 ky	1 Bg	Large plants
500 y	500 Mg	Invertebrates, amphibians
200 y	200 Mg	Reptiles
50 y	50 Mg	Mammals, monkeys
10 y	10 Mg	Proto-cheela
5 y	5 Mg	Cave dwellers
1 y	1 Mg	Nomad hunters, hand axes
1 mo	100 kg	Neanderthal, stone tools, cemeteries
15 d	40 kg	Homo sapiens, hunting and gathering, cave art
5 d	14 kg	Neolithic, writing, farming, churches
2 d	5 kg	Bronze, cities, writing, mounds, war
1 d	2,500 g	Iron, Persia, Greece, Roman empire
12 h	1,400 g	Medieval
2 h	250 g	10 generations
30 m	60 g	Active life span
15 m	30 g	Professional life span
1 m	2 g	
29 s	1	great = 144 turns
200 ms	1	turn of Egg

INFORMATION STORAGE AND TRANSFER

Human transmission rate: The laser communication link from Dragon Slayer (see Dragon Slayer) up to St. George (see St. George) had a transmission rate of 400 MHz. This gave a bit rate of 200 megabits/sec., assuming good error correction practices.

Cheela reception rate: Since the cheela effectively live a million times faster, the human messages from the 400 MHz laser communication link were received at a maximum of 200 bits/cheela sec., which is about 5 words/cheela sec. This is a slow facsimile rate (a little slower than you can read).

Total bits transmitted: In 0.5 human day (43,200 seconds) the humans transmitted 10 trillion bits from the 25 HoloMem crystals in their ship's library down to the cheela.

HoloMem Storage: Each HoloMem holds about 0.4 trillion bits. Since the HoloMem crystals are cubes 5 cm on a side, their volume is 125 cc. This means that each bit has the equivalent of a cube 7 microns on a side for storage. In that 7 micron cube there are about a trillion atoms.

Total HoloMem storage: A printed page holds roughly 350 words, 2100 characters or 15,000 bits. A book of 330 pages is about 5 million bits. The HoloMems could hold about 2 million books. For comparison, in 2050, the United States Library of Congress held about 50 million items (books, newspapers, trade publications, copyright items, etc.).

ST. GEORGE

The spaceship that took the humans to Dragon's Egg was a primitive monopole-catalyst fusion rocket. Its basic structure was a cylinder 500 meters long and 20 meters in diameter, with large spherical external tanks of liquid deuterium fuel. The mass ratio was about 10. St. George accelerated at 0.035 gees, and reached a speed of 0.035 the speed of light at its turnover point. The total trip time out to the neutron star was 1.94 years.

DRAGON SLAYER

The scientific spacecraft used for the close approach to the neutron star was a seven-meter sphere with a spinning tower 1.6 m in diameter and 2.5 m tall, containing the microwave sounder, infrared telescope, laser radar, star image telescope mirror, and other star-oriented instruments. When in synchronous orbit about the star, the science instrument tower on the top of the ship was aligned in the direction of the north spin pole of the neutron star. The bottom end of the science sphere had a viewing port that looked southward toward the distant Solar System.

Around the equator of the ship were six viewing ports that looked out at the neutron star whirling about the ship. The ship was inertially stabilized, so that the distant stars stayed fixed in the viewing ports. The ship, being in orbit around the neutron star with a period of 0.1993 seconds (5.018 rps), rotated with respect to the neutron star at 5 times a second. The science turret was de-spun at the orbital rate so that the instruments pointed to the star at all times. (The entire spaceship could not be rotated at those speeds; had it been, the crew would have been thrown against the outer wall with a force of 350 gees.)

Figure 9 through 12 are diagrams of the three decks and a side view of the scientific spacecraft, Dragon Slayer. The steady component of the residual gravitational tidal fields around and inside the ship are shown by arrows. In addition to the steady component, there is an alternating acceleration component of about the same magnitude as the steady component, which varies twenty times a second as the four-lobed gravity pattern of the neutron star and tidal compensator masses rotates about the ship five times a second.

DEORBITER AND COMPENSATOR MASSES

The human explorers of Dragon's Egg used gravitational techniques to move into and survive in a synchronous orbit around the neutron star. The prime mover for all of the gravitational maneuvers near Dragon's Egg was the large deorbiter mass. Originally a small planetoid about 1000 kilometers across, it had been picked up (along with other asteroidal debris) by the neutron star in its wanderings. The planetoid was condensed by the humans into an ultra-dense mass one kilometer in diameter by injection of magnetic monopoles.

There were actually two large condensed asteroids made at the same time. One was used in a close-encounter gravity whip to drop the deorbiter down from its original orbit out in the "asteroid belt" of the neutron star into the desired orbit. This orbit was a highly elliptical one with a perihelion at 406 km and aphelion at 100,000 km, where the human interstellar ship, St. George, moved in a 12.82-minute circular orbit.

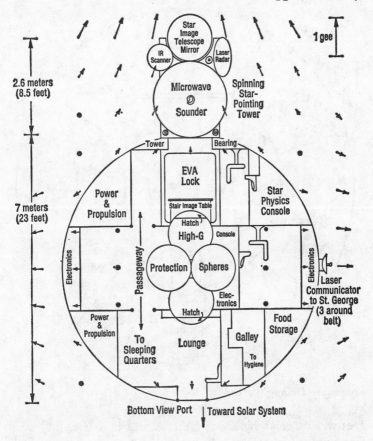

Figure 9. Dragon Slayer—Side View (Arrows indicate steady component of gravity tides)

The elliptical orbit of the deorbiter mass (called Bright's Messenger by precontact cheela) had a period of 4.56 minutes or 9.53 greats of turns of the neutron star. It thus took it only 2.28 minutes or 4.77 greats of turns to drop from the safe circular orbit of St. George to the dangerous synchronous orbit at 406 km above Dragon's Egg.

The gravity field of the neutron star is 40 million gees at the 406 kilometer altitude of Dragon Slayer. However, since the spacecraft was in orbit around the star, most of that 40 million

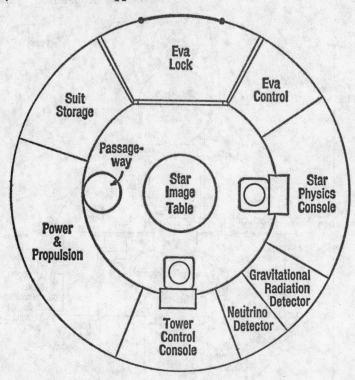

Figure 10. Dragon Slayer—Top Deck

gees was canceled by the fact that it was in a "free-fall" orbit. However, an object is only in free fall at its exact center of mass. When the middle of your body is in a free-fall orbit around a neutron star at 406332 m distance it will feel nothing. But if you are oriented with your feet toward the star, your feet, which are at 406331 m away from the star, are pulled by a gravity force that is 202 gees more than your middle, while your head, at 406333 m distance, is being pulled by a force that is 202 gees less than your middle. If your body is oriented in a direction tangent to the neutron star, your head and feet will feel a 101-gee compression instead of a 202-gee pull. A human cannot survive at a distance of 400 km from a neutron star without some kind of protection from these tidal forces.

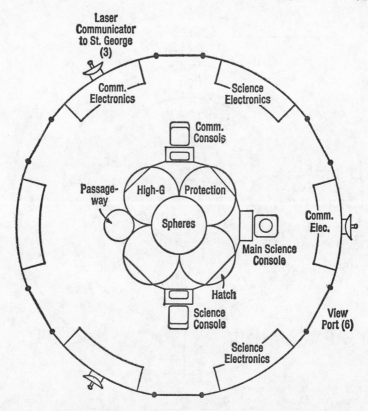

Figure 11. Dragon Slayer—Main Deck

To protect the humans in Dragon Slayer from these residual gravity tidal forces, six tidal compensator masses were placed in a 200-meter radius ring about the science capsule and arranged so that the plane of the six masses was always at right angles to the direction to the neutron star. The compensator masses were made from asteroids about 250 km in diameter that were condensed to 100 m in diameter.

In the center of that ring of ultra-dense spheres, the masses are attempting to pull anything at the center out toward them. At the exact center of the ring all the forces cancel. However, if your head or feet are in the plane of the ring, since they are about one meter away from the exact center of the ring, they

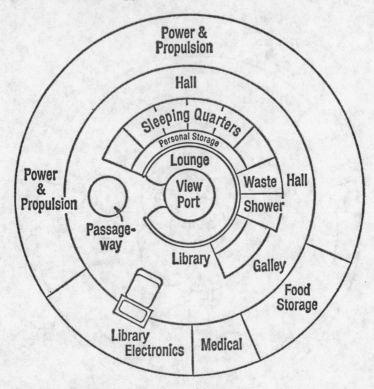

Figure 12. Dragon Slayer—Lower Deck

will be pulled with a force of 101 gees. If you try to orient your body to point along the axis of the ring, your head and feet will be compressed with a force of 202 gees. If made dense enough and placed at the right distances, the six compensator masses will cancel the neutron star tidal forces over a seven-meter diameter spherical region. (See Figure 9 which shows the residual tidal forces around Dragon Slayer.)

In operation, the six compensators rotate about Dragon Slayer as it orbits the star at 5.018 rps. The individual orbits of the compensator masses are almost in a natural gravitational orbit, but require that the masses change speed slightly each half orbit to maintain the circular formation. This is accomplished by magnetic interactions between the magnetically charged compensators, assisted by trimming maneuvers carried out by robotic herder probes using monopole-catalyzed fusion rockets.

VISIT

The only significant personal contact between the cheela and the humans occurred for a period of 1.2 seconds on 20 June 2050 between Clear-Thinker of the cheela and Pierre Carnot Niven of the humans. This was a short interval during the occasion of a ten-second visit by a cheela expedition to examine the human spacecraft and the humans inside.

The cheela had to go to great lengths to protect themselves and the humans from the effects of gravity. The cheela would explode if their bodies were not kept under sufficient gravity to keep their matter in a degenerate state, and the gravitational fields that were comfortable to the cheela were destructive to human flesh.

The main cheela spacecraft was a crystal shell 4 cm in diameter. With its large number of docking pits for the smaller instrumental shells and individual flyers, it had the size and appearance of a golf ball. The main ship had a black hole of 11 billion tons mass at its center that kept the surface of the cheela ship at a gravitational level of 0.2 million gees. Although nowhere near the gravitational field strength on their neutron star home, the gravity was enough to keep the cheela from exploding. The gravity field on the humans inside the Dragon Slayer at a distance of 15 m away from the main cheela spacecraft was a reasonable 1/3 gee.

Clear-Thinker used a smaller individual flitter with a much smaller black hole of only 0.22 billion tons mass. This flitter was only 5 mm in diameter (just slightly larger than a cheela body) and the surface gravity again was sufficient to keep Clear-Thinker's body from exploding. This smaller personal flitter could come within 70 cm of a human, so that the human eyes could actually see some detail of the glowing-hot cheela body. (For a well-written description of this unique scene, see Reference 4.) Even at that, the gravitational field on the nose of the human, P. C. Niven, was over three gees.

We do not know the propulsion technique used by the cheela

to lift their spacecraft off the surface of the neutron star (the escape velocity of Dragon's Egg is 39% the speed of light). We also do not know the propulsion technique that they use in space. The human observers during the Visit, P. C. Niven and A. S. Drake, saw no evidence of any rocket-type mechanism in the cheela spacecraft. From their conversations with the cheela communicators, they suspect that the cheela used some sort of antigravity catapult to get off the star, and some form of inertia drive in space. Our only clues are some old speculative papers (see References 5 and 6) based on the now-suspect Einstein theory of gravity.

At the time of this writing (2063), the knowledge of the antigravity and other space drives, including a faster-than-light drive, remains locked in the encrypted sections of the HoloMem crystals containing the knowledge of the cheela after they surpassed the human race in development. Present estimates are that we will be able to duplicate the cheela antigravity catapult (and decode that section of the HoloMem) in another 10 years. We have only a few clues on the inertia drive. Scientists estimate that it will take us at least two more decades before we learn enough to find the code to that section.

REFERENCES

1. V. Sawlinski et al., "A nearby short period pulsar," *Astrophysical Journal*, *561*, 268 (2020)

2. S-Y Wang, "The Egg of the Dragon—Sol's Nearest Neighbor," *Astro. Sinica*, *83*, 1789 (2020)

3. F. D. Drake, "Life on a Neutron Star," *Astronomy*, Vol. 1, No. 5, 5 (Dec. 1973)

4. P. C. Niven, *My Visit with Our Nucleonic Friends*, Ballantine Interplanetary, New York, Earth and Washington, Mars (2053)

5. R. L. Forward, "Guidelines to antigravity," *Am. J. Physics*, *31*, 166 (1963)

6. R. L. Forward, "Far Out Physics," *Analog Science Fiction/ Science Fact*, Vol. XCV, No. 8, 147 (August 1975)

ABOUT THE AUTHOR

DR. ROBERT L. FORWARD is a Senior Scientist at the Hughes Research Labs in Malibu, California. Dr. Forward is one of the pioneers in the field of gravitational astronomy, participating at Maryland University in the construction of the first antenna for detection of gravitational radiation from supernovas, black holes and neutron stars. (The antenna now resides in the Smithsonian Museum.) At Hughes, Dr. Forward constructed the first laser gravity antenna and invented the rotating gravitational mass sensor. Dr. Forward has an ideal position in the "Malibu Hilton." Those of his far-out ideas which can be accomplished using present technology—such as gravity sensors, laser propulsion and electronic cooling—he does as research projects. Those ideas that are too far out, he writes about in speculative science articles or uses in fiction stories. In addition to publishing over forty technical papers in scientific journals, Dr. Forward has given numerous popular lectures on gravitation, astronomy and interstellar flight, and has written many science fact/fiction articles for magazines such as *Analog, Galaxy, Galileo,* and *OMNI.* His home in Oxnard contains his contumacious wife Martha, his youngest daughter Eve, the sometimes-used beds of three college students, Robert D., Mary Lois, and Julie, and a computer terminal in the final stages of thermal overload.